MOTHERING SUNDAY

Sunday Small was abandoned on the workhouse steps at birth. The regime is cruel. If it were not for the kindly Miss Beau who comes in every week to teach the inmate children their letters, and her dear little friend Daisy, Sunday's life would barely be worth living. And as Sunday grows into a comely girl, she begins to attract the unwelcome attention of the workhouse master... When the time comes for Sunday to strike out alone, she's driven on by a promise she makes to Daisy, and her secret dream of one day being reunited with her long-lost mother. But the brutal world of the workhouse hangs over her...

MOTHERING SUNDAY

MOTHERING SUNDAY

by

Rosie Goodwin

Magna Large Print Books
Long Preston, North Yorkshire,
BD23 4ND, England.

British Library Cataloguing in Publication Data.

A catalogue record of this book is
available from the British Library

ISBN   978-0-7505-4661-4

First published in Great Britain in 2017 by Zaffre Publishing

Published in Large Print 2018 by arrangement with
Bonnier Zaffre Ltd.

Magna Large Print is an imprint of Library Magna Books Ltd.

Printed and bound in Great Britain by
T.J. (International) Ltd., Cornwall, PL28 8RW

Find out more about Rosie by visiting her website: www.rosiegoodwin.co.uk

Follow Rosie on Twitter: @rosiegoodwin

For Zillah

*But the child who is born on the Sabbath day is
bonnie and blithe and good and gay.*

Prologue

Treetops Manor, Hartshill near Nuneaton,
September 1870

'*Still* no news?'

The maid paused to stare coldly at the tall, handsome man who was pacing up and down the long landing like a caged animal, before answering, 'No, more's the pity. The poor lamb is havin' a terrible time of it.'

'It will all be worth it if it is a boy,' Sir Ashley Huntley said unfeelingly.

She glared at him, making no attempt to hide her dislike. Zillah had never wanted her young mistress to marry him in the first place but the girl had been besotted by him. 'She should at least have had a proper doctor to attend her,' she grumbled as she made to pass him.

He caught her arm in a grip that made her wince with pain and his handsome face turned ugly as he ground out, 'The midwife I selected is *more* than capable.'

Aye, of keepin' her mouth shut, the maid thought, but she didn't say it aloud.

'And just remember, if it *is* a girl...'

A shudder ran through her as he went on, 'You know what you must do otherwise it will be the asylum for your darling and the workhouse for you. A woman who can't provide me with an heir

15

is no good to me nor any other man.'

Shrugging her arm from his grip, she stamped away downstairs for more hot water. He was a devil, that's what he was, and God willing one day he would get his comeuppance. But for now, all she could do was pray that the poor mistress would give birth to a male. What Zillah was being ordered to do – should the child not be a boy – was just too awful to contemplate.

Minutes later she tramped breathlessly back into her mistress's bedroom and placed the large jug she had just fetched from the kitchen down on to the table that had been placed at the side of the bed. The hot water and the towels would be used to wash mother and baby when the birth was finally over; dear God, let it be soon.

The house was quiet as a graveyard. The master had given the rest of the staff the day off, the moment his wife had gone into labour. He had told them all it was so that she could have some privacy – but Zillah knew better. The less that they saw of what was going on the better, as far as he was concerned. Most of them had gone to church, it being Sunday, and then to visit family.

Now she took the young woman's hand and stared down into her face. Strands of Lavinia's fine blonde hair were sticking to her damp forehead and she looked exhausted.

'Wi-will it be much longer?' she gasped.

The midwife who was attending her – a plump, hard-faced woman with a beaked nose – answered shortly, 'Not if yer do as yer told an' save yer breath.'

The maid gritted her teeth. There was nothing

she would have liked to do more than land the woman a clout but instead she plastered a smile on her face and told her mistress, 'Almost there now, sweet'eart. Just bear down when the nurse tells yer an' yer'll be holdin' a fine son in yer arms in no time.'

'B-but what if it's not a son?' Lavinia moved her head restlessly.

'Shush now an' pay heed,' Zillah urged, and almost before the words had left her mouth another sharp contraction ripped through the poor soul on the bed and she arched her back as she screamed in agony.

Two long hours had passed when the midwife announced triumphantly, 'Here it comes! The head is crownin'. The next good push should do it.'

By then the mother-to-be was slipping in and out of consciousness, barely aware of what was happening.

'That's it, pet. Did yer hear?' her maid asked gently. 'Just one more good push now on the next pain an' it'll all be over.'

But her beloved girl was too far gone to respond so the nurse lifted a wickedly sharp knife and did what had to be done ... and seconds later the sound of a newborn's wails echoed around the room.

The child was quite exquisite, with eyes the colour of bluebells and a head full of soft, blonde, downy curls exactly the same colour as its mother's but Zillah's heart sank as she saw that it was a girl. And then the door suddenly crashed inwards and the father was standing there, demanding, 'Well?'

'It … it's a little lass,' the maid told him fearfully and watched as his hands clenched into fists of rage.

'Then you know what you must do – get rid of it!' He picked up a pillow and threw it at her. 'And you also know what will happen if you ever speak of this to anyone.' He cast one withering glance at his wife then marched from the room, saying, 'I shall tell Matthews to prepare the grave.'

The midwife rinsed her hands in the bowl that was placed ready for her. When the master finally sent for the doctor she would testify that the child had been born dead and he would then issue the death certificate. But right now she felt the need for the large glass of gin that Sir Ashley had promised would be waiting for her in the kitchen so, leaving the maid to clear up, she gathered her things and departed. As far as she was concerned, her job was done and she didn't much care one way or another what happened to the mother or the baby now.

An hour later, Zillah carried a tiny bundle through the kitchen and past the stable block until she came to the orchard where lay two other tiny graves. Within them rested the latest baby's two sisters who had been born a year apart. Unlike this one, they really had been born dead and she almost wished that this one had been too. Matthews, the master's valet, was waiting for her at the side of a gaping hole, leaning heavily on his shovel.

'About bloody time,' he grumbled and the maid looked down her nose at him. She was sure that he would have jumped off a cliff if his master had told him to and she disliked the man intensely. Most of the staff did too, if truth were to be told.

'Give it here then and let's get this over with.' He reached out for her precious bundle but she slapped his hand away and clutched it to her ample bosom.

'She's not an *it*, she's a little lass,' she snapped as tears slid down her cheeks. 'And I shall lay her in the grave meself, so you keep yer hands to yerself.'

Regardless of the muddy earth, she dropped to her knees and tenderly leaned into the grave to lay the pathetic bundle within.

'Sleep tight, me little one,' she whispered brokenly, then standing again she gave him a curt nod. 'So get on with it then!'

Matthews began to shovel earth across the tiny form as the maid looked on, and in no time at all the job was done and he patted the ground level with the back of his spade.

'That's it then,' he muttered, and leaving her standing there, he hurried back to the warmth of the kitchen. Once he'd gone, she followed him back to the house. Her mistress could regain consciousness at any time and then it would be Zillah's unfortunate duty to inform Lady Lavinia Huntley that she had given birth to yet another stillborn little lass. Better that than for the beloved girl to ever discover the truth.

Chapter One

Nuneaton Union Workhouse, November 1880

As the cane whistled through the air and cracked down across the crouching child's back she started but not a sound left her lips; instead she stared up at her attacker with a mutinous expression on her small face.

'What do you think you're doing, Small? I told Daisy to do that, not you!'

The small girl tucked into ten-year-old Sunday Small's side began to whimper with terror but Sunday continued to stare back at the woman undaunted.

'I've already finished my job, Miss Frost, so I thought I'd help Daisy. She's only little and this is a big floor for her to scrub.'

Miss Frost – aptly named, for she didn't have a warm feeling in her body – seemed to swell to twice her already considerable size. The matron, and housemother to the girls, was a tall, well-made woman with steel-grey hair which she wore in a tight bun at the nape of her neck, and cold, steel-grey eyes.

'You,' she stabbed a finger towards Daisy, 'get on with what you were told to do. And don't think I won't be back to check on it. If it isn't done to my standard, it will be the punishment room for you and no supper. Do you understand?'

'Y-yes, miss.' The child snatched the heavy scrubbing brush from Sunday and began to swipe the floor as if her life depended on it, while the housemother grabbed Sunday by the arm and hauled her to her feet before shaking her much as a dog would have shaken a rat.

'How many times do I have to warn you not to interfere with my orders?' she raged, her cheeks flushed with anger. 'Let's see if a day or two in the punishment room will get you to be a little more obedient, shall we?' The woman began to drag Sunday along and the child went without protest. She had learned long ago that to argue only made things ten times worse.

At the end of the long, gloomy corridor Miss Frost paused to select a key from the chatelaine about her waist, then after unlocking a heavy wooden door she pushed Sunday ahead of her down a stone staircase. The steps were worn in the middle where feet had trodden on them over many years and the walls were damp and smelled fusty. By now, most of the children in the work-house would have been screaming blue murder, but not Sunday. Her chin jutted with defiance and her deep-blue eyes looked straight ahead with not a tear in sight. This only incensed the woman more, and once at the bottom of the steps she unlocked yet another door and flung the child into a tiny dark room.

'There then.' She was panting with exertion now. 'At least you'll be company for the spiders and the rats,' she added spitefully, and with that she slammed the door resoundingly shut leaving Sunday to cower in the darkness.

21

The child had fallen heavily on her elbow and now she leaned against the rough-plastered wall and rubbed it, wincing with pain. She could hear Miss Frost's footsteps receding and then there was nothing but deep darkness and biting cold – but still she wouldn't cry. Her main concern was for Daisy and how the little girl might cope without her. Ever since Daisy and her brother, Tommy, had been admitted to the workhouse some months before, following the death of their mother, Sunday had taken the pair under her wing. She felt fiercely protective of them and, whenever she could, she'd try to find ways to make things easier for the two of them. Having never known any other life than that of the workhouse, Sunday expected nothing – but Daisy and Tommy had known love and missed it sorely, poor little mites.

Sunday centred her thoughts on her friends as she huddled on the damp floor, wrapping her arms about her knees to try and keep warm. A worn wooden bench stood against one wall, but she knew from past experience that if she chose to sit on it she risked splinters so she preferred to stay where she was on the floor. There was no window so the darkness was all-consuming. She shivered. The other children would all be going into the dining room soon for their evening meal, such as it was. Probably some thin, greasy gruel with a few chunks of vegetables floating in it and dry, grey bread washed down with cold water. Meat was only served three times a week and even then it was so gristly that Sunday often wondered how she didn't break her teeth on it. Sometimes at night as they cuddled down in their beds, which were next to each other, shivering under their one thin blanket, Daisy would whisper to her about the wonderful meals her mother had used to cook, and the cakes she would bake before she became ill, and the cosy little house they had lived in. It had opened up a whole new world to Sunday, who would listen enviously.

Now she tried to ignore her rumbling stomach as she rocked to and fro. She doubted very much whether Miss Frost would let her out before the next morning at least. Miss Beau, who came to the workhouse each day for two hours to teach the children, had told her that the guardians of the workhouse had ruled that the punishment room should only be used as a last resort for short periods at a time, but as Sunday knew to her cost, what did Miss Frost care for rules? As far as the housemother was concerned, what the guardians didn't see wouldn't hurt them and none of the children were brave enough to tell them what really went on. Miss Frost seemed to enjoy making their miserable lives even more bleak. Over the years Sunday had seen at least two children locked away, never to be seen again. Shortly after, two small new graves had appeared in the graveyard at the back of the workhouse. When questioned, Miss Frost had stated that the children had died of influenza. Sunday had her own thoughts about that. She firmly believed that the already undernourished children had been left to starve, but who would have listened to her, had she voiced her opinion – and would she be left to the same fate?

She tried to think of something nice as her breath floated on the cold air in front of her. *Think of Sunday School*, she told herself. Sunday was the highlight of the week, for on that day the children were only made to work until it was time to attend the morning service at the church at 11 a.m. Even the lunch they were served was slightly better on a Sunday. They had meat, albeit gristly, and potatoes and vegetables if they were lucky; sometimes they even got a bowl of rice pudding to follow, but not very often. Now she tried to imagine the sweetness of the rice pudding on her tongue but she was shivering so hard she couldn't manage to do it.

After lunch, when the children had washed and dried all the pots and returned them to their rightful places in the kitchen, the girls would be lined up for inspection and Miss Frost would walk along, inspecting them. Anyone who hadn't taken the trouble to brush their hair or change into their Sunday-best clothes would be sent back to their room. If they offended twice in the same month they would be whipped. Those that passed muster would then be frogmarched down the Bull Ring to All Saints Church at Chilvers Coton and left to the tender ministration of Miss Beau for an hour in the afternoon. Sunday loved the walk in the fresh air, past the florist's shop on the corner, which always smelled wonderful, over the canal bridge and under the Coton Arches, a huge viaduct that spanned the road.

The girl sighed as she thought of Miss Beau. The kindly teacher would read the workhouse children wonderful stories from the Bible. Sun-

24

day's favourite story was about baby Moses being found in the bulrushes, and with Miss Beau's help she could read it all by herself now – a fact of which she was very proud. The guardians insisted that all the children should learn to read and write, and Sunday was like a little sponge, eager to read anything and everything she could get her hands on. It was Miss Beau who had told her of the town's history. Until not so very long ago, Nuneaton had been the heart of the ribbon-weaving industry and had housed many ribbon-weaving factories; the ribbons that were made there had been transported all over the world. Some of them had gone to the hat factories in nearby Atherstone to trim the hats for which they were famous; others had gone to London. But now the town relied mainly on the local brick-works and the pits.

Despite the bitter cold and her hunger pangs, Sunday smiled into the darkness. She was beautiful, was Miss Beau, just like her name, inside and out. Her bouncy brown hair matched soft brown eyes that always seemed to be smiling. The child would have walked over hot coals for her if asked, for Verity Beau was the only adult who had ever shown Sunday an ounce of affection. As well as teaching the girls, Miss Beau spent time in the nursery with the babies and also helped out in the sick wing. She had often told Sunday tales of how, when she was a baby in the nursery after being found on the steps of the workhouse, Sunday was the only one who ever cried.

'The other babies soon learned that crying achieved nothing,' Miss Beau said sadly. Though

25

Verity did what she could for them whilst she was there, no one ever came to them apart from to feed and change them occasionally. The shocking fact was that the majority of them never made it to their first birthday. All except for Sunday, that was, and Miss Beau had told the girl that even as a small child she could always be heard protesting loudly about the lack of care shown to the infants. 'You were a force to be reckoned with even back then,' the woman had informed her with a grin as they sat in the makeshift schoolroom for a small snatched moment after the other children had been dismissed one afternoon.

'And who gave me my name?' Sunday had asked.

'Well, I think you were named Sunday for obvious reasons,' Miss Beau informed her. 'And you were given the surname Small because you were so tiny.'

Miss Frost and Miss Beau were quite regularly at odds; the latter's questions or forthright suggestions enraged the other woman. Miss Beau was the only one, as far as Sunday could see, who ever stood up to Miss Frost or dared to question her disciplinary methods or matters such as the children's diets. Sunday sometimes wondered why her idol had never been dismissed. No doubt it was because Miss Beau was engaged to Mr Lockett, the local vicar, who gave the orphans religious instruction at Sunday School with his fiancée. Even the formidable matron wouldn't dare to upset him, because he was a very influential man in the community.

The girl was so deeply lost in her thoughts that

26

for a moment she wasn't aware of the approaching footsteps – and when she did become aware of them her heart began to pound with fear. Could it be Miss Frost coming back with her cane to mete out yet more punishment? Sunday was the only child in the workhouse who refused to show her fear of the sadistic housemother – and this usually caused her punishment to be much more severe than if she had cried and shown remorse as the others did. She often went without a meal or was whipped and she knew that she sorely tried Miss Frost's patience, but she didn't care and would rather die than weaken and shed a tear in front of her.

Now she watched with trepidation as the key turned in the lock. As the door inched open, the gloomy light from the corridor filtered down into the room and suddenly there was Miss Beau, standing at the top of the stairs, holding a wooden tray.

Sunday let out a long sigh of relief.

'Oh, you naughty girl, whatever am I going to do with you?' Miss Beau said kindly. 'What have you done to upset Miss Frost now?'

'I were only helping Daisy to scrub the floor,' Sunday told her indignantly. 'Daisy's only little an' there was too much for her to do all on her own.'

Miss Beau tutted sympathetically as she handed the tray to the child.

'Eat this up as quickly as you can so I can get the tray back to the kitchen,' she urged. 'Daisy managed to whisper to me where you were when I missed you in class, but if Miss Frost should catch me down here I shall be in trouble too, for flouting her authority.'

Sunday obediently lifted the bowl and quickly drank the thin gruel before emptying the water glass. The gruel was lukewarm and salty but she was grateful for it. She then sat back with the chunk of bread in her hands to chew on when she was alone again.

Miss Beau stared sadly down at her. Sunday knew that Miss Beau cared for her and seeing how she was picked on upset her.

'Why can't you try to be a little more subservient to Miss Frost, dear?' she said now. 'It would make life so much easier for you.'

Sunday sniffed. 'I don't like bullies,' she replied simply, and the teacher shook her head. The child had spirit and Verity Beau knew that it was going to take a lot more than Miss Frost to break her.

'I have to go now.' Bestowing one last smile on the girl she went back up the stone steps and slowly closed the door again. As the key turned in the lock, Sunday was left once more in darkness. Something warm with a long tail ran across her foot and she hastily kicked it out of the way. It was a rat, no doubt after any crumbs she might drop. She shuddered, then began to chew on her chunk of bread. At least her hunger had subsided and after all the cleaning she had done she was tired now. Eventually she lay down on the cold floor, using her unhurt arm as a pillow, and in no time at all was fast asleep, dreaming of the day when, with her best friends Daisy and Tommy, she would leave the workhouse for ever.

Sunday had no idea how long she stayed in the

punishment room. There was no way of determining night from day down there but she supposed that she had been there for at least a day and a night before she heard footsteps again, for her stomach was growling ominously.

The door creaked open as Sunday peered up through bleary eyes to see Miss Frost staring down at her.

'So, are you ready to do as you are told yet?'

Sunday opened her mouth to tell her captor to go away but then thought better of it. Daisy might need her and she couldn't help her while she was locked away. She was also afraid that Miss Frost might leave her there for ever if she didn't agree with her.

She forced herself to nod although it went sorely against the grain and the woman smiled a cold smile.

'Come along then. There is work waiting to be done. You know the saying "idle hands make work for the devil". But first you must clean yourself up. You smell like a sewer.'

It was hardly surprising, Sunday thought, seeing as there was only a bucket to use as a chamber pot. It was half-full now and the smell rising from it in the confined area was overpowering.

'Bring that with you,' the woman snapped. 'And make sure it is emptied and thoroughly washed out.'

Sunday lifted it, feeling as weak as a kitten, but she didn't say a word. She knew all too well that Miss Frost only needed the slightest excuse to push her back into the room and leave her there again.

Once she had lugged the heavy bucket upstairs she found that it was afternoon. There was no sign of any of the children so she assumed they would all be at their lessons with Miss Beau. She trudged outside to the privy block and emptied the contents of the bucket then washed it out at the pump as she'd been instructed before heading for the grey stone wash-house. Normally she would have loved to be out in the fresh air but she was so cold that her teeth were chattering and she just wanted to get back inside. She was almost halfway there when she realised that she would need some clean clothes so she darted back to the dormitory that she shared with Daisy and six other girls. Like the rest of the building the dormitory was a bleak place. It contained eight iron beds on which lay thin straw mattresses and one ragged blanket each, four on either side of the room. Between each bed was a small wooden locker to house the girls' meagre belongings, and on the end wall was a window set high up, through which the wind whistled. There were no pictures or ornaments of any description to soften the austere surroundings but Sunday didn't miss them for she had never known any different. She had expected to find the room empty at this time of the day so was shocked to see a slight form huddled beneath the blanket on the bed next to hers.

'Daisy, is that you?' she asked, instantly forgetting what she had come there for.

A tiny voice moaned, 'Yes.'

'But what are you doing in here at this time of day? Are you feeling ill?'

There was no answer so Sunday approached the bed and gently drew back the blanket.

'Oh, poor Daisy – what's happened to you?' The child was naked save for her faded cotton bloomers, and angry red weals made a striped pattern across her back.

'It … it was Miss Frost,' Daisy whimpered. 'She punished me for allowing you to do my work for me.'

Sunday swallowed the lump that had risen in her throat before tenderly placing her arm about the skinny shoulders.

'For as long as we're here I'll try to protect you, Daisy, and one day we're going to get out of here,' she promised in a voice that trembled with rage. 'We'll go somewhere where Miss Frost can never hurt any of us again, you just see if we don't!'

There was such determination in her friend's voice that Daisy allowed herself to believe her as the girls clung together, drawing what comfort they could from one another.

Chapter Two

Miss Beau was tidying the empty schoolroom later that afternoon, for her pupils had returned to their chores, when a little voice interrupted her and she spun around to see Sunday standing in the doorway, nervously wringing her hands. For most of the time the child put a brave face on things but just now and again something happened to remind the kindly teacher that Sunday Small was just a little girl.

'Miss Beau, will you come and look at Daisy, please? She's in a lot of pain and I don't know what to do for her.'

The young woman was just about to leave for the day and it was the first chance Sunday had found to get her alone for a private word.

'What do you mean, dear?' Verity asked. 'What's wrong with her?'

Sunday licked her lips and glanced furtively around to make sure they couldn't be overheard before whispering, 'While I was in the punishment room Miss Frost caned her for allowing me to help her with her work. She didn't seem too bad yesterday but now I think she's running a fever and she's very poorly.'

Miss Beau's pretty face darkened as she replied, 'I see, then you go about your work, Sunday. I don't want you getting into even more trouble. I shall go and check on her.'

Sunday let out a huge breath of relief before she hurried back to the entrance, dropped to her knees and began the unenviable task of scrubbing the foyer floor again. A thankless task, for no sooner was it done than people traipsed in from outside and it was dirty again. Today, however, Sunday was so concerned about Daisy that she was glad of the diversion, and at least Miss Beau was going to look at her now. When she had told Miss Frost earlier on that she feared Daisy was really ill, all she'd got in return was a good clout around the ear.

Keeping one eye on the stairs, Sunday worked

on and at last Miss Beau reappeared, heading purposefully for the housemaster's office. Sunday rose and tiptoed after her, hiding behind the stairs and able to hear all that followed.

'Ah, Miss Beau. What can I do for you, dear lady?' Sunday heard Albert Pinnegar enquire sweetly. His table was loaded with all manner of treats and as Miss Beau pictured the disgusting food that was served to the children every meal-time she eyed him disdainfully.

'I fear young Daisy Branning is very ill,' she told him. 'She's running a high fever and I believe she should be in the sick quarters.'

'What concern is that of mine, Miss Beau? I suggest you inform the housemother.' The work-house master popped a sweetmeat into his mouth and licked his fingers noisily.

'That is not possible,' Miss Beau replied, clearly trying her best to hide her feelings as she stared at his plump figure. His waistcoat was straining across his fat stomach and the buttons on it looked in danger of popping off at any second. He was quite short and almost as far round as he was high with a bald head, a large red nose and a thick handlebar moustache that was usually full of morsels of food. All in all, he was quite repulsive. 'I believe the fever was caused due to a severe beating,' the teacher went on.

'A beating?'

'Yes. Miss Frost thrashed Daisy the day before yesterday and it appears she was a little over-zealous.'

At that precise moment Miss Frost herself appeared as if she had been conjured up by black

33

magic. 'Is something amiss?' she enquired. 'If so, you should have come to me to discuss it, Miss Beau, rather than bother dear Mr Pinnegar.'

'It's Daisy Branning,' Miss Beau informed her tersely. 'She should be in the sick quarters. Her temperature is dangerously high.' She would have liked nothing better than to be able to tell the matron what a wicked woman she was, but Miss Beau had long since learned that if she gave vent, it was inevitably the girls who would suffer.

'I see.' Miss Frost turned to the housemaster with a simpering smile. 'I'm afraid I had no choice but to chastise her,' she explained. 'Daisy would try the patience of a saint. Nevertheless, if she needs medical attention you may rest assured that she will receive it. But now, Miss Beau, isn't it time you left?'

Clenching her teeth, Verity Beau nodded, turned abruptly and blindly left the office without seeing or acknowledging Sunday on her way out.

All the way home Verity fumed as she thought of the way the workhouse children were treated. If only she could do something about it! Miss Frost was clearly in awe of Albert Pinnegar. He resided in a small cottage in the grounds of the work-house and it was common knowledge that the matron idolised him, though what she saw in him Verity had no idea. The thought of the pair made her shudder but once again she was powerless to do more than she was already doing. She couldn't afford to lose her job.

With a sigh, Verity moved on across the frosty ground. She had lived in a small rented room in a terraced house in Henry Street for some years, but all that would change soon when she married dear Edgar and would go to live in the vicarage with him. The thought brought a smile back to her face. The Reverend Edgar Lockett was the kindest of men, handsome too, and sometimes she could hardly believe that he had looked upon her as suitable wife material. Verity had become orphaned herself in her late teens and for a time had gone into service in one of the big houses on the outskirts of Nuneaton as a governess before taking a post teaching the girls in the workhouse. As the years passed by and she realised she was fast approaching thirty, she had sadly resigned herself to becoming an old maid, but then she had met Edgar when she started helping out at the Sunday school, and everything had changed. Edgar was some ten years older than herself and had tragically lost his first wife in childbirth some years before, but there had been an instant rapport between them. She had been so happy when he had asked for her hand last summer and now Verity could hardly wait to become his wife. They had already discussed her post at the work-house. Edgar understood that she was very fond of some of the children there and he was happy for her to continue volunteering for a few hours each week, in her capacity as the vicar's wife.

Verity's footsteps quickened as she remembered it was Wednesday – the night she helped Edgar with choir practice in the church hall – and she went on her way feeling a little better and humming softly, vowing that she'd go to see Daisy first thing in the morning.

Back in her dormitory in the workhouse, Sunday was lying in bed staring morosely at Daisy's empty bed. She missed her little friend more than she could say but at least Daisy was in the best place now. While she was in the sick bay she would be excused work duties and the wounds on her poor back would receive attention. Shivering, Sunday snuggled further down beneath the holey blanket. One of the other younger girls in the room had started to sniffle and soon the sniffles turned to full-blown sobs.

'Shush, Susan,' Sunday urged her, but it was too late. The door was already opening and Miss Frost was marching towards the weeping girl's bed. Sunday screwed her eyes up tight and pretended to be asleep. The girl was beyond her help for now.

There was the sound of a faint tussle then suddenly everything became silent again. Sunday was aware of someone standing at the end of her bed and she lay as still as a stone. She heard Miss Frost sniff then the housemother stalked out of the room and relocked the door, leaving a foul smell behind her that Sunday recognised all too well. The rag that the woman used to quieten the children by pressing it across their nose and mouth would have been soaked in some bitter-smelling stuff, and little Susan would be out for the count for the rest of the night now. Her entire family was in the workhouse after losing their tied cottage in Bedworth when Susan's father had been crippled in a pit fall.

Sunday waited until she was quite sure that

Miss Frost had gone before sneaking out of bed and hurrying across to the child, sighing with relief to find that, although comatose, Susan was still breathing. She remembered an incident from the previous year when one little girl had not woken up after such treatment. When sent for, the doctor simply said that she had died of a weak heart and her small body had been interred in the graveyard at the back of the workhouse. However, Sunday had always had her own doubts about why the girl had passed away that night. Now she always tried to soothe the ones who were becoming upset, in order to try and avoid such a situation happening again but sometimes, like tonight in Susan's case, she didn't succeed. Thank goodness Susan was a strong little girl.

Sighing, Sunday glanced towards the window and to quiet her anxiety allowed herself to indulge in her favourite daydream. One day soon her mother would come to claim her and would take her to live in a splendid house surrounded by sweet-smelling flowers and green, green grass, where birds sang in the trees and the sun always shone. They would have wonderful things to eat every single day; she would never be hungry again and in that beautiful place she would be treated like a princess. The lonely girl had convinced herself that her mother had wanted desperately to keep her, but that some circumstance had made it impossible. Perhaps she had been too ill to keep her when she was born but was recovered now? And one day, Sunday told herself, she *will* come and we'll live happily ever after. On that happy note her eyelids drooped and at last sleep claimed her.

The harsh ringing of a bell brought Sunday snapping awake early the next morning and she blinked. Surely it couldn't be six o'clock already?

'Come along, all of you. Let's have you into the washroom.'

Miss Frost looked exactly as she had the evening before and Sunday wondered if she had even been to bed. Her greying hair was pulled back into the usual severe bun, and in her dark clothes and with her hook nose she reminded the child of one of the huge blackbirds that sometimes flew into the workhouse garden.

The girls hastily fell out of their beds and formed a line, blinking the sleep from their eyes before following Miss Frost along to the austere wash-room. A row of tin bowls full of ice-cold water with a slice of carbolic soap, a wash rag and a rough piece of huckaback to dry themselves on placed at the side of each one was waiting for them on a long trestle and the woman pointed at them, barking, 'Get to it now.'

The girls stumbled in their long drab nightgowns in their haste to do as they were told and within minutes they had all stripped naked to the waist and were shivering as they scrubbed themselves down from top to toe in the freezing water. It was either that or feel the length of the evil-looking split cane Miss Frost was slapping against the sides of her long black bombazine skirts. There was no room for modesty here. Saturday evening was the ultimate humiliation, when they were each forced to strip completely naked and sit in the rows of tin hip-baths spaced along the opposite wall whilst whichever members of staff who were on duty that night scrubbed at their hair with vile-smelling soap before wielding the dreaded lice combs. The least sign of lice and the girls' heads would be shorn like lambs. It was worse still for the older girls who had begun their courses. They would throw their bloody rags into a soak bucket in the corner that would be taken to the laundry the next morning, and many of the younger girls found the sight frightening. Strangely, this routine didn't overly concern Sunday, for she had never known anything else. But she knew that some of the girls who were newly admitted often cringed with misery and embarrassment.

The workhouse was divided into four sections, women in one part, then boys, girls and the men in the others. During work days some of the able-bodied men and the stronger boys were set to work oakum picking, which involved teasing out the fibres from old hemp ropes into threads; these were then sold to shipbuilders who would coat them with tar and use them to seal the lining on wooden ships. The rest of the men were put to work at bone crushing which, Sunday knew, was a particularly unpleasant job if the smell that issued from the large shed where the men were working was anything to go by. The bones were delivered daily from the local slaughterhouse and once they were crushed they would be sold to farmers for fertilizer. The luckier of the men and boys worked in the gardens growing the fruit and vegetables for the workhouse meals. The women and girls were also made to work hard at a variety of jobs. They

39

had a sewing room where they made the work-house uniforms. The more skilled needlewomen were set to making clothes for the better off of the parish or doing repairs; others worked in the kitchens cooking or cleaning or were sent to slave in the laundry. The inmates rarely came together apart from on Sundays when they were allowed to go to church, and Sunday had seen too many times the devastating effect this separation could have on families.

Now, she hurried through the morning ritual and then was led with the other girls back to their dormitories where they hastily dressed and brushed their hair before making their beds. God help any of them who didn't do it properly, for Miss Frost inspected their rooms each morning when they went down to breakfast.

In the dining room they silently took their seats as the staff seated themselves at the top table with the housemaster and Miss Frost who led them in prayer. Today the matron from the sick bay was present, along with the head of the nursery, but sometimes one of the guardians might stay for a meal or even the vicar, Mr Lockett, on the rare occasion.

'For what we are about to receive, may the Lord make us truly thankful,' Miss Frost intoned.

'Amen,' the children chorused, then lifting their tin bowls and spoons they formed an orderly queue before the table where women were slopping dollops of porridge into each dish. When they reached the end of the table they each took a wedge of grey bread before resuming their seats and beginning their breakfast. It was utterly tasteless but Sunday cleared her dish. Anything was better than suffering hunger pangs and she had long since ceased expecting anything better. Each child had a tin mug full of watered-down milk, and all the time those at the staff table were being served with plentiful rashers of sizzling bacon and fried eggs with bright yellow yolks.

One day when my mother comes for me I shall have a breakfast like that every day, Sunday thought and a little smile lifted the corners of her mouth, but then some instinct made her glance up, to see Miss Frost glaring at her, and she hastily lowered her head and began to chew on the bread.

As soon as the meal was over Miss Frost rose from her seat and began to read out the list of duties for that day.

'Small, kitchen duties,' she rapped out when it came to Sunday's turn and again Sunday stifled a smile. Her hands were already sore and chapped from scrubbing the floors the day before, but at least it was warm in the kitchen with her arms up to her elbows in hot water as she washed the piles of dishes. It could have been worse; she might have been allocated gardening duties, for summer or winter there were always jobs to do out there. Her favourite job was working upstairs in the nursery with the babies but she never told Miss Frost that, for she knew that had she done so, the woman would never have let her go up there out of spite. She was only allowed up there occasionally as it was.

The children filed away to their various chores as Sunday collected a large wooden tray and began to pile the empty dishes onto it. She actually liked

41

working in the kitchen. Some of the local women came in during the day to help the female inmates with the cooking and many of them were kind. They would chat to each other about their families and their homes and it gave Sunday an insight into what family life must be like; she would sigh and wish again that her mother and father had kept her.

She was in the process of unloading the second tray of pots onto the side of the huge stone sink when Miss Beau suddenly appeared in the kitchen. Spotting Sunday, she hurried over to her.

'Ah, I'm glad I've caught you, dear.' She smiled. 'I just wanted to let you know that Daisy is a little better today so you can stop worrying. Her fever has come down although I fear her back will be scarred.' The smile disappeared then and she frowned. 'I really don't know why Miss Frost has to be so heavy-handed and I've told her so as well. Not that it will do any good.'

'Thank you, miss.' Sunday stared up at her adoringly.

'Well, that's all I came to say. I must get about my duties now,' Miss Beau said then. 'Oh, and make sure you wear your shawl when you go out for your airing. It's bitterly cold out there. In fact, I wouldn't be surprised if we didn't have some snow.'

It was mid-morning before Sunday had washed and dried all the dishes and returned them to their rightful places and she raced upstairs to her room to fetch her shawl. The garment was a drab brown colour like the rest of the shapeless uniform she was forced to wear, but at least it kept her warm.

She then went to stand in the hallway with the rest of the girls until they were led outside to a yard that was divided by a high wire fence through which they could see the boys also taking their airing in the other side.

'All right, *walk* – no dawdling! The whole purpose of this is for you all to get some exercise,' Miss Frost barked but then luckily she left them under the watchful eye of another member of staff who was not nearly as strict as she was whilst she went back into the building to enjoy mid-morning tea and biscuits with Mr Pinnegar. The girls, of various ages, began to stamp their feet and blow on their hands as Sunday sidled over to the fence hoping for a sight of Tommy, Daisy's brother. She was soon rewarded when she saw him hurrying towards her.

'Where's our Daisy then?' he asked anxiously, looking over her shoulder.

'It's all right. She's in the sickbay because she had a fever but she's over the worst now,' Sunday assured him.

She watched his face fall and wasn't surprised; he was fiercely protective of his little sister. At eleven, Tommy was tall for his age, although he was dangerously thin, and had deep-brown eyes and unruly hair that had a tendency to curl. He was two years older than Daisy, and a year older than herself. 'Do yer promise?' he said.

Sunday nodded solemnly. 'Cross my heart. She'll be back here before you know it. But are *you* all right, Tommy?' She stared at his latest black eye. Scuffles often broke out in the boys' quarters, but noting her concern he grinned.

43

'I'm fine. You don't have to worry about me – I can take care o' meself.' He winked at her boldly as if to add emphasis to his words but then as he thought of his little sister lying in the sickbay his face crumpled.

He looked so miserable that Sunday's heart went out to him. Both he and Daisy had taken their mother's death very badly. Tommy looked remarkably like his sister. Daisy also had curly brown hair and brown eyes, and if Tommy had been a girl Sunday thought it would have been difficult to tell them apart.

'Will they let me go an' see 'er?' he asked then.

'I doubt it,' Sunday said honestly, 'but if she's better you'll get to see her at church – so it's not so bad, is it?'

His bottom lip wobbled perilously and Sunday felt like ripping down the fence that separated them so she could give him a cuddle.

'Look after her for me, won't you, Sunday?'

'Course I will,' she mumbled, feeling helpless.

He brightened slightly then as he told her, 'I've been in the workshop today learning carpentry and I've really enjoyed it. I think I might like to work with wood when I get out of here… *If* I ever get out of here, that is.' He glanced at the dismal surroundings, the cold grey walls that made them all feel as if they were in prison and the horrible wire fence that separated them. Even the sky overhead was grey today.

'You will get out,' she promised. 'We all will one day and we'll go to work on a farm. We'll look after the animals and grow our own food and never be hungry and no one will ever hurt us again.' She

44

flushed slightly following her outburst as he stared at her intently, praying that what she had said would come true.

The moment passed and all she could do was watch as Tommy walked away, his shoulders sagging.

I will *get us all away from here one day,* she silently vowed as she too turned and began to walk about the yard.

Chapter Three

Over the next few days, Sunday waited patiently for Daisy to return to their dormitory. The weather had taken a turn for the worse and now everywhere was under thick snow, which looked pretty but made the daily airing even more miserable. Many of the children came down with bad coughs and colds but still the dreadful monotony of the workhouse routine went on. Rise at 6 a.m., wash in the icy cold washroom before hurrying back to the dormitories to get dressed, empty the disgusting chamber pots and rinse them thoroughly, (each child was responsible for doing their own from the age of three onwards), breakfast in the unheated dining room, then on to chores before the daily airing. After that it was more chores until lunchtime then lessons for two hours in the afternoon with Miss Beau.

Because it was her favourite time of the day, Sunday almost skipped into the room where

Miss Beau taught them, her face alight. The teacher was already there and today she had a treat for them. She was going to read to them from Charles Kingsley's *The Water Babies.*

'Please take your seats, children, and then I'll begin,' Miss Beau invited and there was a scraping of chair legs on the floor as the girls hastily did as they were asked. This was just one of the things Sunday loved about Miss Beau. She never ordered you to do anything, she always asked. Soon the children were lost in a fantasy world as Miss Beau read the beginning of the story to them. Eventually she closed the book. 'There, wasn't that lovely? I'll read you some more tomorrow. But now who can tell me what happened in the first chapter?'

Sunday's hand fluttered in the air but Miss Beau wasn't surprised. Sunday was always one of the first ready with an answer, and the teacher was impressed with her keen young mind and her ability to learn.

When the lessons were over the girls returned to their chores. And so it went on until at last, exhausted, the children were sent to bed for lights out at seven o'clock sharp.

'And it will be woe betide any of you if I hear so much as a whimper,' Miss Frost warned as she hovered in the dormitory doorway. Thankfully, by then many of them were so tired that they slept like the dead anyway beneath their scratchy blankets.

Sunday's patience was finally rewarded one day when she entered the dining hall to see Daisy sit-

46

ting waiting for her. Her first instinct was to fly across to her friend and give her a hug, but knowing that this would only bring Miss Frost's wrath down on her head, she instead demurely took her seat beside her, daring to give the child's hand a little squeeze beneath the table. Daisy looked desperately pale and winced each time she moved so Sunday knew that her back must still be hurting her, but the child never uttered a word of complaint. She didn't want to risk more of the same.

The day brightened somewhat when Miss Frost announced after prayers that the guardians would be joining them all for a meal later in the week. 'We will also be welcoming a new guardian, so I shall expect you all to be on your very best behaviour,' she went on.

'Why does everyone always look so happy when they know the guardians are coming?' Daisy whispered, keeping her head low.

'It's 'cos on the days they join us we get to have a slap-up meal,' Sunday whispered back. 'The staff here wouldn't want 'em to know what muck they usually serve us, would they? At least we get to eat decently once a month.'

After breakfast, Miss Frost began to read out the list of chores and told Sunday that she was to be on sluice duty in the elderly bedridden women's quarters. The girl couldn't help but wrinkle her nose. It was a duty usually assigned to someone who had upset the housemother and she wondered what she might have done to deserve this now? She didn't argue, however; all the children knew that it was futile: Miss Frost's word was law.

Daisy was then told that she was to scrub the floors ... and as Sunday recoiled in shock, to her great great relief Miss Beau spoke up at that point.

'Do you think that is wise?' she questioned, staring at the older woman fearlessly. 'Daisy is only just out of the sickbay and I fear that all that bending and stretching will do her back no good at all.'

Miss Frost's chest swelled with barely suppressed rage but after a few moments she plastered a smile on her face and said smoothly, 'Of course, you are quite right, Miss Beau. I was forgetting. Sunday and Daisy may exchange duties.'

Daisy's face fell a mile but Miss Beau wasn't done yet.

'I feel lifting all those heavy chamber pots may be too heavy for her too. May I suggest that you put her on light kitchen duties for the next few days? After all, we wouldn't want her back in the sickbay when the guardians are due to visit, now would we?'

All the children held their breath as Miss Frost clearly struggled with herself, but once more she managed to rein in her feelings. 'Of course,' she answered in a clipped voice. 'Cissie Burns, you will do sluice duties. Daisy, you go into the kitchen until further notice.'

Even then Miss Frost's humiliation at having her authority challenged wasn't complete, for Mr Pinnegar, who was seated beside her at the head table, piped up, 'Actually, I would like to have Cissie in to clean my office this morning, Miss Frost.'

The matron looked shocked but, recovering herself, she turned to him and simpered, 'I'm sure I can allocate that task to one of the younger girls, Mr Pinnegar.'

Cissie was now approaching fourteen years old and was blossoming into a very attractive young woman, a fact that clearly hadn't escaped the housemaster's attention. Soon she would be found a place to work, probably in one of the big houses in the town or on a nearby country estate where she would be employed as a maid. Sunday saw Miss Beau shudder when the housemaster looked towards Cissie and licked his lips.

He answered, 'No. I insist, Miss Frost. Cissie is stronger than the younger girls. See that she reports to my office immediately after breakfast.'

Clasping her hands tightly at her waist, a habit she always adopted when she was annoyed, which seemed to Sunday to be for most of the time, Miss Frost reluctantly nodded. 'Very well, sir.' Then, addressing Cissie who had risen to her feet and whose face was beetroot red, she rapped out, 'Report to Mr Pinnegar's office straight after breakfast, Burns.'

The housemaster leaned back in his seat and leered as Cissie shuffled uncomfortably from foot to foot. All the girls knew to steer clear of the housemaster, especially as they got older, and now poor Cissie was filled with dread. She didn't argue, however; she knew that she must do as she was told.

Sunday chewed on her lip feeling heart sorry for the girl and relieved that Mr Pinnegar had never looked at her. She just hoped that Cissie would be strong enough to fend off his unwanted advances. Miss Beau looked none too pleased with the latest developments either but having already upset Miss Frost she wisely chose to remain silent.

'Poor sod,' Sunday muttered to Daisy as they left the room side-by-side and then they separated to go about their chores.

It was bedtime before any of them saw Cissie again and Sunday couldn't help but notice her red eyes and trembling lip as they hastily changed into their nightclothes in the freezing dormitory.

'Are you all right?' she whispered as Cissie removed the ugly calico cap they were all forced to wear during the daytime. It was a rule Miss Frost had invented, insisting that it helped to slow the spread of head lice, or nits as they were called. The caps were tied with coarse ribbons beneath the chin and everyone had a sore patch there because of them. Now, as Cissie removed hers, her hair fell to her shoulders in thick auburn waves.

'I'm all right, thanks,' she whispered back as she pulled her dress over her head and hastily yanked on her nightdress – but not before Sunday had noticed the bruises appearing across her buttocks and her small breasts.

Then Miss Frost appeared and, staring at Cissie, she barked, 'Your hair is becoming far too long, Burns. Report to me first thing in the morning for a haircut. The rest of you, into bed immediately before I turn the light out.' The light she was referring to was a solitary oil lamp that stood on a table below the small barred window which was the only source of natural light. The girls obediently tumbled into bed and the woman extinguished the light, plunging them into darkness.

'Now, not a peep out of any of you,' she threatened as she marched to the door, her full skirts rustling. Seconds later the darkness was complete as she slammed the door and they heard the key turn in the lock. Once the sound of her footsteps had receded, Sunday leaned up on her elbow and hissed, 'The mean old bitch. She's only takin' the scissors to your lovely hair 'cos she knows old Pinnegar has taken a fancy to you.'

'She can scalp me for all I care if it makes the dirty sod keep his hands to himself,' Cissie answered tearfully, and then slowly the room became silent as the worn-out children drifted off to sleep.

It was the following night before the other girls saw the results of Miss Frost's handiwork on Cissie's hair ... and they were horrified. As she removed her cap and flung it onto the bed, Sunday's mouth dropped open. Miss Frost had cut chunks of it here, there and everywhere – and now what was left of Cissie's once-beautiful hair stood out in clumps close to her scalp.

'Look what she's done! You should complain to Miss Beau,' Sunday gasped, but Cissie merely shrugged.

'It's not worth it. Frosty will just say I had nits and that she did it for all our goods, to stop 'em spreading. Anyway, with luck I'll be out of here soon when they find me a position somewhere an' it'll grow again, so it ain't the end of the world.'

Sunday sniffed. She supposed Cissie was right and admired her for being brave about it. Most girls cried their eyes out when the matron got a spiteful mood on her and took the scissors to their hair. Even so, as she lay there in the darkness she was more determined than ever that one day she would get herself, Daisy and Tommy out of this place, and until then, they'd stay out of Mr Pinnegar's way as much as they possibly could. She could hear Daisy snoring softly, the poor soul. Even light kitchen duties had reopened some of the weals on her back, although the soothing salve Miss Beau had insisted should be spread across them had at least eased her suffering.

With a sigh, Sunday burrowed further down in the bed and tried to lose herself in her favourite daydream. Her mother would be tall and slender with fair hair exactly the same colour as her own, and her eyes would be as blue as bluebells. She would come and take her to live in a lovely house where they would have wonderful food each day. Real meat that wasn't full of gristle, and fresh fruit like they'd seen at the market, and vegetables that hadn't been boiled to mush. There would be no more lumpy porridge and they would sleep together in a big bed with soft sheets and silken pillows and she would never be cold again. There would be no more chores. On Mothering Sunday, when the children in the workhouse who were lucky enough to have mothers were allowed to go to church with them, Sunday and *her* mother would go too and Sunday would present her with a bunch of wildflowers. Every year when Mothering Sunday came around, the lonely girl would watch the other children's rituals enviously and the way the mothers and children beamed at one another: this was the best part of her favourite daydream. The church was always filled to capacity on this special day, for even the daughters in service from other parishes would be allowed the day off to attend the service with their mothers.

Sunday was so lost in the dream now that she forgot that her hands and feet were stiff with cold, and as her eyes grew heavy she fell asleep with a smile on her face.

Unfortunately, Miss Frost's savage haircut did nothing to deter Mr Pinnegar's interest in Cissie, and over the following weeks she was forced to spend more and more time in his office with him. His floor needed mopping, he would inform Miss Frost, and Cissie was his choice to do it. The woman had seen his fixation with the girls many times before and was powerless to do anything about it. Sunday suspected that the matron was insanely jealous that Cissie was getting the attention she wanted so much for herself ... so it was the rest of the girls who suffered for it. Cissie meanwhile was becoming more and more withdrawn and then the week before Christmas, Sunday woke to find her being violently sick into her chamber pot.

'Crikey, shall I fetch someone?' she asked, but the girl shook her head and stared at her from frightened eyes.

The other girls had clustered into a worried little group and Cissie addressed them all. 'Please don't get mentionin' this to no one,' she pleaded. 'It'll only make things worse.'

The girls all silently nodded. Thankfully, by the time Miss Frost appeared to lead them to the wash-room Cissie had managed to compose herself, and though she looked pale she went about her ablutions without a word of complaint.

With one week to go until Christmas, an air of excitement began to ripple through the work-house. On Christmas Day a number of the local women volunteered to provide a meal and come in and cook it for them. On top of that the work-house guardians always provided a treat for each and every child. The year before, Sunday had been given a small orange and she was sure that she had never tasted anything so sweet. It had been followed by a meal that she would never forget. Crisp roast potatoes and a slice of juicy goose with vegetables that tasted unlike anything that was normally slopped into their bowls. Now all the children were hoping fervently that they would be fortunate enough to get the same this year.

The only cloud on the horizon for Sunday was Cissie, who continued to be ill each morning. Daisy especially was concerned about their friend, for although she had only been very young at the time, she could remember her mother being sick like this each morning when she was having their last baby brother. Sadly, he hadn't survived the birth but that couldn't be what was the matter with Cissie, of course. Everyone knew that you had to be married to have a baby, so perhaps Cissie was really ill?

The poor girl's vomiting had become such a regular thing that most of the children didn't even notice it any more, but then one morning

Miss Frost came into their room, wrinkled her nose and demanded, 'Has someone in here been sick? There's a terrible smell of vomit.'

The children stood as still as statues as Miss Frost's eyes roamed over them before coming to rest on Cissie.

'Was it you, Burns?' she rasped.

'Yes, miss,' Cissie answered timidly.

Miss Frost frowned. 'And how long has this been going on?'

Cissie gulped. 'A … a few weeks now, miss.'

'I see.' Miss Frost glared round at the others before snapping, 'Get yourselves along to the wash-room, NOW! Do you hear me – or do I need to use this?' She brandished the split cane that was never far from her side and the seven other girls who shared the room scurried away as quickly as their legs would take them.

'Poor old Cissie, it ain't as if she can help bein' ill, is it?' Daisy whispered to Sunday when they were safely out of earshot in the wash-room.

Sunday shrugged. She had no idea what the problem might be and was terrified that Cissie might be seriously ill.

'You err … don't think that Cissie might be having a baby, do you?' Daisy asked then and Sunday was shocked. Just like Daisy she had thought that you had to be married to have babies.

'I shouldn't think so,' she replied doubtfully.

'Well, I only asked 'cos my mum was sick like Cissie every morning when she had her last baby.'

'I see.' Daisy and Sunday huddled together, praying that Daisy's suspicions weren't right.

Chapter Four

After a busy day, Sunday found Cissie sitting miserably on her bed with her head in her hands.

'What's wrong?' she asked, and Cissie immediately dried her tears and gave her a watery smile.

'Nothing for you to worry about,' she told Sunday kindly.

'I saw them taking you into the sickroom earlier on,' Sunday persisted. 'Did the doctor find out what's wrong with you?'

Cissie glanced fearfully towards the door. 'Yes, they did,' she said in a small voice. 'But if I tell yer what it is, yer must promise not to tell anybody else.'

'Cross my heart!' Sunday duly made the sign on her chest.

Lowering her voice still further, Cissie confided, 'I'm gonna have a baby.'

'A baby!' Sunday's eyes stretched wide. 'But how? I mean – where did it come from?'

'Huh!' Cissie snorted. 'That all depends on whether some dirty old man gets his maulers on yer. But it ain't so bad really. The doctor is sendin' me to a special place in the countryside where I'll be well looked after, an' when the baby is born at least I'll have somethin' of me very own to love.'

The conversation was stopped from going any further when the rest of the girls trooped into the

56

room, closely followed by Miss Frost. She eyed Cissie disdainfully.

'Get your belongings packed. You will be leaving first thing tomorrow,' she told Cissie. 'And the rest of you – get changed immediately. I shall be back in five minutes and it will be woe betide anyone who isn't in bed.'

There was a mad scramble then and by the time the stern matron returned, the room was in silence. She extinguished the oil lamp without another word and swept from the room as the girls lay like corpses pretending to be asleep.

'When are you coming back?' Sunday asked when she deemed it safe.

'I don't know. Never, I 'ope,' Cissie squeaked in reply. 'But don't get worrying about me. And, Sunday … try an' keep out of old Pinnegar's way, eh?'

All was quiet then and soon there was nothing to be heard but the sound of gentle snores echoing around the room.

The following morning after breakfast, Cissie was sent to her room to collect her things and Sunday was despatched to help the laundry women for the day. The two girls had said their goodbyes and Sunday was feeling sad as she went to the dreaded laundry room. It was one of her least favourite jobs as the steam from the coppers made her sweat and by the end of each day her hands were red raw from the soda crystals and hot water in which they were submerged for most of the day. It was also back-breaking and by lunchtime her spine and arms would be aching painfully after turning the handles of the heavy mangle.

She was still sorting the washing into various piles when she heard the caretaker opening the enormous wooden gates that led into the back yard and a horse and carriage clip-clopped through them. Both she and the other girl she was working with hurried to the door just in time to see two men descend from the carriage. Seconds later, Cissie emerged from the back door with Miss Frost. At the sight of the carriage, she froze.

'B-but that's the asylum carriage,' they heard Cissie gasp. 'I know because I've seen it before when they've come to take some of the old 'uns away.' She turned terrified eyes on Miss Frost but the woman remained impassive as the two men advanced on the girl.

'B-but you promised I was going somewhere nice – somewhere where I'd be allowed to care for my baby!' Cissie was openly sobbing now. It was well known that once she was incarcerated in the asylum she would never be let out again, for she had no one to come for her. It was the fate of many unmarried mothers – and many of them lost heart and died within that godforsaken place.

'Fetch Mr Pinnegar,' Cissie demanded then as she shrank away until her back was against the wall. '*He* did this to me! He won't let you send me there – *he won't!*'

'You *wicked* girl, saying such things!' Miss Frost grabbed Cissie's arms and her pitiful bundle hit the floor, her possessions scattering as Miss Frost shook her until her teeth rattled. 'Don't you *dare* go making such accusations against the dear man when we all know that you've been free with your favours with any number of the male inmates. Why, I'll wager you don't even have a clue who your bastard's father is!'

'That's not *true*,' Cissie screeched. 'You know we're never even allowed to mingle with the male inmates, so when would I 'ave found the chance to 'ave anythin' to do with any of them?' As she continued to sob and struggle to get away, the two men wrestled her to the ground. Then one of them ran back to the carriage and returned with a straitjacket as Cissie put up the fight of her life. It was then that Sunday rushed forward to put in her two penn'orth.

The men were trying to force Cissie's arms into the straitjacket now. So, bringing her foot back, Sunday kicked the nearest one as hard as she could in his calf, making him temporarily let go of Cissie as he yelped with pain.

'Get that little hellcat off me!' he panted. 'Else we'll be takin' her along of us an' all!'

Miss Frost made to grab her but Sunday wasn't done yet, not by a long shot. Even as Miss Frost tried to pull her away, Sunday grasped a handful of the man's hair and yanked with all her might. A chunk of it came away in her hand as he howled with pain and indignation but Sunday didn't care now … and all hell broke loose, bringing female staff running from the rear entrance.

Within minutes they had Sunday tightly secured between two of them and she could only watch helplessly as they manhandled poor Cissie, who was trussed up like a chicken, into the back of the carriage. Minutes later it rattled out of the yard and the caretaker heaved the gates to.

'Right, madam.' Miss Frost was so angry that she was breathing heavily. 'I'll teach you what happens when you interfere in things that don't concern you.' She turned to the two members of staff who were restraining Sunday and told them tersely, 'Take her to the punishment room – and there's to be nothing to eat or drink for her until I decide otherwise!'

The two women hastened to do as they were told. They were too afraid to do otherwise but Sunday fought them every inch of the way. When they reached the stone steps that led down to the punishment room they had no choice but to drag her kicking and screaming down them, so that by the time they reached the bottom the girl's knees were skinned and bleeding.

'You're wicked, the whole lot of you!' she shouted hoarsely as they finally managed to throw her into the damp little cell. 'You'll all go to hell; you just see if you don't!' But then the door was slammed and she found herself raging at an empty room. Dropping to the floor, she leaned with her back against the wall as she tried to regain her composure, barely able to believe what she had just seen with her own eyes.

Poor, dear Cissie. *The asylum!* No one knew what happened to the unfortunate people once they entered Hatter's Hall on the outskirts of the town. They were rarely seen again. And then, as she hugged her sore knees, Sunday allowed herself to do something she rarely did. She cried for her lost friend as if her heart would break.

It was three days later before the door to the

60

punishment room creaked open.

Sunday blinked in the dim light that flooded the stinking little room. Her lips were dry and cracked from lack of water. She had even considered sipping the urine from the slop bucket to wet them but the smell from it had made her retch. The blood on her knees had dried and caked and her hands and feet were blue with cold although thankfully she had long since lost all feeling in them. Even the hunger pains had settled into a dull ache now but she was so weak that she could barely move.

'Oh, Sunday, whatever have they done to you?' Miss Beau cried as she hurried down into the cell. 'I've been at home for two days with a chill and didn't know they'd put you in here until I arrived this morning. Come along, dear. Let's get you upstairs and cleaned up. Have you had anything to eat or drink?'

'No,' Sunday croaked. She felt curiously light-headed and as she tried to stand, her legs buckled and she slumped back to the floor.

Miss Beau gently lifted her to her feet, wrinkling her nose as the stench from the slop bucket hit her full force. Then with Sunday leaning heavily against her, she helped her slowly up the steps and straight to the sickroom, where she insisted the doctor should be sent for. She stayed close to her until the man arrived and when he had examined Sunday, he took the kindly woman to one side, saying, 'She'll survive – but how long had she been kept down there? I understood that that room should only be used as a last resort for very short periods of time?'

'Three days she's been down there,' Verity Beau fumed. 'And with not even a drop of water to drink. It's downright cruel, and I dread to think what might have happened had I stayed off any longer.'

The doctor secretly agreed with her but, like so many others, was too afraid to speak out and voice his opinion. The guardians of the workhouse paid him well and he couldn't afford to upset them. There was a chain of secrecy and collusion here that went from high to low.

'Well, just give her a warm bath and get plenty of sips of water and some food into her. That should do the trick,' he advised, then closing his black bag with a snap he pulled his top hat on and left the room.

'What on earth happened?' Miss Beau asked later as she tenderly bathed the blood from Sunday's knees. She had expected the girl to be cowed and broken after such a dreadful ordeal but soon found out she was wrong.

'I was trying to help Cissie,' Sunday said, her eyes flashing dangerously. 'The carriage from the asylum came and took her away.'

'*What?*' Miss Beau looked horrified so Sunday told her what had happened.

'I see,' Verity said when Sunday had finished her tale. She believed every word of it and was frustrated to realise that there was so little she could do. If she caused too much of a stir she might be dismissed – and that would never do. Until she married Edgar, she had rent to pay and food to buy.

'Well, unfortunately you will have to try and

put it from your mind now,' she told the child sadly. 'Cissie is a strong young woman. She'll survive.'

'She may well do – but what sort of a life will she have in that place?' Sunday spat. She'd heard the local women speak of what a dreadful place Hatter's Hall was; of how newborn babies were wrenched from their mothers' arms at birth and sold for adoption. Despite the way the child had been forced upon her, Cissie had been looking forward to having her own baby, but now that might never happen, if the rumours were true.

'One day, Daisy, Tommy and I will escape – and then we'll get her out of there,' Sunday vowed, and knew from looking into Miss Beau's face that the teacher almost believed that she just might do it.

Miss Beau insisted that Sunday stayed in the sick-bay for the rest of that day to rest and recuperate quietly. She then stormed off to confront Miss Frost, much to Daisy's delight, who overheard them arguing as she scrubbed the floor in the corridor.

It was bedtime before Sunday returned to the dormitory to find her friend anxiously waiting for her.

'I've been so worried about yer,' Daisy said, nestling into Sunday's side as she threw her arms about her waist. It was hard for Sunday to remember sometimes that Daisy was only nine, a year younger than herself. 'Are you all right?'

'I'm fine,' Sunday sighed. Her old fighting spirit had returned already, thanks to Miss Beau's tender loving care.

'I heard Miss Beau giving Miss Frost a right old telling-off about locking you away for so long. She were really brave,' Daisy confided, before asking, 'But what's happened to Cissie? All the girls that saw what happened are whisperin' that they've carted her off to the lunatic asylum.'

Never one to tell lies, Sunday nodded. 'They have, but don't you worry. We'll get out of here one day an' when we do, we'll go an' get her out of there as well.'

'But that's a long way away yet,' Daisy fretted. 'You're so brave, Sunday. I won't be afraid with you by my side.'

'The time will pass, you'll see,' Sunday assured her as they clung together, drawing comfort from each other.

Chapter Five

March 1884

'Isn't it lovely to be out in the open air,' Daisy said, as she and Sunday walked in file to All Saints Church for the Sunday-morning service, admiring the spring flowers that were peeping from beneath the hedgerows and the birds twittering in the trees. How Sunday envied them their freedom.

Miss Beau had become Mrs Lockett, the vicar's wife, over two years before, and soon she would bear her first child so she was spending less and less time volunteering at the workhouse. They would see her today though, which added to their pleasure on this sunny morning.

Sunday had shot up in height over the last few years and although she would never be tall she was now at thirteen one of the oldest girls in the workhouse. She was also one of the prettiest. Her skin was like peaches and cream and her blue eyes had a sparkle to them. But it was her nature that endeared her to most people. As Mrs Lockett had often told her, 'You live up to the day of the week you were born on, Sunday.' She would then repeat the rhyme, 'But the child who is born on the Sabbath day is bonny and blithe and good and gay', much to Sunday's embarrassment.

Sunday had already asked Miss Frost to look for suitable employment for her and she often thought with amusement that the woman would be only too happy to see the back of her. She certainly hadn't made the matron's life easy. Over the last four years there had been another three stretches in the punishment room for Sunday, along with two or three beatings – one of them quite severe – but through it all Sunday had concentrated on the time she could spend with Miss Beau, now Mrs Lockett, and had distracted herself with the lovely books the woman had lent to her. By blocking out as best she could how awful her life in the workhouse really was, she had managed to make it through. Had it not been for parting from Daisy and Tommy, Sunday would have been looking forward to leaving even more than she already was, but she was wise enough to know that once she was out, she stood more chance of finding a place for all of them. Even so, as things stood she was dreading having to leave them behind.

'Still, it won't be for long,' she constantly reassured Daisy. 'I shall save every single penny I earn and as soon as I have enough money to rent a place where we can live I shall ask Mrs Lockett to help me get you and Tommy out of here, I promise.' Tommy had actually been found a position on a farm the year before but had been returned to the workhouse within weeks by the farmer, who had stated he was worthless and workshy. Sunday knew that wasn't true and suspected that Tommy hadn't tried on the farm because he was fretting about leaving his little sister behind in the workhouse.

The two girls were moving across the Boot Bridge that crossed the Coventry Canal now and Daisy pointed excitedly to a boat that was moored there.

'Probably water gypsies,' Sunday told her. 'They earn their living transporting coal and other goods along the canals.'

'What a wonderful way to live.' Daisy sighed blissfully and Sunday grinned. Daisy was a hopeless romantic. They moved on and passed beneath the Coton Arches and soon they were in the church staring up at the beautiful stained-glass windows.

As they were ushered onto the pews that were set aside for the workhouse inmates, Mrs Lockett waddled down the aisle with a wide smile on her face to greet them. She nodded politely at Miss Frost, who was looking severe in her Sunday-best black bonnet that would have been more suited to wear for a funeral, before turning her attention to Sunday and Daisy.

'How are you?' Sunday enquired and Mrs Lockett giggled.

'Feeling very, very fat,' she replied, much to Miss Frost's disgust. She clearly didn't consider it was etiquette to discuss such delicate conditions in public.

'And my ankles are so swollen I can barely get my shoes on now,' she went on, ignoring the matron's disapproving stare. She tenderly stroked her swollen stomach and Sunday couldn't help but feel a pang of envy. This baby would be blessed indeed to be born to two such wonderful people who wanted it with all their heart, would love it and might even bring brothers and sisters into the world for it to grow up with.

She glanced up to see the vicar take his place in the pulpit and after his wife had toddled away to take her seat the service began. The congregation sang hymns and said prayers before the vicar preached to them about Loving Thy Neighbour. Sunday grinned wryly to herself, hoping Miss Frost might take note.

They were all in a happy mood as they made their way back to the workhouse afterwards, partly due to the fact that the guardians would be joining them for lunch in the dining hall today. The smell of roast lamb wafted to them as they entered the building and Daisy and Sunday smiled at each other expectantly.

'Come along, girls,' Miss Frost trilled with a forced smile as she ushered them all to their seats. She was always the model of caring in front of the guardians but the girls just wished that the board of guardians could know what she was really like when they were not present. Of course, Mrs Lockett had tried to speak to them about her concerns but the majority of the guardians were elderly, somewhat old-fashioned and not really interested. Sunday hoped that now Lady Huntley, who Mrs Lockett had told her was a much younger lady, had joined them, she might take notice and bring about some changes.

The girls collected their plates and formed an orderly queue. The dinner ladies then placed a succulent slice of sizzling roast lamb along with a selection of vegetables and potatoes on each plate, and by the time the girls had carried their food back to the tables their mouths were watering and it was painful to have to wait for Miss Frost to say grace before they tucked in. Within seconds of them sitting down the only sound to be heard in the room was that of the cutlery scraping their plates.

Now and again Sunday glanced up at the woman who was seated at the head table between the other three male guardians. *She must be the new guardian,* Sunday deduced. She certainly hadn't ever seen her before; she would have remembered her if she had. The woman was pretty in a fragile sort of way. Of medium height with fair hair coiled becomingly about her head, she looked as if one good puff of wind might blow her away. Her blue silk day dress, which was the colour of a summer sky and exactly the same shade as her eyes, was the height of fashion – a wide crinoline with a bustle –

and the majority of the girls could hardly keep their eyes off her. Everything she wore looked expensive but Sunday noted that she merely picked at her food like a little bird as her gaze roved about the room. At one stage their eyes met briefly and the woman smiled, completely transforming her face before Sunday quickly lowered her eyes. They had all been taught to keep their eyes averted when in the presence of the guardians but Sunday could have gone on staring at her for ever.

Following dinner, the inmates were served with a slice of apple pie and custard, a rare treat indeed, and suddenly the room was full of happy faces as Miss Frost dismissed them to go to their chores, which thankfully they would finish early today because it was the Sabbath.

As Sunday trailed past the female guardian she dared to peek up and they exchanged a little smile.

The woman then turned to Miss Frost and commented, 'That girl, the fair-haired one – what age is she? She looks as if she might be old enough to find work soon.'

Miss Frost pursed her lips and nodded in agreement. Against her better judgement, she could barely disguise the fact that Sunday had been a thorn in her flesh for some long time. She was the only child whose spirit she had not been able to break.

'She will be fourteen in September, but I fear it will not be easy.'

When the woman raised an eyebrow Miss Frost went on, 'Sunday Small can be a very difficult girl. Probably the best we can hope for her is the position of a laundry maid somewhere.'

'Really?' the woman said as she rose from her seat. 'I thought what a pleasant girl she looked.'

'Hmm, well, looks can be deceptive, milady,' Miss Frost replied, before ushering her away on a tour of inspection.

At that moment, Sunday was just beginning her work again back in the laundry. Because that and cleaning the sluice rooms were the worst possible jobs, Miss Frost made sure that they were often allocated to Sunday. Today, however, the girl didn't mind. After such a wonderful meal and the visit to the church that morning she was in a happy mood. Even more so because Daisy was working in the laundry with her and they could chatter together as long as they were quiet.

'Weren't that dinner grand?' Daisy said as she plunged her hands into a sink full of hot water and began to scrub at the aprons soaking there. 'And weren't Lady Huntley, the new guardian, beautiful.' She sighed as she pictured the pretty woman in her beautiful clothes. 'I never knew that women could be guardians before.'

Sunday nodded as she humped a load of clean washing over to the rinsing sinks. She had lit the fires in the pits beneath the enormous coppers early that morning before they left for church and now the steam from the coppers was making them sweat.

'Let's open the door,' Daisy suggested as she pushed a lock of hair back under the ugly caps they were forced to wear. Sometime later she and Sunday carried the first lot of wet washing out into the yard. They were just hanging the items from the lines that were suspended there when the board of guardians appeared.

'Daisy and Sunday are on laundry duties today,' Miss Frost informed the small group.

The woman who had claimed Sunday's attention smiled and said, 'Sunday – what a curious name.'

'She was left on the workhouse steps on a Sunday,' Miss Frost said politely, meanwhile glaring at the young woman they were talking about. 'It seemed as good a name as any for her.'

When they'd passed by, Sunday grinned as she started pegging the washing to the line.

'They couldn't even be bothered to make an effort to come up with a proper name for me, could they? It's a good job I wasn't born on a Saturday.'

Daisy giggled. 'I like your name,' she told her sincerely. 'It's different and it makes me think of sunshine and light. My mum told me she called me Daisy because I reminded her of a tiny flower when I was born.'

'Oh, that's lovely,' Sunday agreed with an affectionate smile.

Daisy adored Sunday and wouldn't have a word said against her but as Sunday's birthday grew closer the younger girl was beginning to fret. How would she cope in the workhouse without her friend if Miss Frost were to find Sunday a position? But then remembering the delicious dinner they had just had and the happy time in church, she pushed the thought to the back of her mind. She would cross that bridge when she came to it and, anyway, Sunday had promised that she would come back for her and Tommy – and Daisy believed every word she said.

Later that afternoon when the guardians had left, Miss Frost entered Mr Pinnegar's office and said, 'Have you started to seek a position for the Small girl yet, Mr Pinnegar?' She had asked him to begin looking a few times now but on each occasion he had cleverly changed the subject.

The housemaster was seated in the comfortable leather chair behind his desk with a large glass of port in his hand.

'Ah ... well, not yet,' he admitted. 'These things take time.'

Miss Frost sniffed. She had noticed the way his eyes had started to follow the Small girl about and the way she saw it, the sooner she was gone now the better.

'Very well, I shall leave it in your capable hands,' she told him and with an insincere smile she turned and left the room as Mr Pinnegar stared thoughtfully at the cracks on the ceiling.

Albert Pinnegar had behaved himself for some long time now, ever since the unfortunate dalliance with Cissie, which had resulted in her being locked away in the asylum, but now he was hungry to feel young flesh again and the Small girl fitted the bill. He'd best not leave it too long though, he thought. Now that old Frosty was keen to get rid of her, time was running out and soon he'd be forced to seek employment for her.

Chapter Six

As they were going into breakfast one morning early in April, Mr Pinnegar told the house-mother, 'I shall need a girl today, Miss Frost. I wish to have some administrative help.'

Miss Frost looked momentarily dismayed; she knew only too well what this might mean. However, the housemaster had to be obeyed so she replied, 'Of course. I shall get one of the girls to report to you after breakfast.'

'I want the Small girl.' He stared at her in a way that brooked no argument. 'Mrs Lockett informs me that she excels at her lessons and I need someone well able to read.'

Suppressing her rage, Miss Frost nodded. 'Very well,' she told him primly, then with her hands gripped at her waist she stamped away.

When the matron read out the list of chores following the midday meal, the colour drained out of Sunday's face. She was no happier about the arrangement than Miss Frost was, although she didn't argue. Sunday glanced at Daisy and gave her a defiant smile; they were both clearly thinking of what had happened to Cissie four years ago. But Sunday had no intention of letting history repeat itself.

'Don't worry, I'll kick the fat sod where it hurts if he tries to lay a finger on me,' she whispered to Daisy as they filed out of the dining hall. They

73

parted then, with Daisy going off to the kitchen gardens where at least she might see Tommy, and Sunday reluctantly heading for Pinnegar's office. She tapped on the door.

'Come in,' a voice boomed and Sunday stepped into the room, purposely leaving the door wide open behind her.

'Close the door, my dear,' he said in a sugar-sweet voice and the girl had no choice than to do as she was told.

'How may I help, sir?' she asked politely as he licked his thick lips and eyed her greedily up and down.

'I thought we might tidy up some of the files – I'm afraid they have become in rather a muddle. Mrs Lockett informs me that you are very good at reading, so this job should be easy for you. So much nicer than being stuck in that laundry, don't you think?'

'I don't mind working in the laundry,' Sunday told him, her gaze steady.

The man looked slightly taken aback that she had dared to answer him so boldly but then quickly recovered himself.

'Ah well… We'll make a start, shall we? But first, why don't you remove that cap? It must be terribly uncomfortable when it's hot.'

Sunday reluctantly undid the coarse ribbon beneath her chin and when she removed the cap, as requested, her fair hair spilled onto her shoulders in soft, gleaming waves.

Mr Pinnegar came to stand beside her and fingered one of her curls with his fat fingers as she shuffled uneasily from foot to foot.

'Such pretty hair,' he murmured. 'It's a crime to hide it away.'

His breathing had become rapid so Sunday quickly suggested, 'Shall we make a start on the files then, sir?' As she spoke she took a step away from him and he seemed to pull himself together.

'What? Oh yes ... yes, of course.' Crossing to a tall wooden filing cabinet he yanked open a drawer and told her, 'I want all these files placed in alphabetical order. Do you understand what that means?'

'Of course.' Sunday stared at him disdainfully. What did he think she was – a simpleton? She was horrified to see that there was a whole wall full of cabinets. If she had to tidy them all she might be trapped in here with him for days ... but she then turned to the job in hand and was soon so absorbed in her task that she forgot all about Mr Pinnegar. It was actually quite nice to be doing something that taxed her brain a little rather than menial cleaning jobs.

By mid-morning she had finished the first drawer and was working on the second when Miss Frost appeared, balancing a tray containing tea and a plate of shortbread.

'Your elevenses,' she trilled, placing them on the housemaster's desk. She then glared at Sunday, who quickly got on with what she was doing.

'Why aren't you wearing your cap, girl?' Miss Frost said harshly.

Before Sunday could answer, Mr Pinnegar told her, 'I gave Small permission to remove it, Matron. It's rather warm in here.'

'Put it back on *immediately*,' the woman hissed

75

at Sunday, and as the girl rushed to do as she was told she turned her attention back to Mr Pinnegar. 'I'm afraid it's rules that the girls wear their caps at all times. It helps to prevent the spread of head lice.'

'Very well. Thank you, Miss Frost, that will be all,' he told her, and with an angry flush on her cheeks, the woman turned about and stalked out of the room.

Mr Pinnegar asked, 'Won't you come and share a cup of tea with me, my dear? You must be thirsty by now. And how about one of Cook's home-made biscuits?'

'I'm perfectly all right, thank you,' Sunday told him primly although she would dearly have loved a cup of sweet tea and one of the fresh-baked biscuits. However, there was only one cup. 'I'll just get on with the job if you don't mind.'

'But I *do* mind, my dear.' His face was straight now as he stared at her. 'You will discover that I can be very generous if you are nice to me.'

Sunday had a very good idea of what being nice to him might entail if what had happened to Cissie was anything to go by. Her stomach began to churn but she merely stared back at him with an innocent expression on her face as she replied, 'But I *am* being nice, sir. See, I've almost finished the second drawer now.'

Containing his impatience as best he could, he ordered, 'Stop that for a moment. Pour this tea for me.'

Feeling like a rat caught in a trap, Sunday slowly approached the desk and lifted the heavy brown teapot. Almost instantly his hand shot out to stroke hers and she jerked in shock. Some of the tea sloshed out over the tray and over some of his plump, sausage-like fingers.

He howled with pain as he shook his hand. 'Now look what you've done! You burned me!'

'S-sorry, sir. You startled me.' Sunday wasn't sorry at all and watched as he rammed the scalded fingers into his rubbery lips and sucked them.

'There, that's better – you may try again now, but please be more careful this time,' he said as he tried to plaster a smile onto his face.

Now she carefully poured the tea into the cup before adding milk and sugar, painfully aware of his eyes on her. He reminded her of a big fat cat about to pounce on a mouse and her heart was in her throat as she handed the cup and saucer to him.

'Perfect, just as I like it,' he praised before slurping at the drink noisily. 'Are you *quite* sure you wouldn't like to taste it?' His voice was cajoling but Sunday shook her head and turned back to the filing cabinet to continue with her work.

Sunday was actually quite enjoying rearranging the files. She had even managed to glance through a few of them and was sad at the tales they told of some of the workhouse inmates. So much heartache written on those pages. It was just a shame that she had to be in the room with Pinnegar. She was grateful when the bell sounded for lunch and she was able to escape.

'Be sure to come straight back after your meal now,' he called after her. 'You are doing an excellent job, my dear.'

She gulped as she closed the door between them, then hurried off to the dining hall where she found Miss Frost waiting for her with a face like a dark thundercloud.

'I hope you have almost finished,' she snapped.

'I'm afraid not, Matron. I've not even quite finished the second drawer yet. The filing system was in a terrible mess.'

'You had better finish the task after dinner then, but don't you *dare* take a second longer than you need to or you'll have me to answer to.'

Sunday's spirits sank. There was a whole wall full of drawers. There was no way she could work her way through them all in one afternoon.

Over dinner she merely played with her food and Daisy whispered, 'Is he behaving?'

'Only just,' Sunday muttered. 'I can feel his eyes boring into my back the whole time I'm working. He tried to stroke my hand once so I slopped hot tea all over him.' She saw Daisy's eyes light up with amusement at that and had to stifle a giggle. 'He didn't half jump!'

'Serves the old devil right,' Daisy snorted, and then becoming aware that Miss Frost was watching them the girls fell silent. It was with great reluctance that Sunday returned to her job after dinner to find Mr Pinnegar waiting expectantly for her.

'Ah, back to continue with the good work, I see,' he said cheerily as Sunday ignored him and got on with her task. Three times that afternoon he brushed up against her until Sunday's nerves were so on edge she felt like screaming at him.

At two o'clock she asked if she might be excused for her two hours of lessons with Mrs Lockett but he shook his head.

'You can miss one day,' he told her. 'In fact, you have clearly been a good student and I doubt there would be any more Mrs Lockett could teach you at your age. We should think of employing you in a clerical job right here in the workhouse.'

Sunday's spirits sank even lower but she got on with what she was doing without a word. She would rather take the lowliest of jobs outside of the workhouse than have to spend every day ensconced here with him.

The afternoon dragged on interminably but, at last, the bell for supper sounded and Sunday inched towards the door.

'Will that be all, sir?'

'Until tomorrow. Report back here first thing after breakfast.' His eyes raked her up and down and she got the strangest feeling that he could see right through her clothes. Her cheeks grew hot. She felt angry and powerless.

Daisy noticed that she was not her usual self over their evening meal and Sunday's mood became worse when Mr Pinnegar, who appeared to be lingering in the corridor, stopped her as they were making their way back to their dormitory.

'Ah, Miss Small. Would you just spare me a few moments, my dear? I can't seem to put my hand on the Bates family file.'

Sunday tried to hide her hostility as she told him, 'It will be in the top drawer under the Bs unless it's in one of the drawers I haven't addressed yet.'

'Perhaps you could—'

79

'What's this about?'

Sunday had never been so pleased to see the housemother in all her life. 'Mr Pinnegar wants to me go to his office to look for a file,' she said.

'Absolutely not. It would upset the girls' routine and you know how strict we are about maintaining rules, Mr Pinnegar,' Miss Frost told him in a no-nonsense sort of voice. 'It will have to wait until the morning. I could come and help you look for them if it's so important.'

'Oh no … no, there's no need for that,' he coughed, running his hand across his hair which was flattened to his scalp with Macassar oil. 'I dare say it will wait until morning.'

Sunday and Daisy grinned at each other before lifting their skirts and escaping up the stairs as fast as their legs would take them. For the first time in her life, Sunday had something to thank Miss Frost for, and she decided she would worry about tomorrow when it dawned.

Meanwhile, over in his office, the bulge in Albert Pinnegar's trousers was throbbing painfully. But he didn't want to frighten her. Sunday Small clearly wasn't going to be as easy a conquest as Cissie had been, but she was such a bonny little lass that he was prepared to bide his time... For a while at least. There was something about her that he found irresistible and he was already imagining her lying in his arms, her virginity his for the taking.

Chapter Seven

The girls had just entered their dormitory when Miss Frost followed them in and told Sunday, 'Small, come along to the wash-room.'

'But I was just about to get undressed,' Sunday said with a frown.

'This *minute.*'

Giving Daisy a reassuring smile, Sunday followed the woman along the corridor. The second they entered the wash-room Miss Frost removed a large pair of scissors from the deep pocket of her gown and, brandishing them, she told Sunday, 'Sit down here.' As she motioned to a wooden chair, the only seat in the room, the girl guessed what was about to happen.

'I thought I saw something move in your hair earlier on in Mr Pinnegar's office,' Miss Frost told her, and before Sunday could object she grasped a handful of her hair and began to part it. 'Ah, just as I thought,' she said gleefully. 'You do have nitties!'

'*I do not!*' Sunday was furious. She had always taken special care to keep her hair clean. 'If I had, a member of staff would have noticed when they went through my hair on Sunday evening with the nit comb.' But it was useless. Before she could say another word, the woman had lifted the scissors and a large clump of Sunday's beautiful hair drifted to the floor. The girl's hands clenched into fists and she blinked to hold back the tears. Was there nothing this woman wouldn't do to hurt her?

'Cleanliness is next to godliness,' the woman chanted and Sunday was powerless to stop her as she hacked away at her hair with a vengeance. Within minutes, Sunday's hair stood out around her head in clumps and the woman sighed with satisfaction.

'Now get yourself back to your bed.' Miss Frost bent to retrieve the locks of hair from the floor, muttering to herself, 'I should get a good price for this from the wigmaker.' And with that she strode away, leaving Sunday to stare at the few remnants of hair spread across the floor. Taking a deep breath, she then rose and slunk away to the dormitory, very aware of the sympathetic glances she was receiving from the girls she passed on the way.

'Oh, no!' Daisy's hand flew to her mouth as she gazed in horror at what the housemother had done to her friend. 'The jealous old crow has done this because Mr Pinnegar has shown an interest in you. Your poor, beautiful hair!'

Sunday shrugged. 'It'll grow again, and to be honest I'll thank her if it makes him keep his hands off me.' Thankfully, Sunday had never been a vain girl but Daisy was devastated for her.

'Well, I just wish we could do the same to her,' she said tearfully as she yanked her nightdress over her head.

Sunday changed and hopped into bed then tentatively ran her fingers across her bare neck. It felt cold without the thick curtain of hair but no doubt she would get used to it, and as she'd said, it would soon grow again. At the moment she was more worried about Mr Pinnegar's wandering hands but at least for now she was safe from him. Even he wouldn't risk entering the girls' dormitories.

Following breakfast the next morning, much to Miss Frost's disgust, Sunday was told to once again report to Mr Pinnegar's office. She had felt his eyes on her all throughout the meal and couldn't eat a thing – not that she had missed much. The porridge was particularly vile that morning.

'Ah, here you are then on this bright sunny morning, my dear,' he greeted her as she entered his room. She had her cap pulled tightly down over her ears but she couldn't prevent the straggly clumps from poking out from beneath it here and there. Then: 'What has happened to your hair, my dear? Remove your cap, please.'

Sunday did as she was told and once the full extent of Miss Frost's handiwork was revealed, the corpulent house-father gasped with horror. He didn't ask who had done it, however, but he clearly guessed and was outraged.

'What a shame,' he said, opening his palm to reveal a beautiful length of scarlet ribbon. 'I had bought you this to tie your curls back with, but it appears you won't be needing it for a while. Still, your hair will soon grow back, so take it and put it away safely.' She flinched away from him when his hand snaked out to stroke her shorn scalp.

'Thank you, sir, but Miss Frost will not take

83

kindly to my accepting gifts and, as you said, it will be some time now before I would need it.' Sunday rammed her cap back on, her cheeks suffused with colour, and hastily tied the ribbons beneath her chin. She then walked past him, pulled one of the drawers on the filing cabinet open and instantly got to work.

Mr Pinnegar scowled but thankfully turned his attention to some papers on his desk and for a while there was nothing to be heard but the sound of birdsong filtering through the window from the kitchen gardens outside.

If only I were out there, Sunday thought longingly. She knew that Daisy loved being out there too, especially if Tommy was working outside and they could all be together. During the spring and summer, the vegetables and fruit were grown and harvested for the workhouse kitchens. There was also a small orchard where berries and apples were cultivated. The male inmates of the workhouse and the boys did most of the outdoor work but just occasionally the girls were allowed to help, and the few times Sunday had worked out there stuck in her mind as being some of the happiest times of her life. She loved the fresh air and begrudged being shut away indoors. However, she continued with her task, continually interrupted by Miss Frost who was making any excuse she could to visit the house-master's office. Sunday was actually glad of the woman's presence although it was clear from his face that Mr Pinnegar was becoming increasingly irritated. Just before lunchtime, he lost his temper and, following Miss Frost's latest departure, he stamped over to the door and turned the key in the lock. Sunday gulped deep in her throat. There was no chance of them being unexpectedly interrupted now and she stiffened as he pulled his chair closer to her and began to stare at her with a strange light in his eyes.

'So what would you like to do when you leave here?' he asked pleasantly.

'I err … I suppose I'd like a job where I was working outdoors, perhaps on a farm if that were possible,' Sunday told him nervously.

'Hmm, unfortunately it's usually the boys the farmers prefer … but if you were to be *nice* to me I'm sure I could be nice to you too and pull a few strings.' He inched even closer, and as his hand settled on her backside, Sunday jumped as if she had been scalded and leaped away from him.

'I … I don't know what you mean, sir,' she stuttered as her heart beat a tattoo in her chest.

'No? Then let me show you. You see, one day some young man will come along and want to marry you… I could show you the way to keep him happy. Come a little closer, girl, and give me your hand.'

'It's quite all right,' Sunday said breathlessly. 'I'm happy to learn as I go along, when that day comes.'

Suddenly someone tried the office door, then finding it locked began to pound on it.

'*Mr Pinnegar! Mr Pinnegar!* Why is the door locked? Let me in at once!'

The man groaned with frustration as he went to open the door before confronting Miss Frost with: 'What on earth do you want now, woman?'

'A signature on this, if you please.' She pushed past him into the room and eyed Sunday coldly before slapping a paper down on his desk. 'It's the payment for the coal delivery. And why is the door locked, may I ask? It's most irregular. Myself and the rest of the staff should have access to you at all times – you are needed, sir!'

'I am a very busy man and I locked it to prevent these constant interruptions,' he replied in a high ill-humour. He then bent to the paper and after dipping his pen in the inkwell he signed it and thrust it back towards the woman. 'There. Now for goodness sake leave me in peace to get on with my work.'

'Very well, but in future please leave the door unlocked,' she told him, then with a final glare at Sunday she glided from the room like a ship in full sail.

Sunday kept her eyes on the files in front of her and thankfully Mr Pinnegar returned to his paperwork although he looked far from happy. She was relieved when the bell sounded for dinner and scooted away as fast as her legs would carry her. Daisy was waiting for her outside the dining hall and she whispered urgently, 'Are you all right?'

'Just about, but his hands have started to stray now. Still, I can handle him so don't you get worrying, and thankfully Miss Frost has insisted to him that I attend lessons today.'

Mrs Lockett was coming more infrequently now, for her baby was due at any time. The guardians had appointed a new teacher to take her place when she was absent. The girls missed her terribly although they didn't begrudge her her happiness. Sunday was subdued during lunchtime and when she trooped into the room that served as a classroom Mrs Lockett peered at her and asked, 'Are you feeling unwell, dear? You don't appear to be your usual cheery self.' Her eyes then strayed to the clumps of hair on Sunday's forehead and she gasped, 'Whatever have you done to your hair? Take your bonnet off this instant.'

The other girls were already seated and they stared at Sunday in sympathy as she revealed the extent of Miss Frost's spite just as the woman herself entered the room.

'I noticed that the girl was scratching and on inspection I found that she had a bad infestation of head lice so it is I who is responsible for her haircut,' she said self-righteously.

Mrs Lockett was so angry that she was visibly shaking as she retorted, 'I find that very hard to believe, Miss Frost. Sunday is always punctilious about her hygiene and I certainly wouldn't call that outrage a haircut! It's more of a barbaric scalping.'

Miss Frost sneered. 'Well, I was only trying to prevent an outbreak of nits so I think you'll find I was quite within my rights to do it. But now shouldn't you be doing what you came here to do rather than stand here disagreeing with me?' She smiled sweetly then turned her back and left the room as Mrs Lockett's hands clenched into fists.

Sunday rushed over to her side. 'Please don't get distressed over me,' she pleaded. 'It's only hair and it will grow back in no time.'

Mrs Lockett nodded and made a conscious effort to pull herself together before addressing the girls, saying, 'Right, today we are going to look at verbs...' She broke off suddenly and with a groan leaned across the table, clutching her stomach.

Some of the younger girls in the class began to whimper. Mrs Lockett was one of the very few people who ever showed them any kindness and they were terrified to see her in distress.

'I'll go and fetch Miss Frost. She can't have gone far,' Sunday gabbled and she shot from the room like a bullet from a musket. The woman was just about to enter the housemaster's office yet again when Sunday finally tracked her down.

'What on earth do you think you are doing, running in the corridors indeed like a common hoyden. You know it's forbidden.'

'It's Mrs Lockett,' Sunday told her breathlessly. 'I think her baby is coming.'

'What?' Miss Frost hastily followed Sunday back to the classroom and after one glance at the teacher she told Sunday, 'Run outside and tell the caretaker to get the cart ready. It is an emergency. We have to get Mrs Lockett back to the vicarage. As soon as you've done that, run and try to find the vicar and tell him to send for the midwife and the doctor immediately.'

Minutes later, after gabbling instructions to Barker, the ancient workhouse caretaker, Sunday was running across the Boot Hill as fast as her legs would carry her. Thankfully, as she approached the church, she saw Reverend Lockett in the churchyard. He had just finished conducting a

88

funeral and looked like he was heading home for a well-earned cup of tea.

'Whatever is wrong, my dear?' he asked as he saw her racing towards him.

'It's your wife.' Sunday skidded to a halt and clutched the stitch in her side. 'The baby is coming. Mrs Lockett is on her way home now in the cart and Miss Frost says you're to get the midwife and the doctor straight away.'

Lockett's face paled to the colour of bleached linen. 'Right ... thank you. I'll get back to the vicarage right away and see to it.' He was clearly all of a fluster and as he hastened away, Sunday paused for long enough to get her breath back. She then made her way back to the workhouse at a more leisurely pace. It was the first time in her whole life that she had ever been allowed out unaccompanied, and under other circumstances she would have enjoyed it, but as it was, she was too concerned about Mrs Lockett to even think about it.

She was almost back to the Bull Ring when she passed the horse and cart taking Mrs Lockett back to the vicarage. The woman looked very pale and uncomfortable but when Sunday waved she waved back, and the girl prayed that all would be well. There was nothing more she could do to help her now.

Miss Frost was waiting for her when she arrived back at the workhouse. 'You took your time,' she scolded. 'Now get back to work. And just remember ... I'm watching you, Small.'

'Yes, Miss Frost – but will you tell me when there's any news on Mrs Lockett's baby?'

'I most certainly will not.' The woman bridled. 'Mrs Lockett's private affairs are nothing to do with the likes of you. Now get out of my sight.'

Sunday reluctantly returned to Mr Pinnegar's office. Thankfully, the housemaster virtually ignored her, which was one blessing at least. *I could have run away this afternoon,* she found herself thinking, but knew deep down that she wouldn't have done so. It would have meant leaving Daisy and Tommy, and she would never abandon them. Also, she had nowhere to go as yet.

The following day at lunchtime, as the girls stood in the queue waiting to be served, one of the kindly local ladies who came in on a part-time basis to help the workhouse women leaned slightly towards her and informed her, 'Mrs Lockett gave birth to a fine healthy little lass last night, dearie, an' mother an' baby are both doin' well. The vicar asked me to tell yer, should I see yer.'

'Oh thank you!' Sunday's eyes sparkled. *A tiny new life,* she thought joyously. *Thanks be to God that she will not have the kind of childhood that I and the other girls in here have been forced to endure.*

Chapter Eight

The next two weeks were torture for Sunday. Each morning she was forced to report to Mr Pinnegar's office. Some days he'd watch her, some days he'd ignore her completely and some days she'd have to fight off his straying hands. She had just begun on the unending filing system one morning when Miss Frost appeared in the doorway wearing her best day dress and bonnet to inform the housemaster, 'I am going into town today. I have some personal items that I need to purchase but I shall be back for lunch, God willing.'

'Take as long as you need, dear lady, and don't rush back. It is officially your day off, after all,' he told her, rubbing his hands together gleefully. Albert Pinnegar was thrilled at the unexpected opportunity to lock his door and be uninterrupted for a few hours. Sunday had become an obsession with him and the more she rebuffed him, the more he wanted her. The young girls he had abused before – and there had been many of them over the years – had always been too afraid of him to refuse his advances, but Sunday was made of much sterner stuff. But *today*, he decided, today he would have her!

As soon as Miss Frost had left, Pinnegar turned the key in the lock. He sat in his leather chair watching Sunday avidly from the corner of his eye and thought how very pretty she was, though she seemed totally unaware of it. The harsh haircut that Miss Frost had administered had softened into sweet blonde curls that framed her heart-shaped face and peeped from beneath her bonnet. Her small developing breasts pressed promisingly against the hard calico of her workhouse uniform and already she had a womanly shape about her; in a few years' time she would be a real beauty. No doubt some young blade would snap her up and wed her in no time once she had left the work-house, thought Pinnegar, but he was determined that he should have her first. He dreamed about her at night and now he felt himself hardening just looking at her. She seemed oblivious to his presence as she concentrated on her work. When he crept behind her and began to fondle her thigh, Sunday started as if she had been stung and sprang away from him, putting the desk between them.

'Leave me alone!' she cried, but he was beyond reasoning now. He had tried to tempt her with all manner of treats over the previous weeks but she had refused them all, politely but firmly. Now he was prepared to take her by force if need be, and as they circled the desk his eyes, tight on her, reminded Sunday of a picture she had seen in a book of a snake that was about to strike.

'Don't touch me,' she threatened, her eyes sparking fire.

Pinnegar made a sudden dash around the desk and grabbed at Sunday's dress, causing it to tear and reveal part of her bare back. The sight of her flesh incited him more and now he swung her about and pressed her to him as Sunday fought like a little alley cat. Then his wet slobbery lips found her mouth and she started to retch.

'Stop fighting me,' he said breathlessly as he hung onto her but she ignored him and continued to wriggle. She was all too aware of what might happen. Her strength was no match for his but he wouldn't take her easily. She managed to push herself slightly away from him then and before he had time to realise what she was doing she brought her knee back then thrust it upwards into his genitals with every ounce of strength she possessed. There was a tortured cry as he released her and bent forward in agony as he clutched at his private parts and the blood drained from his face.

'*You – little – hell-cat!*'

Sunday gripped her torn dress tightly to her and raced to stand with her back against the door as she fumbled behind her for the key. 'Help! Help!' she cried, but no one was coming. If only she could manage to turn the key she would escape into the corridor and scream blue murder. But already he was beginning to straighten... Amidst the panic an idea occurred to her and she told him threateningly, 'If you lay so much as one finger on me again I shall tell Mrs Lockett what you tried to do. What do you think her husband will make of that, eh, not to mention the board of governors!'

Sunday was feeling confident now. The housemaster wouldn't dare upset the vicar, surely? And if the board of guardians were to find out what he did to the girls, he would soon be out of a job and out on his ear. The thought made her relax slightly as she saw him hesitate ... but then his face became dark as he ground out, 'Very well, my dear. If you don't wish to play there are others that will. I'll find a pliant little girl – your friend Daisy, for example. There's many a young thing in here who I'm sure wouldn't be averse to a few treats for supplying a favour or two. It's up to you, Sunday. Shall it be them, or you?'

Sunday's jaw dropped as she stared at him in horror, and seeing that he had shocked her he went on, 'Of course, should you decide to be nice to me I wouldn't dream of touching any of your little friends … so what is it to be?'

The fight went out of Sunday. She believed every word he said, and she could never subject another girl to that – so what choice did she have?

She remained silent as he advanced on her, although every nerve edge she had was tingling with disgust.

'That's better.' He undid the ribbons beneath her chin and removed her cap as she stood tensely then he began to fondle the short curls. 'Such pretty hair,' he murmured. 'Even Miss Frost could not spoil it.'

Sunday closed her eyes and wished she were dead. She could smell stale alcohol, sweat and Macassar oil, and it was almost overpowering. His hot breath was fanning her cheek and then his hand dropped to the tear in her dress and he was stroking the soft skin of her back and his breathing was becoming irregular. His other hand had unbuttoned the flies on his trousers and much to her disgust she realised that he was playing with himself. The hand on her back moved up to the coarse vest beneath her dress and round to her front before closing over her breast. Sunday felt as if she was caught in the grip of a nightmare but she remained rigid. Far better this happened to her than Daisy. He began to knead her tender nipple viciously and it was all she could do not to cry out with pain but he almost seemed to have forgotten she was there now as he started to pant. Then suddenly he stiffened and jerked and almost in the same moment he turned his back on her, saying thickly, 'That will be all for now. Report back here after lunch.'

Sunday almost stumbled in her haste to unlock the door and get away. She raced towards the wash-room, heedless of who might see her. As chance had it, the corridors were deserted apart from the women and girls who were down on their hands and knees scrubbing them, and they paid her no heed. The wash-room was empty too and once there Sunday leaned heavily against the wall until her heart-rate had slowed to a steadier rhythm. Sobbing with humiliation and disgust, she stripped off the torn dress and scrubbed herself from head to toe so vigorously that angry red patches appeared on her skin – and yet still she felt dirty and knew that she would never be able to wash away the feel of his revolting hands on her. A large bruise was already forming around her breast and she fought down the urge to cry. *What good would that do?* she asked herself.

At last she took a deep breath and crept back to the dormitory to change into her other dress. Luckily the girls were all issued with two each. She would drop the torn one into the sewing room on her way to dinner and tell them that she had ripped it when she had caught it on a nail. Perching on the end of the bed she tried to think logically. She supposed that she had got off lightly this morning. But for how long would the horrible man be content with simply pawing her? Cissie was proof that he wouldn't settle for just that and Sunday didn't know how she was going to bear it. Everything about him revolted her but he had her exactly where he wanted her, knowing how fond she was of Daisy…

Sunday was so lost in thought that she started when the bell sounded for dinner and snatching up her torn dress she made her way downstairs. *Just a few months until my birthday in September and I would have been gone from here,* she thought desolately. She wished with all her heart that Mrs Lockett were still there, but Verity was resting after the baby's birth and even when she did return it would only be occasionally. Of course, Sunday was well aware now that she couldn't have told the woman what was going on because of the risk to other young girls, but at least she had felt comforted when Verity was there, for she was the only constant person she had had in her life. It would have been useless trying to speak to the guardians; they would never have believed her so she was trapped.

She found Daisy hovering at the entrance to the dining hall waiting for her.

'Are you all right?' the younger girl whispered as they entered the room side by side. Miss Frost was back and already sitting at the top table watching them like a big black crow.

'*Oh,* I think I might be coming down with a bit of a cold,' Sunday muttered back and Daisy frowned, puzzled. A cold in this glorious weather? But she was aware that Miss Frost was glaring at them so she said no more as they went to take their seats.

Thankfully, Mr Pinnegar had an appointment with the guardians that afternoon and so Sunday was left to work in peace. She didn't stop for a second, aware that the sooner she could escape

96

his company the better, after which it would be more difficult for the master to catch her alone.

She was very low and depressed when she retired to the dormitory that evening and Daisy eyed her worriedly. Sunday didn't seem to be her usual self at all; she had stayed as close to the other girls as she could all evening – and then it occurred to Daisy what the problem might be.

'Has Pinnegar been trying to maul you again?' she enquired in a low voice so that the other half-dozen girls who were preparing for bed wouldn't hear.

'No more than usual – and he'll never get the better of me,' Sunday answered nonchalantly but then a member of the night staff appeared in the doorway.

'Into bed, girls, if you please.'

There was a rush as all the girls tumbled beneath their blankets then silence as Sunday turned on her side and pretended to be asleep. The nights were lighter now but their bedtime never varied. It didn't really matter, for the girls were so tired they were asleep within minutes of their heads hitting their pillows and Sunday was usually no exception, but tonight sleep evaded her. She lay there counting down the days and months until her birthday, wishing the time away so that she might escape from this dreadful place. The stars were riding high in the sky before she finally managed to rest.

The next few days took on a nightmare quality for Sunday. She was working as quickly as she possibly could to finish work on the files but there were so many of them. Quite a few of them had to

97

be removed into separate drawers, for some of the people had died or left the workhouse, and this only added to the work. And throughout it all, Sunday had to keep a constant eye on Mr Pinnegar, for although for now he had confined himself to just watching her, she was almost certain that he was planning his next attack.

Chapter Nine

In the sunny morning room in the vicarage at Coton, Lady Lavinia Huntley was admiring Verity Lockett's new arrival.

'You're *so* lucky, Verity.' Her blue eyes looked dangerously close to tears as she stared down at the baby's perfect little face.

'Thank you, Lady Huntley.' Verity's expression was serene as she stood at the other side of the lace-trimmed crib. 'And she's such a good baby. She only ever cries when she wants feeding or changing. I think Edgar wishes she was awake more.' She tittered. 'I swear he would sit and hold her all day long if he could.'

'I think I would too.'

They were interrupted at that moment when a maid knocked and carried a tray of tea into the room. 'Ah, thank you, Minnie.' Verity smiled at the maid before asking Lavinia, 'You will take a cup of tea with me, won't you? And some of Cook's delicious walnut cake?'

'Well, I only popped in to bring the baby her

presents. I don't want to put you to any trouble.'

'It's no trouble at all,' Verity assured her as she lifted the china teapot, then she confided, 'I must confess, having a maid and a cook has taken some getting used to. I've told Edgar that I'm quite capable of cooking and doing the household chores myself, but the cook has been with him for years and the maid came here from the workhouse so he won't hear of them leaving.'

'Quite right too.' Lavinia graciously accepted the china cup and saucer and added milk and sugar. 'And does this little darling have a name yet or is it not decided?'

'Oh yes, Edgar and I chose the names for a boy and a girl before she was born. Her name will be Phoebe Mary Lockett. Phoebe was my mother's name and Mary was Edgar's mother's.'

Lavinia beamed her approval. 'Quite beautiful, and I dare say you will be having her christened soon. Will Edgar conduct the service himself?'

Verity nodded, smiling radiantly, and they then went on to talk of the workhouse. They had become quite close friends over the last year or so since Lavinia Huntley had joined the board of guardians. Before that she had become quite reclusive, spending most of her time in Treetops Manor. Since the loss of her last stillborn daughter in 1870 she had been a semi-invalid with little inclination to venture away from home, but the outside interest had given her something to focus on and appeared to have done her the world of good.

'I would like to see some changes in the workhouse in the near future,' Lavinia told Verity.

There was something about the dear woman that made her feel she could trust her.

'For a start, I abhor the thought of families who have fallen on hard times having to be split up when they enter the place. It's humiliating enough for them having to throw themselves on the mercy of the parish, without them being prevented from living as a family any more. And those *poor* foundlings! Surely more could be done to find them homes with loving families? There are so many childless couples who would jump at the chance of taking a child in, especially the babies.' *Like me,* she could have added, for over the years she had begged her husband to allow her to do this, but he had consistently refused.

'You are probably right,' Verity agreed. 'But the majority of the little ones who do get taken in usually go to houses and farms where they are trained to work.'

'Well, because I am relatively new on the board of guardians I have held my counsel up to now but I intend to suggest a few changes in the not too distant future. I just get the feeling when I visit the place that all is not as it seems. For one thing, the matron, Miss Frost, seems to be overly strict with the children.'

Verity would have liked to tell Lavinia just *how* strict – but perhaps this was not the right time. However, she sensed that in Lavinia Huntley she had found someone who would strive with her to improve conditions for all the inmates at the workhouse and she felt heartened.

Lavinia interrupted her thoughts then when she said, 'Anyway, the reason I came today is to bring a few small gifts for the baby. I hope you will accept them.' Lifting a large parcel wrapped in brown paper and tied with string, she placed it on the table and intrigued, Verity began to open it.

'Oh my goodness!' she gasped as she lifted a beautiful white woollen shawl that was as fine as cobwebs. She then unfolded a lovely little lawn nightdress with a heavily embroidered yoke, along with a number of other baby clothes. They all bore the label of a very expensive London store in Mayfair. 'But this is far too much,' she objected.

Lavinia shrugged. 'They have lain in a drawer in the nursery at Treetops Manor for many years,' she said quietly. 'I have accepted that I will never need them now and so I decided that they should be used.'

Verity saw the sadness on the other woman's face and her heart went out to her.

'Then I can only thank you sincerely.' She reached out to squeeze the woman's hand gently, then wishing to change the subject she asked, 'And how is my Aunt Zillah?'

Verity's aunt was Lavinia's personal maid and prior to that she had been her nanny, so they were very close indeed.

Lavinia's face instantly brightened. 'Oh, she is fine. To be honest it was she who encouraged me to join the board of guardians and I'm so glad she did now. I'm afraid I had become something of a recluse. After the loss of my last child I found it very difficult to even think of venturing out of the house.'

The baby stirred then and lifting her from her

crib Verity placed her in Lavinia's arms and they talked of other things for a time until Lavinia reluctantly passed the child back to her mother, saying, 'I really should be going now. Ashley's attorney is coming to dinner this evening and my husband insists that everything is just so.'

It was clear that Lavinia was not too happy about the visit but Verity wisely didn't comment on it and saw her to the door herself instead of calling for Minnie.

'Do come again soon,' she urged. 'It's been lovely to see you, and you are welcome any time. Oh, and do please tell my aunt I'm looking forward to seeing her on her day off.'

'I most certainly will – and thank you.' Lavinia leaned forward to plant a tender kiss on the baby's forehead then hurried away to the carriage that was waiting outside for her.

Treetops Manor, Lavinia's home, nestled on a hilltop close to Hartshill Hayes, a village on the outskirts of town, hence its name. It was a large, imposing house, with a breathtaking view of three counties on a fine day. It had stood the test of time and also withstood the elements, and Lavinia loved every red brick of it. The Manor had been a present from her late father on her marriage to Ashley and on the day they had moved in after returning from their honeymoon in Italy she had imagined all of the nine bedrooms ringing with children's laughter. But it wasn't meant to be and now she was resigned to being childless. She tended the three tiny graves of her stillborn daughters religiously and knew only too well that, had it not been for Zillah, she would probably have ended up in Hatter's Hall by now. Her marriage had been a bitter disappointment to her and now she kept to her own wing of the Manor for much of the time, only seeing her husband when it was absolutely necessary. The couple lived on a generous allowance that had been left to Lavinia by her paternal grandmother and she was all too aware that Ashley blamed her for not presenting him with a son. Had she done so, he too, would have inherited a business and a large fortune from his late uncle – but only on condition that there was a live male heir. Lavinia knew perfectly well that Ashley kept a mistress in a small cottage in Stockingford, but it had long since stopped troubling her. And the woman in question had obviously never conceived or someone would have informed her.

On their wedding day, which had been a grand affair, she had floated down the aisle in a flurry of silk and lace on her father's arm to marry the man she loved and who she believed loved her. It had been one of the happiest days of her life but, sadly, soon afterwards her father had passed away. Her mother had died some years before, leaving her father to bring her up alone, and she missed him dreadfully. As she was an only child he had adored her and they had been very close, but she had consoled herself that she still at least had a loving husband. However, she had soon realised that Ashley had only married her for her wealth and the son she would bear him. It had come as a bitter blow for Lavinia had been besotted with him but, over the years, thanks to her beloved maid, Zillah, she had come to accept her way of life. It was only on days such as today when she saw a newborn infant, or when she visited the workhouse, that she realised all over again just how much she had missed by being childless. Had it been left up to her she would have taken a baby from the workhouse and brought it up as her own years ago, but Ashley would not agree to it and so her arms, and her heart, had remained empty.

Now she leaned back against the leather squabs in the carriage and sighed as she absent-mindedly straightened a crease in her gown. The carriage moved on and eventually pulled onto the tree-lined drive leading to Treetops Manor. As always, Lavinia craned from the window for her first glimpse of it, for even now she loved the grand old house as much as she had on the day she went to live in it. It finally came into view; the bricks had mellowed to a soft golden colour over the years and the long windows sparkled in the sunlight. A gardener was rhythmically scything the grass of the lawns that ran down to it and the flower beds were ablaze with spring blooms.

The driver drew the pair of matched horses to a halt in front of curved stone steps that led up to two heavily carved oak doors, set between towering marble pillars.

'Thank you, Briers, that will be all for today.'

'Yes, my lady.' Briers touched his cap as he helped her down from the carriage then began to lead the geldings towards the stables.

The two oak doors opened as if by magic as Lavinia reached them and a little maid in a frilled white apron and mob cap bobbed her knee in greeting.

'Good afternoon, my lady. The master is in the drawing room waiting for you.'

'Is he?' Lavinia frowned as she removed her bonnet and gloves and handed them to the maid. It was unusual for Ashley to be in during the day – or night, for that matter. Crossing to the mirror, she patted her fair hair into place then approached the drawing room in a rustle of silk skirts.

Ashley was standing looking out through the window with his hands clasped behind his back, and as he turned she noticed the new, expensively tailored waistcoat he was wearing. No doubt she would be getting the bill for it very soon, she thought wryly.

'You wished to see me, Ashley?'

He scowled. 'Yes, I did, but you were out. You're always out lately. No doubt at that stinking workhouse again. Why you should wish to consort with such people is a mystery to me.'

Crossing to an elegant little velvet chair with spindly legs she perched on it and folded her hands neatly in her lap. 'As it happens I went to visit the vicar's wife and took her some gifts for their new baby. But what did you wish to see me about?'

'I wanted to speak to you before Mr Wilde arrives for dinner tonight.' He began to pace up and down and she could see that he was agitated. Ashley's uncle had died some fifteen years before and left a complicated will. In it he had stated that his vast wealth should pass to the first of his two nephews to produce a male heir – and Ashley was devastated that as yet it hadn't been him. His

105

younger brother Lewis was still a bachelor, thank God.

He paused to stare at Lavinia closely for a moment. Something had changed. Now that she was getting out and about again and taking a pride in herself once more, he realised with a little shock that his wife was still an extremely attractive woman.

'I just wanted to verify that you had spoken to Cook about the menu this evening. You know how fussy Mr Wilde is with his food.'

She nodded. 'Don't worry. She will be cooking all his favourites.'

As he resumed his pacing she got the idea that there was something more he wanted to say so she waited patiently and eventually he began, 'I've been thinking ... this living in separate rooms at our age is silly. Perhaps it is time we thought of sleeping together again?'

Lavinia turned pale as she saw in her mind's eye the three tiny graves in the orchard. She wasn't sure that she was strong enough to go through all that heartache again. But then Ashley was her husband ... how could she refuse him if he wished to come to her bed?

'I think perhaps we should give this some thought. You know how the other times turned out, and how angry and upset you were,' she reminded him gently.

'That doesn't mean to say that the same thing would happen this time.' He stopped in front of her once more. 'Don't you *want* a child? Are you unnatural?'

'That isn't fair – you know I do,' she objected

hotly as colour flooded her cheeks.

'Then that's an end to it. Tell Zillah that I will be sleeping in your room this evening and when Mr Wilde arrives we shall present to him as a loving couple.'

Lavinia knew better than to argue with him when he was in this mood, and a tiny part of her still loved him for all she knew that he was unfaithful and shallow.

'Very well,' she agreed quietly, and with a satisfied smirk on his face her husband strode from the room, leaving his wife to her thoughts.

Chapter Ten

As he sat at the head table in the workhouse, Albert Pinnegar kept his eyes firmly fixed on Sunday as he wolfed down his meal, a fact that was not missed by Miss Frost who found that for once she couldn't eat a morsel. Over the last few days he had come up with any excuse he could drum up to have Sunday sent to his room and now the matron could hardly wait for the girl to be gone. She glowered at her now, for sitting there looking so pretty. Even the harsh haircut she had administered had done nothing to spoil the girl's beauty. Now that it had grown slightly it curled softly about her head like a golden halo and peeped from beneath the ugly cap to frame her heart-shaped face.

I'll have the little temptress on her hands and knees

scrubbing floors today, Miss Frost vowed as she viciously speared one of the fat, juicy sausages on her plate before pushing it aside.

'I was thinking that the walls in my office could do with a lick of whitewash.'

Mr Pinnegar's voice interrupted her thoughts. 'But of course. I shall send one of the boys in to do it immediately,' she told him ingratiatingly.

'No, there will be no need for that.' He waved her offer aside. 'The boys tend to be so clumsy. You can send Sunday Small to my office after breakfast. At least I know she will do a good job.'

The smile slid from the woman's face and ugly red patches appeared on her cheeks. She wanted to protest but in this domain the housemaster's word was law; should she upset him, she could find herself dismissed and forced to be apart from her beloved. Instead she merely inclined her head.

When she read out the list of chores after breakfast and told Sunday to report to Mr Pinnegar's office, the girl's face fell. *What on earth can he have found for me to do now?* Sunday thought gloomily, but like Miss Frost she knew she had to do as she was told.

She knocked on his office door with her heart in her mouth, dreading the day ahead. Most of it would probably be spent submitting to his lewd attentions, but within minutes of entering the room she discovered she was wrong.

'Ah, there you are, my dear.' He smiled pleasantly and motioned to a bucket of whitewash and a large brush he had ready. 'I know how conscientious you are. I fear one of the boys would

108

have slopped it everywhere and it wouldn't do if it were to get onto my paperwork.'

'No, sir.' Sunday lifted the brush and began to paint the nearest wall, keeping a watchful eye on him all the time, but as the morning wore on he behaved like a perfect gentleman, even plying her with tea when Miss Frost personally brought in the tea tray – containing a china cup for him and a tin mug for the girl, as requested.

His plan meantime was growing in his head. He had already located a small cottage that was for sale in Coton and if his plans came to fruition he intended to install Sunday in it as his young mistress just as soon as she reached her fourteenth birthday in September and could officially leave the workhouse. No other young woman had ever fascinated him as she did, and just the thought of being able to visit her at will made him excited. But first he must win her trust, although it was hard to keep his hands off her.

'So how's the smelly old toad behaved?' Daisy hissed as they sat together at lunchtime.

Dipping her dry grey bread into the slimy vegetable soup, Sunday grinned. 'Good as gold, as it happens. Perhaps he's finally realised that I can't stand him.'

Daisy glanced towards him. The housemaster was shovelling food into his mouth as if he hadn't eaten for a month and the sight nauseated her. 'Let's hope it lasts then,' she muttered. 'I've had quite a good day too, as it happens. I've been working out in the garden and Tommy was there as well so we managed to spend a little time together.'

Sunday was pleased for her and wished she could have been there with them.

Thankfully, the afternoon in Albert Pinnegar's office continued in exactly the same way. Sunday had completed half the room by then and the fat man had even helped her to move the cupboards so that she could reach behind them. Miss Frost continued to find excuses to enter the room at every opportunity but each time she came in she found Mr Pinnegar seated at his desk and Sunday busily sloshing the whitewash onto the walls. All appeared to be just as it should be, and the woman gradually relaxed as the day progressed. It seemed to her that the housemaster's latest obsession had finally burned itself out, much to her relief.

Sunday completed the task by the middle of the following afternoon and Mr Pinnegar was profuse with his praise.

'I am sure that not even a professional could have done a better job,' he said, gazing around the room as if at some great work of art.

'It's only a bit of whitewashing,' Sunday replied as she wiped her hands on a piece of rag. 'I'm sure anyone could have done the same.'

'No, no, credit where it is due. And now I must reward you.'

Sunday frowned as he began to rummage in the drawer of the desk, and then he produced a small bag with a flourish and held it out to her.

'Please take it as a sign of my appreciation,' he urged.

When Sunday made no move towards him he sighed and tipped the contents of the bag into his hand, revealing a small brooch in the shape of a flower. He had purchased it from the market and it had no monetary value whatsoever but to Sunday, who had never owned pretty things, it was beautiful. Even so, she shook her head vehemently and backed away from the desk.

'Thank you, sir. It's very nice of you but I'm afraid I can't take it. Can you imagine what Miss Frost would say, were she to see it?'

'Miss Frost needn't know about it,' he assured her smoothly and this unnerved her even more. Turning away, she lifted the bucket containing the remainder of the whitewash and inched towards the door. Before Pinnegar could say another word she was gone and he scowled as he flung the brooch down onto his desk. Seconds later there was a tap on the door and Miss Frost slid into the room, glancing around at Sunday's handiwork.

'Ah, I see it is all finished.'

'Yes, yes, it is.'

Her sharp gaze then settled on the brooch, which he hadn't had time to return to the bag, and her eyes lit up.

'Oh, Albert!' She pounced on it much as a cat would have on a mouse. 'Is this for *me*, you dear man? But how did you know it was my birthday?'

She was already pinning it to the bodice of her austere bombazine dress and the man was at a loss as to what he should do. He could hardly tell her that he had bought it for Sunday, could he?

'I err ... knew it was round about now but couldn't remember exactly what day it was,' he blustered as he nervously fingered his moustache.

She was positively beaming as she admired her new bauble.

111

'Well, it is most thoughtful of you and now I must do something for you in return. Would you join me for a glass of sherry in my rooms this evening when we have attended to all our duties? I must not let the day pass uncelebrated after you've gone to so much trouble for me.'

Albert inwardly cringed although he managed to keep his smile in place. It was bad enough having her interrupt him throughout the day, he thought, without having to spend his free time with her as well. However, he could see no way out of it so he answered politely, 'That would be very pleasant. Shall we say eight o'clock, Miss Frost?'

She simpered coquettishly as she turned about. 'That would be perfect. And please, Albert … when we are alone, surely we could cease with the formalities after having known each other for so long? My name is Fanny.'

He almost choked as she swept from the room and had to run his finger about his stiff, starched collar to loosen it. *Fanny Frost!* The name 'Fanny' always conjured up images of wanton whores to him, whereas Miss Frost was as cold as a fish. But then he supposed she could not be blamed for what her mother had chosen to call her. A picture of Sunday's heart-shaped face and deep blue eyes flashed before him then and he wiped his forehead. His first attempt to woo her hadn't gone at all as he had planned but he wasn't finished yet, not by a long shot!

They were all at supper in the dining hall that evening when Sunday noticed the brooch pinned

112

to Miss Frost's chest and spluttered on a mouthful of tea as she wondered how Mr Pinnegar had managed to talk himself out of that one.

She was in a happy mood today because Daisy had told her that their temporary teacher, Mr Jacques, had informed them that Mrs Lockett would be paying them a visit the following day. Sunday could hardly wait and wondered if Verity would bring the new baby along. She was longing to meet her. The board of guardians were also paying them a visit tomorrow, which meant that the children would all eat well, so Sunday was humming softly to herself as she made to leave the dining hall. She had gone no more than a few paces, however, when Miss Frost called her back. What now? Sunday wondered. The woman found fault in everything she did, but she was used to it by now.

'Yes, Matron?'

'One of the local women who comes in of an evening to work in the nursery is off sick,' the woman informed her tightly. 'So tonight you will take her place. I'm sure you are quite old enough to be trusted to do that now. The other member of staff who is on duty up there will show you what to do.'

'Very well, Matron.' Sunday was actually quite happy at the prospect but was careful to keep her face expressionless as she left the hall and headed for the stairs. The nursery was located in the attics and when she arrived there she tapped on the door gently.

It was opened by an elderly lady who appeared to be quite unsteady on her feet as she ushered

Sunday inside. Sunday had not been in the nursery for years and she glanced around. Eight crude wooden cots were lined up regimentally below the sloping eaves and there was not a sound to be heard.

'Are the babies all asleep?' she whispered and the woman laughed as she swiped snot from her red nose on the back of her sleeve.

'Are they 'ell as like,' she cackled. 'The little buggers know better'n to disturb me. If they do yark, I gives 'em a swill o' this – an' that soon shuts 'em up.'

She brandished a bottle of clear liquid at Sunday and the girl saw that it was sloe gin. *No wonder the poor little souls are so quiet,* she thought as she began to walk along the row of cots. The babies stared up at her beseechingly and Sunday felt like crying. The smell issuing from some of them was overpowering and she asked, 'Where do you keep their binders? I think some of them might need changing.'

The woman had settled onto the only chair in the room by now and was swigging away from the bottle as if her life depended on it.

'They's in that cupboard over there.' She gestured with the bottle. 'But don't you get spoilin' 'em, mind. They'll expect this sort o' treatment all the time.' She cackled again as Sunday went to the cupboard and collected an armful of clean binders before working her way methodically along the row. The reek of stale urine was making her retch and she was horrified to find that most of the tiny bottoms she changed were so sore they were bleeding. The dirty binders were dropped into a

114

large bucket of cold water to soak in the corner of the room and would be taken to the laundry room to be boiled in the copper the next morning. By the time she had tended to the last baby there were tears in her eyes but this was no time for giving in to her emotions. Most of the babies had tried to suckle her hand while she was changing them so she knew that they were hungry. They seemed to range from newborn up to a few months old and the sight of them lying there too afraid to even whimper almost broke her heart.

'I'll start to feed them now. Where is the milk?' she asked then. It was obvious that the old woman had no intention of doing it and it was clear to Sunday now why so many of the infants never reached their first birthdays.

'There's a pan full of it an' the bottles over there.' The woman gestured towards a small stove. 'There's some vestas to light the stove an' all if you've a mind to but I just give it the little buggers cold. They's that hungry it don't much bother 'em which way it comes.'

Ignoring her comment, Sunday struck a vesta and lit the gas to warm the milk. She then poured it into the banana-shaped glass bottles with a rubber teat either end and lifted the nearest baby from his cot. He stared up at her silently but when she placed the teat near his lips and he tasted the warm milk he began to slurp it so greedily that he almost choked.

Sunday rocked him as she fed him and in minutes he had drained the bottle and gave a satisfied burp. *The poor little lambs are starving,* Sunday thought as she laid him gently back in his cot. The old woman was snoring loudly by the time Sunday had finished and so were most of the babies if it came to that, but at least she had the satisfaction of knowing that they were all content, for now at least. She repeated the whole process again in the early hours of the morning by candlelight and then again as the dawn was breaking, and just as she was finishing tending to the last infant the old woman started awake.

'What time is it?' she asked, knuckling the sleep from her eyes.

'I should imagine it's approaching six o'clock,' Sunday answered as she looked towards the only grimy window in the room.

'That's us done then, the day shift'll be 'ere in a minute.' She dragged herself to her feet as Sunday eyed her with contempt. She hadn't lifted so much as a finger to help with any of the babies all night long.

With a sigh Sunday glanced at the sleeping infants for one last time then made her way to the wash-room but found that she couldn't stop thinking about them. They were all so deserving of someone's love, and from now on she would volunteer to work in the nursery as often as she was allowed. She hadn't had a scrap of sleep all night so it looked set to be a very long day ahead. But the one thing the night shift in the nursery had achieved was to make Sunday determined that, one day, she would make a difference to these poor babies' lives and others like them. Perhaps some time in the future she could open a foundling home of her own, where she could love and care for unfortunate children like these?

The idea took root and began to grow. The night marked a turning-point in her life: Sunday Small had found her vocation.

Chapter Eleven

As Lady Huntley breezed purposefully into the workhouse on a hot day in late July 1884, Miss Frost appeared from the shadows. There were no visits from the guardians expected as far as she knew, and if there were it was very remiss of Mr Pinnegar not to have told her.

'May I help you, Lady Huntley?' she asked primly as the woman hovered in the entrance hallway.

'Ah, Miss Frost – yes, you may. I wish to see Mr Pinnegar. Is he in?'

'Err ... well, yes he is. But it is usual to make an appointment.' Miss Frost hadn't taken to Lady Huntley at all – the woman was too nosy by half. Always asking to see into different rooms and enquiring about routines that had nothing to do with her. The gentlemen were so much easier to deal with as far as she was concerned.

'Nevertheless, I still wish to see him.' Lavinia Huntley stared back at her haughtily. She hadn't taken to Miss Frost either. For one thing, she was far too ready to use that damned cane she carried about with her, if what she had heard whispered was true. 'So would you kindly inform him I am here, please?' And when the woman hesitated,

'*Now*, if you will.'

Miss Frost bristled, but inclined her head all the same as she stalked away to do as she was asked.

'Mr Pinnegar will see you now,' she informed the visitor when she returned.

Lavinia Huntley followed her along the corridor until Miss Frost paused at the housemaster's door and tapped on it lightly. She then stood aside for the guest to enter the room but swiftly followed her in, closing the door behind them.

'Lady Huntley, what an unexpected pleasure. How are you, dear lady?' Mr Pinnegar extended his hand and after shaking it Lavinia Huntley took a seat and spread her skirts about her while Miss Frost stood back to listen to what had brought her there.

'I have heard of a position that might suit one of the older girls who is due to leave the workhouse shortly,' Lady Huntley told him without preamble. 'There is an elderly lady who runs a lodging house in Whittleford and I heard at church that she needs a young woman to help out as it is all getting a little too much for her. She is offering board and lodgings as well as a small wage to the right person.'

'I see.' Mr Pinnegar tapped his double chin thoughtfully. 'As you say, it might well be suitable for one of our leavers. They have all been taught to sew and clean and keep house.'

To skivvy, more like, Lavinia thought, but she remained silent as he digested the idea before adding, 'I do, in fact, already have someone in mind. I've seen her a few times when I've visited here lately and Mrs Lockett has provided her with an excellent reference.'

'Oh yes, and who would that be?'

'I don't know her name but she has short fair hair and very blue eyes.'

'It's the Small girl,' Miss Frost interrupted, delighted at the prospect of getting rid of her.

Mr Pinnegar's face, meanwhile, fell a mile. He had very different plans for Sunday.

'I think you are absolutely right,' Miss Frost hurried on. 'She would be perfect, Lady Huntley, and she is due to leave here in September anyway.'

'It's out of the question. She must remain here!' Mr Pinnegar snapped.

'Nonsense.' Miss Frost waved his objections aside and Mr Pinnegar looked outraged. How dare she dismiss him this way!

Addressing Lady Huntley, Miss Frost asked, 'When would the lady like her to begin? It would be quite all right to let her leave a few weeks early if the position is suitable for her.'

'The lady in question needs someone as soon as possible. But perhaps we should ask the girl how she feels about it first?'

'Well, I hardly think—' Mr Pinnegar protested.

'That would be an excellent idea, Lady Huntley,' Miss Frost gushed, once more ignoring Mr Pinnegar's attempts to speak. 'She's working in the laundry today, I believe. Shall we go and put the proposition to her?'

Mr Pinnegar's face turned an ugly dark red but neither woman noticed as they left the room.

Miss Frost showed the visitor into the day room where the inmates received their visitors each

119

Sunday before hurrying away to fetch Sunday. She found her sweating profusely with her arms up to the elbows in hot soapsuds and with her apron covered in blood. Today the unfortunate task of washing the rags that the women used for their monthly courses had fallen to Sunday. It was a task she detested but she supposed someone had to do it. In the winter she quite enjoyed working in there but in the summer it was so hot that it was torture – a fact of which Miss Frost was well aware. She had kept Sunday in the laundry for two whole weeks out of sheer spite. Now, when Miss Frost advanced on her, Sunday braced herself, wishing that the woman would just go away and leave her alone!

'Ah, here you are, Small.'

Sunday was shocked to see that the house-mother appeared to be in a good humour.

'Dry your hands, change your apron and follow me. Someone wishes to see you.'

'*Me?*' Sunday was amazed. She could never remember having a visitor before and wondered who it might be. Could it be that her mother had come for her at last? Her heart began to pound with joy.

Hastily she straightened and dried her hands on her skirt then quickly swapped her apron for a clean, starched one before following Miss Frost at a smart pace across the yard and back into the workhouse.

'She is in here,' Miss Frost told her, holding open the door to the day room, and Sunday's hopes died as she recognised the pretty woman sitting there. She was the new guardian, but what could she possibly want with her?

'Hello, my dear. It's Sunday, isn't it? Such an unusual name.'

Sunday stared back at her, well aware of what a mess she must look. Her cheeks were glowing from the steam and her hair had sprung into tight curls. Hiding her reddened hands behind her back she bowed her knee.

'Good day, my lady.'

Lady Huntley patted the seat at the side of her, inviting, 'Come and sit down here by me then we can have a little chat.'

Sunday glanced anxiously at Miss Frost but for once she was grinning like a Cheshire cat so Sunday did as she was told.

'Perhaps we could have a tray of tea, Miss Frost? I'm sure Sunday must be thirsty working in all that steam,' the woman suggested then, and Sunday had the satisfaction of seeing the smile slide from the housemother's hatchet-like face.

A tray of tea indeed! Miss Frost thought resentfully as she stamped out of the room. *Who did the woman think she was anyway – visiting royalty?*

Left alone, Lady Huntley gave Sunday her undivided attention. 'I came to see you today because I heard of a position that might just be perfect for you,' she explained and went on to tell Sunday all about it. 'Of course, dear Mrs Spooner is a little eccentric,' she ended. 'But do you think it might be something you would consider?'

Sunday chewed on her lip. It sounded perfect, and to be away from the confines of the workhouse at last would be a dream come true – but

121

would there be any room for Daisy and Tommy?

'Do you think Mrs Spooner would be able to afford to employ three of us?' she asked tentatively then rushed on to tell Lady Huntley how close the three of them were and how much they wanted to stay together.

Lady Huntley frowned. The story of how Sunday had taken the two under her wing when they were orphaned had touched her heart and she was glad the three of them were firm friends, but she doubted that Mrs Spooner would want all of them.

'I suppose I could ask her,' she replied cautiously. 'But you really should think of yourself. Daisy and Tommy will still have each other and Tommy will be out of here again soon, anyway. He's slightly older than you, isn't he? And he's a fine strong lad. I've no doubt a farmer will employ him. As for Daisy, she might find a position as a maid somewhere when the time comes.' Then seeing Sunday's downcast expression, she went on gently, 'The problem is, we can't find everyone a place all at once.'

Miss Frost bustled back in then with a tray loaded with the special china that was kept especially for the guardians' visits, and so for the first time in her life Sunday found herself drinking from something other than a tin mug, although the look Miss Frost gave her was poisonous.

'So, would you at least like to meet Mrs Spooner, dear?' Lady Huntley asked eventually.

'That isn't the normal pattern we follow,' Miss Frost interrupted peevishly. 'The young people don't usually have a choice. They simply go

122

where they are sent and are grateful for it.'

'Really?' Lady Huntley raised an eyebrow. 'How absolutely dreadful. I'm sure we can do better than that.' She then turned to look questioningly back at Sunday, who was feeling a number of emotions. Part of her was still worried about leaving her friends behind but the other part of her couldn't help but be excited at the prospect of getting away from the hated workhouse. She nodded.

'Excellent.' Lady Huntley carefully placed her cup and saucer back on the tray and rose from her seat. 'I shall collect you at two o'clock sharp tomorrow afternoon then, if that is satisfactory to you, Miss Frost?'

The woman was simmering with rage but she said tightly, 'Of course. I shall see that the girl is ready and waiting.'

Lady Huntley smiled at Sunday and took her leave and the second she was out of sight, Miss Frost barked, 'Well, what are you sitting there like a lady of leisure for? Get back to work this instant.'

Sunday stood up and sauntered from the room, which only incensed the woman even more. *That girl is too big for her boots,* she fumed, *and the sooner she is gone the better!*

As they were lying in bed that evening, Sunday told Daisy all about Lady Huntley's visit and was surprised at her friend's reaction.

'Of course you must go, if you like the woman when you meet her,' Daisy encouraged. 'I'm sure it will be a far nicer position than old Frosty would have found for you.'

123

'But what about you and Tommy?' Sunday fretted.

Daisy blinked back tears and answered bravely, 'Any time now they could find Tommy a new position on a farm or something, where he's allowed to come and visit me, and next year I shall get out of here too. The time will pass in the blink of an eye. And you can always come and see us on Sunday afternoons. Me and Tommy have never had anyone to visit us before and it'll be something to look forward to each week.'

'Hmm.' Sunday's emotions were in turmoil. Her friends were like her very own brother and sister. 'Well, I'll go and meet her then,' she agreed. 'But if I don't like her I'll say so.'

'Oh yes? And then what will happen? Frosty will find you somewhere ten times worse,' Daisy pointed out sagely.

Sunday knew that she was right. The matron made no secret of the fact that she couldn't wait to be rid of her. Not surprisingly, the feeling was mutual.

The next day dawned bright and clear although it didn't make much difference to Sunday. Once again she was sent to work in the laundry. But at least she had her outing with Lady Huntley to look forward to, so she hummed as she worked. It was a rare treat to be allowed out of the work-house other than to visit the church.

Half an hour before Lady Huntley was due to call for her, Miss Frost allowed Sunday to go to the wash-room and change into her Sunday clothes. They were barely better than the ones she was forced to wear each day but she washed herself from head to toe and brushed her hair until it gleamed and at least she felt clean.

She was in the day room nervously waiting when Lady Huntley arrived.

'Ah, you're all ready, I see.' The woman smiled at her kindly. 'Shall we go then?' She held out her hand to Sunday as Miss Frost scowled at them both.

'I'm not sure how long this will take but rest assured I shall see that Sunday is safely delivered back to you,' Lady Huntley told her as she drew the girl out of the room.

Too angry to speak, Miss Frost tossed her head. *Delivered safely back, indeed!* Anyone would think the foundling was made of delicate china!

Outside the confines of the workhouse, Sunday paused to breathe deeply. It was such a treat to be out in the fresh air instead of being trapped in the gloomy laundry. A carriage stood outside pulled by two beautifully matched dapple-grey horses who were pawing the ground impatiently. The driver was sitting high above them and as Sunday caught his eye he winked at her. He clambered down then to help Lady Huntley and Sunday inside, and for the first time Sunday had the pleasure of a ride in a carriage. The smell of leather wafted to her and she gazed in awe from the window. She was so absorbed in looking out that she started when Lady Huntley laughed softly.

'Am I to take it that you've never been in a carriage before?'

'No, Mrs … err … ma'am,' she stuttered, feeling totally out of her depth.

'I see.' Lady Huntley stared at Sunday's ugly clothes and the heavy boots that encased her feet. *The girl could be quite beautiful if she were dressed in pretty clothes,* she found herself thinking. *And she must be about the same age as my last daughter would have been...* She abruptly stopped her thoughts from going along that route. Even now it was much too painful to think about.

'So,' she said instead, pulling herself together with an enormous effort, 'let's go and meet Mrs Spooner then, shall we? You never know, my dear. This could well be the beginning of a wonderful new chapter in your life.'

Chapter Twelve

They pulled up some time later in front of Whittleford Lodge on the Stockingford side of town.

Sunday stared at it from the window. The house was enormous, with three storeys that seemed to stretch up into the sky. Wide stone steps led up to a stout wooden front door. A large brass door-knocker was attached to it in the shape of a lion's head but Sunday saw that it was badly tarnished. In fact, the whole of the house, which must once have been beautiful, now had a sad, neglected air. Dirty white paint was peeling from the window frames and the lace curtains that covered the panes were tattered and grey. Low, wrought-iron railings ran along the front of the Lodge with steps to one side of them that Sunday rightly guessed must lead down to the basement kitchen.

'Are you ready then, my dear?' Lady Huntley gently squeezed her hand, sensing the girl's nervousness. 'Don't be afraid. I am assured that Mrs Spooner's bark is much worse than her bite.'

Sunday gulped deep in her throat then straightened her back as the driver came to assist them from the carriage. They climbed the steps side by side and shortly after Lady Huntley had rapped on the door with the lion's head knocker they heard footsteps on the other side of it shuffling towards them.

'Yes? Whadda yer want?'

They were confronted by an old woman who might have been a witch straight from the pages of the fairy-story books Mrs Lockett had occasionally read to them.

'I am here to see Mrs Spooner and she is expecting me,' Lady Huntley told her imperiously as she dabbed at her nose with a tiny scrap of handkerchief scented with rose-water. The smell of stale sweat that was issuing from the woman was eye-watering. 'Would you kindly inform her that I am here.'

The woman sniffed. 'I dare say yer'd best come in then.'

Lady Huntley and Sunday stepped into a spacious hallway that looked just as neglected as the exterior of the property. Sunday thought the tiles on the floor might be black and white but they were so grubby it was hard to be sure, and cobwebs hung from the ceiling.

'I'm afraid if you do decide to take this position you are going to have your work cut out for some time to come,' Lady Huntley whispered as the old woman shuffled away to tell the lady of the house that they were there.

'Hard work never hurt no one,' Sunday told her with a determined air and Lady Huntley smiled to herself. Without a doubt the girl had spirit.

A door along the narrow passageway that ran off the entrance hall opened then and the old woman who had admitted them reappeared and crooked an arthritic finger in their direction.

'The missus says as she'll see yer now. Come this way an' be quick about it. I ain't got all day, yet know.'

Lady Huntley sailed ahead, her full skirts trailing across the dirty tiles with Sunday close on her heel. The two found themselves in a large drawing room which must have been quite magnificent at some stage. There were two enormous windows, one at either end of the room, framed by thick curtains that were so dusty it was difficult to assess what colour they were. Fine-fringed Turkish rugs were scattered about the floor and a marble fireplace graced the centre of the opposite wall. China dogs stood at each end of the deep mantelshelf with a collection of other china trinkets dividing them. The whole room was cluttered with imposing items of furniture but again, in here the air of neglect continued. There were heavy mirrors and paintings on the walls, tiny rosewood tables containing yet more trinkets scattered about, and on either side of the fireplace stood a pair of magnificent wing-backed leather chairs. A velvet settee stood between them and after a while the voice that issued from it made them both start.

'Well, are you coming in or ain't you then?'

Tentatively they both stepped forward and Sunday got her first glimpse of the woman who could possibly soon be her employer. It was a shock, to say the least, for to describe her as 'flamboyant' would have been putting it mildly.

An elderly woman of indeterminate age was glaring fiercely up at them as she clung to an ebony-topped walking stick with one hand and gesticulated to them irritably with the other.

'Sit down,' she ordered. 'It hurts me neck to have to look up at you.'

The two newcomers obediently sank onto the leather chairs, and now that they were on a level with the woman, Sunday stared at her curiously. Her face was heavy with powder and rouge that had sunk into her wrinkles, and a ridiculous wig adorned her head. Her dress was a mass of frills and lace, and bangles jangled on both her arms every time she moved. There was also a heavy jewelled ring on each finger and, about her neck, a stunning necklace made of blue and white stones that caught and reflected every sliver of light that managed to fight its way through the murky windows.

'So this is the wench you have in mind to help me with the lodgers, is it?' she asked Lady Huntley.

'Yes, Mrs Spooner. This is Sunday Small, from the Union Workhouse.'

'Hmm!'

Most young people would have been alarmed as the old woman stared at her closely but Sunday merely stared calmly right back.

'An' what sort of a name is that then? *Sunday,* indeed!'

'It's the only one I have,' Sunday replied coolly, and to her surprise the old woman grinned.

'Hmm, an' what are you like at cooking an' cleaning?'

'I'm very good at cleaning. I've had lots of practice in the workhouse. I'm not so good at cooking though, as I haven't had a lot of practice at that, but I'd be very willing to learn,' Sunday replied honestly.

Mrs Spooner suddenly hooted with laughter and started to bang her stick on the floor as Lady Huntley and Sunday looked at each other in bewilderment. The old woman who had admitted them stuck her head around the door and Mrs Spooner told her, 'Fetch us a tray o' tea in, would you, Annie?'

Annie gave the guests a nasty look as she swiped her hands down the front of her grubby apron, saying rudely to her employer: 'An' what did yer last servant die of then, eh?' Still mumbling, she disappeared and Mrs Spooner again turned her attention to Sunday.

'Can you read an' write?'

'Of course I can. And I'm told that I'm very good at it,' Sunday answered indignantly.

The woman laughed again. 'You can stick up fer yourself, I'll say that for you. An' you'd probably look respectable enough if we were to get you a few decent togs to wear.'

'Sunday is a very hardworking, intelligent girl,' Lady Huntley interjected quickly. 'She is also very conscientious and caring, as Mrs Lockett, the vicar's wife, will gladly testify. I truly believe she will be an enormous help to you.'

They chatted for a few moments more, before Annie butted the door open with her backside, then dumped a tray down on a small table placed close to Mrs Spooner, sloshing tea all over the place.

'Do yer reckon yer can manage to pour it?' she asked sarcastically.

Mrs Spooner waved her hand graciously. 'I should think so, Annie. That'll be all.'

'Don't you come yer airs an' graces wi' me, Biddy Spooner,' Annie warned angrily, waggling a finger at her. 'Don't forget I know where yer come from. Yer were just a kid from the Ford, same as me, till your Herbert made an 'onest woman o' yer.'

At that moment a large golden spaniel bounded into the room, almost knocking Annie over in the process, and to Sunday's amazement Mrs Spooner greeted it with open arms.

'Ah, come here to Mammy, my sweet girl,' she crooned, then looking at Sunday she told her, 'I'd sooner have animals than people any day o' the week. Animals love you and are loyal whereas people can hurt and betray you.'

Apart from a stray cat that had used to call regularly at the workhouse looking for scraps of food, Sunday had never been in such close proximity to an animal before and she was a little nervous. She had become very fond of the cat and

131

had used to sneak it titbits from the table until Miss Frost had caught her at it one day. It had cost Sunday a day in the punishment room and, she remembered sadly, two days later she had found the cat dead outside the laundry room. It had been poisoned, no doubt by Miss Frost who thought all animals were vermin, and Sunday had been inconsolable for days. The dog looked friendly enough, however, and after a few moments when it wagged across to her she tentatively stroked it. To her amazement it dropped to the floor and after rolling onto its back at her feet, it raised its legs into the air.

'She wants a belly rub,' Mrs Spooner informed her with a laugh. 'An' you can think yourself highly honoured. She only usually does that for me.'

'Dirty creatures, dogs,' Annie grunted, looking disgusted.

'My Mabel is *not* dirty,' Mrs Spooner snapped. 'It's just a pity as you're not so pertic'lar about keeping clean as she is, Annie – if the smell o' you is anything to go by!'

Annie glared at her and for a moment Sunday feared that the two women might come to blows.

'Shut yer mouth, yer silly old bat!' Annie retaliated. 'I'll be glad when yer get somebody to take over from me, so I will, though I doubt that there's any bloody daft enough.' With that she stomped from the room with her nose in the air as Sunday and Lady Huntley looked on, speechless.

'She doesn't mean it – not really,' Mrs Spooner confided when she had left the room. 'Me an' Annie knew each other as girls. But now, lass, would you pour the tea.' It was said more as a command and Sunday hastily began to do as she was told. 'An' while yer doin' it yer can tell me a bit about yourself.'

'There's not much to tell really,' Sunday admitted as she poured milk into the cups. 'I was found on the steps of the workhouse as a newborn and I've lived there ever since. I liked working in the nursery there with the babies but I didn't like the punishment room. We were locked in there if Miss Frost thought we had misbehaved. My best friends, who are still there, are called Daisy and Tommy Branning, they're brother and sister.' She looked sad for a second as she handed Mrs Spooner her tea before going on, 'I love reading and writing and arithmetic and that's about it.'

'Hmm, and have you no idea who your parents were?'

When Sunday silently shook her head the old woman concluded, 'So you have no one then.'

'I have Daisy and Tommy. They're like family to me.'

'Well, I couldn't afford to take them in as well,' Mrs Spooner told her in her forthright way. 'Would you still be allowed to go and see them?'

'Every Sunday afternoon if I was allowed,' Sunday told her hopefully.

'So what you're saying is, if I take you on – and I say *if* – you would want every Sunday afternoon off?'

Sunday nodded, 'Yes, and a couple of hours every Sunday morning so I could go to church to see Mrs Lockett. She's always been ever so kind to me for as far back as I can remember.'

'Anything else?' Mrs Spooner asked caustically. She had to hand it to the girl, she knew what she wanted and wasn't afraid to ask for it, although she had had every intention of allowing her to have her Sunday afternoons off anyway. In actual fact she reminded Biddy Spooner very much of herself at that age. But would she be up to the job that was going, that was the question. She was only a little scrap of a thing and looked as if a hard day's work would see her off.

She chewed on her heavily painted lips for a moment as she stared thoughtfully down into the cup of tea that Sunday had poured for her, then making a decision she suggested, 'How about you start on Monday and do a month's trial for me? You'd get your bed and board and a couple of shillings a week to start with, that would be the best I could do. If at the end of the month you ain't come up to scratch, you go back to where you've come from. How does that sound?'

Sunday glanced at Lady Huntley and when the woman gave an imperceptible nod of the head, Sunday turned back to Mrs Spooner.

'Very well. But would I get my time off on Sundays as I requested?'

'You ain't backward at coming forward, are you, girl?' Mrs Spooner said, but there was a twinkle in her eye. 'And yes, you can have your time off on Sunday. But now we'll start as we mean to go on. I think Sunday is a silly name so I shall call you Sunny – is it agreed?'

Sunday nodded as Mrs Spooner turned back to Lady Huntley, asking, 'Can I leave it to you to make all the necessary arrangements?'

'Of course,' Lavinia told her. 'There will be release papers to sign but I can do them on your behalf if that is agreeable to you?'

Mrs Spooner inclined her head. 'Thank you, Lady Huntley. It might be for the best. Old Annie grumbles a lot but she's a good sort really. I know she's about ready to clear off though, an' then I'll be up the creek wi'out a paddle wi' all them lodgers to care for so the sooner we can get this sorted the happier I'll be.'

And so it was decided.

Chapter Thirteen

They arrived back at the workhouse to find Daisy down on her knees scrubbing the floors, but the younger girl didn't ask how things had gone. Miss Frost was hovering close by and she didn't want to give the woman another excuse to punish her.

The housemother came to greet Lady Huntley, studiously ignoring Sunday to ask, 'Well, how did it go?'

'It went very well indeed, thank you. But now I must discuss the situation with the housemaster. Excuse me, Miss Frost.' With that, she set off in the direction of the housemaster's office.

Sunday hastily lowered her eyes so that Miss Frost wouldn't see the devilment in them. It was nice to see her being put in her place for a change.

'Ah, so you're back then. Good afternoon,

135

Lady Huntley.' Mr Pinnegar was in the process of eating a huge slice of fruit cake and crumbs were sprayed about the desk. 'Do sit down,' he invited her and she graciously did as he requested whilst Sunday stood meekly at the side of her.

'So was the lady in question interested in employing Sunday?'

When Lady Huntley nodded, he swallowed a morsel down the wrong way and had a fit of coughing.

'Very interested indeed, sir,' Lavinia replied once he had mopped his streaming eyes. 'She would like her to start in her employ next Monday, for a trial period of one month.'

If she had been expecting him to be happy with the outcome she was disappointed when he spluttered, 'Next Monday? But that is quite out of the question, madam! Sunday isn't fourteen for a few weeks yet.'

'I am aware of that,' she answered with a steely glint in her eye. 'But that is neither here nor there if a good position is being offered.'

Albert Pinnegar could see the chances of having Sunday as his secret mistress slipping away. The girl continued to fill his thoughts as no other before her ever had – but how could he argue with one of the guardians?

'Is the lady in question respectable?' he enquired, desperately looking for some excuse to stop Sunday leaving.

'Of course. I would never have entertained the idea of a young person going to her if she wasn't,' Lady Huntley replied indignantly.

There was a tap on the door then and Miss

Frost entered. 'So will Small be leaving us then?' she asked bluntly. Unlike Mr Pinnegar she could hardly wait to see the back of the dratted girl, as was obvious from her manner.

'I can see no valid reason why she shouldn't,' Lady Huntley answered haughtily.

'Excellent.' Miss Frost glanced at the house-master who looked like a mouse that had been trapped in a corner by a cat. He yanked at the collar of his shirt and ran his tongue across his thick wet lips.

Sunday could see small crumbs of fruit cake trapped in his moustache and felt as if she might be sick. If she never had to clap eyes on him again it would be too soon for her, but she still regretted the fact that she would be leaving Daisy and Tommy behind.

'So may I inform Mrs Spooner that Sunday will start on Monday?' Lady Huntley asked. Something was making her feel vaguely uneasy. Mr Pinnegar was clearly not a happy man – but why? It didn't make sense.

'Of course you may,' Miss Frost answered for him as the colour in his face changed from pink to red.

'Then that is settled.' Lady Huntley rose from her seat in a rose-scented flurry of skirts that floated about her like a cloud. 'I shall personally call for Sunday early on Monday morning to escort her to her new home, and as Mrs Spooner is elderly and fairly housebound now I shall also sign any necessary release papers on her behalf.'

'Thank you, that will be most acceptable.' Miss Frost stared at Sunday then and said, 'You may go back to your work now, girl. You still have to earn your keep until you leave.'

'Yes, ma'am.' Sunday flashed a grateful smile at Lady Huntley and sidled from the room, then raced towards the laundry with her thoughts all over the place.

Just a few more days then she would be gone from this place for ever – if her month's trial worked out, that was, but she was determined that it would. Mrs Spooner could no doubt be a bit of a tartar but anyone would be easy compared to Frosty. And better still, Sunday would never have to feel Pinnegar's fat fingers on her again.

Once the office door had closed, Albert Pinnegar sat silently seething. Throughout his recent advances, Small had merely stood as still as a statue with no sign whatsoever on her face of what she was feeling. Physically she was quite fragile but her spirit was strong and he admired that. As yet he had not dared to try and deflower her, for there was always the risk that Miss Frost might appear at any moment. But now he was painfully aware that time was running out. In just a few short days, Sunday would be gone from the workhouse for good. It was time to put the next part of his plan into operation.

Daisy was bursting with curiosity to hear all about the visit, and when the girls retired to bed that evening, Sunday had to relate every tiny bit of the afternoon that she could remember at least twice.

'It was a bit of a shock, my first sight of the old lady,' she confided with a giggle. 'She looks like one of those china-faced dolls with the bright red cheeks you see in the toy-shop windows, and tries to talk la-di-da but every now and again she forgets. Apparently she was just a normal girl from a miner's house in the Ford until she married her husband who was the manager at the brickworks. Lady Huntley told me about her in the carriage on the way home.'

She sighed dreamily as she remembered the carriage ride. 'It was *so* wonderful,' she told her friend who was hanging on her every word. 'We passed the canal and so many lovely green fields I lost count. There were cows and sheep grazing in them and everywhere looked so clean once we got out of the town.'

Daisy had seen such wonders many times before but for Sunday, who had been raised in the grim confines of the workhouse, it was all new. 'And Mrs Spooner has a dog,' she went on. 'Her name is Mabel and she's a golden cocker spaniel and quite beautiful. I always wanted a dog, you know. Lady Huntley told me that Mrs Spooner has a number of cats too. I wonder if it will be up to me to care for them? I do hope so.'

'I think you're going to be really happy there,' Daisy told her, pushing her own feelings aside. Every time she thought of Sunday leaving she had to blink back tears but she didn't want her friend to lose this wonderful opportunity.

'Well, I'm not daft and I know it's going to be hard work,' Sunday said. 'The whole house is filthy from what I could see of it and has been allowed to get into a rare old state. Goodness knows how long it will take me to get it back to rights. But she did say I could go to church every Sunday morning before coming to see you and Tommy in the afternoons, so that's something, isn't it?'

Daisy gave a wry smile. 'You mustn't get worrying about me and Tommy, and if you can't always get to see us we'll quite understand.'

Pulling herself up onto one elbow, Sunday scowled at her. 'Of course I'll come,' she whispered hotly. 'You and Tommy are like family to me. The only family I've ever known, in fact!'

'Well, we'll see. I know we'll both miss you dreadfully. Tommy is pining for you already.' She grinned then. 'You do know he worships you, don't you?'

'I think a lot of him too,' Sunday answered but Daisy shook her head impatiently.

'No – you misunderstand me. I mean he *loves* you! He always has.'

Sunday was flabbergasted. She had always looked upon him as the brother she had never had.

Daisy giggled. 'Didn't you guess?'

Sunday shook her head.

'Well, love will strike when and where it will. That's what our mum always used to say. Love has no respect for age or position.' Daisy shrugged as Sunday lay back against her lumpy pillow and stared at the ceiling. 'I think he's loved you from the first moment he clapped eyes on you. He wants to become apprenticed to a carpenter so that he can start his own business up eventually, and knowing him as I do I've no doubt he'll do it. My big brother can be a determined little devil when he sets his mind to something.'

Seeing that Sunday was frowning, she asked, 'What's wrong?'

'Nothing, really. It's just that I've just suddenly realised I won't be here if my mother comes looking for me.' This had only just occurred to her but then she sighed. 'Not that that's likely to happen now. Perhaps she's died? Or perhaps she never intended to come for me anyway.'

'I'm sure she would have come if she could,' Daisy said comfortingly, stifling a yawn. She desperately wanted to hear every single detail of Sunday's adventure all over again, but it had been another long hard day and, before she knew it, she was fast asleep.

The next morning, as the girls took their daily exercise in the airing yard, Tommy approached the fence that divided them and after Daisy's revelation of the night before, Sunday found herself looking at him through different eyes. Tommy had had a growth spurt over the last twelve months and was now taller than she was, a gangly youth who seemed to be all arms and legs. But somehow Sunday couldn't imagine him as anything other than a friend. With his deep brown eyes that could change from the colour of warm treacle to almost black depending on his mood, and his thick mane of dark brown hair he looked set to be a handsome man one day but still Sunday couldn't picture him as a suitor.

'Daisy tells me you'll be going on Monday,' he whispered mournfully as they strolled up and down the fence keeping a watchful eye on the member of staff who was supervising them.

'Yes, but I shall be back to see you and Daisy every Sunday afternoon come hell or high water,' she promised.

He nodded. 'Well, I just hope this woman you're going to work for treats you right, else she'll have me to answer to when I get out of here,' he said self-consciously.

Sunday blushed.

'And if you're worried about anythin', make sure you speak to Mrs Lockett or Lady Huntley. They'll look out for you.'

Sunday was deeply touched at his concern and was about to reply when a voice yelled, *'Branning – Small*, get away from that fence!'

Tommy winked then strolled away to join the rest of the boys with his hands in his pockets as Sunday re-joined Daisy.

Mrs Lockett was waiting for Sunday at the entrance to the church with her baby in her arms when the workhouse children arrived there on Sunday. Ignoring Miss Frost's forbidding expression she pulled Sunday to one side and told her, 'Lavinia Huntley told me you'll be going to work for Mrs Spooner tomorrow. I'm so thrilled for you and I hope it works out. But just remember I'm here for you if you should ever need me.'

Sunday was mesmerised by the baby and beamed as the tiny girl gripped one of her fingers. She really was the most beautiful baby and the girl had never seen Mrs Lockett looking so happy. She appeared to have taken to motherhood like a duck to water.

'Mrs Spooner says I can still come to church

every week so I shall still see you.'

'Excellent.' Mrs Lockett smiled at her warmly. 'Now shall we go in before Miss Frost drops in a fit?'

They giggled as they hurried into the church side by side.

That night, as Sunday lay in her bed in the dormitory beneath the thin scratchy blanket for what she hoped would be the very last time, she had to sniff back tears. She had realised long ago that tears achieved nothing and was far too proud to show any weakness, but tonight she was choked with emotions. The workhouse was a grim, austere place but it was the only home she had ever known and the prospect of change, as well as being exciting, was also alarming. There was a big wide world out there that she had been protected from until now, up to a point. She had said her goodbyes to Tommy that morning through the wire fence in the airing yard and had been shocked to see that there were genuine tears in his eyes.

'You take care o' yourself now,' he had told her gruffly and she had nodded.

'I will, but you're talking as if we are never going to see each other again when I shall be here to visit you both every Sunday.'

Her parting from Daisy had been no easier and the girl had clung to her as if she would never let her go. 'Don't forget us,' she had begged.

'As if I ever could,' Sunday had responded emotionally. Then she had slipped away to the dormitory to pack the very few clothes she pos-

143

sessed into a bundle. She stripped the sheet and blanket from the bed, wondering what poor soul would take her place in it, then carried them downstairs and headed along the corridor to the laundry. She had almost reached the end of it when Albert Pinnegar's voice halted her and the hairs on the back of her neck stood on end. She had hoped she would never have to speak to him again.

'Yes, sir?' She faced him boldly although her stomach felt as if it was tied in a knot.

'Step into my office.'

Sunday glanced up and down the corridor, for once in her life hoping for a sight of Miss Frost but the matron was nowhere to be seen so she reluctantly did as she was told.

'Are you quite sure that you're happy about this position?' he asked, and she was so surprised that her mouth gaped open.

'Yes, sir, I am, thank you.'

'Hmm...' He stroked his moustache as he eyed her hungrily then said, 'I must admit that I had better things in mind for you.'

'Really?' Sunday was intrigued.

'The thing is...' He appeared to be choosing his words carefully and she waited patiently.

'The thing is ... I have found a very nice little cottage in Coton that is for sale. It would be perfect for me when I retire but in the meantime I was thinking that perhaps you could live in it and keep it clean and tidy for me. I would pay you, of course.'

I bet you would, Sunday thought but she didn't say it. She had a fair idea of what he had in mind, for although she had led a sheltered life she had heard the workhouse women gossiping from time to time.

'I think I'm happy with the position Lady Huntley has found for me, thank you, sir,' she answered politely and now he scowled as he thrust a small package wrapped in brown paper and string towards her.

'Every person who leaves the workhouse takes with them what they arrived with,' he told her shortly. 'These are the clothes that you were wearing when you were left on the doorstep, for what good they will do you. Sign here to say that you've received them.'

Sunday quickly did as she was asked then looked at him. 'Will that be all, sir?'

'Yes – but if you should change your mind about my proposition...'

'I won't,' she informed him, snatching up the bundle. 'Goodbye, sir.'

She was about to leave the office when Pinnegar suddenly shot round the desk with a speed that was quite surprising for a man of his size. He had tried the gentle approach and she had scorned him, so now he would take what he wanted.

Before she knew what was happening he had pushed her across the desk and as she opened her mouth to scream he clamped his fat hand across it whilst he fiddled with the buttons on his flies with the other.

'I've tried to be nice to you,' he gasped, red in the face. 'But now I'm going to make a woman of you, you little bitch!'

145

Terror coursed through her as she tried to fight him off but she was no match for him and now she could feel his hand on the soft skin at the top of her leg as he tried to yank her drawers to one side. He was panting and Sunday felt vomit rise in her throat. His hot flesh was pressed throbbing on her skin and she closed her eyes, knowing that there was nothing more she could do to stop what was about to happen.

Then suddenly, like a miracle, there came a loud knocking on the door and Pinnegar jerked upright like a puppet on a string.

'Stand up and not a word, do you understand,' he hissed, 'else some other girl will take your place later today.' All the time he was talking he was putting his clothes back in order and, badly shaken, Sunday rose and did the same.

'Mr Pinnegar! Lady Huntley has arrived early.' Miss Frost's voice reached them through the door. 'Why is the door locked? And where is the Small girl?'

'Ah, I locked the door to give us some privacy while I handed over her possessions,' he answered, hurriedly going to unlock it.

Miss Frost glared at Sunday suspiciously before asking, 'Are you ready, Small?'

Sunday was shaking so badly she feared the woman would notice but she kept her voice steady as she answered, 'Yes, miss.'

She then sailed past the housemaster without giving him so much as a second glance and once the door had closed behind her he slammed his fist onto the desk, upsetting the inkwell, and let out a string of oaths. The little minx had got under his skin and he'd be damned if he'd rest till he had her, by fair means or foul!

'Ah, here you are, my dear. Are you all ready to go?' Lady Huntley asked and when Sunday nodded she smiled approvingly as she smoothed her cream gloves up her arm. 'Good, well, all the necessary forms have been signed so we'll be on our way, shall we?'

Miss Frost escorted them to the door. Unlike Mr Pinnegar it was a case of good riddance to bad rubbish as far as she was concerned.

'Goodbye then, Small,' she said as Lady Huntley led Sunday out onto the steps. 'And good luck.'

'Goodbye, Miss Frost,' Sunday answered with dignity. The woman had just saved her from being raped, could she have known it, which was one thing Sunday had to be thankful to her for. Miss Frost then slammed the door so hard that it danced on its hinges.

Sunday stood for a moment staring at it, hardly able to believe what a lucky escape she had had, then turning to Lady Huntley she took a deep breath.

'I'm ready.' It was time to go and start her new life.

Chapter Fourteen

'You're very quiet, dear,' Lady Huntley commented, as the carriage rattled along. 'Are you feeling nervous?'

'A little,' the girl confessed. 'But I shall be fine.'

Lady Huntley had no doubt about it. Sunday was a plucky young thing and she couldn't help but admire her.

'You could perhaps take your cap off now,' she suggested kindly. 'There's no need to wear it any more if you have no wish to, and it's such a shame to cover your glorious hair.'

That's the first perk of being away from the work-house, Sunday thought as she did as she was told and promptly lobbed the dratted thing out of the open carriage window. No more sore chins – hurrah. She then glanced down at the ugly uniform she was wearing. Perhaps when she had saved some of her wages she could go to the rag stall on the market and get herself something nicer to wear?

Lady Huntley, who appeared to have been able to read her thoughts, said, 'I have a portmanteau full of clothes that I never wear any more here for you, Sunday. Miss Frost informed me that you had been taught how to sew, so perhaps you will be able to adapt some of them to fit you – just until you have time to get some new ones, of course,' she added tactfully, knowing how proud

148

Sunday could be.

'Thank you, ma'am.' Sunday blushed with excitement at the thought of wearing something other than the workhouse uniform she had worn all her life. Anything would be an improvement on that, surely? She gazed wide-eyed at all the unfamiliar places they were passing through. Never having gone further than the church in Coton or the marketplace, she felt as if a whole new world was spreading out before her and it was too much to take in.

Soon after, the coachman drew the horses to a halt in front of Mrs Spooner's residence and helped both passengers down from the carriage. Today Lavinia was dressed in a pale lemon crinoline that was trimmed with navy blue to match the bonnet. It was adorned with lemon silk roses and Sunday was sure she had never seen anything more pretty. No doubt it had cost all she could earn in a whole year at least. Not that she begrudged Lady Huntley owning it. She had proved beyond a doubt already what a kind, generous lady she was.

'Here we are then,' Lady Huntley chirped cheerfully when they were standing at the bottom of the steps. Sunday was clutching the brown paper bundle that Mr Pinnegar had given her and despite the brave face she was presenting, her teeth were chattering with nerves and delayed shock following his attempted rape.

The same elderly woman that they had seen before opened the door to them. Jerking a tobacco-stained finger down the hallway, she announced, 'Biddy's in there. She's expectin' yer.'

'Thank you.' Lady Huntley set off in the direction she had indicated, Sunday at her side, as the coachman set down the portmanteau she had mentioned just inside the door and went back outside to the horses.

'Ah, so yer here then.' Mrs Spooner stared at Sunday. 'And all ready to knuckle down and do some work, I hope?'

'Yes, ma'am.'

'Right then, well, while me an' Lady Huntley 'ere have a sup o' tea I'll get Annie to show you where you'll be sleeping. From now on, the main of the housework will fall to you. But Annie will continue to come in until you've learned how to cook.' She then turned her attention to Annie who had appeared in the doorway and told her, 'Take the lass up to her room, would you, then you can show her round the rest of the house.'

Annie sniffed. 'Anythin' else yer want doin'?' she grumbled as Sunday followed her towards the staircase.

As they climbed the stairs, the girl noticed that the banister was heavily carved from mahogany and was probably quite beautiful beneath the layers of dust. They arrived on the first-floor landing with Annie puffing and panting.

'This is where all the lodgers sleep,' she informed Sunday breathlessly, pointing to a number of doors that led off it. 'You'll be up in the servants' quarters. Not that there's been any servants 'cept me 'ere fer many a long day.' She shambled off to a door at the very end of the long landing and when it was opened they were confronted with yet another set of steep stairs. Unlike the first flight, which had a carpet running up the centre, held in place by brass runners, these steps were bare wood and their feet echoed hollowly on them as they climbed.

'Phew, I'm glad I don't 'ave to come up 'ere very often,' Annie gasped when they reached the top. 'My poor old dicky ticker ain't up to it any more.' She stood for a moment getting her breath back then set off again, stopping at the second door she came to. The corridor wasn't so long here and Sunday realised that they must be under the eaves, for the roof sloped slightly on either side of them.

'Ah, just as I thought. There's a bed in 'ere,' Annie announced with satisfaction. 'Most o' the other rooms are full o' junk that's been brought up 'ere over the years. It ain't posh admittedly but I dare say it'll do when it's had a bit of a clean-up.'

Sunday stood in the doorway and looked around. An iron-framed bed stood against one wall with a small table with an oil lamp on it at the side of it. On the opposite wall was a large chest of drawers and on the back of the door were a number of nails where she could hang her clothes – *when I have some to hang up!* she thought wryly. All she had was what she stood up in at the moment until she unpacked the items Lady Huntley had kindly given to her. She crossed the room to the window and after wiping a little circle in the grime she saw that it gave a wonderful view across open fields. There was another slightly bigger table that housed a jug and bowl beneath it and although her steps had created a cloud of dust, the girl could have wept for joy.

151

For the first time in her whole life she would have a room all to herself!

'It's perfect,' she told Annie with a lump in her throat and the woman scowled.

'Well, I'd 'ardly call it that, lass. But then if yer happy wi' it that's all that counts. I dare say it'll scrub up nicely enough wi' a bit o' spit an' polish an' a dollop of elbow grease. I'll see as the missus gives yer time to get that done first so yer can settle in afore you do owt else.'

For the first time, Sunday realised that Annie wasn't as harsh as she made out and she smiled at her. Then, throwing her small bundle into the deep bottom drawer, she followed Annie to begin her tour of the house.

'I'll show yer the downstairs first,' Annie wheezed as she tackled the stairs again. 'The lodgers 'ave bed, breakfast an' evenin' meal an' they're out fer most o' the day workin', but you'll get to meet 'em all, given time.'

Finally, back on the ground floor again, Annie headed for the back of the house and entered an enormous kitchen. On one wall was a huge black-leaded range, although Sunday noted that it hadn't been cleaned for many a long day. A large oak table stood in the centre of the room sur-rounded by a number of wooden ladder-backed chairs, which again all looked in need of a good scrub. Next to the back door was a deep stone sink with a pump attached to it that pumped in water from a well outside.

That should save some time, Sunday thought approvingly. Attached to the sink was a deeply grooved wooden draining board but it was covered in dirty pots and pans. Two large ginger cats lay asleep in front of the range and they flicked their tails and eyed Sunday suspiciously as she passed them. Glancing down at the floor she assumed it was covered in red quarry tiles but again, they were covered in the dirt of ages and so she couldn't be certain.

'Yer needn't look like that,' Annie bridled, seeing the expression on Sunday's face. 'This is a big place fer one woman to keep clean an' I ain't no spring chicken no more! It takes me all me time to get the meals on the table an' see to the lodgers' bedrooms, so it does.'

'Oh, I wasn't blaming you,' Sunday assured her hastily. The last thing she wanted to do was offend the woman. 'I was just wondering how you've managed, that's all. It's such a big, rambling place.'

'It is that,' Annie huffed, slightly appeased. 'But now why don't yer get what cleanin' things yer need an' go an' get yer room ready? I've got to start preparin' the lodgers' evenin' meal.'

After scouting around for a while Sunday found all she needed. A bucket and a somewhat dingy mop, some soda crystals and lye soap and a number of old rags. Annie was already seated at the kitchen table shelling peas by then so she silently made her way back up to her room. She was breathless by the time she got there. It had been no easy task balancing the bucket up two flights of stairs but she was eager to make a start. So much so that she forgot all about going to say goodbye and thank you to Lady Huntley. First of all, she gathered up the rugs that were scattered about the floor and placed them by the door. Later

153

on she would take them outside and give them a good beating. She then opened the window as wide as it would go and set to with a vengeance, coughing and spluttering as the dust swirled around her in clouds. She was so absorbed in what she was doing that she started when Annie appeared in the doorway some two hours later.

'Are yer deaf or what?' she grumbled. 'I've been bawlin' me lungs out fer you to come down an' 'ave something to eat.' She looked around in amazement. The floorboards were gleaming damply in the light from the window that Sunday had cleaned, the whole room was spick and span, and the furniture smelled of beeswax polish.

'Well, I'll be...' she said, greatly impressed. 'You've certainly transformed this room, lass.'

Sunday sat back on her heels and grinned. She was in the process of wiping down the chest of drawers now, before cleaning inside the drawers, lining them with newspaper and then giving the whole thing a good polish.

'I've almost finished. I hung the flock mattress out of the window and gave it a good shake but I forgot to ask you where I might find some bedding. I want to give the rugs a good beating too – and once that's done you can tell me where else you want me to start.'

'I'll show yer where the linen cupboard is an' yer can help yerself to whatever yer need. But leave this fer now an' come an' get somethin' inside yer. We only 'ave a light meal midday but it'll keep yer goin' till yer dinner tonight.'

Sunday stood up and wiped her hands on her apron before following Annie downstairs.

'I've taken a tray in to the missus,' Annie informed her, 'but she'll eat in the dinin' room wi' the lodgers this evenin'. You'll eat in the kitchen wi' me.'

As they entered the kitchen the smell of new-baked bread reached Sunday and her stomach growled ominously. She suddenly realised that she hadn't eaten at all that day; she had been too nervous at breakfast, not that she had missed much. The porridge that was served to them in the workhouse always left a nasty after-taste and often made her feel nauseous.

Now she gazed in amazement at the two loaves that were cooling on a rack on the table. They looked nothing at all like the dry grey bread that she was used to and her mouth watered at the sight of them.

'I do me own bakin' at least three times a week,' Annie informed her proudly. 'There's one thing I'll say fer the missus, she don't skimp when it comes to feedin' her lodgers – an' though I say it meself, I'm a fair old cook.' She chuckled then. 'I've 'ad to be. I 'ad eleven nippers to see to an' they was always hungry so I 'ad to make me money go a long way. They've all long since grown up an' flown the nest but I still pride meself on keepin' a good table. Now sit yerself down an' stick in, lass.'

Sunday plonked herself down on one of the kitchen chairs and stared at the food spread out before her.

'That's the remains o' the leg o' pork left over from last night's dinner,' Annie informed her. 'An' there's some pickled onions an' cheese there

155

along wi' the butter. That should keep yer goin' till later.'

As she spoke she was sawing off a great wedge of the fresh-baked bread and she placed it on Sunday's plate along with a thick slice of succulent pork and the most enormous pickled onion the girl had ever seen. She then added a good-sized wedge of cheese and told her, 'Well, get stuck in then.'

As Sunday bit into the bread, liberally spread with golden-yellow butter, she sighed with delight. She had never tasted anything like it in her life and before she knew it she had made a pig of herself.

'Oh dear,' she apologised. 'I'm afraid I've been rather greedy, but your food is so tasty, Annie.'

Annie grinned as she swiped a straggle of grey hair behind her ear. 'Never you mind. I like to see a lass wi' a good appetite. I used to tell my lot they'd got 'ollow legs. I could never fill the little bleeders up. It ain't the same when yer only 'ave yerself to see to, that's why I offered to come an' help the missus out when her old man died.' As she spoke she was filling a mug with tea to which she then added milk and a liberal amount of sugar before pushing it across the table to Sunday. 'Now get that down yer an' then per'aps yer'd like to tackle the washin' up afore yer finish yer room. I'm going to put me feet up at the side o' the range fer an hour or two now afore I have to get the meat in fer tonight's dinner. We're 'aving lamb an' roast potatoes.'

Sunday happily began to add the dirty pots to the pile already teetering on the draining board. The back door was open and the only sound to be heard was the birds singing in the trees. The girl felt a sensation of well-being wash over her. Perhaps it wasn't going to be so bad living here after all, she found herself thinking.

Chapter Fifteen

As she had been told, Sunday dined in the kitchen that evening with Annie and when they had eaten Annie donned her coat and set off for home, telling Sunday, 'I can leave you to clear up the pots, can't I, lass?'

'Of course.' Sunday wished her good evening then, left to her own devices she set to with a will. After washing up every pot in sight and transferring the clean ones to the table, she then scrubbed down the huge oak dresser that took up almost one wall before putting them away. The floor was next, and after giving it its second thorough mopping she was gratified to see the red-brick tiles shining through the dirt. She would have liked to tackle the heavily tarnished copper pans that were suspended all along the shelf in the fireplace but it was growing dusk by then and she was so tired that she was sure she could have fallen asleep on her feet.

Still, at least I've made a good start, she thought as she glanced around appreciatively. Already she could picture what a lovely kitchen it would be when everything in it was bright and shining. It was at that moment that the door leading into the hall swung open and Mrs Spooner appeared, making her jump.

'Ah, I was wondering if I'd catch you before you went to bed, Sunny. I was going to ring the bell in the parlour but I thought you might have already gone up.' She stared about her for a moment but she didn't make any comment before turning her attention back to Sunday and saying, 'I was aware that you might need some clean clothes to change into so I got my dressmaker to run these up for you. I had to guess the size, of course, but they'll be good enough to wear about the house no doubt, and Lady Huntley tells me she's given you some clothes that might be suitable for walking out in once you've had time to alter them.'

Colour burned into the girl's cheeks as she gratefully accepted the clothes that were folded across the old woman's arm. Biddy Spooner was gripping her walking stick and told Sunday then, 'You may turn in whenever you wish now. No doubt you will be tired. Good night, Sunny.'

'Good night, ma'am.'

The minute the old lady had left the room, Sunday laid the clothes across the now clean table-top and began to examine them. There were two identical gowns made of a thick cotton material in a navy-blue colour trimmed with white piping. They were fairly plain but by far the finest that she had ever worn and she stroked the material reverently. There were also a number of white petticoats and undergarments as well as two fine lawn nightdresses. Sunday's eyes shone as she examined them and she could hardly wait to try them on. But then she caught sight of herself in the mirror above the fireplace. Her hair was thick with dust and there were smuts of dirt on her cheeks. It would be a crime to put these clothes on in the state she was in. Making a hasty decision, she filled the kettle and put it on the range to heat. Before she went to bed she would wash her hair and every inch of herself from top to toe. It was unlikely she would be disturbed as Annie had told her no one ever ventured into the kitchen of an evening.

An hour later, after laying the fire ready to be lit the next morning, she wearily made her way up to her room, clutching her precious new clothes and feeling clean as a new pin. She lit the oil lamp in her room with the candle she had carried up there, then after taking off the hated uniform she flung it into a corner and slipped one of her new nightdresses over her head. There was an old pitted mirror hanging above the washstand and as she caught sight of herself in her new finery she did a little twirl about the room. The nightdress was slightly long, with full sleeves and a tiny collar trimmed with lace. She felt like a princess and was very grateful to the woman who had supplied her with the first brand-new item of clothing she had ever owned. She yawned then as the long day caught up with her and the smile slid from her face as she thought of Daisy and Tommy still trapped in the workhouse. They would have been in bed for hours now and suddenly she missed them desperately.

Crossing to the newly made bed she turned back the covers and again realised how lucky she was. The pillow was feather-filled and the sheets were crisp white cotton. The blankets were soft and thick and Sunday wished with all her heart that her friends were there to share such luxury with her as she slid into the bed. For a while she lay there listening to the night noises and trying to adjust to her change of circumstances. She loved the feeling of the open space all around her. Eventually she snuggled down and within seconds exhaustion claimed her and she slept.

The sound of a cock crowing woke her early the next morning and for a second she blinked, wondering where she was. And then it all came back to her and she hastily scuttled out of bed and washed in the jug of water she had placed ready, realising she hadn't asked her new employer what time she was expected downstairs. It wouldn't do to turn up late on her very first day. Once she had dressed in her new finery she brushed her hair and glanced into the mirror. Her hair had grown back to chin-length now and hung in soft curls about her face, and her eyes were glowing. The dress, which fitted tight into the waist, was far more flattering on than off, and again she did a little twirl of pure pleasure. It was a shame about the ugly boots but there was nothing to be done about them for now so she hastily tidied her bed and hurried downstairs.

She was making her way along the first-floor landing when Mrs Spooner suddenly emerged from one of the bedrooms there and she stared at Sunday in amazement.

'I hardly recognised you,' she remarked eventually. 'That dress fits very well, considering I had to guess your size. But don't let it go to your head, mind. You have to earn what those clothes cost me now.'

'Oh, I will, Mrs Spooner,' Sunday promised. 'Do you need any help getting down the stairs?'

She held her hand out to assist her but the old woman slapped it away. 'When I want your help I'll ask for it,' she told her peevishly. 'Now go an' see if Annie's arrived yet an' make yerself useful. I haven't employed you to stand about lookin' pretty. An' tomorrow morning I'll expect you to be up a bit earlier to light the fires afore everyone gets up.'

'Yes, Mrs Spooner.' Sunday clattered away down the stairs, stifling a giggle. She could be a crusty old devil that was for sure but already Sunday had discovered she had a good heart. She had almost reached the kitchen when a young man with a newspaper folded under his arm appeared from Mrs Spooner's drawing room.

'Ah, you must be Sunny.' He gave her a smile and extended his hand and Sunday cautiously shook it as colour flooded into her cheeks.

'My aunt has told me all about you. How did your first evening here go? I trust you slept well? Oh, and I'm Jacob Bartlett, by the way.'

'I slept very well, thank you, sir,' Sunday replied, taking in his neat suit and cravat. 'Now I err … really ought to get on,' she mumbled.

'Of course.' He gallantly stepped aside and Sunday almost tripped over her skirt in her haste to reach the kitchen and close the door between them.

Now why did I behave like that? He'll think I'm

some sort of a simpleton, she silently scolded herself. She had never been addressed by a young man like that before but she didn't have long to think about it, for at that moment, Annie bustled in saying, 'Phew, I swear that walk down Church Road gets longer every day. Either that or me old legs are wearin' out good an' proper.' Looking Sunday up and down then she smiled her approval before suggesting, 'I should get yer apron on if I were you, lass. Yer wouldn't want to go spoilin' that nice new frock, now would yer?'

Sunday hurried over to take her apron from the nail on the back of the door as Annie threw some coal into the range and placed the kettle on top of it.

'We'll 'ave us a nice cuppa, I think, afore I start the breakfasts,' she said, sliding her shawl from her shoulders. 'An' you can look lively an' go an' set a match to the fire in the dinin' room.' She cocked her thumb towards the ceiling then. 'Sounds like everybody's up an' about now. They'll be comin' down like a pack o' vultures soon, you just mark my words. You can carry the food into the dinin' room an' place it on the sideboard for 'em this morning. They help 'emselves from there. It'll be one less job fer me to do.'

'Of course,' Sunday agreed willingly as she hurried away to light the fire. When she returned she set out two cups and saucers. Soon the kettle was singing and once Annie had made the tea she carried the teapot to the table and set it aside to mash.

'So does Mrs Spooner's nephew live here?' Sunday asked curiously. 'I just met him in the hallway.'

162

'Ah, yes he does, that's young Jacob,' Annie replied, lifting the lid of the teapot and giving it a good stir. She glanced towards the door then to ensure that they were alone and confided, 'His mother were Biddy's sister – an' a right little madam she were an' all if yer get me drift.' She tapped the side of her nose as Sunday stared at her blankly then sighed. How could she explain to a thirteen year old? 'He were born on the wrong side o' the blanket so to speak, then Biddy's sister dumped him an' ran off when he were no more than knee-high to a grasshopper! No one's seen hide nor hair of her since, so Biddy an' the mister brought him up as their own. An' a right good job they did of it an' all. Sadly, they couldn't 'ave any of their own so young Jacob fulfilled a need in 'em.'

'How sad.' *But at least his mother didn't dump him on the steps of the workhouse like mine did,* Sunday found herself thinking as her idyllic picture of her mother slipped for just a moment.

They drank their tea then Annie started breakfast and for a time they didn't think of anything but the job in hand. Soon Sunday was carrying platters of sizzling eggs, bacon, kidneys and all manner of treats into the dining room and placing them on the sideboard, which she noted was just as neglected as the rest of the house. *I'll tackle this room next,* she decided before scuttling away as the first of the lodgers entered the room.

'So who does all the laundry?' she asked Annie when breakfast was over.

'The lodgers have local women do their washin' and ironin' for 'em, an' all the bedding gets collected once a week by a laundry in town, but I've always done the missus's and Jacob's washing for 'em. Per'aps that's another job you could take off me hands?' she suggested. 'There's a washroom in the yard out the back with a dolly tub, a copper an' a mangle. I usually tackle it on a Monday, weather permittin'. You could do your own at the same time.'

'Yes, I could,' Sunday agreed. She was just beginning to realise how enormous Annie's workload was. It was no wonder the house had got into a state.

When the table had been cleared and the dirty pots had been washed, dried and put away, Sunday headed off to clean the dining room. Standing on a chair, she first unhooked the heavy curtains and carried them outside where she hung them across the line and gave them a good beating. As the dust flew into the air she was shocked to see a colour emerging. They were a lovely royal blue and by the time she carried them back indoors and rehung them they looked very smart indeed. She did the same with the rugs that were scattered about, then put them to one side as she tackled the floor. It was a beautiful wooden parquet and by lunchtime it was gleaming, having had a thorough mop and a polish. Annie came to the door then to summon her to the kitchen for something to eat and she looked around approvingly. The sideboard was shining with beeswax polish and Sunday had already made a start on the rest of the furniture. She'd also washed the windows, and now the sunshine was flooding into the room.

'Blimey! I ain't seen it look like this for many a long year,' the old lady remarked. 'I'll hand it to you, lass, you ain't afraid of hard work.'

Sunday smiled at the praise as she followed her back to the kitchen. 'I should have it all finished for when the lodgers come home tonight,' she told her. 'I'm going to get through one of the downstairs rooms each day this week, then next week I can make a start upstairs, then I'll have to go back and begin at the beginning again with a house this size.'

Lunch consisted of delicious fried eggs that Annie informed her had been bought from a local farm.

'Biddy used to have half a dozen chickens of her own out the back,' she informed the girl. 'An' there's a lovely walled vegetable garden too, but sadly it's all gone to ruin since the master died. He loved potterin' about in there, he did, but these days I have to buy the veg from the market. It plays 'avoc wi' my old legs, havin' to go all that way into town.'

'So you thought perhaps that could be another job I could take off your hands?' Sunday said with a cheeky grin before Annie could suggest it.

Annie chuckled. 'Well, the thought 'ad crossed me mind,' she confessed. She liked someone with a lively sense of humour.

By Saturday of Sunday's first week at Whittleford Lodge the whole of the downstairs had been transformed into a clean and orderly living space. She was tired but satisfied with what she had achieved, but now she was looking forward to seeing Mrs Lockett at church in the morning and

Daisy and Tommy in the workhouse the same afternoon.

'I have a carriage come to take me to church each Sunday morning so you can travel with me,' Mrs Spooner said, and Sunday willingly accepted the kind offer although she did wonder why Mrs Spooner attended Chilvers Coton All Saints Church when St Paul's was close by in Church Road. She had started to explore the area a little now when she had any spare time and was shocked at just how many different parishes there were in the town. Up until she had come to live with Mrs Spooner her whole world had revolved around the parish of Coton.

'The master were born an' bred in Coton,' Annie explained when Sunday commented on it. 'An' they were wed at Chilvers Coton so she's attended there ever since. So did he while he was alive, God rest his soul. He were a good man, were the master. They used to have their own pony an' trap that they travelled about in but the missus let 'em go when the mister died.'

That night, Sunday again washed her hair and every inch of herself, ready for the outings the next day. Sewing by the light of the oil lamp in her room she had worked on one of the dresses Lady Huntley had given her for a couple of hours each night and now it was hanging up on the back of the door, all ready to be worn.

As Sunday lay in bed she admired it and could hardly wait to put it on. It was made of heavy cotton with a full skirt that cinched in tight to the waist. It was a very pale lemon colour sprigged with tiny blue forget-me-not flowers that exactly matched her eyes, and Sunday knew that she was going to feel like a princess in it. She yawned as she wondered what Daisy and Tommy would think of her in her new attire and fell asleep with a happy smile on her face.

Chapter Sixteen

Sunday was up early the next morning and by the time the carriage arrived to take her and Mrs Spooner to church she had cleared the dining room and washed and dried the breakfast pots. The carriage was nowhere near as grand as the one she had arrived in with Lady Huntley, but all the same Sunday felt like royalty when it deposited them at the lych-gate of the church.

People were hurrying up the path, keen not to be late for the service, and they eyed Sunday curiously, wondering where they had seen her before. In her pretty new clothes, she looked completely different to the girl from the work-house in the drab uniform they were accustomed to seeing.

Mrs Lockett was greeting the congregation with her husband at the door with baby Phoebe in her arms.

'Why, just look at you! Don't you look grand?' she said as she pulled Sunday aside to have a private word. 'But how is it going? Are they treating you all right?'

Sunday was quick to reassure her. 'I'm fine and

167

settling in very well, thank you. It's hard work admittedly and I don't get much time to myself but it's a hundred times better than being shut away in the workhouse.'

Relief washed across the woman's features but then she saw the party from the workhouse advancing up the path in a straight regimental line supervised by Miss Frost and murmured hastily, 'I'll come and have a word with you when the service is over, and perhaps you can introduce me to Mrs Spooner?' She hurried back to her husband's side then as Sunday quickly scanned the line for a sight of Daisy and Tommy. And then there they were and it would have been hard to tell who was the most delighted to see each other again. Sunday would have liked nothing more than to run up to them and tell them all her news. But this would only get them into trouble with the matron so she kept her eyes downcast as they filed past her. They would have to wait for a catch-up until she visited them in the workhouse later that afternoon. At the very back of the line was Mr Pinnegar, and when he came abreast of her he paused to ask, 'How are you, Small?'

Just the sight of her looking so clean and pretty set his pulses throbbing. He had thought she had been an attractive girl dressed in the workhouse garb, but with her hair and her eyes shining and in that dress, it was all he could do to keep his hands off her.

'I shall be calling to see you tomorrow to ask your new mistress how you are shaping up,' he informed her and Sunday's heart beat with alarm.

'Mrs Spooner is here today, sir. Perhaps you could ask her now to save yourself a journey?' she suggested tactfully. But the organ struck up a tune then and there was no more time for niceties so they both hurried into the church and took their seats in the pews.

As always, it was a lovely service and the voices of the congregation echoed from the rafters as they sang the much-loved hymns and listened to Edgar's reading. When it was over, the vicar and his wife stood at the door saying goodbye to their parishioners as they left, and Sunday herself waited quietly for Mrs Spooner.

The workhouse inmates trooped past her, glancing at her curiously as she smiled at them, followed last of all by Miss Frost and Mr Pinnegar.

'She looks well, does she not, Miss Frost?' the housefather said as he eyed Sunday covetously.

Miss Frost sniffed and looked Sunday up and down as if she were of no worth whatsoever.

'Let us just hope she remembers who it was who gave her a start in life,' she answered repressively, then taking the man's arm she led him away without so much as a backward glance.

Minutes later Mrs Spooner arrived and hobbled painfully back to the lych-gate where the carriage was waiting for them. 'It's a shame the visiting hours at the workhouse aren't earlier in the day. As it is you'll have to come all the way back home only to return later,' the woman commented and Sunday nodded in agreement. It was a fair walk back from Whittleford to the workhouse admittedly, but she would gladly have walked twice the distance if it meant being able

169

to see her friends. If she could find her way there, that was!

Annie had a delicious roast dinner waiting for them and for once the house seemed full, as the lodgers had no work to go to on the Sabbath. Sunday still hadn't been formally introduced to them all as yet, but Mrs Spooner intended to rectify that when she returned from visiting an old friend later that afternoon. Sunday was looking forward to it; they seemed a nice group of people and she had no doubt that she would soon get to know them if she was to live there.

After dinner she washed the pots, leaving them to drain and promising Annie that she would dry them and put them away when she returned.

'Will you just tell me the directions again?' she asked Annie for at least the tenth time in as many minutes and the old woman sighed.

'Out the front door and down the hill till you come to Church Road, left into that, straight to the top and turn left again, then when you reach Heath Road turn right an' keep goin' an' you'll come to the workhouse on the bend. Got it?'

Sunday nodded apologetically. She was not used to finding her way outside the workhouse but she didn't want to be late for her visit and so she set off, allowing herself plenty of time to be there before two o'clock. It was a glorious day with the sun riding high in a cloudless blue sky and despite the fact that her boots were rubbing her heels, Sunday quite enjoyed the walk, promising herself that she would treat her feet to some new footwear just as soon as she was paid.

She sighed with relief when the workhouse

came into view. At least she had managed to find her way there. A number of people were already assembled on the workhouse steps and it felt strange to be going there as a visitor rather than as a resident. At two o'clock sharp they heard the sound of the bolts being drawn and they began to file in. Sunday glanced ruefully down at the floor, wondering how many times she had been down on her hands and knees scrubbing it. That job would fall to some other poor soul now.

Miss Frost was waiting in the day room and when Sunday appeared she ignored her before telling one of the girls, 'Go and fetch Daisy and Tommy Branning.' She had no need to ask who Sunday had come to see. The girl scuttled away as Sunday settled on a chair at one of the tables to wait.

Tommy and Daisy soon appeared and hurried happily over to join her.

'You look wonderful,' Daisy said enviously as she stared at Sunday's dress and Tommy blushed as he nodded in agreement. But the awkward moment soon passed as Sunday told them all about her new home.

'There's a lovely dog called Mabel and some cats,' she said excitedly. 'And they used to have their own chickens too. There's a big walled vegetable garden as well and an orchard, but sadly there's no one to tend it now and it's all overgrown.'

'I could tend it,' Tommy muttered. 'I like gardening.'

'I'm sure you could,' Sunday agreed, wishing with all her heart that she could just pick both her friends up and run away with them. She hated to think of them still there while she had her freedom. 'But what have you both been doing?'

Daisy grimaced. 'I've been on nursery duty for the last three nights. Ugh, all those soiled bindings to change. I don't know how you enjoyed working up there, I really don't.'

Tommy grinned at Sunday. 'Our Daisy doesn't seem to have the same maternal instincts you have,' he teased his sister and she playfully slapped at his arm. There was so much to say and not enough time to say it in before Sunday would be gone again for another week.

The hour seemed to pass in a flash and when Miss Frost appeared and rang the bell to herald the end of visiting time, Daisy had to blink back tears.

'I miss you something awful,' she said chokily. 'There's no one else in the girls' quarters I can really talk to now 'cos they're all much younger than me.' And Sunday's kind heart went out to her.

'I miss you too but it won't be for ever. Somehow I'm going to get you out of here,' she promised.

They said their goodbyes and Sunday left on legs that suddenly felt as heavy as lead. The return journey to Whittleford seemed to take twice as long and she constantly fretted that she was going the wrong way. When she eventually entered the house by the back door, Annie took one look at her and asked, 'What's wrong, lass? You look like yer lost a bob an' found a tanner. Did the visit not go very well?'

'Oh, it went very well. It's just so hard to leave my friends there, I suppose,' Sunday said miserably.

There was no answer to that so Annie went back to preparing the Sunday tea. There were hard-boiled eggs, a chicken pie, fresh-baked bread and pickles, as well as a large sponge cake oozing jam and cream that Annie had baked that afternoon. Already in just a few days, the elderly lady could see a change in Sunday. She was losing the sallow complexion so evident in people who came from the workhouse and now there were some roses in her cheeks. Annie thought her face had filled out slightly too, due to the good food she was now eating, and she just wished that she could help all the children that were incarcerated in that terrible place. Thank God her own eleven childer had escaped that fate.

After tea, Mrs Spooner called Sunday into the drawing room and introduced her to the lodgers. Sunday didn't really think of them as lodgers at all as Annie had confided that many of them had lived there for some years.

'This is Mr Greaves, Sunny,' Mrs Spooner told her, referring to an elderly gentleman who looked as neat as a new pin. He was sitting in the window seat reading a newspaper. His hair and moustache looked as if they had been painted silver but his twinkling grey eyes were lively and alert.

He extended his hand. 'I'm very pleased to meet you I'm sure, my dear. And may I say what a wonderful job you've done of tidying up the downstairs rooms? It's a pleasure to come home

173

each day now.'

'Thank you kindly for noticing, sir.' Sunday bobbed her knee respectfully and he beamed.

'Mrs Spooner's husband Herbert and I were great friends and worked together for many years at the brickworks,' he told her then. 'Sadly, this dear lady and I lost our spouses within weeks of each other so I decided to sell my house and move in here.' He winked at her then. 'I'm afraid we men are not much use on our own and Annie's culinary skills are legendary around here.'

'She is a wonderful cook,' Sunday agreed, smiling back at him.

'And this here is Miss Bailey,' Mrs Spooner said, introducing a very elderly lady who was busily working on an embroidery frame. 'Miss Bailey used to be the headmistress at Stockingford School until she retired.'

Sunday was struck by the difference in the two women. Where Mrs Spooner was very flamboyant and extrovert in her dress, Miss Bailey was the complete opposite and looked every inch the spinster in a severely cut high-necked gown that had no adornment of any kind. Her grey hair was pinned back from her face and she reminded Sunday of a little bird.

'Good afternoon,' Miss Bailey said politely. 'Mrs Spooner informs me that you enjoy reading and writing, Miss Small.'

Sunday nodded. 'Yes, indeed I do, Miss Bailey. But please call me Sunday.'

'Pah!' Mrs Spooner waved her hand airily. 'Sunday indeed! It's Sunny while you live here.' She then turned to a much younger woman who seemed to be a bundle of nerves. 'This is Miss Falconer. She's only been with us for a few months and she's working in the solicitor's office in town.'

'How do you do,' the woman said, and shook her hand. 'I would like to add my praise to that of Mr Greaves. The house is looking wonderful. You've done remarkably well with it in less than a week.' Sunday noted that she was very tall for a woman, and quite plain, but she seemed pleasant enough. She looked to be in her early to mid-twenties and Sunday wondered why such a young woman was living in a lodging house, although she didn't dare to question her until she had got to know her a little better. Her soft brown hair was brushed into a neat, shining arrangement, and her dress was a pale dove grey and rather reserved for someone so young. Through the gold-framed spectacles she wore, Sunday could see that her eyes were a lovely shade of green and she found herself thinking that the woman could be quite attractive. Everyone had a past and a story, the girl found herself thinking.

'And finally my nephew, Jacob Bartlett – but I think you've already met, haven't you?'

'Yes, we have.' Sunday blushed as he looked up from the book he was reading on the couch and smiled at her, and now that the introductions had been made, she turned to go back to the kitchen. Annie would be leaving any time now and the rest of the evening was hers to do what she liked with, once she had prepared the dining-room table for breakfast and tidied the kitchen. Already she was getting into a routine. Strangely, even though she

175

could now go to bed at whatever time she liked within reason, Sunday found that her body was used to workhouse hours and after seven o'clock she couldn't seem to stop yawning. But then she had lived by such a strict regime that she realised with a little shock that it was going to take some time to get used to her new way of life.

'So you've met the crew then?' Annie chirped when Sunday entered the kitchen.

'Yes, and they all seem very nice.'

Annie sighed as she stabbed a hat-pin into her old felt hat. 'They are, but there was a time when every room in this place were full. Trouble is, there's too much to do for one person to see to any more lodgers, so there's four rooms stood empty. An' the jobs that need doin' about the place ... the front needs a lick o' paint, the gardens are over-grown. Huh! We could do wi' a live-in handy-man-cum-gardener. It's costin' the missus a small fortune to keep havin' tradesmen in.'

Sunday stared at her as an idea began to form in her mind. Annie might just have given her the answer to all her prayers but she would have to do some careful thinking before she put the idea to the mistress.

'Annie, you're an angel in disguise!' she de-clared, planting a smacking kiss on the woman's wrinkled cheek.

'Gerroff, yer daft ha'porth,' Annie objected, but she blushed with pleasure. She was a good girl, was young Sunny, and her coming here was the best thing that had happened for some long time as far as she was concerned. Now the burden of housework had been lifted from her shoulders,

176

she felt ten years younger and had even started to take more care of herself.

'Can I just ask you something very cheeky before you go?' Sunday asked then. 'Do you happen to know how much Mrs Spooner charges her lodgers each week?'

'Four an' sixpence if they have all their meals in,' Annie replied, thinking it rather a strange question. 'Why do you ask?'

'Oh, I was just curious.'

'Right, well, my bed's callin' me. G'night, Sunny, love. See yer in the mornin', God willin'.'

As Annie bustled away, Sunday began to do some quick calculations. Of course, she hadn't been at Whittleford Lodge nearly long enough as yet to make the suggestion that was growing in her head, but just maybe in a few months' time...

Chapter Seventeen

It was mid-morning the next day as Sunday was polishing the banister rails that someone rapped loudly on the front door.

'Get that would yer, lass?' Annie bawled from the kitchen and placing the tin of beeswax polish down, Sunday hurried to the door. To her consternation she found Mr Pinnegar standing on the step.

'Aren't you going to ask me in then?' he asked as he leered at her and Sunday held the door wide so that he could pass. As he did so he

177

rubbed up against her and she shuddered.

At that moment, Mrs Spooner's voice reached them from the drawing room where she was enjoying a tray of tea. 'Is that somebody fer me?'

Mabel came bounding out of the door then and at sight of the visitor her hackles suddenly rose and she began to growl deep in her throat.

'Is it err ... vicious?' Mr Pinnegar asked nervously as he removed his hat.

'Not usually – and the missus is in there if you'd care to go through,' Sunday told him shortly.

Feeling that he had no other option he tiptoed past the dog, giving it as wide a berth as he could, then disappeared into the drawing room, quickly closing the door behind him.

Sunday patted Mabel's silky head, crooning, 'Good girl, seems like you're a good judge of character,' before going back to the job in hand.

She kept her eye on the door, wondering what the housemaster had come for and praying that he hadn't come to persuade Mrs Spooner to let him take her back with him. Becoming accustomed to the outside world was taking some getting used to but she didn't want to go back, not ever.

At last the drawing-room door opened and he appeared in the hallway again with Mrs Spooner close on his heels. She was dressed colourfully as usual and the French perfume that she favoured was almost overpowering.

'So we'll leave it at that then, shall we?' Sunday heard her ask. 'If I'm not satisfied wi' young Sunny's work I'll let you know. There's no need fer you to come here. I'm sure you've got better things to do with your time.'

'But as I explained, dear lady, we do like to know that our young people are well and happy in their new positions,' he purred. Biddy Spooner stared at him suspiciously, wondering why he should be taking such an interest in the girl.

'I'll soon let you know if she ain't,' she said smartly. 'An' now I'll wish you a good day, sir. Sunny, show the gentleman out.'

Only too happy to oblige, Sunday tripped down the stairs and held the door open for him. He paused as if there was something else he would have liked to say, but he was very aware of Mrs Spooner watching his every move so instead he placed his hat back on, bowed slightly and left with a face as dark as a thundercloud.

'I don't like that man,' Mrs Spooner declared when he had gone. 'There's somethin' about him that gives me the willies, so it does.' Still muttering to herself she retreated back to the drawing room leaving Sunday to get on with her work.

Their next visitor later that week was Lady Huntley, looking charming in a very pretty gown fashioned from pale pink satin and the flounces trimmed with navy-blue ribbons.

As it happened Sunday was passing the front door on her way upstairs to tackle yet another of the bedrooms when she knocked, so Sunday answered it with a welcoming smile just as Mrs Spooner was coming out of the drawing room with Mabel at her heels.

Lady Huntley had stepped into the hallway and was standing next to Sunday.

'Well, good mor…' Mrs Spooner's voice trailed away for a second as she stared at the two of them

179

but then quickly composing herself she rushed on, 'It's nice to see you, Lady Huntley. Sunny, could you fetch us a tray of tea please, lass?'

'Of course.' Sunday darted away obligingly as Mrs Spooner led her guest back into the drawing room. The sun was streaming through the window and Lavinia looked around in amazement. The furniture was gleaming and the wholesome smell of beeswax polish greeted her.

Mrs Spooner chuckled as she saw the woman's reaction. 'It looks a bit better now, don't it?' she said in her usual forthright way.

Not wishing to offend her, Lady Huntley chose her words carefully. 'It certainly looks very welcoming,' she said tactfully.

'Sunny has worked really hard since the second she arrived,' Mrs Spooner informed her. 'She's got the whole o' the downstairs lookin' neat as a new pin an' she's workin' on the upstairs now, bless 'er. She might be only a little scrap of a thing but she can't 'alf work. An' she's pleasant to 'ave about the place an' all. The lodgers 'ave all taken to her.'

'I'm pleased to hear it.' Lady Huntley smiled. It seemed that everything was going well and she couldn't have been more pleased. She had taken to Sunday at first sight and was thrilled that the poor girl was finally away from the dreadful Nuneaton Union Workhouse. Now Lavinia was working tirelessly to improve the lives of the rest of the people there – although of course she was all too aware that the changes she was suggesting were not going to happen overnight. Unfortunately, the other guardians were male, older and set in their ways, not even prepared to listen to her suggestions half of the time, but she was determined to go on trying. Only the day before, she had placed another boy from the workhouse in a position on a farm and the boy had been ecstatic about it as he had always longed to work outdoors. Verity Lockett was also keen to see long-overdue changes made now, and so Lavinia Huntley was sure that with their combined efforts, they would succeed in the end.

'Actually, I was hoping to have a word with Sunday – if you have no objections. It's why I came – as well as to see how she is settling in, of course,' she added hastily.

Mrs Spooner shrugged. 'That's fine by me. She'll be back in with the tea in a minute.' She thought Lady Huntley looked pale but was too polite to comment.

It wasn't long before Sunday bustled back in with a laden tea tray.

'Annie sent you some arrowroot biscuits made from Mrs Beeton's recipe to go with your tea,' she told the women cheerfully, then after placing the tray down she immediately turned to leave the room.

'Hold on! Is yer tail on fire, lass?' Mrs Spooner halted her. 'Lady Huntley 'ere wanted a word with you.'

When Sunday paused and looked anxious the woman instantly said, 'It's all right, you haven't done anything wrong.' She patted the seat at the side of her. 'Come and sit down here by me for a moment.'

Sunday looked at Mrs Spooner for permission

and when the woman nodded she quietly did as she was told, perching nervously on the very edge of the seat.

'I'm going to be honest with you, my dear, and tell you that I've been rather disturbed by some of the things I've seen at the workhouse,' Lavinia began. 'For a start, the guardians contribute a princely sum of money to ensure that everyone there is fed well. Admittedly, whenever I have visited that appears to be the case but I wondered … could you confirm that you were always that well fed?'

Sunday took a deep breath as she deliberated what she should say. Lady Huntley had produced a small notebook from the depths of her bag and was clearly going to make notes of anything that she said, but then deciding that she had nothing to lose now that she no longer resided there, Sunday chose to tell the true story. Perhaps her honesty now would improve things for the people who still were enduring conditions there.

'The meals were awful for most of the time.' She pulled a face as she remembered them. 'Dry grey bread and thick greasy porridge for break-fast and most times soup with bits of vegetables floating around in it for dinner. Even when there was meat in it, which was usually twice a week, three times if we were lucky, it was so gristly that you couldn't chew it.'

'Hmm, I thought so. And I've heard rumours of a punishment room. Could you tell me more about that?'

'It's down in the cellars and all that's in there is a bucket for your necessities.' Sunday blushed.

'There's not even a bed or a blanket. Once they close the door it's pitch black and you can't see your hand in front of you. The mice, rats and spiders run over you if you fall asleep and it's very cold and damp.'

Trying to hide her dismay, and scribbling furiously in her notepad, Lady Huntley simply nodded although she was appalled at what she was hearing. 'And how long would someone be left in there?'

'The longest I was down there for was three days,' Sunday said in a low voice, shuddering. 'I think I'd have been down there longer if Mrs Lockett hadn't come looking for me. I was so weak when she fetched me out that I had to go into the sickbay overnight. I'd had nothing to eat or drink in all that time, you see? Once, two little girls were locked down there and we never saw them again. When someone asked Miss Frost where they had gone she told them the children had died of influenza. They're buried in the little graveyard at the back of the workhouse but I can't remember anyone saying they'd had a proper funeral.'

Even Mrs Spooner was frowning now, hardly able to believe what she was hearing.

'And was any other form of punishment enforced?'

Sunday nodded. 'Oh yes – the cane. Miss Frost never goes anywhere without it. It is a split cane, so whenever she used it we could barely stand straight for a day or two. I think you'll find a lot of the orphans in there bear the scars from that – myself included.' As she spoke, she inched the skirt of her dress up and exposed some shiny white scars across the tops of her legs and her thighs.

Lady Huntley screwed her eyes up for a moment at the thought of such cruelty and then she asked her final question. 'And was Mr Pinnegar a kind master?'

She saw a flash of panic in Sunday's eyes just for a moment but then Sunday thought of Cissie and it all came pouring out of her like a torrent.

'No! He's a *horrible* man! A devil! I had a friend called Cissie and Mr Pinnegar started to take an interest in her, inviting her to work in his office and whatnot. Cissie hated him but she was too afraid to refuse and then suddenly she got ill. She started to be sick each morning and finally she told me that she thought she might be having a baby and that it was his. He'd forced her to ... you know?' Sunday stopped to take a long breath before going on. 'When Miss Frost found out about it, she told Cissie that she was going to send her away to somewhere nice where she and the baby would be looked after. But on the day she was leaving, the carriage from Hatter's Hall asylum turned up and Cissie got hysterical. She knew then that they were going to lock her away with the lunatics. She put up a really brave fight but they took her anyway, and I've never heard from her since.' A sob ripped out of her then.

'That's a very serious accusation to make,' Lady Huntley said quietly. 'Do you think Cissie was telling the truth, Sunday?'

'Yes, I do!' Sunday's chin came up and her eyes sparked. 'They told everyone that it was one of the men from the workhouse who'd interfered with her – but that would have been impossible. The only time we ever saw them was on Sunday when we went to church or when we were having our daily airing in the yard, and then we were separated by a high wire fence. Mr Pinnegar likes the girls as they get a little older. He … he even tried … you know … to do things to me.' Sunday lowered her head in shame as she recalled the feel of his filthy hands on her most private parts.

'I see.' Lady Huntley looked visibly shocked.

'Look, if you don't believe me, go to Hatter's Hall and ask to see Cissie Burns,' Sunday pleaded. 'She's bound to still be there because she had no one to fetch her out, and in cases like that the people who go in there stay in there for the rest of their lives.'

'Well, thank you for being honest with me,' Lady Huntley said then, snapping her notebook shut and returning it to her bag. 'Just leave it with me, Sunday. I vow to do all I can to make it better for everyone there in the workhouse in the future.'

'But what about Cissie?'

Lady Huntley shrugged despondently. 'I shall have to give that some thought,' she answered truthfully. 'If Cissie has been there for a while… Well, the chances are she won't be the same any more – and even if she was and I made accusations, it would be her word against Mr Pinnegar's. Who do you think everyone would believe? Even so, I promise you I will pursue it when I've decided the best way to proceed.'

Sunday's shoulders sagged as she realised the

185

truth of what the woman was saying. Mr Pinnegar would *definitely* deny any involvement and Miss Frost would back him to the death. It was hopeless.

'Please ... trust me,' the woman said then, laying her hand gently on Sunday's arm. 'If there is anything that can possibly be done to get her out of there then I'll do it – but I can make you no promises, I'm afraid.'

Sunday left the room then to continue with her chores but for the rest of the day thoughts of Cissie would not be banished and everyone noticed that her usual cheery smile was nowhere to be seen.

Chapter Eighteen

The day got progressively worse for Lavinia Huntley, for when she got home she found that once again she had started her monthly course. She was usually as regular as clockwork and this month was no exception.

It was three months now since Ashley had taken to coming to her bed again, and every month he asked, 'Is there any sign of a child yet?' And each month she was forced to confess that there was not. Now this month would be no different.

She sighed as she straightened her hair in her dressing-table mirror. He would be home soon and she supposed it was best to get it over and done with. She had not enjoyed resuming a

186

sexual relationship with her husband – but then she was no longer the starry-eyed young girl who had once been swept off her feet by his charm and wit all those years ago. He was still a handsome man, admittedly, but only on the outside – as she had learned to her cost. Inside he was narcissistic and weak with no thought for anyone but himself.

Ashley Huntley had never done a single day's work in his life. He spent his time in leisurely pursuits – drinking at his club, studying horse-racing form, gambling and attending shoots. Lavinia knew all too well that she had merely been a means to an end for her husband. He had known that she could keep him in the manner he craved until his wealthy late uncle made him his heir – as soon as she presented him with a healthy son, that was. All she had managed to present him with up until now, however, was three tiny stillborn daughters, for whom she still continued to grieve every single day. Following the birth – and death – of the last one she had sunk into a profound, unending melancholy, but now once again she had something to focus on, and Lavinia felt as if she was wakening after a long, deep sleep.

Her thoughts moved back to the talk she had had with Sunday earlier in the day. The girl's revelations had been horrifying, particularly the story about poor Cissie, yet Lavinia believed every single word she had said. It was what she was to do about it now that was concerning her. She knew it would be no use discussing Sunday's disclosures with the rest of the guardians. They were all older, staider gentlemen who thought the sun rose and set with the housemaster and the matron. Should she bring this to their attention, Mr Pinnegar would strenuously deny the allegation and she had no doubt that Miss Frost would defend him to her last breath. Before she did anything at all, Lavinia realised that she would have to give the situation her serious consideration. Perhaps she could talk it over with Verity? Yes, she decided, that was what she would do before making any decisions.

Her thoughts drifted back to her own position. Ashley's sudden need to father a son again had been brought about due to his younger brother Lewis having recently announced his engagement to a very respectable young lady. Ashley was all too aware that, should his brother produce a son now before he did, the inheritance would pass to him and he thought it was grossly unfair. The way he saw it, he was the oldest living relative of his uncle and therefore the inheritance should automatically come to him. Lavinia shuddered as she glanced at the bed. She didn't know if she could go through the birth process again, for her fear of producing another dead child and the heartache that would entail far outweighed the chance of having a child.

The sound of hooves thundering towards the house disturbed her thoughts, and she crossed to the window to see Ashley on his stallion flying up the drive like the wind. *The groom will not be too happy about that,* she thought. The animal was foaming at the bit and the groom regularly complained to her about the master's treatment of the poor horse. Ashley cared for no one but himself, neither man nor beast, and took no notice of criticism. She had just got downstairs when the maid opened the door and Ashley strode in, having flung the horse's reins to the waiting groom.

He stared at his wife in an obvious ill-humour. 'Matthews informs me that you were out earlier again,' he snapped as he headed for the day room.

She followed him and watched as he went straight to the decanter on a silver tray, poured himself a generous measure of whisky and tossed it back in one go, his hair shining in the sun that was streaming through the window.

'Well – where were you?' He was already in the process of pouring himself another drink.

'I visited the young girl I found a position for, from the workhouse,' she answered.

'Huh! Your time would be better spent in the nursery attending to a brood of your own children. Speaking of which, is there any sign yet?'

'I'm afraid not,' she told him, sitting down gracefully in a chair next to the fireplace.

'What sort of a woman are you if you can't even present me with a son?' he spat, and she visibly winced. Each time he said it, it was like a knife being thrust into her heart.

'Lewis informed me today that he and Felicity have set the date for their wedding,' he snarled then. 'It's going to be two days before Christmas this year, so that gives us a few more months.'

When she merely stared down at her joined hands he growled and stormed from the room, and once he was gone she sighed with relief, praying that he would be off out again soon and she wouldn't have to see him again until that evening. Better still, he might stay away all night.

Zillah, her maid, came into the room then and seeing the look on her mistress's face she went to her and placed her arm about her shoulders. 'I just passed him in the hallway,' she said. 'Has he upset you again?'

Lavinia nodded, distressed. 'Yes. I just had to tell him that there is no baby again this month. What is wrong with me, Zillah? Other women give birth to fine healthy children, so why can't I?'

'It's just the way it is, pet. Some women can get with child and give birth as easily as shellin' peas, for others it's harder,' the woman told her practically. 'But come along now. It's time you had a little rest, you look tired. How did your morning go?'

On the way upstairs, Lavinia told her all about her visit to Sunday and the things she'd learned about the way the children in the workhouse were treated. When she told her Cissie's tale, the kindly maid frowned.

'What do you think I should do about it?' Lavinia asked. They were in her room by then and Zillah was helping her off with her shoes.

'I can't rightly say but it's a sad kettle of fish from what you've told me. That poor girl. Would it be worth you visiting the asylum to see if she's still locked away there?'

'But what reason could I give?'

Zillah sat next to her mistress on the end of the bed and stared thoughtfully off into space for a moment before suggesting, 'I suppose you could

190

say you knew a relative of hers and you would like her to come and work for you? I heard the housekeeper saying that our laundry maid, Meggie, would be leaving soon to get married. We'll be needing another one then and although it's the lowliest of positions I dare say it's better than being locked away in an asylum. That's if the poor lamb is still of sound mind, of course. Many people go in there sane and end up as bad as the rest of the inmates, from what I've heard of it. If you went along that route you needn't make any accusations about the housemaster, unless you have evidence and we know we've got her safe.'

'Hmm, you could be right,' Lavinia answered, swinging her legs up onto the bed. 'I shall certainly give it some thought. Thank you, Zillah. I really don't know what I'd do without you.'

'I hope it'll be some long time afore you have to.' Zillah laid a warm rug across her mistress then crept from the room leaving her to get some rest.

When Lavinia went down to dinner that evening Ashley had not returned from his afternoon jaunt so after waiting another half an hour for him she dined alone then went to the drawing room where she played the piano for a time before retiring. Thankfully he did not come home at all that evening but she slept badly, for she had nightmares about the terrible stories that Sunday had told her.

Zillah found her pale and wan the next morning when she went in to open her curtains.

'I've no need to ask how you slept. You're as white as a ghost. Come on, up onto your pillows now and eat some of this breakfast I've brought you.'

She laid a tray across Lavinia's lap but the woman merely picked at the food like a little bird before finally pushing it away.

'I'm sorry, Zillah, but I don't seem to have much of an appetite this morning,' she apologised.

Zillah shook her head. It had taken years to coax her mistress from the lethargic state she had sunk into following the loss of her last baby and she was determined that she wasn't going to go back there.

'In that case you can get up and get dressed and go and see our Verity,' she ordered bossily. 'It's too nice a day for you to be stuck indoors.'

Lavinia smiled wryly. And yet it was mid-morning before she made a decision and asked Zillah, 'Would you ask for the carriage to be brought around, please? I'm going out.'

Zillah paused; she was just making the room tidy and she beamed. 'That's the spirit,' she said approvingly and hastened away to do as she was asked.

Twenty minutes later Lavinia went out to the carriage and told the driver, 'Hatter's Hall, please, Jenkins.'

'You mean the asylum, ma'am?' He looked surprised but made no comment as he handed her into the carriage. There was still no sign of Ashley but Lavinia wasn't overly concerned. He'd taken to staying away for days at a time now, often only coming back when he ran out of money from betting on horses or to force himself on her in the hope of getting her with child. Sometimes she felt guilty for hoping that he might never come home again!

The carriage rattled along as she stared at the fields through the window. It was another beautiful day but autumn would be upon them before they knew it. Lavinia had no idea whatsoever what she was going to say when she arrived at the asylum, but she decided that she would face that problem when they got there. Very soon, Jenkins drew the horses to a stop outside two enormous iron gates set in a high brick wall. Lavinia felt a pain as she thought of all the poor people who must have entered through them, never to come out again. It was rumoured that at night the sound of the demented souls could be heard wailing and the local people avoided the area like the plague.

A porter appeared from a small gatehouse at the side of the gates and, lowering the window, Lavinia informed him imperiously, 'I am here to see the person in charge.'

'Are you expected?' the man asked and Lavinia shook her head.

'Well, usually visitors are only admitted by appointment,' he informed her worriedly.

Lavinia looked steadily back at him before saying, 'I suggest you open the gates immediately, my good man, or it will be the worse for you when I am admitted.'

He looked uncertain for a moment longer but seeing she was obviously a high-class lady, he rushed to admit her.

The carriage rattled down the drive as Lavinia stared at the house ahead from the window. The red-brick walls were heavily covered in trailing ivy and Virginia creeper, but she noted that there were bars on all the windows and it looked dark, forbidding and totally unwelcoming, much like some of the houses that she had read about in Gothic novels.

Jenkins pulled the horses to a halt at the entrance and after handing her down from the carriage he asked, 'Would you like me to come in with you, my lady?'

Putting on a brave face, she replied in a hushed voice. It was so quiet here, as if even the birds were afraid to sing in such a sad place. 'No, thank you. Just wait here for me.'

She tugged at a rusty chain that hung at the side of the door. A bell clanged somewhere inside and she heard the sound of heavy bolts being drawn back. When the door creaked open, the waft of stale urine and vomit assailed her, and it was all she could do to stop herself from retching as she told the little maid who appeared, 'I have come to see the superintendent. Kindly inform them that Lady Lavinia Huntley is here.'

'Step inside, ma'am.'

Lavinia found herself in a cavernous foyer with several corridors leading off it. From the centre of the foyer rose a staircase that led up to a galleried landing. There were red and white patterned tiles on the floor and Lavinia was shocked at the sheer size of the place.

'Would you wait here, please?' The little maid hurried away and as she stood there the faint sounds of crying and wailing echoed down the staircase.

Lavinia shuddered. This was surely hell on earth!

Chapter Nineteen

'Could you come this way?'

Lavinia started as the maid's voice interrupted her gloomy thoughts. Then, bracing herself to face whatever lay ahead, she forced herself to follow the girl. She was feeling dizzy and claustrophobic, and worried that she was going to have a fainting attack. She'd had a number of those following the death of her last daughter.

The walls were all painted a sludgy brown colour which did nothing to lift the gloomy atmosphere of the place and as they set off along the corridor the sounds of crying and intermittent screaming grew louder.

'That's just some of the inmates having their daily treatments,' the maid told her, noting the shocked look on Lavinia's face. To the latter, it sounded more like they were being tortured than treated.

At last the girl stopped before a door, again painted in the same dull colour. Attached to it was a plaque which read: *Augustus Crackett, Super-intendent*. She tapped then opened it to allow Lavinia to pass into what proved to be a very spacious office.

A painfully thin gentleman with wispy grey hair and pince-nez spectacles perched on the end of his bulbous nose stared back at her from behind an enormous mahogany desk.

'It is customary to make an appointment when coming here, madam,' he informed her coldly. 'What is it I can help you with?'

'I've come to enquire about a Miss Cissie...' Lavinia paused here. Now what had Sunday said her surname was? And then it came to her. 'Burns,' she finished hastily.

'May I ask why?' He steepled his fingers and stared at her with a stern expression on his face.

Again, Lavinia felt temporarily at a loss as to how best to answer but then she lied, 'I knew a member of her family some time ago and I have come to offer her a position as laundry maid in my household. But first I wish to talk to her.'

'I see.' The man scowled. 'Could you tell me when this person was admitted? You must realise that we have many patients here.'

Once more, Lavinia realised just how ill-prepared she was for this interview. She hadn't thought to ask Cissie's exact date of admission either.

'Forgive me.' She fluttered her eyelashes becomingly at him although it seemed to make no impression whatsoever. 'I can't remember the exact date but it was some time ago, perhaps three or four years? She was admitted here from the Union Workhouse and at the time she was in ... shall we say ... a delicate condition.'

He rose and crossed to one of a row of cupboards that stood against the back wall. 'And you say her name was Burns?'

Crossing her fingers in her lap, she nodded.

Mr Crackett delved through a number of files before drawing one out as Lavinia held her breath. So many girls died in childbirth, particularly in this godforsaken place. It could be that poor Cissie hadn't survived the birth of her child.

'I think this might be the person you are enquiring about. She is in the West wing. And you say you wish to see her?'

'Yes, please.'

'This is highly irregular.' He stroked his chin thoughtfully as Lavinia rummaged in her small reticule. She produced a folded five-pound bank-note, and as she placed it on the table and fully unfolded it, his eyes lit up greedily.

'However, I suppose just this once...' He swiftly pocketed the money and rang a small bell on his desk, and within seconds the little maid who had admitted Lavinia appeared as if by magic.

'Evans, take Lady Huntley to the West wing,' he instructed her, 'and tell the officer there that I gave permission for her to visit Cissie Burns.'

'Yes, sir.' The maid bobbed her knee as Lavinia rose hastily to follow her. She was led up the sweeping staircase and found herself thinking how beautiful it must have been once upon a time. A number of locked doors confronted the pair at the top of the stairs. The maid rapped on one, which was opened by a plain-faced woman in a limp grey gown. Her expression was sour. The noise was louder here, people sobbing and whimpering, and Lavinia tried hard not to hear it for fear of bursting into tears herself. The maid

197

explained why they were there and the woman looked askance but ushered Lavinia through the door all the same. Lady Huntley found herself in yet another long corridor with doors leading off on either side and she began to tremble, instinctively knowing that people were locked away behind each one.

'Follow me, dear,' the woman ordered and set off, the keys in a bunch at her waist clanking together.

Each door had a small open panel covered in iron bars, and as Lavinia peeped inside her sense of despair increased. The rooms were like prison cells, and the blank-eyed women within stared back at her like lost souls. One woman was wailing and doing her best to tear her eyes out, and one was rocking vigorously to and fro as she chanted something beneath her breath.

At last the woman stopped in front of a door at the far end of the corridor and selecting a key she told Lavinia, 'She's just come back from having her treatment so don't expect to get any sense out of her. This one can be dangerous so we have to keep her chained.'

'What sort of treatment?' Lavinia asked, aghast.

'Water treatment. The patients are dipped and held under. It soon quietens them down and stops their nonsense.' She laughed harshly.

Lavinia could hardly believe what she was hearing. It sounded utterly barbaric but the door was opening now so she held her tongue.

'I'll give you five minutes.' As the woman strode away Lavinia wondered if she had an ounce of compassion in her body. It didn't appear so!

She looked towards the girl who was shackled to the walls by chains then and her breath caught in her throat. Cissie had curled herself into a ball and was dripping wet from head to toe and shaking uncontrollably with cold. Lavinia was shaking too, with outrage. She couldn't even begin to imagine how one human being could treat another like this. This was far, far worse than anything she had ever dreamed of.

'It's all right, my dear. I haven't come to hurt you.' She slowly approached the girl, then, heedless of the filthy floor, she dropped to her knees to be on her level. Her skirts settled like a golden cloud around her as she tried to think what to say. Cissie was painfully thin and her large eyes seemed to be sunken into her face. When Lavinia stretched out a hand to her, the girl shrank away and cried, 'What do yer want?' She was clearly terrified.

'I've come to help you,' Lavinia soothed as tears sprang to her eyes.

The girl shook her head, her eyes deep pools of misery. 'No one can 'elp me.'

Lavinia didn't know what she could say to comfort her until she whispered, 'Sunday told me about you.'

'*Sunday!*' Now there was some life in her eyes again. 'So she remembered me then?'

'Of course she did and she's never stopped worrying about you, which is why I've come to try and get you out of here. I have a position at my house for you. It's only in the laundry but it's yours if you'd like it.'

The light dulled in the girl's eyes again. 'They'd

199

never let me go,' she said hoarsely. 'They've told me I'll be in here for always.' Her voice was without hope but now anger was stirring in Lavinia's breast. The way this girl was being treated was inhuman. She rose and brushed down her skirt just as the nurse-gaoler reappeared.

'Kindly take me back to the superintendent's office.' Gone was the timid woman who had entered only minutes before and now in her place was someone who was on a mission. Noting the change in her the woman stared at her curiously before gesturing her from the cell and locking the door behind them.

'Don't worry,' Lavinia murmured through the open bars to Cissie and with that she strode purposefully back down the corridor.

Back in Mr Crackett's office she towered over him at his desk and refused a seat. 'Why has Cissie been classed as dangerous?' she demanded to know.

'Well, err … she can get very upset and needs restraining,' he muttered.

'And what happened to her baby?'

He coughed as he bent quickly to the files on his desk. 'It appears that it died at birth.'

More likely it was sold for a good sum to a childless couple, Lavinia thought. 'Well, as I informed you, I have a position ready and waiting for Cissie and I'd like to take her out of here with me – *this instant!*'

'I'm afraid that is quite out of the question,' he blustered. 'It has to be a member of the inmate's family or the person who put them in here, who must sign them out. In this case it was the master of the workhouse, a Mr Pinnegar.'

'And *I* happen to sit on the board of governors at the workhouse,' Lavinia told him imperiously with her chin in the air.

Still he hesitated, so once more Lavinia dipped into her reticule and produced another banknote, which she held up in front of him. 'I am, of course, prepared to make a generous donation towards the running costs of the asylum,' she told him silkily, nodding towards the money. 'And I am also prepared to take full responsibility for the girl. It will be one less patient for you to worry about.'

'Well, when you put it like that I suppose it would be all right.' He reached out for the money but Lavinia held onto it. Rifling through a drawer in his desk, Augustus Crackett took out a legal-looking paper. 'This is the release form,' he told her solemnly. 'Whilst you fill it in I shall go and send the maid to fetch Burns.'

Lavinia filled the form in quickly then sat impatiently waiting until the superintendent appeared again with the young maid close behind him. Clad now in a dry smock, Cissie was leaning heavily on her arm and looked as if she was about to collapse at any moment. She was blinking in the light and there was a glazed expression on her waxen face as if she hardly dared to allow herself to believe what was happening.

'Ah, here you are.' Lavinia smiled at her encouragingly. She then pushed the release form towards the superintendent, with the banknote peeping out beneath it. 'I think you will find this is all in order, and now if there's nothing else you require me to do I shall wish you good day, sir.'

'Of course, my lady.' He clicked his fingers at the maid, ordering, 'Help this young lady out to the carriage immediately, Evans!' It was clear that Cissie was in no state to get there without help.

Lavinia left the room without bestowing so much as a backward glance on the man. What an obnoxious creature he was! Even animals were kept in better conditions than those she had witnessed today. The things she had seen and heard in this dreadful place would stay with her for ever and she could hardly wait to get away.

Taking Cissie's other arm, with the help of the maid she managed to get her down the steps and to the coach as Cissie's legs buckled beneath her. Jenkins looked mildly surprised to see the girl with his mistress. The young lass was in a rare old state but without a word he lifted her and gently placed her in the carriage. And then at last the carriage was rolling away down the drive and once the gateman had let them out, Lavinia breathed a huge sigh of relief.

Cissie looked dazed and disorientated, and in the bright light of day Lavinia was horrified to note that her hair was matted to her head. The smell that was issuing from her was rancid too and Lavinia wondered how long it was since she had been allowed access to soap. She reached out to take the girl's hand but at the sudden movement Cissie flinched away from her. As she did so the sleeve of the shapeless shift dress she was wearing slid up her arm, revealing a multitude of bruises ranging from older yellow ones to more recent vivid purple ones.

'Oh, you poor thing.' Tears were sliding down Lavinia's cheeks. 'Please don't be afraid of me. I'm going to get you well again and then you'll be safe working at my house for as long as you wish to.'

Cissie stared back at her for a moment from wide, frightened eyes but then her eyelids started to droop and before Lavinia could say another word her head had lolled to the side and she was fast asleep.

'I believe she has been drugged,' Lavinia muttered. A number of the inmates had been asleep, she recalled. They too had probably been sedated to keep them quiet. But never mind, once they got Cissie home and she'd been handed into Mrs Roundtree's tender care she'd be as right as rain again in no time. The housekeeper was a kindly woman and Lavinia had no doubt at all that she, and her darling Zillah, would gladly take Cissie under her wing.

They arrived back home and Mrs Roundtree was led outside to meet the still slumbering Cissie. The girl was slumped on the seat in the carriage and as Lavinia hastily whispered what had happened to her the housekeeper's mouth set in a grim line as she flicked a tear away.

'Carry her into the kitchen for me would you, George?' she asked Jenkins, taking control of the situation. 'This little lady needs a good bath and a clean nightgown. I'll get some decent food into her then and put her to bed till I deem she's well enough to get up again.'

'Thank you, Mrs Roundtree,' Lavinia said

gratefully as the groom lifted Cissie down from the carriage, and the woman beamed.

'You just leave it with me, ma'am. Zillah and I will have her better in no time. Well, her body at least. The Good Lord only knows how long it will take for her mind to heal.' She clicked her tongue disapprovingly and ushered Jenkins towards the back entrance, warning, 'Be gentle with her now.'

Suddenly Lavinia felt exhausted. It had been a very trying morning but thankfully she could share it all with Zillah. She had achieved what she had set out to do and now it was down to Cissie and time – the great healer. She pictured Sunday's face when she gave her the news. The girl would be ecstatic.

Chapter Twenty

The next weekend rolled around in no time and once again Sunday found herself looking forward to going to church with Mrs Spooner and visiting Daisy and Tommy in the workhouse.

'Time seems to fly by,' Annie remarked as she put her coat on ready to go home on Saturday evening. She had given Sunday a lesson in baking that afternoon and the results of their efforts were now cooling on racks on the table. There were two fresh loaves for breakfast the next morning and a number of scones. Old Mr Greaves was very partial to a scone or two slathered with butter and jam and so was Miss Bailey.

204

Sunday was very pleased with her attempt and couldn't stop smiling. She had followed Annie's instructions to the letter and everything had turned out far better than when she'd been taught in the workhouse. Not that she felt anywhere near ready to attempt it on her own yet, and even when she did, she doubted she would ever be as good a cook as Annie was.

Annie, who had smartened herself up considerably since the welcome arrival of Sunday at Whittleford Lodge, had just put her hat on when there was a knock on the front door.

'Now who would that be at this time on a Saturday evenin'? It's an odd time to call, an' just as I were about to leave an' all.'

'You get off, Annie,' Sunday urged. 'I'll go and answer the door. It's probably someone to see the missus.'

'All right, lass. If yer sure.' Annie lifted her bag and disappeared out of the back door as Sunday hurried along the hallway.

She found Lady Huntley standing on the step. 'Good evening,' Sunday said, a little surprised. 'Was it Mrs Spooner you were wanting to see, ma'am?'

Lady Huntley beamed excitedly at her. 'No, actually, it was you I wanted a word with, Sunday dear. May I come in?'

'Yes, of course.' Sunday was all of a dither. 'Perhaps we should go through to the kitchen?' She didn't feel it would be right to show her into one of Mrs Spooner's best rooms, but thankfully the lady herself appeared in the doorway of the dining room just then.

'How nice to see you, Lady Huntley,' she welcomed her guest. This evening, Biddy Spooner was at her most flamboyant. The gown she had squeezed into had so many frills and was so heavily adorned with lace that Lady Huntley didn't quite know which part of it to look at first. The jewels on the old woman's fingers were sparkling and every time she moved, the many gold bangles on her arms jangled. Her face, as always, was heavily made up.

Lady Huntley smiled at her politely, saying, 'I hope you'll excuse me calling at such an unusual hour. I wouldn't dream of disturbing you at such a time normally but there was something I wished to tell Sunday. I would have called earlier in the week but my husband has been entertaining friends and—'

'Oh, my dear, you are most welcome here any time. But did you wish to see Sunny in private? There is nothing amiss, I hope?' She was consumed with curiosity and so was pleased when Lady Huntley shook her head and explained the situation.

'No, there is nothing amiss, I assure you. In fact, it's quite the opposite. At least, I hope Sunday will think so. And I'd be delighted to share my news with you too.'

Intrigued, Mrs Spooner took her elbow. 'In that case, let's go into the day room. My lodgers are in the drawing room at present and we'll have some privacy in there.'

She led the way along the corridor and once they were all in the room Sunday and Mrs Spooner looked at the woman expectantly.

'The thing is, following our talk when you told me about poor Cissie,' Lady Huntley began, addressing Sunday, 'I took it upon myself to visit Hatter's Hall.' She then went on to tell them all that had transpired and when the story was told, Sunday's face lit up brighter than a ray of sunshine.

'You mean Cissie is really out of that dreadful place?' She hardly dared believe what she had just heard. 'Oh, thank you, Lady Huntley. Thank you so, so much!'

'She certainly is out of there, and even as we speak my dear housekeeper, Mrs Roundtree, is fussing over her like a mother hen. She's really taken to her.'

'And how is Cissie?'

Lady Huntley's face became sombre then. 'Well, physically she is on the mend. We are making sure she gets lots of rest and good food, but...' She gave a little shake of her head. 'I fear being in that place for so long has left a lasting impression on her – and I'm not surprised after what I saw whilst I was there.' She shuddered. 'Up to now she hasn't uttered so much as a single word since leaving Hatter's Hall, which is why I was hoping, dear Mrs Spooner' – she looked at Biddy – 'you might allow Sunday to visit her? Seeing a familiar face might bring her back from the dark place to which she seems to have retreated.'

'Of course she can,' Mrs Spooner said immediately. 'What about this evening?'

'But I haven't washed the supper pots up yet,' Sunday pointed out. She longed to see Cissie but

207

didn't want to neglect her duties.

'Pah! What's a few dirty pots?' Mrs Spooner wiggled a heavily ringed hand in the air. 'They can wait till morning. You can go right now if Lady Huntley has no objections, although I'd like you to be seen safely home after the visit. It stays light till late, but nevertheless...'

'I would make sure she was escorted right to the door,' Lady Huntley assured her. 'So what do you think, my dear? Would you like to come with me now to see your friend?'

'Oh yes, please!' Sunday was so excited she could barely contain herself and without even thinking about it she suddenly flung her arms about Lavinia's neck and planted a sloppy kiss on her cheek.

Lavinia Huntley flushed with pleasure. Mrs Spooner watched the two of them together and once again it struck her how alike they looked. Their hair was almost the identical colour and they both had a heart-shaped face. They were both blue-eyed as well, although Sunday's eyes were a much deeper colour, more of a violet blue than a sky blue. *What a pretty picture they make*, the old lady found herself thinking.

'Oh ... sorry,' Sunday said self-consciously then as her cheeks turned a rosy pink. 'I didn't mean to be so familiar.'

'Don't apologise, I liked it,' Lady Huntley told her with a warm smile and Mrs Spooner thought how cruel life could be. Here was a woman who would have loved a daughter, and a young girl who would have loved to have a mother.

'Well, go an' make yourself presentable then,

Sunny, if you're goin' out,' Mrs Spooner ordered her bossily. 'Run a comb through yer hair an' take your apron off quick smart else it'll be dark before you even get there.'

Only too happy to oblige, Sunday skipped away to do as she was told as the two women looked fondly on.

'She's such a lovely girl, isn't she?' Lady Huntley said and Mrs Spooner nodded in agreement.

'She is that, though she can be a young madam too. But then I suppose she had to learn how to stick up for herself, being brought up in the workhouse. Do you know, I've never seen her shed a tear?'

They wandered into the hallway then and Sunday soon reappeared with her eyes glowing and her hair freshly brushed. She had changed into one of the dresses that Lady Huntley had given her and the women thought how pretty she looked.

'What time do you want her home?' Lavinia asked.

Mrs Spooner shrugged. 'Whenever you like, so long as you see her back safely.'

She stood on the steps in all her finery waving as the carriage rolled away, then went back to the drawing room to enjoy a game of cards with Mr Greaves.

By the time the carriage arrived at Treetops Manor, Sunday was squirming with anticipation. Her mouth fell open at the first glimpse of Lady Huntley's home. She could never imagine living in such a place in a thousand years. After the con-

209

fines of the workhouse she had thought Mrs Spooner's residence was wonderful, but this was like something out of one of the pages of the books she had looked at with Mrs Lockett. Tall chimneys stretched into the sky with the smoke curling lazily from them and the many long windows reflected the early-evening light. Soft lamps in the rooms beyond gave the place a welcoming appearance. Virginia creeper and ivy grew in wild profusion up the facade. Sunday was sure she had never seen such a beautiful building. But then the carriage was drawing to a halt and she forgot all about the house and suddenly remembered why she had come here – and all she could think of was seeing Cissie now. She had to keep pinching herself to make sure that this was really happening, although her excitement was laced with apprehension. After all poor Cissie had been through, would she have changed?

As if she had picked up on her thoughts Lady Huntley said, 'I ought to warn you that Cissie is...' She paused to choose her words carefully. 'Perhaps not quite as you'll remember her,' she warned gently. 'She's been locked away for a long while but I have every hope that within time she'll make a full recovery. I'm sure that seeing you again will help.'

She led Sunday inside and the girl gaped at the luxurious interior. It was every bit as impressive as the outside of the house. A portly round-faced woman hurried to meet them and smiled at Sunday kindly.

'Hello, my dear,' she greeted Sunday. 'My name is Mrs Roundtree and I'm the housekeeper here.

You must be Cissie's little friend? I'm sure she'll be very pleased to see you. I've put her in the room next to mine where I can keep my eye on her and she's doing quite well, considering.'

She nodded politely at Lady Huntley, who left them then, and led Sunday away down a long corridor. 'My rooms are along here,' she told her. 'And this one here is Cissie's room for now. When she's well and able to start work, she'll go up into the servants' quarters.'

She opened a door and ushered Sunday into a small room. In the window, which overlooked the front of the house, was a chair. Someone was sitting in it gazing quietly out across the lawns with her back to them, and after glancing at the house-keeper, who gave her an encouraging nod, Sunday approached it, saying tentatively, 'Cissie?'

The person sat very still for what seemed like a very long time, showing no signs of having heard her, but then she turned slightly towards her and Sunday found herself staring into two dead eyes that were sunk deep into the girl's head.

'Oh, Cissie. It really *is* you! I never thought I'd see you again.'

Dropping to her knees, she took the girl's hands in her own and smiled from ear to ear although she felt like crying. Goodness only knew what the poor soul must have endured in Hatter's Hall to bring her to this state. Cissie had never been the most robust of girls, for few thrived in the work-house on the meagre rations they were served. But now she seemed to have shrunk to half her original size and every bone that was visible was prominent as if her skin had been stretched across them.

211

'Cissie … it's me, Sunday.' She held her breath as her friend continued to stare blankly back at her but then suddenly Cissie's lip trembled and recognition dawned in her eyes.

'Su-Sunday.' Her voice was hoarse as if she had not used it properly for some long time. 'They took my baby away!'

And then, with no warning, the tears came and she fell into Sunday's waiting arms and began to sob.

Mrs Roundtree nodded her approval. 'That's it, lass. You have a good cry and get it all out now. Tears are healing!'

Sunday held her tightly for a long time until the sobs finally turned to dull hiccuping whimpers and then, gently wiping the damp hair from her brow, she smiled at her dear friend as she told her, 'It's all right. It's all over now, Cissie, I promise.'

With a large lump in her throat, the house-keeper crept away to give the two girls some time alone to talk in private.

'Was it awful?' Sunday asked eventually as Cissie lay like a limp rag in her arms.

Cissie nodded miserably as she swiped her nose along her sleeve – some things never changed, it seemed.

'Do you know what was the strangest thing?' she said brokenly. 'Once they locked me away I hated the baby I was carrying and I knew that I was going to hate it because it was forced on me. Yet when he was born and I held him I had feelings run through me that I've never felt before. He was a part of me and suddenly it didn't matter who his father was. I loved him. I'd never

212

had anyone of my very own to love before, you see.' Her eyes were so bleak when she looked at Sunday that the girl's heart ached for her.

'I only got to hold him for a couple of minutes and then they took him away and I never saw him again. I don't even know where he is or who he's with. I know they will never love him as I would have though.'

'One day when you meet someone special there will be other babies to love,' Sunday promised but Cissie shook her head.

'No. I'll never let another man touch me for as long as I live.' She trembled as she recalled the feel of Mr Pinnegar's hands on her bare skin.

'You will, you'll see. It will be completely different if it's someone you respect and love.'

They fell silent then as Sunday held her close, and after a while Sunday asked, 'Would you like to hear what's been happening to me since you left? I no longer live in the workhouse. A lovely lady called Mrs Spooner has employed me to work in her home at Whittleford and I love it there.'

For the first time, Cissie noticed the neat dress Sunday was wearing and a spark of interest flared in her eyes so Sunday hurried on to tell her all that had happened in the years they had been forced to be apart.

Sometime later, leaving a slightly calmer Cissie behind, Sunday descended the stairs to find Lady Huntley waiting for her in the enormous hallway. Seeing the sad expression on the girl's face she gently took her hands. 'I did try to warn you that she is still quite altered by all that's happened to

213

her, didn't I? But never fear, she will get the best of care here, I assure you.'

Sunday managed a weak, grateful smile as the woman turned to lift some books she had ready on a hall table.

'I thought you might enjoy these,' she said. 'When you've read them, simply return them and you're welcome to borrow some more from the library.'

Sunday glanced through the books eagerly. The first one was *Heidi* by Johanna Spyri, the second was Jane Austen's *Pride and Prejudice*. Her whole face lit up with pleasure as she clutched them and she could hardly wait to start reading them.

'Right, I think I had better get Jenkins to take you home now,' Lady Huntley said then. 'Mrs Spooner will be thinking you've got lost. But do feel free to come and visit Cissie whenever you are able to. I'm sure seeing you will help to speed her recovery.'

'I will – and thank you for everything you have done, Lady Huntley.' One last smile then Sunday tripped down the steps and soon the carriage was bowling back to Whittleford again. It had been quite a day, one way or another, she thought. To see Cissie, freed from Hatter's Hall, was like a kind of miracle; and behind it all was Lavinia Huntley, an angel of mercy if ever there was one.

Chapter Twenty-One

Sunday was in a more subdued mood when the carriage arrived back at Whittleford Lodge. Although she was thrilled that Cissie was finally free, her poor friend had been through so much... Sunday wondered if she would ever completely get over it.

Mrs Spooner was waiting for her. 'How was she, lass?' she asked immediately.

As Sunday told her some of the things Cissie had confided to her the old woman's eyes smarted with tears and she wagged her head from side to side in shocked disbelief. 'To think that those poor people get treated like that. And as for that housemaster ... why, he should be run out of town. I hope Lady Huntley is going to address what he's done with the board of governors?'

Sunday shrugged. 'I'm not sure what she intends to do,' she said tiredly. 'The problem is, it would be his word against Cissie's – and as she pointed out, who would believe her? They'd think she was just out to cause trouble – although from rumours I've heard, Cissie wasn't the first. He even tried it on with me, though he didn't go so far as to...' Her voice trailed away as she blushed furiously and Mrs Spooner bristled.

'He should be stopped. The man is a menace to young girls!' And with that she stomped away, leaning heavily on her silver-topped stick. She had almost crossed the hall when she paused to look back over her shoulder and say, 'And by the way, Sunny, when your friend is recovered enough, she can come here to visit you. I was only saying to Mr Greaves earlier on that it would do you the power of good to spend some time with people your own age.'

'Thank you, Mrs Spooner.' Her employer's kindness made a lump come into her throat.

Sunday had had every intention of washing up the supper pots when she got back but now she decided that they could wait until the morning, as Mrs Spooner had said. She felt completely drained emotionally and was now worrying about who Mr Pinnegar might target next. Mrs Spooner was quite right: he needed stopping – but *how?*

The next morning, she attended church with Mrs Spooner and after the service, as they were saying goodbye to the vicar, Mrs Lockett allowed Sunday to hold Phoebe for a moment. She was such a contented baby and nestled in Sunday's arms, staring up at her from her lovely blue eyes.

Sunday commented on the beautiful shawl she was wrapped in and Mrs Lockett told her proudly, 'It was a gift, among many other baby things, from Lady Huntley. It's quite exquisite, isn't it, and I dread to think what it must have cost. It's so fine I suppose I should save it for her christening day really, but then I don't want it to lie in a drawer and not be used.'

'Quite right,' Mrs Spooner agreed, adjusting the enormous red and yellow silk flowered hat that she was wearing. It was so wide that Sunday

216

had feared she'd never get through the church door in it, and so richly adorned that she knew it must be very heavy. But then that was Biddy Spooner – the more colourful the better, as far as she was concerned.

Mrs Spooner's nephew had accompanied them to church that morning and as he stood patiently waiting for them he noticed Sunday blinking at his aunt's hat.

'It's monstrous, isn't it?' He chuckled as his eyes followed hers and Sunday grinned as she reluctantly handed baby Phoebe back to her adoring mother. She and Jacob were getting on very well and because he was the nearest person in age to her in the house they always managed to find something to talk about.

'I was wondering, if next week, you might like to stay and have lunch with us after the morning service, my dear?' Mrs Lockett said then. 'It would be much easier for you to get to the workhouse from the vicarage to see Daisy and Tommy, and it would save you having to go home and come all the way back again. But only if Mrs Spooner doesn't mind, of course.'

Sunday was delighted at the request but glanced anxiously at Mrs Spooner. She didn't want to take advantage of her good nature. She needn't have worried, however, for the woman thought it was an excellent idea and gave her permission straight away.

'But what about the dinner pots?' Sunday fretted.

Mrs Spooner laughed. 'They'll be waiting for you when you finally get home, never you fear.

I'm not goin' to do 'em meself.'

Sunday looked back at Mrs Lockett. 'Then in that case I'd love to come. Thank you very much.' And so it was decided and something for her to look forward to.

She set off to visit her friends that afternoon in a cheerful frame of mind, but the moment she went through the door she felt as if a great weight had been placed on her shoulders again. The workhouse would always have that effect on her.

But she told herself that things were looking up. She was happy in her new position and Cissie was out of the asylum. She would be fourteen years old in just three short weeks now and soon after Christmas, Daisy would be too – so hopefully she would be out of the workhouse as well then. And then there was Jacob, of course ... she felt bashful just thinking of him.

She settled herself at a table and before long her friends joined her. Tommy seemed to have shot up, she observed as he entered the room. He wasn't quite sixteen yet but already he was much taller than herself and Daisy. He was rapidly changing from a young boy into a young man and seemed to be all gangly arms and legs. His voice had changed too, recently – it was much deeper now. The minute they were seated, Sunday burst out with her news about Cissie and they were both thrilled for her, although she noted that Daisy didn't seem her usual chirpy self.

'Is everything all right?' she asked, and Daisy gave her a sad sort of smile that didn't quite reach her eyes.

'Oh yes, I'm fine. Just got a bit of a headache, that's all.'

Sunday could well believe it as she stared at the dark circles beneath her friend's eyes.

'She's been down in the dumps for a while now,' Tommy informed Sunday with an anxious glance at his sister. 'But she won't tell me what's wrong.'

'There's nothing wrong,' Daisy said irritably, and seeing that she was becoming upset he quickly shut up, giving Sunday a meaningful look. They then went on to talk of other things until the bell sounded to herald the end of visiting time. Sunday took her leave, promising that she would be there at the same time the following week.

A few days later, Mrs Spooner gave Sunday permission to go and visit Cissie again. She had seen Lady Huntley earlier in the day, and Lavinia had encouraged it, saying that Sunday seemed to do the girl more good than any of the remedies and tonics that Mrs Roundtree was pouring into her.

With all her chores done, Sunday set off for Treetops Manor but had barely reached the brick-works when she bumped into Jacob, who had just finished work.

He smiled at her in greeting. 'And where are you off to, looking so chirpy?'

She told him where she was going and he said immediately, 'Then in that case I shall come up there and walk you home. It's almost seven o'clock already so it will be at least nine by the time you leave. The nights are beginning to draw in a little now and it wouldn't do for you to be

219

walking home in the dark alone.'

Sunday flushed becomingly. Jacob was such a nice young man, and handsome too.

'I shall be quite all right,' she assured him but he wouldn't be put off so they agreed that he would be waiting for her at the end of the drive leading to Treetops Manor at nine o'clock sharp.

Sunday was delighted to find Cissie in a much happier frame of mind and looking a great deal better. Zillah had washed and combed out her matted hair and dressed it in a simple but agreeable style, with pins and tortoiseshell combs.

'I've told Mrs Roundtree that I'm well enough to start work but she says I'm to rest for at least another week.' The girl was still painfully thin but at least there was a little colour in her cheeks. The haunted look was still there, lurking in the back of her eyes, but she seemed to be much more her old self – although the kindly housekeeper had confided to Sunday that she still had dreadful nightmares.

'I can never thank you enough for telling Lady Huntley about me and getting me out of that awful place,' Cissie said to Sunday just before she left, giving her an affectionate hug. 'I think I would have ended up as mad as some of the poor souls in there if I'd had to stay much longer. I'd lost all hope, you see, after they took away my baby son.'

'You have to try and put it all behind you now and get on with the rest of your life,' Sunday told her with a wisdom way beyond her years, and Cissie nodded. She knew that Sunday was right but doubted that she would ever be able to forget those traumatic years in Hatter's Hall.

As promised, Jacob was waiting for Sunday at the end of the drive; her heart did a little flutter at the sight of him. The walk home seemed to be over in a flash as they chatted easily about anything and everything. Sunday had taken to reading the newspapers that Miss Bailey left lying about when she had read them, and now she could converse on many different topics, including politics. Jacob enjoyed being with Sunday; it was nice to have someone young about the house. He had taken on the role of a protective older brother – after all, he was almost nineteen years old and viewed her as still just a very young girl – but he liked her company all the same.

When they got back, Sunday went to make sure that all was tidy in the kitchen before retiring to her room to alter another of the gowns that Lady Huntley had passed on to her; this time it was for Cissie. She hoped that it would help to cheer her friend up.

The following weeks raced by and in no time they were into September. Sunday's birthday came and went without any kind of celebration. This was nothing new. She had never celebrated it in the workhouse and she didn't mention it now.

She had settled in very happily at Mrs Spooner's. The kindly lady had increased her wages to half a crown a week, a small fortune to Sunday, who was saving every penny she could. All she had spent up to now was a shilling on a pair of second-hand boots from the rag stall in the market and another shilling on a warm woollen shawl now that the days were getting colder. Although the items were used, these were the first clothes she had ever bought for herself and she was thrilled with them. The boots had had very little wear and were the finest she had ever owned, and the shawl, which was in a pretty shade of blue that matched her eyes, was her pride and joy and made her feel very grand when she wore it. The only dark cloud on her horizon was Daisy, for every time she visited the workhouse, she sensed that all was not well with her. The girl had lost weight and seemed nervy and on edge, but would not tell Sunday what the matter was, insisting that all was well. Sunday suspected that Miss Frost might have turned her bullying attentions onto Daisy and longed for the day when her friend could get away from the Union Workhouse for good.

Cissie, on the other hand, was thriving under Mrs Roundtree's tender loving care. She was now working in the laundry at Treetops Manor and had joined the other staff in the servants' quarters upstairs; after the harsh regime she had endured at the workhouse, she found her duties easy. Zillah and the housekeeper were keeping a close eye on her and ensuring that she didn't overdo things and that she ate well, and Cissie was settling in nicely. However, she was still prone to burst into floods of tears whenever she remembered the baby that had been snatched away from her at birth and the years of privations, 'treatments' and cruel confinement that had followed.

Little Phoebe, Mrs Lockett's baby, was thriving too and now Sunday looked forward to the church services each week so that she could spend a little time with her. Verity and the Reverend were looking rather tired as Phoebe was teething now and causing them sleepless nights but even so, anyone could see how devoted they were to the little girl.

Sunday, her name-day, was the girl's favourite day of the week now. She would wear the blue dress that Lady Huntley had given to her and her lovely blue shawl, and feel like the bee's knees.

One particular Sunday, she came down ready to travel to the church with Mrs Spooner and found the old woman waiting for her in the hall.

'Here,' Biddy said self-consciously, thrusting something into Sunday's hand. 'The tallyman called yesterday and when I saw this I thought it might be just the right colour to go with your shawl.'

Sunday looked down to find a length of blue ribbon and she beamed with pleasure. It was the first she had ever owned and was so lovely that she almost didn't want to wear it, although her hair, which she wore loose, had grown to shoulder-length again now. It would soon be time to put it up in a more womanly way.

'You shouldn't go spending your money on me,' she protested, unable to tear her eyes away from the beautiful gift. No one, apart from Mrs Spooner, had ever bought her anything that was unworn and brand new before – apart from Albert Pinnegar, that was, and she didn't want to think of him now. And then, not wishing to appear ungrateful she rushed on, 'But thank you so much. I shall put it on right now and only wear it when we go to church.'

She then leaned over and kissed Mrs Spooner soundly on the cheek, making the old woman flush beneath her layers of paint and powder. For the first time in her life Sunday was truly happy – and she hoped it would last for ever.

Chapter Twenty-Two

Sunday's happy mood lapsed a little when she visited Daisy and Tommy that afternoon. Daisy seemed even more tense than the week before and her eyes kept flicking nervously towards the door. For the whole time Sunday was there, Daisy sat plucking at the skirts of her drab dress and seemed totally preoccupied, barely contributing to the conversation. She did manage a smile and a peck on the cheek when Sunday left, but on her way home Sunday frowned thoughtfully. Daisy's strange behaviour bothered her, and it was then she decided that it was time to put the proposition that had been steadily growing in her mind for some time to Mrs Spooner.

The perfect opportunity came after the light tea that Annie had prepared for them all.

'Mrs Spooner, could I have a word, please?' As always, Sunday was polite. The lodgers had all adjourned to the drawing room and Biddy was the only one left in the dining room.

She sat looking up at Sunday, who was hovering around, then told her bluntly, 'Sit down, can't you, Sunny? It's hurtin' me neck looking up at you.'

Sunday sat opposite her and licked her lips which were suddenly dry. 'The thing is, I have an idea to put to you,' she began cautiously.

'Oh yes, an' what would that be?' Mrs Spooner tried to guess what was coming.

'Well...' Sunday paused, wondering as she absent-mindedly stroked Mabel if she might be being a little too forward. But then an image of Daisy's unhappy face flashed in front of her eyes and she plunged on. It was a case of nothing ventured, nothing gained. 'As you know, I've taken over a lot of Annie's work now and in the not too distant future I'm hoping to take over all the cooking as well so that Annie can properly retire.'

'Yes, you've done well, I'll grant you that. But what's this leading up to?' Her employer narrowed her eyes suspiciously.

'It's quite a large house for one person to keep – not that I'm complaining,' Sunday hastened to assure her. 'I just wondered if you might consider taking on another maid.' When Mrs Spooner frowned she rushed on: 'It wouldn't cost you a penny – well, only what you paid me when I first came here. But the thing is, if I had a little help we could let out the other bedrooms that are standing empty so you'd actually be considerably in pocket with their rents coming in.'

'Hmm...' Mrs Spooner tapped her chin thoughtfully. She could see the sense in what the girl was saying. And then she said casually, 'And did you by any chance happen to have anyone in particular in mind to help you?'

'I did, as it happens,' Sunday confessed. 'My friend Daisy Branning from the workhouse. She's

225

just a few months younger than me and a *very* hard worker. She could share my room if you liked. She has a brother too. His name is Tommy and I wondered if you might like to employ him as well. The vegetable garden and the orchard are sadly overgrown, as you know, and he could bring them back to life. He loves gardening and it would save a lot of money if we could grow our own fruit and vegetables. It would save lots of time on trips to the market too. And he's very handy at other things as well: he could paint the outside of the house for you for a start-off. You did say you were going to employ someone to do it.'

'There is that, I dare say,' Mrs Spooner said. 'But what would he do during the winter months when there's no gardening to be done?'

'I've thought of that too.' Sunday couldn't suppress her eagerness now. 'He's very handy. All the boys in the workhouse are taught to do lots of things so he could do all the odd jobs about the place, which would mean you wouldn't have to call in tradesmen when anything went wrong. I also thought that perhaps if there were a boy to see to them we could get some pigs for the empty sty and some chickens too, so we can have our own freshly laid eggs. And we could get a little pony for the empty stable to pull your cart again so you could get out and about more easily. With all the animals to tend to and maintaining the house, Tommy would have more than enough to keep him busy all year round then.'

Mrs Spooner's eyes were alight with amusement now. 'It seems to me you've given this a lot of thought, young lady.'

'I have – and for some time.' Sunday smiled disarmingly back at her. 'But think of what we could save for the sake of two wages if we let the other rooms out.'

'I suppose you do have a point,' Mrs Spooner conceded, 'but you'll have to give me a little time to think on it. And I'd want to talk it over with Jacob an' all.'

'Of course.' Sunday helped the old lady to her feet and as she hobbled away, leaning heavily on her silver-topped walking stick, Sunday hugged herself with excitement. It would be wonderful if she, Daisy and Tommy could all be under the same roof again – but now all she could do was wait to see what Mrs Spooner decided.

The next morning, as soon as breakfast was over, Sunday carried all the washing out to the wash-house and lit the firepits beneath the two copper boilers. Her own laundry and Jacob's took next to no time to do, but Mrs Spooner's frilled and flounced garments were another matter entirely; once dry, they took forever to press. Not that Sunday was complaining. She had grown very fond of her employer and would have done anything for her now. She was on tenterhooks waiting for Mrs Spooner's decision about Daisy and Tommy and hoped that she wouldn't take too long to make up her mind.

It was the next evening following dinner as Sunday was carrying the dirty pots from the dining room to the kitchen on a tray that Mrs Spooner told her, 'I've been thinking about your idea, lass, and I've also spoken to Jacob about it and we both think it could work – having your friends here, I mean.'

Plonking down onto the nearest chair, she leaned both hands on her stick and went on: 'I like someone who can use their initiative. You won't know this but when me and my husband were first married we went to live in the West Indies – Jamaica it was. My Herbert had work there, you see. He kept the accounts at a sugarcane plantation and the sugar that was harvested there was then shipped to London. It was a very responsible job for him but soon I got bored of being on my own all day, waited on hand and foot by the local ladies, so decided to start up a little business of my own. I employed those same ladies to help me and I set up my first boarding house. It was a great success.' She puffed out her chest proudly. 'Eventually, Herbert started pining for England so we came back and bought this place and then when I lost him I adapted it into a lodging house. You're quite right, Sunny, when you point out that with a little more staff we could take in more lodgers, so the next time I see Lady Huntley I'll ask her to approach Mr Pinnegar about it. I reckon she'll be the best one to sort it out. I don't want no larking about, mind! Your pals'll be here to work so you'd best all remember that.'

Slightly offended, Sunday raised herself up to her full height. 'I'd rather hoped you knew me better than that by now, ma'am,' she said peevishly, which brought the smile back to Mrs Spooner's face.

'Now there's no need to get on your high horse.' She waved a finger at the girl but her eyes

228

were twinkling with amusement. Sunny could be a fierce little lass, there was no doubt about it. But then that was one of the things that the old lady liked about her. She admired people with a bit of spirit. In fact, Sunny reminded Biddy very much of herself at that age, and later as a young bride in the West Indies. There had been no room for shrinking violets there.

Mabel came bounding in then and Sunday bent to pet her as Mrs Spooner watched them with a thoughtful expression on her face.

'You'll have to clean out a couple more rooms up in the attic for them. Your room is too small to share,' she instructed. 'But don't get building your hopes up too high. The housemaster may well have other plans for them so let's just wait an' see, eh?'

She whistled and called Mabel to heel then, and Sunday took this as a signal to get on with her work. But it was hard for her to concentrate on what she was doing because she was so excited.

In Treetops Manor, Lavinia Huntley was playing the piano in the drawing room. It was three days now since her husband had been home but rather than be concerned she was enjoying not having to worry about what mood he would be in. He was no doubt with his mistress in the small cottage he had rented for her on the outskirts of the town, ironically paid for with his wife's money. Unfortunately, as his brother's wedding grew closer his efforts to produce a son had become almost frenzied and he had taken to coming to Lavinia's room on a regular basis again. She was still bruised and aching from his last attack on her and 'attack' was the only word she could think of to describe their coming together now. It certainly could never be classed as making love.

Her trusted maid, Zillah, had been horrified to find her crying the last time he had come to her room; it made Zillah see red, and sometimes she wondered how she had managed not to strangle him. She loved Lavinia as a daughter and hated the man she had married with all her heart. She knew how hard it was for her mistress to be childless. All Lavinia had ever wanted was a baby to love and cherish, and sometimes the terrible secret Zillah was forced to carry was almost more than she could bear. Even so, she knew she had no choice. She believed every word of Ashley's threat and knew that he was heartless enough to carry it through. Their doctor was a great friend of his, and should she betray him, Ashley would have no hesitation in tricking the doctor into pronouncing Lavinia insane. She would then be locked away in Hatter's Hall, and Zillah herself would be packed off to a living death in the workhouse.

As Zillah turned back her mistress's bed now, she sighed as she looked towards the tallboy in the corner of the room. If her suspicions were confirmed she feared there could be yet more heartache ahead, for in there she kept the cloths that Lavinia used for her courses each month and just the day before, she had realised that the latest course was now more than two weeks overdue. Lavinia clearly hadn't noticed and it could just be a case that the monthly visitor was late. Zillah chewed on her lip. But if it wasn't...

She thought back to the state Lavinia had been in after the Mothering Day service earlier in the year. It was always a beautiful service where the Reverend Lockett gave thanks to the mothers in the congregation, and the children and daughters in service returned to their home parish to bring their mothers little gifts, usually bunches of wild-flowers. Each year it affected Lavinia terribly. None of her daughters had survived to bring her flowers and yet she would willingly have given up everything she possessed for just one healthy child. Perhaps if Lavinia was with child again she would get her wish this time? *But what if it is another daughter?* a little voice asked and Zillah shuddered at the thought. She was sad for the first two Huntley babies and, getting older, doubted she could be strong enough to do again what she had been forced to do with their third daughter. Pushing the disturbing thoughts aside she continued to get her mistress's room ready for her to retire to. What would be would be, and all she could do now was carry on caring for her dear Lavinia as best she could.

It was much later that evening when Ashley returned, badly the worse for drink, staggering and swearing at the maid who rushed forward to take his cape. Zillah was in the hall with a tray of cocoa that she had just been about to take up to Lavinia and she glared at him.

'I suggest you stay in your own room tonight,' she said. They had long since stopped trying to hide their mutual dislike. 'The mistress is just about to settle down.'

His clothes were crumpled, she noted, and he reeked of spirits and another woman's bed.

'Thish is my house and I'll shleep where I want. And don't you forget it elshe you'll find yourself out on your arse,' he slurred.

Zillah scowled at him fearlessly. Thankfully that was the one thing Lavinia would never allow him to do – get rid of her. It had been agreed as part of the marriage settlement that Zillah could stay with her for as long as she wished; it was the one thing that Lavinia had refused to budge on.

She watched as he staggered drunkenly towards the stairs and prayed that he might fall and break his worthless neck. She knew she should feel guilty for having such evil thoughts but she couldn't help herself. However, he finally reached the top and shambled off in the direction of his own quarters and Zillah breathed a sigh of relief. At least he wouldn't trouble her dear girl tonight and she was thankful for small blessings.

Chapter Twenty-Three

It was midweek when Lavinia Huntley woke one morning feeling sick and slid aside the breakfast tray that Zillah had carried up for her.

'I won't eat anything just yet if you don't mind, dear,' she said apologetically. 'I think I must have a little tummy upset.'

232

Zillah frowned as her worst fears were realised and decided that she would have to voice her suspicions. 'I rather think it might be more than a tummy upset, my love.'

She lifted the tray and placed it on a small table as Lavinia raised an eyebrow. 'What do you mean?'

Sitting down on the bed at the side of her, Zillah gently took her hand. 'Have you noticed that you've missed a course? I did when I was putting a petticoat away the other day. You haven't had to use your cloths for some weeks.'

Lavinia thought about it, then as comprehension dawned she gasped and her hand flew to her mouth. 'You don't think I might be with child again, do you?' she asked.

Her face solemn, Zillah nodded. 'I think there may be a very good possibility.'

'B-but I'm in my mid-thirties now; I thought I was too old to have a child. And what if it is another girl? Ashley would never forgive me. Worse still, what if it is stillborn like the others? I know I agreed to try again but only because I never dreamed it would happen!' Tears started to roll down her cheeks as Zillah wrapped her arms protectively about her.

'I don't think I can face going all through that heartache again,' Lavinia sobbed.

'I'm afraid you don't have much choice,' Zillah said matter-of-factly. 'Perhaps we should get the doctor to call in and have a look at you, just to be sure? Though it might be too early for him to tell just yet. Even so, I think you should inform the master that there's a possibility that you're with child. That way, he'll leave you alone till we're sure, which will be one blessing at least.'

With her emotions in turmoil, Lavinia nodded. Half of her still longed for a child yet the other half was terrified of history repeating itself.

'But for now there's no sense working yourself up into a tizzy,' Zillah soothed sensibly, mopping the tears from Lavinia's cheeks with a large white handkerchief that she took from her apron pocket. 'Let's get you up and dressed then you can go about your business as normal, for now at least. Weren't you going to see Mrs Spooner today?'

She helped the woman dress then styled her hair as Lavinia sat staring blankly into her dressing-table mirror. She could hardly take it in. But then she knew that Zillah was right, she usually was. She must speak to Ashley then try to go on as normally as she could until it could be confirmed one way or another.

When a sullen Matthews, Sir Ashley's valet, tapped on her door an hour later to tell her that the groom had brought the carriage round to the front, Lavinia nodded at him coolly. Sometimes when Ashley went missing for any length of time he would take Matthews with him; at other times the valet was left to skulk about the house with nothing much to do and was a constant thorn in Lavinia's side. She always felt that he was spying on her and reporting back to his master, not that he would ever have anything untoward to tell him.

As she stepped out of the house, Jenkins helped her into the carriage. Unlike Matthews, George Jenkins was a lovely young man who had only joined them the year before when their former groom had retired to live with his daughter in Somerset. He clearly loved the horses he cared for, which was why he got so upset when the master ill-treated his stallion, and he always had a friendly smile and a good word for everyone. All in all, he had settled very well into the rooms above the stables and was very popular with the rest of the staff.

'Where to, ma'am?'

'Whittleford Lodge, if you please, Jenkins.'

He tipped his cap as he closed the door and soon the carriage was rattling away down the drive as Lavinia stared thoughtfully across the rolling fields. Absent-mindedly she placed a hand on her stomach and wondered if it could be true. Only time would tell now.

When she reached Mrs Spooner's house and Sunday opened the door to her, the girl's face lit up.

'Oh, I'm *so* pleased to see you,' she said.

Lady Huntley teased, 'Well, if I'm to have a greeting like that every time I call, I shall have to come more often.'

'Mrs Spooner has something she wants to talk to you about.' Sunday was clad in an enormous calico apron and there was a smudge of dirt on her nose, yet still she managed to look pretty.

'I'm quite intrigued. Is she in the drawing room?'

'Yes, ma'am. She's doing her accounts. I'll tell her you're here then show you in to her.'

Sunday raced away as Lady Huntley smiled indulgently. She was so happy that she'd got the girl out of the workhouse. Everyone seemed really pleased with her and now that Lavinia herself had got to know the girl she could understand why.

'Ah, I'm right pleased you've come,' Mrs Spooner greeted her when Lady Huntley entered the room. 'Young Sunny put an idea to me t'other day an' I reckon it might be a good one. I've just been lookin' at my books and would like to know what you think.'

A number of ledgers were spread out before her and she pushed one towards her visitor as she quickly told her of Sunday's proposition.

'This here is what we have coming in now,' she said, pointing a gnarled, heavily ringed finger at a row of figures. 'And this here is what I could earn if I were to let the other rooms out after paying out two more lots of wages to Sunny's workhouse friends Tommy and Daisy Branning. So what are your thoughts on it?'

'I must say it certainly looks plausible.' Lady Huntley studied the figures carefully. 'You would clearly be well in profit.'

'That's what I thought!' Mrs Spooner beamed, her bright red lips a scarlet slash in her heavily powdered face. 'So do you reckon you could get Pinnegar to agree to the pair of 'em coming here?'

'I can certainly do my best,' Lavinia promised. She would be glad of the diversion. It might take her mind off her own predicament for a time. 'Sunday is doing really well here with you so there's no reason for him to refuse. I will go to the workhouse to see him today.'

Mrs Spooner smiled with satisfaction and yanked on the bell-pull at the side of the fire-place. To Lady Huntley's amusement, Sunday appeared instantly, as if by magic. It was obvious that she had been listening at the door – which was an indication of how much they meant to her, the two young people she was trying to free from the workhouse.

'Yes, Mrs Spooner?' she asked innocently as she fidgeted from foot to foot.

'Lady Huntley likes your idea,' Mrs Spooner told her. 'But then I imagine you already know that if you were earwigging! But now go an' make yourself useful an' fetch us a tray o' tea. An' some of Annie's raisin flapjacks wouldn't go amiss neither.'

Sunday had the good grace to flush as she turned tail and scuttled away, and her heart was singing. Oh, *if only* Lady Huntley could get Mr Pinnegar to allow her friends to join her, she would be the happiest girl in the world.

Lady Huntley didn't receive such an enthusiastic greeting, however, when she arrived at the Union Workhouse early that afternoon. In fact, Miss Frost stared at her suspiciously. She had not been made aware that any of the guardians were due to visit and bitterly resented the intrusion.

'I hope you haven't come to inform us that the Small girl isn't suitable for her new position,' she said as she faced Lady Huntley in the entrance hall.

'Quite the contrary, Sunday is performing her duties well,' Lady Huntley said with a charming

237

smile which only made the woman glare more, although underneath she was secretly relieved. She could not have endured to have the girl back on her hands.

'Then may I ask why you have called without an appointment? Mr Pinnegar is rather busy at present.'

'Oh, I'm sure he'll spare a few minutes to see me,' Lady Huntley replied airily as she peeled off her long lace gloves. 'Kindly inform him that I am here.'

Miss Frost bristled. Just who did this woman think she was, coming here and giving out her orders? Turning her attention to the girl who was down on her hands and knees scrubbing the floor, she barked, *'You!* Go and ask Mr Pinnegar if he has time to see Lady Huntley.'

'Yes, ma'am.' Daisy dropped her scrubbing brush and scrambled to her feet then shot away as if Old Nick himself was at her heels. Mere seconds later she was back, and skidding to a halt she said breathlessly, 'Mr Pinnegar says he will see her now, Miss Frost.'

Sniffing her disapproval, the matron wondered if he would have been so keen to break the rules had it been one of the male guardians who had turned up out of the blue. 'You'd better come this way,' she said and marched down the hallway. Quite unnecessarily, Lady Huntley thought. She knew perfectly well where the housefather's office was and would have been more than capable of finding her own way there. The woman probably just wanted to be nosy.

Her suspicions were confirmed when Miss

Frost tapped at his door, then followed Lavinia inside.

'My dear Lady Huntley.' Mr Pinnegar rose and offered his hand, ushering her towards a chair.

'I'm so sorry to call unannounced,' Lady Huntley apologised. 'Miss Frost has pointed out how remiss it is of me but I wanted a word with you.'

'Nonsense. It is a pleasure to see you at any time,' he assured her, much to Miss Frost's disgust. Then, 'You may leave us now, Matron.'

Miss Frost twirled about and stalked from the room in a sulky display that would have been better suited to one of the younger residents.

'Now, how may I help you, ma'am?' he asked when the door had closed noisily behind her.

'First of all I thought you might like to know how well Sunday Small is doing in her new home.'

She saw a quick spark of interest flame in his eyes and swallowed her disgust.

He didn't really need her to tell him that, if truth be known. He saw the girl each Sunday at church and just the sight of her could still make his loins tingle, especially now she was dressing in pretty clothes and developing into a young woman. However, his voice was polite and impartial when he answered, 'But of course.'

'She has settled into her new position very well, which leads me to a proposition I have been asked to put to you.' She hurried on to explain what Mrs Spooner had suggested and the man stroked his moustache thoughtfully as he listened intently. Meanwhile it was all Lavinia Huntley could do not to lose control and scream at him, knowing what he had done to Cissie. But her time would come, she promised herself, and when it did, she would expose him for the perverted, lecherous scoundrel he was.

When she had finished, he strummed his fingers on the desk. 'I suppose there could be no harm in what you are proposing. I would home another two orphans, which will please your fellow guardians. But you are aware that one of the children you are talking about is not fourteen yet?' he enquired. 'It is usual for us to start finding them positions then.'

She nodded. 'Yes, I am aware of that, but you may recall that Sunday herself wasn't quite fourteen either when I placed her with Mrs Spooner and she's done extremely well. So I really think if the positions are there for these two, it is worth considering at least?'

He hesitated for another moment or two then smiled. 'In that case, how can I refuse, dear lady? I'm quite sure it would be in order – and of course we must put the interests of the children first. I have always found it difficult to say no to a pretty face.'

Lavinia Huntley squirmed as she stared into his repulsive face. Did she detect a hint of relief in his voice? The man was an absolute menace but for now at least she must try to keep on the right side of him. 'Then perhaps we should put the proposition to the children, and if they are happy with the idea they could maybe go to their new placement early next week. Would that give you enough time to get the necessary paperwork ready? I shall of course sign it myself again.'

'It would give me more than enough time – and don't trouble yourself about speaking to Thomas and Daisy. I'm sure they will be grateful for such an opportunity. And now may I offer you some refreshments?'

Lavinia shuddered at the thought of taking tea with him. She would rather have supped with the devil.

'Thank you, but no. I've taken up quite enough of your time as it is,' she told him as she began to pull her gloves back on. She could hardly wait to be away from this place now. 'Unless I hear from you to the contrary I shall be here to pick the children up at eleven o'clock sharp next Monday morning, and then I shall personally escort them to Whittleford Lodge. Good day, Mr Pinnegar.'

He raced ahead of her to open the door and as she passed him, the rank smell of him assailed her nostrils. But at least her mission had been successful and she could hardly wait to tell Sunday and Mrs Spooner the good news.

Chapter Twenty-Four

Sunday was so thrilled to hear Lady Huntley's report from the workhouse that she did a little dance on the spot.

'I shall start to get their rooms ready straight away,' she said joyously, then added, 'But only when I've done the rest of my jobs, of course.'

'It's only a trial though, remember, young

241

Sunny,' Mrs Spooner warned, wagging her finger although her eyes were smiling. The house had been a happier place since the girl had come to live there.

'Oh yes, I understand that, but I'm sure Daisy and Tommy won't let you down,' Sunday said hastily. She didn't want the woman to think that she was taking advantage of her good nature.

'Very well. Then go and make yourself useful and fetch me and Lady Huntley a tray of coffee.'

'Yes, ma'am.' Sunday skipped from the room; she was so happy that she would have walked over hot coals for either of the women at that moment. She burst into the kitchen to share the good news with Annie.

'We'll have 'alf the workhouse 'ere at this rate,' the old woman commented, but she was pleased to see Sunday looking so excited.

That night when all her chores were done, Sunday set to on making two more of the rooms up in the attic habitable for Daisy and Tommy. She hummed contentedly as she worked. In just a few short days they would all be back together again! She put a bed for Daisy in the room next to hers. At Mrs Spooner's insistence, Tommy would be right at the end of the landing. The very last room in the attic was full of old furniture that had been abandoned and stored there over the years, and after Mrs Spooner had told her to help herself to anything that might be needed, Sunday managed to make their bedrooms very comfortable indeed; she could hardly wait to see their faces when they came up here. Once she was done, Sunday rubbed her hands down her apron and sighed with satisfaction. The rooms could by no means be called luxurious, but after sharing dormitories in the workhouse she was sure her friends would be pleased with them. Of course, she was aware that before their parents had died they had lived in a loving family home and so had probably known better, but she had done the best she could for them. Now all she had to do was somehow contain her anticipation until they arrived.

Over the last few weeks, Mrs Spooner had sent her into the market each Wednesday with a list of food to buy. Annie had accompanied her for the first couple of times to make sure that she knew her way and to show her the cost of things. Having never had to handle money before, Sunday had no idea of prices but she had been a willing student and Annie felt that she was capable of going alone now. Today she set off with a large wicker basket slung across her arm. She was getting to know her way about a little better now and could never get enough of walking through the fields and marvelling at the wildflowers and the wildlife. Jacob had pointed out some of the birds that landed in the garden and told her what they were called, and for the first time in her life she had seen a real live fox. Sometimes she felt as if she had been set free from prison and was making the most of every moment.

Her happy mood continued as she walked amongst the market stalls with her list clutched tightly in her hand. She loved the atmosphere there although she wasn't so keen on the cattle market. She always felt sorry for the animals that were being sold there and had to stifle the urge to open the pens and set them free. There were chickens squawking indignantly and cows, sheep and pigs crammed side by side in pens. They were prisoners, she thought, just as she had been in the workhouse. She purchased the fruit and vegetables that Annie had asked for and was just heading for the butcher's when suddenly a large figure loomed up in front of her and her heart skipped a beat.

'Why, Sunday, what a pleasant surprise. What are you doing here? And looking very pretty, may I add.'

Sunday stared up into Mr Pinnegar's hated face feeling like one of the caged beasts she had just passed.

'I'm just doing some shopping for Mrs Spooner,' she answered calmly although she was quaking inside. There was no way she would let him see how afraid of him she was; her pride would not allow it.

'I hear you have settled in very well,' he went on, as if they were the best of friends.

She nodded and began to inch away from him but suddenly his hand shot out and his fat fingers grasped her arm as he leaned towards her.

'You don't *have* to work there, you know.' His tongue flicked out to lick his lips. Just being close to her had made his manhood harden. She was like a drug that he couldn't get out of his system. 'If you were to let me set you up in my little cottage you could be a lady of leisure and I'm sure you'd come to care for me in time.' He was careful to keep his voice down so that no one could hear him as Sunday yanked her arm from his grasp and stepped away from him.

'I would rather *die* than *ever* let you set your hands on me again,' she spat as her eyes flashed fire, then turning about she hurried away. The day was spoiled and now all she wanted to do was get back to the safety of Whittleford Lodge.

She did the rest of the shopping as quickly as she could, frequently glancing across her shoulder to make sure that Mr Pinnegar wasn't following her, then she set off for home, feeling far more shaken than she cared to admit.

When she arrived in the kitchen, Annie glanced up from the pastry she was rolling on the table and frowned. 'What's up, lass? Yer look a bit pasty. Are yer not feelin' well?'

'Oh, I'm fine.' Sunday managed to raise a smile as she plonked the heavy basket down on one of the kitchen chairs. 'I was able to get everything on the list. Shall I start to peel the vegetables for dinner?'

'If you've a mind to.' Annie was watching her closely. Sunday didn't seem to be quite her usual cheery little self at all. Normally when she arrived home from market she was full of what she'd seen and would chat away fifteen to the dozen, but today she seemed very subdued. *Still, I suppose everyone has their off days,* the old lady thought and turned her attention back to the pie she was baking.

At Treetops Manor that night, as Zillah was helping Lavinia to prepare for bed, they heard a commotion downstairs.

'Sounds like his lordship has rolled in drunk again,' the maid said wryly as Lavinia glanced anxiously towards the door, praying that her husband would be too drunk to demand his rights.

All too soon the bedroom door banged inwards and Ashley stood swaying in the doorway.

'Ah, nice to see the little woman ish all ready for me,' he slurred – and something in Lavinia suddenly snapped.

'No, Ashley, I am *not* ready for you,' she informed him coldly. She normally never denied him, but she was not about to risk anything going wrong if there was a chance of a new little life growing inside her. She looked very pretty standing there with her blonde hair tumbling about her slim shoulders and he felt aroused as he advanced into the room. He was unsteady on his feet and the smell of brandy preceded him, making her wrinkle her nose in distaste.

'You'll do ash I say,' he announced as his hand dropped to his belt but she stood her ground.

'Not tonight I won't,' she defied him. 'Nor any other night in the near future if it comes to that. You see ... I think I may be with child and until I have had it confirmed I'm not going to risk anything.'

He came to an abrupt halt.

'So could you kindly leave me in peace?'

His lips curled back in a sneer. 'Gladly, my love. But if you *are* with child it had better be a boy this time.' He seemed to have sobered up very quickly, she thought as he turned and left the room.

Zillah, who had been holding her breath, let out a long sigh. Her mistress was usually so subservi-

246

ent that it was nice to see her standing up to that bullying husband of hers for a change. 'Well, that told him,' she said with a chuckle. 'But now I think we really should get the doctor to examine you. Ashley is going to be none too pleased if this proves to be a false alarm.'

'I'm fairly certain it isn't,' Lavinia confided as she sat down at the dressing table and waited for Zillah to brush her hair. 'My breasts are quite tender and I'm feeling very sickly all of the time now, although it's worst in the mornings.' She turned to her trusted maid with tears brimming in her eyes then. 'I so long for a child yet I'm so afraid of what could go wrong.'

'We'll do all we can to make sure that nothing does go wrong,' Zillah soothed. 'But now come and hop into bed and drink this warm milk. It'll help you to sleep and at least you know you won't be disturbed now.'

Monday morning finally rolled around and, as promised, Lavinia Huntley arrived at the workhouse spot on time to collect Daisy and Tommy, who were waiting wide-eyed in the entrance hall for her.

'Mr Pinnegar has the release papers ready for you to sign,' Miss Frost informed her, tight-lipped, then glaring at the children she ordered, 'Stay right where you are until we return.'

Daisy and Tommy glanced worriedly at each other. No one had bothered to inform them where they were going and their imaginations had been working overtime, although they were at least grateful that wherever it was they were going, they would be staying together.

Daisy slid her hand into her brother's and he squeezed it reassuringly. Although Tommy was only two years older than Daisy he now towered above her and had taken on the role of her protector as best he could from the boys' section of the workhouse. Neither of them had known a single happy day since they had been admitted to this hellish place but whenever they snatched a moment together Daisy seemed even more on edge than usual and she looked gaunt and frail.

'Don't worry, I'll look after you,' he whispered when Frosty was well out of earshot.

'But what happens if they take us to Hatter's Hall?'

'Lady Huntley would never allow that,' he said strongly. 'So let's just wait and see, eh?' And so they stood close together as the minutes on the grandfather clock in the foyer ticked away, clutching the bundles of clothes and the few possessions with which they had arrived.

Lady Huntley was back in a surprisingly short time and she smiled at them kindly as she ushered them towards the door. 'Right, that's the paperwork all done and dusted so now let's go and get you settled into your new home, shall we? Sunday is so excited, she can hardly wait to see you both.'

'*Sunday?*' Tommy paused on the workhouse steps to stare at her in confusion.

'Yes. Surely someone has told you where you're going?' Lady Huntley said with a frown as the door to the workhouse clanged shut behind them.

When the two children looked at her blankly

248

she tutted with annoyance as she led them to the waiting carriage. George was standing with the door open and he gave the children a friendly smile as they clambered inside and looked back at the Nuneaton Union Workhouse for one last time, praying that they would never have to go through its doors again.

Once they were rattling along, Lady Huntley explained what was happening. 'You are going to live and work with Sunday's employer, Mrs Spooner – I know Sunday has told you all about her – and I'm sure you're going to be very happy.' She was gratified when their faces broke into broad smiles.

'Daisy, you will be helping Sunday with cleaning duties about the house, and Tommy, you will be a sort of odd job man, outdoor work mainly, gardening, repairing anything that needs attention, painting, et cetera, which I'm sure will suit you very well. I can't believe that no one bothered to explain to you,' she finished crossly. 'But then I suppose I shouldn't be surprised. Anyway, let's hope that this is the start of better times, eh?'

Daisy and Tommy nodded eagerly.

They received a rapturous welcome from Sunday when the carriage drew up outside Mrs Spooner's residence. The girl was standing on the steps waiting and flew down to greet them. Biddy was watching the proceedings with an indulgent smile on her face and she eyed the youngsters up and down when they came indoors.

'Well, the lad looks strong enough,' she commented. 'But the lass looks like you could knock her over wi' one finger.'

'Oh, Daisy is stronger than she looks, really she is,' Sunday said quickly in her friend's defence.

Meanwhile, Daisy and Tommy were staring at their new employer in amazement. They had seen her from afar at church but never so close up before and didn't quite know what to make of her although she seemed to be kindly enough.

'Come on, I'll take you up and show you your rooms so you can put your things away while the ladies have morning coffee,' Sunday offered brightly and following a nod from Mrs Spooner she took them through the kitchen to the stairs that led to the servants' quarters, introducing them to Annie, who was busy baking bread, on the way.

'I can't believe we're really here,' Daisy said as she stared about her new room. She looked at Sunday with tears on her cheeks. 'We won't ever have to go back, will we?' she whispered.

'Not if I have anything to do with it.' Sunday gave her a warm hug and as she did so, she felt the small mound on Daisy's tummy. She stepped away from her in shock as the girl stared back at her from frightened eyes.

'Oh, Daisy, what's happened to you?' Sunday breathed.

Chapter Twenty-Five

Daisy lowered her head in shame and began to cry.

'*Oh, cor blimey!*' Sunday's hand flew to her mouth as comprehension dawned. She had only ever felt one mound like that before and that had been on Cissie before she had been carted off to Hatter's Hall.

'It was Pinnegar, wasn't it?' she said and Daisy's head bobbed miserably.

'It ... it was just after you left. He started to make me go to his office,' Daisy hiccuped. 'An' then he ... he did bad things to me. He hurt me but when I told him I'd tell, he said he'd send Tommy to Hatter's Hall.'

Sunday was in a quandary. What should she do now? If she were to go down and tell Lady Huntley and Mrs Spooner of her discovery, Daisy could possibly suffer the same fate as Cissie had. She just couldn't take the risk.

'Look,' she said, making a hasty decision, 'we'll say nothing for the time being. If you carry on wearing that loose dress for a while no one will notice and it will give us some time to decide what we're going to do. Don't cry, Daisy, we'll think of something, I promise.' She wrapped Daisy protectively in her arms and felt the girl's heart hammering. She was very thin apart from her slightly swollen stomach, and Sunday was sure she could

251

feel every bone in her body. She could have cried at the injustice of it all. Pinnegar had caused poor Cissie tremendous heartache and now it looked as if Daisy was going to have to suffer too.

There was a tap at the door then and Tommy shouted, 'I've put my things away. What are you two doing in there?'

'We'll be out in a second,' Sunday called back. Then, lowering her voice, she whispered to Daisy, 'Dry your eyes now. We need to go on as if nothing is wrong. Can you do that for me?'

Daisy sniffed and swiped at her eyes with the sleeve of her shapeless dress as she nodded.

'Promise you won't let them lock me away in Hatter's Hall?' she said in a tiny voice. Somehow now that Sunday knew her shameful secret she felt slightly better, although the prospect of being sent to the asylum still terrified her. She had already vowed that she would kill herself before that happened.

'Of course I won't!' Sunday gave her another loving hug. 'That's it,' she said approvingly when Daisy had pulled herself together. 'Now we're going to go down and put a cheerful face on things, eh?'

'I ... I'll try,' Daisy promised with a watery smile and hand in hand the two girls left the room.

Sunday showed them all around the house. She took them outside and Tommy crowed with delight when he saw the empty pigsties and the overgrown gardens.

'It's a bit late to be tryin' to plant anything now,' he said, 'but there's plenty of work to do getting the beds ready for the spring. And then there'll be the animals to tend to as well, when we get some.'

He at least looked as happy as a cat that had got the cream, even more so when Mabel came bounding outside to join them. She skidded to a halt when she saw the strangers but after sniffing them suspiciously her tail began to wag and she allowed Tommy to fuss her.

'We had a dog when we lived at home, didn't we, Dais?' His eyes became sad as he remembered their little mongrel, Dickens. 'But then when we got taken into the workhouse after Mam died, one of the neighbours promised to take him in. I hope she took good care of him.'

'I'm sure she would have,' Sunday said, sensing his pain. 'But now let's go and scrounge something to eat off Annie. She's the most marvellous cook and now that Daisy is here to help I shall be having even more lessons off her.'

They trooped back inside and were soon tucking into scones straight from the oven.

'Blimey, that were good.' Tommy licked his lips appreciatively and rubbed his stomach. After the appalling food they had been served at the workhouse he felt as if he might have died and gone to heaven. 'I reckon I might just go and have a scout round in the outhouse to see what gardening tools there are,' he said when he'd swallowed a second cup of tea. 'Then I might make a start on clearing the vegetable plot, if that's all right?'

'Well, that's what yer 'ere for, lad,' Annie told him. She'd already taken to Tommy but the lass seemed a different kettle of fish altogether. She'd

253

barely said a word – but then, thought Annie, she was probably just a bit shy and overawed at her new surroundings. She'd come out of her shell in time, no doubt.

'So how do you fancy cleanin' some windows?' she asked and was pleased when Daisy nodded obligingly.

'I'm happy to do whatever needs doing, missus.'

'Just Annie will do, lass, an' you'll find the bucket over there along with everything you'll need. You might do the front steps an' all while yer at it. Young Sunday here's been so excited all mornin' that she ain't got round to 'em yet.'

Daisy instantly did as she was told without a murmur and when Sunday entered the kitchen some minutes later Annie remarked, 'Young Daisy is a quiet little thing, ain't she? Is she allus like that?'

'Oh, I suppose it's just because everything is strange to her. She'll soon settle in,' Sunday answered hastily and was relieved when Annie let the subject drop.

Later that afternoon, Mrs Spooner summoned Daisy and Tommy to the drawing room and laid down her house rules.

'You'll both get Sunday afternoon off,' she told them. 'And a few hours on Sunday mornin' an' all if yer want to go to church. I expect yer both to do what you're asked an' show respect to me lodgers. Keep yer rooms tidy an' go to bed at a respectable time. An' no bringin' friends back here, mind!'

Both young people seemed more than happy with that. They'd both worked well since their

254

arrival and now Biddy was feeling very positive about Sunday's suggestion, so much so that she had already written a sign for the front window advertising three more rooms.

'I shall be very choosy who I allow to stay though,' she told Annie. 'We don't want any riff-raff here. I run a respectable house.'

Annie grinned and on the way back to the kitchen allowed herself a reflection. She could still remember the time when Biddy had run the streets barefoot, one of a horde of children who were all packed into two rooms with their mam and dad. All that had changed when Biddy married Herbert Spooner, and he'd whisked her away to live overseas in the West Indies. She'd come back considering herself a lady and now she wore her respectability like a cloak. Annie couldn't blame her really and they had stayed close friends throughout the years despite Biddy's changed circumstances. Sadly, the one thing Biddy had craved most but didn't get was a family, whereas Annie herself had given birth to eleven of the little devils. Not that she regretted it. Annie's brood were all grown and flown the nest now but she had happy memories of their childhoods even if there had been times when she hadn't known where the next ha'penny was coming from. Life was strange, there was no doubt about it, she often thought.

By mid-afternoon every downstairs window was glinting in the late-September sunshine and the front step was so clean Annie told Daisy she was sure she could have eaten her dinner off it. She still didn't quite know what to make of the girl. She was the total opposite to Sunday, being rather reserved and quiet, and she didn't look at all well – but then Annie supposed that Sunday hadn't either when she'd first arrived. It was probably nothing that a few helpings of good wholesome food and a dollop of fresh air wouldn't cure.

After serving Mrs Spooner and the lodgers they all ate together in the kitchen that evening and Annie saw Tommy's face transform at the sight of the steak and kidney pie she had cooked for them. There was apple crumble and thick creamy custard to follow and Tommy ate so much that Annie feared he would make himself ill. He'd come in from the garden thick with mud shortly before and promptly been sent away to wash at the pump in the yard by Annie.

'I'll not 'ave you traipsin' mud all over me nice clean floor, young man,' she had scolded him, much to Sunday's amusement when she thought back to the state the floor had been in when she first arrived.

When the meal was over Sunday cleared the dirty pots from the dining room while Daisy washed them and Tommy dried them for her. Daisy then re-laid the table ready for breakfast the next morning and between them they had the chores done in no time.

Daisy and Tommy were yawning by then. They hadn't adjusted to being away from the workhouse routine yet and were usually tucked up in bed by that time.

'You two go up to bed. I'll be up too, in a minute,' Sunday encouraged and off they went, keen to spend their first night for a long time in a comfortable bed.

There was not a murmur from Tommy's room when Sunday went up some time later but when she paused outside Daisy's room she could hear her crying, so she tapped on the door and whispered, 'Dais – can I come in?'

She found her friend huddled into a ball on the bed and she went and sat next to her.

'It's so unfair,' Daisy sniffed. 'This should have been one o' the happiest days of me life but what's goin' to happen when Mrs Spooner finds out I'm havin' a baby, Sunday? She'll pack me off to Hatter's Hall for sure.'

'But it's not your fault,' Sunday said hotly. 'Pinnegar took advantage of you just as he did to Cissie and me – and countless other girls before us, no doubt.'

'Huh! An' who will everyone believe if we say that?' Daisy sighed. 'It's no use, Sunday, I should run away before they find out.'

'Oh yes? And live on what – fresh air? No, you must stay put while we decide what's best to do. I reckon I'm going to speak to Lady Huntley. She knows what Pinnegar did to Cissie so she'll believe you too. And perhaps if there are three of us who are prepared to stand up and say what he did, the guardians just might have to do something about it. Would you be brave enough to do that, Daisy?'

'I'm not sure,' Daisy said chokily. Just the thought of the workhouse master could make her break out in a cold sweat.

'Well, one thing's for sure, we can't do anything tonight so let's just try and get some sleep, eh?' Sunday pulled the warm woollen blankets up to

257

Daisy's chin; there was a nip in the air at nights now, a sure sign that winter was just around the corner. 'Sleep tight,' she murmured and crept from the room.

She tossed and turned for most of the night as she thought of the dilemma Daisy was in but finally her eyes grew heavy and she slept at last.

The next morning, she found both her friends already washed and dressed and waiting on the landing for her when she left her room.

'Blimey, you're eager,' she teased. 'Come on, let's go and get the fires started so we can have some breakfast. Annie likes the kitchen to be warm by the time she gets here.'

Once downstairs, Sunday pointed Tommy in the direction of the log store while she filled the kettle and fetched the bread from the pantry.

'Once Tommy's got the fire going we'll do us some warm toast and have it with a nice hot cup of tea before breakfast,' she told Daisy. The girl obviously hadn't slept a wink and looked dreadful.

Annie bustled in at just after seven o'clock to a cosy kitchen and a pot of tea waiting for her and she smiled her approval. Over the last couple of weeks she'd taken to coming in early again although there was no need, and Sunday supposed it was because she got lonely on her own.

'I reckon I'm going to like havin' you two here.' She grinned as she slid out of her coat and into her voluminous apron. 'Now which of yer is goin' to pour me a cuppa afore we get started?'

It was mid-morning before Sunday got the chance to have a word alone to Daisy.

'I've been thinking about your situation,' she said. Daisy looked terrified so Sunday touched her hand and hurried on, 'But I'm not going to say anything for a couple of weeks or so. I want Mrs Spooner to see what hard workers you and Tommy are first. You must only be very early on. How many courses have you missed?'

'Just the one,' Daisy whispered. 'Nearly two now, but me chest is tender and I feel really sick in the morning now.'

'Right then, you're certainly not showing yet so let's bide our time, eh? To my reckoning the baby won't be due till early in April.'

Daisy shuddered. 'I *hate* this thing that's growing inside me because it's a part of the man who forced himself on me. I know even now that I will never love it!'

She burst into sobs and Sunday's mouth set in a grim line. 'I'll look after you, Daisy,' she said. 'And then we're going to make sure that Pinnegar finally gets what's coming to him so that he can *never* do this to another girl again.'

She looked so angry and determined that Daisy didn't doubt her for a second.

Chapter Twenty-Six

By the first week in October, Daisy, Tommy and Sunday had got into a routine and everything was running smoothly. The mornings and evenings were dark now so Tommy would be the first

259

up to light all the fires for them. Daisy had taken on the laundry and some of the cleaning and now Sunday had more time to spend with Annie, who was teaching her how to cook various dishes and desserts. Tommy had almost cleared the vegetable patch and was now busily repairing the hen coops in readiness for some chickens and getting the sties cleaned out for some pigs. He'd also made a start on the stable roof that had fallen into disrepair so that Mrs Spooner could purchase a small pony to pull her dog cart once again. In addition, he had painted the front door a lovely cheery red and the window-frames white. The Lodge now looked as good as new.

A young nurse who had started work at the local hospital had joined them in one of the formerly empty rooms, and Daisy and Sunday found it amusing that Jacob seemed to be quite taken with her, although she was engaged to one of the doctors. Sunday was over the crush she had had on Jacob when she first arrived now, thankfully. The only dark spot on the horizon was Daisy's condition, which still hadn't been addressed. Sunday was hoping to leave it as long as she could before telling her employer what had happened, but that decision was taken out of her hands one morning when Annie breezed in unexpectedly just as Daisy returned from the outside privy looking 'like death warmed up', to use Annie's term.

'You've been lookin' peaky ever since yer arrived. Are yer often sick in the mornin's?' she enquired suspiciously. There wasn't much that slipped past Annie.

Daisy stared at Sunday, too terrified to utter a

word and Sunday knew that the game was up. They had no choice but to tell her now.

'W-well…' Daisy stammered.

Annie shook her head. 'You've no need to say any more, lass. I guessed yer condition wi'in a couple o' days of yer bein' here,' she said regretfully.

Daisy burst into tears then and Sunday hurried across the room to put a protective arm about her. 'It's not her fault,' she said heatedly. 'It was Pinnegar again, the housemaster at the workhouse. The one I told you about who had Cissie put into Hatter's Hall.'

'I see.' Annie looked appalled. She believed every word that Sunday said and Daisy certainly didn't look like the sort of girl that would give away favours. She was only a slip of a kid, poor lass. To Annie's mind they should chop the dirty old bugger's pecker off!

'Well, we'll have to get it sorted, lass,' she told Daisy sensibly as the girl sobbed in Sunday's arms. 'It ain't somethin' that yer can hide fer much longer an' the missus needs to know about it. Do you want me to go in an' have a word to her for you? I'll make sure as she knows it weren't your fault.'

'No, thanks, Annie, I'll do it,' Sunday told her decisively. 'And then we have to decide what we can do to stop this happening again. Pinnegar shouldn't be allowed within ten feet of young girls. He interfered with me as well although he didn't…' Hot colour flooded into her cheeks.

'Then let's get the breakfasts out o' the way an' the lodgers off to work an' then yer can go in to

261

her,' Annie said kindly and then to Daisy, 'Try not to worry, pet. Biddy Spooner won't put yer out on the street if I know her. She might be crusty on the outside but she's as soft as clouts on the in, and it ain't your fault what's happened.'

They were all in a very subdued mood as they set about their tasks and Tommy was quick to pick up on it when he entered the kitchen hefting loaded log baskets for the fires in each hand.

'What's happened in here?' He put the baskets down and stared from one to another of them. 'Has somebody died or sommat?'

'We'll explain everything soon as breakfast is done,' Sunday promised as Tommy peered worriedly at his sister's red eyes.

'Has the missus decided that our work isn't satis-factory? Is she going to send us back to the workhouse? If that's the case, then we'll run away. There's no way me or Daisy will ever go back there!'

'It's nothing like that, Tommy. Please be patient,' Sunday appealed, hearing the panic in his voice.

The kitchen was quiet as they prepared the meal save for the sounds of the eggs and bacon sizzling in the frying pan. At last the breakfast was served and eventually the lodgers all went off to work.

'We'll have ours now, shall we?' Annie sug-gested then but Sunday shook her head.

'Would it be all right if we wait a few minutes, Annie? I think I should go through to have a word with the missus and get it over with.' Inside she was quaking at the thought of what Mrs Spooner's reaction might be – but she knew that it couldn't be put off any longer now. It wasn't fair on anyone.

'Get *what* over with?' Tommy asked in exasperation and Daisy managed to tell him what had happened in a shaky voice.

Annie and Sunday saw the flush rise to his cheeks and his hands ball into fists of rage as the sorry story unfolded.

'I'll *kill* the dirty old bastard!' he shocked them all by saying.

'No, yer won't, lad,' Annie told him sternly. 'I know just how yer must feel but it's got to be done proper like.' Then, her voice softening, she went on, 'Don't you worry, we'll all see as he doesn't get away wi' it this time. Go on, Sunday lass, go an' face the music.'

Sunday gulped and nodded, then headed to the door dreading to think what Mrs Spooner's reaction to the news was going to be.

She found her still in the dining room, wiping her mouth on a napkin. Tapping at the half-open door, she said, 'May I have a word, Mrs Spooner?'

'Of course.' Sensing that something was amiss she waited as Sunday entered the room, closing the door quietly behind her.

'Well?' the old woman demanded when Sunday just stood there. 'Spit it out, Sunny lass – or has the cat got yer tongue?'

And so, after taking a deep breath and choosing her words carefully, Sunday slowly told her what had happened. As the story unfolded Mrs Spooner seemed to swell to twice her size. Her ridiculous blonde wig had slipped slightly to one side and the scarlet colour she had plastered onto

263

her lips had smeared into the wrinkles surrounding them, giving her a slightly drunken appearance.

'*So – you – are – telling – me – that – Daisy – is – carrying – a – child!*' she ground out.

When Sunday nodded miserably, the woman exploded. 'Then she'll have to go back to the workhouse. I'll not have her staying here. My poor dear husband would turn in his grave if he knew I had a girl like that beneath my roof. This is a respectable house!'

To their surprise the door suddenly banged open and Annie, who had had her ear pressed to it appeared, her hands planted on her hips.

'Why, Biddy Spooner, I'm ashamed of yer! Ain't yer bin listenin' to a word the girl has told yer? It ain't that poor child's fault she's in the condition she's in. That randy old sod forced hisself on her, an' as fer your husband... Why, that poor dear man would give yer a swift kick up the arse if he knew how uncharitable yer bein', so he would!'

Mrs Spooner sniffed and hitched up her sagging bust, thoroughly chastised. 'Well, what do *you* suggest we do about it then?' she asked peevishly.

'I suggest we get word to Lady Huntley. She's the one to deal wi' this, bein' on the board o' guardians. That man 'as to be stopped in 'is tracks afore he takes any more young lasses down. An' if you can't see yer way clear to lettin' Daisy stop 'ere then she can bloody well come an' stop wi' me. I rattle round in my place like a pea in a pod now the childer have all flown the

264

nest an' I won't see the child out on the street through no fault of her own, Bridget Spooner!'

'Well, I dare say she can stop for the time being,' Mrs Spooner said begrudgingly. 'And you, Sunny, can scoot off to Treetops Manor an' tell Lady Huntley that I need to see her at her earliest convenience. The sooner this mess is sorted the better as far as I'm concerned.'

'Yes, ma'am.' Sunday flashed a grateful smile at Annie then shot from the room, already taking her apron off as she went. It was still quite early in the morning so if she hurried she should catch Lady Huntley before she went out.

She reached Treetops Manor in record time, running all the way and only stopping now and then to grip the stitch in her side.

As she pelted down the drive she saw a carriage pulling up outside and Lady Huntley just emerging from the house. Luckily the woman saw her and paused to wait. Lavinia had been just about to go into town to do a little shopping and visit her dressmaker, but as she saw the look on Sunday's face she sensed an emergency.

'What is it, my dear?' she asked when Sunday panted to a halt in front of her.

Sunday glanced uncomfortably at George the coachman, unwilling to say too much in front of him.

'Mrs Spooner told me to ask you to call on her at your earliest convenience,' she gasped.

'I see, then your timing was just right. I can call in on the way. Hop in, Sunday. I may as well give you a lift back.'

The girl did as she was told, sagging with relief

265

as she sank back on the soft leather seat.

Once the carriage was moving, Lady Huntley asked, 'Can you tell me what's wrong, my dear?'

And so once again, Sunday slowly relayed the story. By the time it was done there were tears in the kindly woman's eyes and she was furious. As far as she was concerned this was the final straw. But now at last she might have enough evidence to ensure that Albert Pinnegar was stopped once and for all.

During her meeting with Mrs Spooner and Annie it was agreed that Daisy should stay where she was for the present at least. 'Meanwhile I'm going to speak to Reverend Lockett and call for an urgent meeting of the board of guardians,' Lady Huntley promised, and when Annie passed this on to Sunday later that morning she was full of gratitude. At last it appeared that Albert Pinnegar might get his just deserts.

Later in the day, Lady Huntley sent word that she had written to each of the guardians, and her groom had personally delivered the letters, requesting an urgent meeting at the workhouse the following Monday morning. Now all Sunday, Daisy, Tommy and everyone involved had to do was wait for the outcome … something that proved to be a lot easier said than done.

Chapter Twenty-Seven

When Monday morning finally arrived, Lavinia Huntley turned up to the meeting looking pale and wan. Her pregnancy had now been confirmed and mornings were never a good time for her. Even so, she was determined that justice should be done.

Miss Frost met her at the door and greeted her dourly. Did the awful woman never smile? Lady Huntley wondered. But she herself wasn't in the best of moods, knowing what lay ahead, so she said sharply, 'I would like the meeting to take place in the day room, Miss Frost.'

The woman drew herself up. She was matron here; she gave the orders. 'But you usually have the meetings in the dining room,' she objected stiffly.

'There is more privacy in the day room, so see to it that it is prepared immediately, if you please!'

The woman stared at her in astonishment. She had never seen Lady Huntley in this mood before. Turning about, she swept away to bark orders at anyone at hand, and once all the guardians were present, she showed them, unsmiling, into the room.

They were all just getting seated when Mr Pinnegar arrived. Before he could sit down, Lady Huntley told him icily, 'I'm afraid you cannot be present, sir. You may wait outside if you wish.'

The unctuous smile slid from his face. 'What do you mean?' he demanded. 'Of course I must be present. I am the housemaster of this establishment.'

Miss Frost was standing at his side and her head bobbed up and down in agreement but Lady Huntley stood her ground. Quite admirably, as it happened. She had a bullying husband whom she was forced to put up with – but she'd be damned if she'd bow down to this deplorable little man and the shrew beside him.

'The meeting that is about to take place involves serious allegations made against you,' she told him with her chin in the air. 'You will be called in at the appropriate moment.'

'Involves *me?*' he blustered as his insides turned to water. 'But I–'

'Please leave us.' She cut him off, at which point Miss Frost stepped forward.

'Then is there any reason why *I* may not be present? I am the matron, after all.'

'You may stay if you wish,' Lady Huntley conceded. *Although you won't like what you hear,* she added silently to herself, having quickly deduced from her time here that Miss Frost was besotted with the vile creature.

Miss Frost took a seat as Albert Pinnegar marched away in a temper. He had never been excluded from a meeting of the guardians before and something told him that there might be trouble ahead.

'I have called this meeting today because of certain disturbing information that has been brought to my attention,' Lady Huntley began, and as she told all those present of her findings, Miss Frost became agitated.

'How dare you try to besmirch Mr Pinnegar's good name!' she cried. 'That Daisy Branning I can tell you now has always been a troublemaker. She's obviously lying because she's got herself into this predicament!'

'Miss Frost, I must insist that you do not interrupt,' Lady Huntley said with authority as she glared in the woman's direction. 'You will have your chance to speak at the appropriate time.'

Miss Frost's mouth gaped open. She wasn't used to being spoken to like this, but like all bullies she was easily cowed by someone stronger and so she remained silent.

'As it happens I also have another young girl who is prepared to testify, in front of magistrates if necessary, that Mr Pinnegar got her with child too,' Lady Huntley went on, 'and yet *another* one who informs me that he interfered with her as well. I'm sure that if I got the files out and dug a little deeper, these unfortunate young girls may not be the only ones either.'

Miss Frost sagged in her seat; the wind had well and truly been sucked out of her sails.

'This is preposterous!' she began but one more glare from Lady Huntley silenced her again.

'I suggest you either remain silent whilst we decide what's to be done about this or leave the room,' Lady Huntley told her with not a scrap of sympathy and for once the woman did as she was told.

'So are you suggesting that we should report this

269

matter to the police?' one of the guardians asked then. Stephen Crowley was a highly respected member of the community who owned a number of businesses about the town and he was reeling with shock at what he had just heard. 'After all, this is supposed to be a sanctuary for foundlings and families who have fallen on hard times.'

'Perhaps at this point we should get Mr Pinnegar in to see what he has to say for himself?' put in Arthur Trewitt, another of the governors and a well-regarded family man.

Without a word Miss Frost rose to go and fetch him. He walked into the day room sweating profusely and looking decidedly uncomfortable.

'Now then,' he said jovially. 'Good morning, ladies and gentlemen. Miss Frost informs me there has been some misunderstanding.'

Lady Huntley stared at him coldly. 'There has been no misunderstanding I assure you, sir, and I have at least three young people who are prepared to stand before the magistrates and say as much.' She then went on to detail what Cissie, Daisy and Sunday had bravely written in their statements and he began to tug at the collar of his shirt as the colour drained from his face.

The Reverend Lockett, whom Lavinia had also asked to be present, then stood up and told the guardians that he was happy to testify to the girls' good characters.

'It's all lies, I tell you,' Albert Pinnegar gasped.

'I believe a court of law will be the judge of that,' Lavinia told him. 'And now if you will leave the room we shall decide what should happen next.'

Obviously deeply distressed he backed away, with Miss Frost in hot pursuit.

'I quite agree that this man should be punished – but the workhouse is funded mainly by donations,' Mr Trewitt pointed out. 'And should the donations dry up, it would have a bad impact on the rest of the inmates, so perhaps we should find a solution to ensure that this doesn't happen?'

A ripple of agreement went around the room and a long discussion ensued. It was almost two hours later when they called the man back in to face them. It had been a great ordeal for Lavinia Huntley. She firmly believed that Pinnegar should go before the magistrates and answer for his crimes, but the board of guardians were concerned about what people would say should it become publicly known that the housemaster of Nuneaton Union Workhouse was a defiler of children, and she understood their reasoning.

'We have reached a decision,' she told him with eyes that were as hard as pebbles as he stood quaking like the coward he was in front of them. Like Miss Frost, he was a bully with the young people in his care but not so brave when faced with a room full of very angry adults.

'Personally, I believe that you, Albert Pinnegar, should be locked away for the wicked things you have done,' she told him sternly. 'Unfortunately, not everyone here agrees with me so we have been forced to reach a compromise. The guardians are concerned that it would be very bad for the workhouse's reputation should this matter become public knowledge, so you will *not* go before the magistrates. However, you must realise that you

271

can no longer reside here, so I must ask you to go and pack your things and leave the premises immediately. It goes without saying that there will be no references given. In fact, should we ever – *any of us* – discover that you are working anywhere near children or young people again, we will instantly inform your employers of what you have done and why you were dismissed. You will also forfeit any pay due to you. Now please leave.'

Panic swept through him as he saw his comfortable way of life slipping away from him and he looked around at all of them – only to be met by a sea of hostile faces. Many of the men in the room had children or grandchildren of similar ages to those he had despoiled and abused, and they were sickened and appalled.

'B-but it's all a terrible m-misunderstanding,' he spluttered desperately.

'Then perhaps we should place it before the magistrates after all.'

'Oh no, no, no – there will be no need for that,' he gabbled and then, defeated, he turned and left the room with Miss Frost hot on his heels.

When they arrived back in his office, Miss Frost told him loyally, 'I don't believe a word of what they've said, Albert. Those wicked girls are out to tarnish your good reputation. But where will you go?'

He was already collecting his personal possessions from the desk. 'I have recently bought a small cottage in Coton in readiness for my retirement,' he told her in a daze. He could hardly believe that his secret sins had finally caught up with him – and he had a very good idea who would have brought it about. It must be that little trollop Sunday Small. And she was the one he had bought the cottage for!

'Then I shall come with you. You must know that I love you. I've always loved you and I feel now is the time to declare it,' Miss Frost told him dramatically.

The man stopped dead in the act of what he was doing and stared at her as if she had taken leave of her senses. '*You?* Come with *me?*' His lips curled back from his teeth in a sneer. 'Why would I want to take a wizened-up old hag like you with me? No, I like my girlies young and fresh. I would never look at you if you were the last woman on earth!'

She stepped back in shock as if he had slapped her as all her hopes and dreams crumbled around her. 'But – but I always thought we had an understanding – that one day...'

'Get out of my way, woman!' He pushed roughly past her with his arms full of papers, sending her stumbling against the wall. 'That's the one good thing about leaving this place. At least I'll never have to look at your ugly face again.' And with that he was gone, leaving Miss Frost sobbing uncontrollably as he made his way to the little cottage at the back of the building that had been his home for more years than he cared to remember.

What am I going to do? he was asking himself. If any of this was ever to leak out, he would be shunned and run out of town – and what would he do for a job now? He had his cottage admittedly, but the cost of it had sadly depleted his savings; there was nowhere near enough money left for him to live on for long. All that would be open to him now was manual work and Albert Pinnegar didn't like the thought of that one little bit! He had never had to get his hands dirty in his whole life, but now that looked set to change. And all because of Sunday Small, that sanctimonious little tease.

Dragging a carpet bag from the bottom of his wardrobe he began to shove his clothes inside, cursing all the time. One day he would make the little chit pay for this if it was the last thing he ever did!

Chapter Twenty-Eight

By the time Lavinia Huntley arrived back at the Spooner residence her nerves were in shreds and her face was the colour of putty.

She found everyone waiting for her, anxious to hear the outcome of the meeting. However, Annie took one look at her and told Sunday, 'Go an' make a nice strong pot o' tea, lass. It looks like Lady Huntley could do wi' one!'

They all sat down in the drawing room and when Sunday had fetched the tea and passed cups round to everyone, along with a slice of Bakewell tart to keep them going as it was nearly lunchtime, Lady Huntley began to tell them all that had gone on.

'So the swine denied it then!' Annie said in her

274

usual forthright way.

Poor Daisy was wringing her hands but Lady Huntley smiled at her kindly.

'Only until I told him that we would put the case before the magistrates. He left quietly enough then, and now we'll never have to set eyes on the despicable man again.'

She reached out and patted Daisy's hand. 'I do, of course, realise that this still leaves you in a terrible position through no fault of your own, my dear, and I said as much to the guardians.' She reached into her reticule and withdrew a small, clinking pouch. 'They thought that this might see you over the coming months at least and took it from the safe. The sum is nowhere near enough to compensate for what you've been through, but use it wisely.' She placed the pouch in Daisy's hand, saying. 'There are twenty gold sovereigns in here.'

Daisy stared down at the money in her hand. To the girl it seemed like a fortune, but Biddy Spooner wasn't so impressed.

'What we have to decide now is what's going to happen to her,' she said gruffly. 'Young Daisy can work for some weeks longer, admittedly – but then where will she go?'

'I've already given that some thought,' Annie butted in with a smile at Daisy. 'She can stay here until she gets too big to work, then she can move in wi' me. By then Sunday will have taken over all the cookin' – yes, you will, my girl – so I'll not be needed. Then when Daisy has had the babby I'll take care of it durin' the day while she comes back to work. How does that sound?'

'It's a lot for you to take on at your age,' Biddy

commented but Annie grinned.

'I ain't past it yet, thank you, Biddy Spooner, an' it'll be quite nice to 'ave a little 'un in the house again so don't get writin' me off just yet. The way I see it, this is the best solution fer all concerned.'

'It does sound viable,' Lady Huntley agreed. 'But are you prepared for the gossip, Annie? People can be very cruel and it won't be easy for you or Daisy, especially as they won't know the circumstances.'

'It'll be a nine-day wonder,' Annie said airily. 'Daisy ain't the first unwed mother an' I've no doubt she won't be the last. Let 'em gossip, that's what I say. It'll be like water off a duck's back as far as I'm concerned, an' while they're talkin' about her they'll be leavin' some other poor bugger alone.'

'Well, that seems to be that then,' Mrs Spooner said grumpily. 'Though I still think the swine has got off too light.'

'We're all in agreement, I'm sure,' Lady Huntley answered. 'But had word got round, it would have been as awful for Daisy as it was for the workhouse and we all wanted to protect her – and all those who live within the workhouse – as much as we possibly could. But never fear, Mr Pinnegar will suffer, don't you doubt it. He has been unmasked and humiliated, and he will find it hard to find a new job. *And* he knows that we are watching him.'

It had to suffice. Eventually they all agreed that the situation had been dealt with as well as it could be, under the circumstances.

Only Daisy remained silent. As she said to Sunday later that night, it was all very well for everyone to sort out her future for her – and she was grateful to them for caring enough to do it. But at the end of the day it would be she herself who would be forced to nurture Pinnegar's child ... and the very thought of it filled her with dread.

Lavinia Huntley was physically and mentally exhausted when she finally arrived home and Zillah insisted that she must put her feet up.

'His lordship's on the rampage,' she warned her mistress. 'He's got his tail up now that the baby's been confirmed an' he's invited Mr Wilde, his late uncle's lawyer, to dinner this evenin' to tell him the good news, so you need to rest, pet.'

'Oh no!' Lavinia groaned. 'Couldn't he have waited a while longer? What if something should go wrong, or if it's another girl?'

'Don't start lookin' fer problems that ain't there,' Zillah scolded, but Lavinia couldn't seem to help it. She had been through so much heart-ache already and still wasn't at all sure how she felt about the coming child. She then went on to tell Zillah all about the meeting she had just attended and about the predicament Daisy was in.

'Poor little mite,' Zillah said compassionately, 'but at least she wasn't at the workhouse long enough to get sent to the asylum like Cissie. Strange, isn't it? Both your babies should be due round about the same time.'

Lavinia nodded in agreement. 'Yes, and the funny thing is, I think both of us have mixed

277

feelings about them.'

Zillah wagged a finger at her. 'That's enough now, my girl, talkin' like that indeed! At least you have a ring on your finger, and isn't a baby what you've always wanted most in the world?'

'Yes, it is,' Lavinia admitted and burst into tears. 'But I'm so afraid that something will go wrong again. Oh, Zillah, I just daren't allow myself to look forward to it.'

Back at Mrs Spooner's, as Sunday helped Daisy peg some washing on the line that was strung across the yard, Daisy was feeling much the same.

'So he got away scot-free,' she said bitterly as the sheet she had just fixed to the line began to dance in the wind. The leaves were falling from the trees like confetti now and as fast as Tommy swept them up, more fluttered down to take their place.

'I'd hardly say that,' Sunday disagreed. 'He's lost his job and a very comfortable living. And at least Lady Huntley ensured that you don't have to worry financially now for some time.'

Still Daisy looked miserable and then suddenly she confided: 'I *hate* this creature that's growing inside me. I know I will never be able to love it and sometimes I wish I could just go to sleep and never wake up, rather than have to have it.'

Like Zillah, Sunday scolded her gently. 'Everyone is doing the very best they can for you, and as Mrs Lockett says, you'll likely feel different when you actually see your baby and hold it for the first time.'

'I won't,' Daisy said with utmost certainty. 'And I don't want to sound ungrateful, really I don't.

Everyone has been so kind, especially Lady Huntley, and Annie for offering me a place to live.'

She looked so dejected that Sunday gave her a hug. 'Well, let's just wait and see how you feel in a while.' It sounded such an inadequate thing to say but she couldn't think of anything else.

Daisy nodded and sighed, then went about her work as if she had the weight of the whole world on her shoulders.

That evening at dinner, when Ashley Huntley told his uncle's attorney of the coming event, the elderly man peered across the table at his hostess.

'Expecting? Again? Why, I would have thought you'd have given up by now.' Jeremiah Wilde had never been the most tactful of men and tonight was clearly going to be no exception. 'Aren't you a little old to be having a child now, my lady?'

Stifling the urge to say something rude, Lavinia dabbed at her lips with a crisp white damask napkin, remarking, 'I'm only in my thirties. Women in their forties frequently give birth.'

'Only the ones who've already turned out a rook of 'em,' he said unfeelingly. 'You haven't yet produced a single live infant, have you?'

Lavinia cringed with a mixture of shame and anger, but held her tongue. She knew that Ashley wouldn't want her upsetting the man; he himself was almost fawning over him.

'Well, you're quite right, Wilde,' he said with forced joviality. 'But let's hope that this time becomes an exception to the rule and that my wife will present me with a fine healthy male.'

'Indeed.' The man then fell on his food with all

279

the manners of a peasant as Lavinia quietly excused herself. Even for Ashley she couldn't endure to be in the man's presence a second longer.

'Yes, you go up and rest, my love,' Ashley told her as she rose from the table. 'We don't want our little mother-to-be to overtire herself, do we? Wilde and I have almost finished anyway so we'll go through to the drawing room for a glass of port and a brandy. Good night.' He hurried ahead of her to open the door and as she passed through it she glared at him. *'My love'* indeed! Ashley was as false as a cartload of monkeys.

In his tiny, draughty cottage in Coton, Albert Pinnegar was also drowning his sorrows in a bottle of brandy. There wasn't a stick of furniture in there as yet, not even a bed, so he would have to sleep on the floor tonight. And all because of that chit Sunday Small.

Pah – women! he thought with disgust. They were being granted far too much power lately. Earlier that very year, he had read in the newspaper that women had been allowed to compete in the Lawn Tennis Championships at Wimbledon for the first time, and back in April a statute had been passed allowing women to sit exams at Oxford University. Who would have believed it! As far as he was concerned women had been put on the earth to serve men. All they were good for was cooking and cleaning and pleasuring the opposite sex. He couldn't be doing with new-fangled ideas about them being men's equals – especially sluts like Sunday Small who had deliberately flaunted herself at him. He took another long swig from the bottle as he gazed sorrowfully around his new home. He supposed he'd have to go out and buy some second-hand furniture tomorrow and that would eat into his savings even more.

He shuddered. The nights had turned cold now and a wind was rattling the windowpanes and finding its way through the gaps around the doors. Had he been at the workhouse he would have been sitting in front of a cosy fire with his feet up reading a newspaper while Miss Frost scurried around fetching him hot cocoa and waiting on him hand and foot. He sniggered as he thought of the proposal she had put to him. Come and live with him indeed! Was she completely mad? As if he would ever look the side that dried-up old stick was on – and he'd have to pay her keep! It was Sunday he wanted even now, but she had betrayed him and he would know no rest until he had made her pay.

Albert Pinnegar took another swallow from the bottle and then another … and soon he had drunk himself into an uneasy doze.

In no time at all they were racing towards Christmas and Sunday was looking forward to it enormously. It would be the first one she had ever spent outside of the workhouse. Tommy was looking forward to it too, but Daisy was still very subdued despite everyone's best efforts to cheer her. The mound of her stomach was quite pronounced now but she still had not bought or made a single thing in readiness for the baby's arrival. Both she and Tommy had had a birthday and Annie had baked them both a cake to celebrate

281

although Daisy hadn't shown much interest in it. She didn't show much interest in anything any more.

On a cold and frosty morning early in December, Annie made Sunday a shopping list to go to the market and suggested to Daisy, 'Why don't you go with 'er, lass? A little outing will do you the power o' good. Sayin' that, it's a bit nippy out so why don't you both go into town on the carrier cart? It'll be passin' any time now.'

Daisy nodded listlessly. Her stomach was expanding but the rest of her seemed to be shrinking by the day and she was all skin and bone. There were dark circles still beneath her eyes and she was hardly eating enough to keep a bird alive despite all Annie's attempts to tempt her with tasty treats.

'Oh, please say you'll come,' Sunday pleaded. She loved the market now it was getting closer to Christmas and enjoyed looking at all the pretty window displays in the shops.

Daisy shrugged. 'All right, but let's walk it. I don't fancy being jostled about on the cart. I'll just go and get my shawl.'

Tommy entered the kitchen then with a broad smile on his face. He was now the delighted keeper of two fine healthy Tamworth pigs, which a farmer had kindly delivered to the Lodge in his cart from the market some weeks before. Mrs Spooner had bought a male and a female and hoped that soon they would be the proud parents of a litter. The pigs were a rich red colour and Tommy doted on them, so much so that Annie sometimes worried how he would cope when they did have piglets and

282

they started to breed them for food. Mabel was like his shadow now, and unlike his sister the boy appeared to be as happy as Larry. They now also had half a dozen chickens and a cockerel that crowed and woke them at the crack of dawn each day. Annie quite liked having fresh-laid eggs again and often teased Tommy that they were the best tended chickens in the Midlands. He had also proved to be very capable at doing odd jobs about the house, which was just as well, for another two lodgers had joined them now. They were a young newly married couple who were saving up enough to rent a house of their own and they had fitted into the household very well. Annie had decided that she would continue to come in to cook the evening meal until after Daisy had given birth and was fit to return to work as there would have been too much for Sunday to do on her own. All in all, everyone at Whittleford Lodge, apart from Daisy, was happy.

Tommy took two fresh-laid eggs from each of his jacket pockets and sidling up to Annie, he said, 'You could perhaps use those to make one of your delicious sponge cakes?'

'Yer cheeky young devil, you!' She swiped him gently round the ear. Tommy had filled out considerably since coming to live there and he was always hungry – not that Annie minded. She liked to see the youngsters enjoying their food.

'While yer in the town yer could perhaps pick me some wool up from the wool shop?' she suggested to Daisy hopefully. Annie had already knitted two tiny matinée coats for the baby but Daisy had shown no interest in them at all.

'All right,' the girl agreed wearily. She couldn't understand what all the fuss was about. The baby wasn't due for months yet.

'I'll come in again with you next week,' Tommy told the girls then. 'I'll have another look for a suitable pony to pull Mrs Spooner's cart. I haven't seen one that's caught me eye yet.'

The girls set off with their shawls wrapped about their heads and shoulders and they had gone some way when Daisy suddenly stopped dead in her tracks and a look of horror crossed her face.

'What's wrong?' Sunday was instantly in a panic.

'It ... it just *moved!*'

'Phew!' Sunday let out a sigh of relief. 'You scared me then. I thought something was wrong. Of course it will start to move about now. Here, let me see if I can feel it.' She reached out her hand to lay it on Daisy's stomach but the girl slapped it away.

'No – no, don't touch it! It's evil.'

Sunday scowled. 'How can it be evil? It's just an innocent baby that can't help who its father is.'

'I don't care.' Daisy's face set. 'It's still going to have a part of *him* in it so I don't want anythin' to do with it.' Tears started to pour down her pale cheeks then as she wept, 'Oh, Sunday, what am I gonna do? Surely we could give it away? Someone must want it!'

It was Sunday's turn to be upset now. 'An' do you have any idea how that child will feel when it's old enough to understand that its own mam didn't want it?' she asked. 'It's all right for you. I know it's sad that they died but at least you *had* a mam and dad that loved you – I never did.

284

Whoever mine was just left me on the steps of the workhouse. I used to pretend to myself that there must have been some good reason and that one day my mam would come for me and we'd go off and live happily ever after – but though I'm content with Mrs Spooner I'm too old to believe in happy endings now, so I've had to accept that either my mother is dead or I was just unwanted. I spent the whole first part of my young life in that workhouse with no one but Mrs Lockett to show me an ounce of kindness. Is that really what you want for this baby?'

Deeply ashamed, Daisy hung her head. She hated herself for how she felt, but nothing anyone said could change that. This was her burden, no one else could carry it, and there was no way out. Dashing a tear from her eye, she trudged on, all hope gone.

Chapter Twenty-Nine

Christmas was only a week away now, and there was a festive mood inside Whittleford Lodge. The week before, Mrs Spooner and Tommy had gone to the market with a handcart so that they could bring back a Christmas tree and they'd had so much fun choosing it. It was even better when they eventually got it home and Mrs Spooner presented the young ones with a box full of beautiful hand-blown glass globes, gold cardboard figurines and tiny candles to decorate it with.

'My husband bought 'em one year for me when we went on a shopping spree to London, God rest his soul,' she had told them sadly. 'So don't you get breaking them now! There are some things as can't be replaced.'

'I'll be really careful,' Sunday had promised as she saw how much they meant to her. Tommy was already outside filling a sturdy bucket with earth to stand the tree in and Sunday had no intentions of letting him near the precious baubles. He had hands like hams already and seemed to be shooting up daily.

She and Daisy spent a pleasant afternoon decorating the tree which now stood in pride of place in the drawing room, and when the lodgers returned from work that evening they all complimented the girls on their efforts.

And now it was time for Sunday's final trip to the market before Christmas. Daisy had offered to go with her, which was nice, and as she got ready for the journey that morning she hummed happily to herself. Even Daisy seemed in slightly better spirits and they set off early, guessing that the marketplace would be crowded. As they walked, the two girls commented on how pretty everywhere looked beneath its crisp white overcoat of frost.

'I wouldn't be at all surprised if we didn't have snow in time for Christmas. It's certainly cold enough,' Daisy said as they approached Queens Road, the main street that ran through the centre of the town. She was huffing and puffing by then, and just as soon as they reached the marketplace, she sighed with relief.

'As much as I enjoy coming with you I reckon this will be my last time now until after... Well, for a while.'

Sunday glanced at her from the corner of her eye. The girl still couldn't even bring herself to think of or speak about the birth. It was as if she thought that by ignoring it, it wouldn't happen. It was very sad but Sunday didn't comment, just nodded in agreement.

When they reached the pie stall, Sunday treated them to a tray of faggots and peas each then they began to walk amongst the stalls, getting the things Annie had asked for. In the background the Salvation Army were playing Christmas carols on brass instruments that boomed out over the town. The shop windows were full of Christmas decorations and Sunday noticed that Daisy seemed to be enjoying herself now and was glad that her friend had wanted to come. Once they'd bought everything on the list, Sunday then began to scout about for a few small presents. It was the first time she had ever been in a position to afford to do this, and she felt quite lighthearted.

The two girls were standing at a stall admiring some pretty little muffs and mittens when Sunday heard Daisy gasp; she glanced around and she too, started when she saw Mr Pinnegar leaning heavily on a large broom glaring at them from across the road. *So he's been reduced to sweeping the streets*, Sunday thought, and she was glad. He deserved no better!

'Ignore him,' she hissed to Daisy but Pinnegar seemed to have other ideas and was already heading towards them.

287

Sunday hastily paid for the fingerless gloves she had just bought but by the time the stall-holder had handed her her three farthings change, Pinnegar was at the side of them.

'*So!*' He leered at Daisy's swollen stomach and it was all that Sunday could do to stop herself from lashing out at him. Daisy had shrunk into her side and she could feel her shaking. She, however, refused to be intimidated.

'Why don't you go back to sweeping the streets and leave us alone?' she demanded fearlessly although she was trembling inside. The man had lost weight and looked in need of a wash and shave. He was wearing heavy boots and a string belt about his heavy overcoat. A far cry from the fancy clothes he had worn in the workhouse.

'*You* have brought me to this and I'm going to make you pay!' he spat.

'No, it was you,' Sunday answered steadily. 'And you've finally been exposed for the despicable person you are. You were in a position of trust and you abused it.' Her voice rang out and the stall-holder glanced round to see what the fuss was about.

Pinnegar looked as if he were about to burst with rage as he gripped the handle of his broom until his knuckles turned white.

'Well, don't think you've seen the last of me. I won't rest till I've had my vengeance on all of you!' he said hoarsely.

'I think you'll find you are in no position to hurt us any more,' Sunday replied, to which he laughed – a harsh sound that grated on her nerves.

'We'll see about that, Sunday Small. Just remember to keep looking over your shoulder – and don't forget ... I know where you live!' He shuffled away then leaving both girls badly shaken although Sunday would have died rather than admit it.

'Take no notice of him, it's all empty threats.' She squeezed Daisy's hand reassuringly and dragged her away. 'Just ignore him. We're safe from him now.' But are we? asked a little voice in her head. Suddenly the day was spoiled, and the only thing the girls wanted to do now was to get back to the sanctuary of Whittleford Lodge.

'So what's up wi' you pair?' Annie asked when they arrived home early that afternoon. They had taken the carrier cart back to the house as Daisy hadn't seemed up to walking and Annie immediately saw that there was something wrong. She glanced at Daisy, saying worriedly, 'You're not feelin' bad are yer, pet?'

'She's fine, just a bit tired,' Sunday answered for her, shooting a warning glance at Daisy. There was no point in speaking about what had happened. As far as she was concerned, Pinnegar's vicious threats were best forgotten.

For the rest of the day, Daisy sat huddled by the fire and Sunday knew that encountering Pinnegar had really set her back – as she pointed out, what could he do to them now? If he were to put in an appearance at Mrs Spooner's he'd soon be sent away with a flea in his ear!

Daisy supposed that she was right – but her fear of him was so deep-rooted that she was still

289

severely unnerved.

'Just look at those two,' Lavinia Huntley said to Zillah. She was sitting with her feet up at her maid's insistence in the drawing room and through the window she could see Cissie and young George chatting to each other. 'Do you suppose we have a budding romance on our hands?'

'I wouldn't be surprised.' Zillah grinned. 'They look well together, don't they?'

Lavinia nodded as she sipped at her coffee. 'They certainly do. Cissie looks like a different girl now that she's put on a little weight. She's got some of her brightness back and I think we can put that down to Mrs Roundtree's care. It looks as if Cissie is returning his clean laundry to him.'

'Yes, she is.' Zillah stood back from the window and watched as Cissie shyly passed the young man a small pile of freshly ironed clothes before skipping away. George's eyes followed her for a time before he headed back in the direction of the stables. Zillah then turned her attention back to Lavinia to ask, 'Is there anything else you'd like?'

Lavinia sighed. 'Yes, I'd like to be able to see my feet again but I don't suppose you can help there, can you?'

Zillah chuckled. This time her mistress's pregnancy seemed to be going really well. She was gaining weight, there was a glow about her and Zillah prayed that this was a sign that at the end of it there would be a happy conclusion. Thankfully they saw little of Ashley these days, and even when he was at home he didn't trouble his wife, which suited her very well.

Strangely, all Lavinia's misgivings about the forthcoming baby had vanished on the day she felt it quicken inside her, and she too, was now looking forward to the birth. Already the nursery, which had lain under dustsheets for so long had been prepared and the tiny clothes that she had kept – for she had not given them all away – had been washed and pressed and were ready to be worn.

Ashley had told her to start advertising for a wet nurse and a nanny but on this Lavinia had stood her ground. She would agree to a nanny but insisted should all go well she would feed her baby herself.

Ashley told her he found the thought of it disgusting but had given way. After all, should she finally present him with a son he would have no need of her any more. He didn't intend to be there that much once his uncle's lawyers had settled a down payment on his inheritance, for he would be too busy out and about enjoying himself. Admittedly, Lavinia was generous with his monthly allowance, but that would be small change compared to his uncle's wealth and he could hardly wait. But God forbid if she should present him with another daughter! It didn't even bear thinking about so he was trying to stay optimistic. His wife had positively blossomed during this confinement once she had got over the morning sickness, so perhaps that was a sign that she was carrying a boy this time? Please God it was so.

It was some weeks since Lavinia had attended

any meetings at the workhouse. It was not common practice for women who were *enceinte* to be seen in public so for now she confined her outings to visiting Mrs Spooner and the vicar's wife, where she would spend hours playing with little Phoebe. She was an adorable baby and Lavinia couldn't get enough of her. Often after such a visit she would wander to the three tiny graves in the orchard and try to imagine what her own baby daughters would have been like. Would they have been fair-haired and blue-eyed like her, or would they have taken after their father? It was something she would never know. The last one would be fourteen now had she lived and she still celebrated each girl's birthday every year by laying flowers on their graves.

'So are you off to visit Mrs Spooner this afternoon?' Zillah asked then and Lavinia nodded.

'Yes, I think so. You could ask George to bring the carriage around to the front at about two o'clock if you wouldn't mind, dear? That is, if it doesn't start to snow. It's certainly cold enough, isn't it? But then there is something quite magical about a white Christmas, I always think. Oh, it's such a pleasure to visit Mrs Spooner now. I swear Sunday, Daisy and Tommy have given her a new lease of life. I do worry about Daisy though. She's out of the workhouse now – yet she seems so subdued.'

'It's hardly any wonder, is it?' the maid answered practically. 'She's only a slip of a girl and carrying a child that's been forced on her through rape by that horrible man. All we can do is hope that she bonds with it when it's born.'

'Hmm. Well, at least now that Pinnegar's gone, no other girls will suffer the same fate,' Lavinia replied. 'Apparently the new housemaster is a different kettle of fish altogether. He and his wife are living in Pinnegar's old cottage and he's very kind, so they say, and so is his wife. I haven't heard what's become of Miss Frost though – not that I have much sympathy with her. I insisted that she should be dismissed too, because of her sadistic mistreatment of the girls. She left shortly after Pinnegar.'

'Well, it's good riddance to bad rubbish so far as I'm concerned,' Zillah sniffed. 'She were little better than him from where I'm standing! But now to change the subject: Cook was asking this morning how many there'll be for Christmas dinner this year?'

'Ah, I meant to talk to you about that.' Lavinia beamed. 'Ashley informed me that he'll be away so I thought you and I could just have it quietly together. It will save a lot of work for the staff and I'd like you to get Mrs Roundtree to tell them that they can all have the afternoon and the evening off once dinner is over. I'm sure you and I can do something light for our evening meal and then the staff can have a little do in the kitchen, or at least, those of them that want to can.'

Zillah smiled approvingly. 'They'll love that. Especially Cissie. She bought some material off the rag stall in the market last week an' she's sewing herself a new gown. Been working on it every night, she has, and it's coming along a fair treat. Happen she'll want to wear that on Christmas Day.'

'Then that's settled,' Lavinia said contentedly. The thought of a quiet Christmas with just her and Zillah was quite appealing. And so Zillah went off happily to pass on the good news.

Chapter Thirty

A tap on the door woke Sunday on Christmas Eve and she started awake, amazed to see that it was already getting light.

'Wh-what time is it?' she asked groggily as Daisy popped her head round the door.

'I don't know but I think it's late,' Daisy answered worriedly. 'The cockerel usually wakes me up with his crowing but I didn't hear a peep out of him this morning.'

She shot off to wake Tommy then before going back to her own room to get dressed. Soon Sunday and Tommy were rushing downstairs with Daisy lumbering on behind them only to find Annie already there with the kitchen fire lit and breakfast well on the go. There was no need whatsoever for her to be there in the mornings any more, but old habits die hard and she often turned up even though Sunday was quite capable of cooking the first meal of the day.

'Ah, here you are, yer sleepyheads,' Annie teased.

'Oh, Annie, I'm so sorry. We all overlay but why didn't you wake us?' Sunday asked as she hurried forward to help.

'A little lie-in now an' again never hurt nobody.' Annie expertly flipped a sizzling rasher of bacon in the huge black-bottomed frying pan on the range. 'It might be a good idea if you got the fires in the drawing room and the dining room goin' though, Tommy, as they'll all be down to breakfast soon,' she suggested and he hurried away to do as he was told.

Luckily he had become an expert at damping all the fires down at night so it never took him too long to coax them back to life each morning; thankfully, today was no exception. The girls had laid the table in preparation for breakfast the night before, so now whilst Sunday set about making a large pot of tea, Daisy took the long-handled fork and began to toast some bread on the fire. They had the house running along like a well-oiled cog now and in no time at all the meal was served. The lodgers were leaving today to spend Christmas with sons and daughters or extended family, and the atmosphere at the table was lighthearted.

It was almost nine o'clock before the staff sat down to their own breakfast but no one was rushing today although there was a huge turkey waiting to be plucked and the stuffing to make. Annie had had the Christmas pudding and the mixture for the Christmas cake soaking in brandy for weeks and today they would be cooked too. Sunday was also going to try her hand at making some mince pies although she doubted the pastry would be half as good as Annie's. Still, as the latter had pointed out on more than one occasion, 'practice makes perfect'.

'Eeh, I reckon this is gonna be one o' the best

Christmases this house has seen fer some long time,' Annie remarked happily as she helped herself to another cup of tea and liberally spooned sugar into it. It was just as she liked it, well brewed and sweet. 'You young 'un's 'ave breathed new life into it.'

They all smiled. It would be a special time for them too, especially for Sunday who had never known a Christmas outside the workhouse.

'Right, I'd best get out and see to the animals now,' Tommy said eventually as he rose from the table patting his full stomach contentedly. He went away whistling merrily as Daisy and Sunday set about the dirty pots but the mood was broken when Tommy burst back in some minutes later with a stricken look on his face.

'Me cockerel's dead.' He held the poor lifeless creature up for them all to see and he was clearly distressed and shocked.

'Eeh, that's a shame, lad,' Annie tutted. 'But then these creatures don't live for ever. Perhaps a fox got him?'

'It weren't no fox and he didn't die of natural causes by the look of it. I reckon someone has broken his neck.'

'Oh no!' Daisy's hand flew to her mouth. She knew how fond her brother was of the animals. 'But who would do such a wicked thing?'

'No one in their right mind. Happen you're mistaken,' Annie said calmly. 'It's a shame but it were only a cockerel at the end o' the day an' he might as well go in the pot as go to waste.'

'I can't let you cook him!' Tommy was horrified at the thought.

'An' why not?' Annie asked, placing her hands on her hips. 'What's the difference 'tween you eatin' him to one you've bought from the butcher?'

Tommy shrugged. He knew she was right but he was heartbroken. He had tended those chickens and the cockerel as if they were his children and would have loved to have got his hands on the person who had killed it.

'It was probably some young 'uns out fer a lark,' Annie concluded. 'Soon as the town is open again after Christmas you can go an' choose another one from the cattle market.'

And so that was the end of that, although Tommy couldn't shift the feeling that there was more to it. The poor bird had been left lying on top of the chicken coop like a sacrifice. Surely if it was just a group of youngsters, they would have taken it home for the pot?

The rest of the day passed pleasantly enough. With none of the lodgers coming home that evening there was less work to do and the atmosphere was relaxed.

On Christmas morning, bright and early, Sunday rose to get dressed. She missed the cockerel waking her but was trying not to think of the unfortunate end to which the poor bird had come. The night before, she had washed her hair and scrubbed herself from head to toe and this morning she brushed her hair until it gleamed and tied it back with the pretty blue ribbon that Mrs Spooner had bought for her and which she kept for church and special occasions. She then put on her prettiest gown, one of those that Lady Huntley had given her, and after collecting her presents she crept down to the kitchen, careful not to wake anyone. There was no reason for her friends to be up early today and Sunday wanted them to have a lie-in – but to her surprise when she got down-stairs, she found Annie, Daisy and Tommy already there.

'I couldn't see the point in stayin' at home on me own,' Annie told her. 'An' me an' Biddy usually spend Christmas Day together any road.'

She was looking very neat and tidy today in her best gown, with jet earrings and matching choker. It was obvious that she had made a special effort for Christmas Day.

'The missus an' Jacob said they'll join us in 'ere fer breakfast today,' she informed them. 'It's not worth layin' the dinin'-room table just for the two of 'em.'

When Mrs Spooner and Jacob did eventually join them, Sunday was amused to see that the old lady almost outshone the baubles on the Christmas tree. There were so many rings on her fingers that she could barely bend them, and the power-ful gusts of her perfume made Daisy cough. The bracelets and bangles that adorned her arms jangled merrily every time she moved, and her face was even more heavily made up than usual but Sunday was used to the sight of her now and was becoming fonder of her by the day.

Breakfast passed quickly with lots of laughter then Mrs Spooner began to hand out the pre-sents she had bought for each of them.

'I know it's usual to wait till after dinner,' she

beamed, 'but I never could wait even as a child.'

For Daisy there was a warm pair of blue woollen mittens, embroidered with a daisy on each one, and a matching scarf. Her thin face lit up when she saw them.

'Ooh ... they're lovely!' she cooed with delight. 'Look – daisies, like me! These will keep me so cosy and warm.' And she promptly wrapped the scarf about her neck and slipped the mittens on.

Tommy opened his gift to find a sturdy pair of boots that would be perfect for wearing when working outside. He was pleased as Punch with them.

'But how did you know my size?' he asked in amazement. They were just what he needed.

'Well, I'd heard you complain that your others were pinchin' your toes so I just looked for some a bit bigger and took pot luck! Those you're wearing are so smelly I don't know how you can bear to put them on,' Mrs Spooner teased him.

Annie was just as pleased with her gift, a very pretty apron trimmed with broderie anglaise. 'Though Lord knows when I'll get to wear it,' she muttered. 'It's far too nice to get it dirty.'

Finally, the old woman handed Sunday her gift. It was a shawl in beautiful autumn colours.

'Oh!' The girl was so overcome that she could think of nothing to say. It would look lovely with the gowns Lady Huntley had given her and she knew that she would treasure it. 'It ... it's like something the toffs might wear,' she whispered eventually and everyone laughed.

'Just wear it in the spirit it was given an' enjoy it,' Mrs Spooner said kindly and then Sunday hastily handed out her presents, to hide the tears in her eyes. *This is just turning out to be the best Christmas ever!* she found herself thinking and couldn't seem to stop herself from smiling.

Even Daisy seemed more her old self that morning, which passed in a blur of laughter and good humour. The young people and Annie ate in the dining room with Mrs Spooner and her nephew for the very first time that day. The turkey was cooked to perfection, as was Annie's sage and onion stuffing, but Sunday noticed that no one made a start on the poor cockerel. They could all still remember him too well strutting round the yard. There was also a selection of vegetables and crispy roast potatoes followed by Annie's Christmas pudding served with brandy butter or thick creamy custard. It was the nearest thing to perfection Sunday had ever tasted.

By the time they had finished all this it was decided that they would have to wait until teatime to try Sunday's mince pies, for they were all too full to manage another mouthful. Mrs Spooner, Jacob and Annie retired to the drawing room then for a snooze as the young people began to clear the table.

'It's been just wonderful,' Sunday declared as she, Daisy and Tommy washed and dried the pots, and her friends nodded in agreement although their pleasure was slightly marred by memories of Christmases past shared with their family. They were sad that those times could never come again but grateful for what they had.

It had also been a happy day at Treetops Manor.

Zillah and Lady Huntley had dined quietly together whilst the staff all enjoyed their Christmas dinner in the kitchen amongst much merriment. Mrs Roundtree was tickled to see that George sat right next to Cissie, making her cheeks flush prettily. It was actually Cissie who found the silver sixpence in her Christmas pudding and when ordered to close her eyes and make a wish, she did so before blushing even more and glancing at George through her eyelashes.

No need to wonder what she was wishing, the housekeeper thought before turning her attention back to her mince pie, and she fervently hoped that something good would come of their meeting.

Later that evening when the staff party was in full swing in the kitchen, Lavinia Huntley climbed to the nursery floor and glanced around with a look of longing in her eyes.

'Please, dear Lord Jesus, let this be the last childless Christmas I ever have to bear,' she prayed as she crossed to the tiny rocking crib. It had a little canopy heavily frilled with lace, and inside it little blankets lay waiting to warm their new occupant. She caressed her bump. This time next year, God willing, she would be spending time in here with her baby. It was all she had ever dreamed of and now once again, and rather unexpectedly, the dream was within her grasp.

301

Chapter Thirty-One

The snow began to fall on New Year's Eve and suddenly everywhere looked as if it had been painted white and was brand new. Not everyone was enamoured of it, however.

'I hope the chickens an' the pigs are warm enough,' Tommy fretted, much to Annie's amusement.

'Well, even if they ain't, they ain't comin' in 'ere,' she told him with a grin. The lodgers had all returned from their Christmas vacations and tonight they would be having a little party. Annie had been busily baking for two whole days and now the dining-room table held an impressive array of meat pies and pickles, a side of ham and a huge roast leg of pork as well as a variety of fresh-baked rolls, jellies and all kinds of cakes.

'I love parties,' Sunday sighed happily as she laid out a number of knives and forks.

'Hmm, well, make the most o' this 'un,' Annie warned her. 'It'll be back to work as normal once we get tomorrow over wi'.'

Sunday just smiled. Nothing could dampen her spirits today and she was curious to see what Jacob's latest young lady looked like. He'd been walking out with her for a few weeks now, according to Annie, but none of them had met her as yet. Her father was one of the managers at the brickworks and supposedly quite well off, which had tickled Mrs Spooner no end.

An hour before the party was about to begin, Sunday slipped upstairs to get ready, only to find Daisy lying on her bed in the dark.

'Come on, Dais,' she urged. 'The party will be starting soon. Don't you want to get changed for it?'

But Daisy merely shook her head. 'I reckon I'll stay up here tonight. I'm not really feelin' in a mood for celebrating.' It had struck her that day that they were almost into a brand-new year – a year that would change the whole of her life for ever, for during that year she would be forced to give birth to the bastard she was carrying.

'In that case I'll stay up here with you. I'll light the lamp and read to you if you like,' Sunday offered, but Daisy again shook her head.

'Thanks, but I'd rather be on my own if you don't mind.' She knew how much Sunday had been looking forward to this evening and she didn't want to spoil it for her. Even so, the other girl was persistent.

'How about I bring you up something to eat on a tray. Is there anything in particular you fancy?'

'Nothing at all. I'm not hungry. Now will you *please* just go and get changed? I'm perfectly comfortable here.'

Sunday sighed. Daisy could be a stubborn little so-and-so when she set her mind to it.

'All right then, I will,' she told her with her hands on her hips. 'But I shall be up to check on you, young lady.' She sloped off to her room then and as she emerged a short time later she almost bumped into Tommy, who was all dressed in his best. He had treated himself to a smart new shirt and a pair of trousers from the rag stall with some of his wages.

'Isn't Dais ready yet?' he asked, glancing appreciatively at Sunday. She really did look a treat, he thought, although he was too shy to tell her so.

'She doesn't want to go to the party,' she answered. Her friend seemed to have slipped back into her slough of despond since Christmas Day and it was so frustrating not being able to do anything about it.

'Still,' she went on then, not wanting to spoil his night too, 'there's nothing to say we shouldn't enjoy ourselves, is there?' Tucking her arm innocently into his she marched him to the head of the stairs, making his heart pound, and soon they had joined the party downstairs.

Jacob's friend, whom he introduced as Miss Rebecca Moreton, turned out to be a very well-dressed pretty brunette with pale green eyes, but Sunday didn't take to her as she appeared to look down on them all, especially Mrs Spooner.

'Jacob's aunt is err … quite colourful, isn't she?' she remarked to Sunday at one stage when Jacob had gone off to get them both a drink of mulled wine.

Sunday giggled. 'Yes, she does like her frills and flounces admittedly but she's got a heart as big as a bucket,' and she glanced affectionately over at the old woman.

'And what relation to Jacob's family are you?' the young woman asked stiffly.

'Me? Oh, I'm not related to them at all,' Sunday told her. 'I'm just a maid here.'

'*A maid!*' Rebecca stared at her in horror. The maids in her house would never have been allowed to join their betters at occasions such as this. They knew their place, her mother made sure of that.

'Would you excuse me,' she said stiltedly then and marched off to voice her dismay to Jacob.

Sunday shrugged and turned her attention back to Mr Greaves who was doing his best to produce a song from Mrs Spooner's rather out of tune piano.

Every time Sunday glanced Rebecca's way after that she saw her hanging possessively onto Jacob's arm and staring at her as if she had some terrible disease. Jacob had obviously noticed and looked decidedly more uncomfortable as the evening wore on until presently Sunday hissed to Tommy, 'I think I might go up. I have a bit of a headache coming on.'

'Oh yes, and would the headache be called Rebecca, by any chance?' he hissed back.

Sunday flushed. So he had noticed how the girl was glaring at her, had he?

'Actually, I think I may go up as well,' Tommy said then. 'I ain't got no time for people who have airs an' graces. God alone knows what Jacob sees in her, and him such a friendly chap an' all. Still, I suppose it's each to us own. Let's say our good nights an' leave 'em all to it, shall we?'

Soon Sunday was leading the way up the stairs that led to their attic rooms, and as she was going in to check on Daisy, Tommy gently caught her arm and told her, 'Don't let that stuck-up little miss upset you, Sunday. You're worth ten of her and you're prettier than her an' all. That's probably why she didn't take to you.'

Sunday grinned. 'I'm sure it wasn't that, Tommy, but thank you all the same.'

Tommy awkwardly swiped a thick lock from his forehead. 'Well, er ... g'night then.'

'Good night, Tommy,' she answered softly as he bustled off to his room and she felt a little warm glow inside. He was still young as yet but he was already kind and hard-working, and one day he was going to make someone a first-rate husband. She was very happy to have him here along with herself and his sister. Tapping on Daisy's door, she slid inside to see the New Year in with her friend.

'Happy New Year, Dais,' Sunday yawned the next morning as she woke up and stretched. She had fallen asleep in Daisy's bed and now she was stiff from lying on the edge of the single mattress. The girls had had to lie back to back otherwise they'd never both have fitted in, with Daisy's bump.

'Crikey, I reckon I'll stick to sleeping in me own bed in future,' Sunday groaned as she slid off the side and tried to stand. Then on a happier note, 'And now it's 1885 and we're not waking up in the workhouse. That's an improvement on last year for a start, isn't it?'

When no reply was forthcoming from the sleeping figure she grabbed her dress from over the back of the chair where she had flung it the night before and, crossing to the door, she gingerly inched it open. It wouldn't do for Tommy to catch her sneaking along the landing in her petticoat and drawers. Thankfully there was no sign of him so

306

she shot along to get washed and changed ready to start the breakfast, although she doubted that anyone would be awake early today after the party last night. Tomorrow would be another matter entirely. Everyone would be going back to work and things would return to normal, which Sunday thought was quite a shame. She'd enjoyed her first Christmas and New Year away from the workhouse.

As she had anticipated, the house was in silence when she got downstairs. It appeared that even Tommy had had a lie-in and there was only Mabel to greet her but she didn't mind and set to, to get the kitchen fire lit. Soon the room was warm and cosy and she put the kettle on to boil for the first cup of tea of the day. No doubt Annie would be arriving any minute and she was never any good until she'd drunk at least two cups. She let Mabel out into the yard and was just getting the cups ready when the dog began to yap furiously. *Drat*, she thought, *she'll wake everybody up at this rate.* Hurrying to the door, she threw it open and warned Mabel, 'Be quiet, will you?' Then she frowned. Mabel was over by the chicken coops and was barking at something that had been laid on top of one of them.

The snow was deep although it wasn't snowing at that present time, so Sunday lifted her skirts and stepped across the yard, shuddering as the snow found its way in over the top of her boots. She had almost reached the coops when she realised what it was lying on top of them and her hand flew to her mouth before she looked about her fearfully. Two more of the chickens had been laid side-by-side with their necks twisted at an unnatural angle. Someone had deliberately fetched them out and cold-bloodedly killed them – and that wasn't all they'd done, for now as she glanced back at the kitchen door she saw that eggs had been thrown all up it and across the windows.

Shuddering, she grabbed Mabel's collar and hauled her back across the yard, closing and locking the door quickly behind her. *What vile person could have done such a thing?* she asked herself. And a little voice in her head answered, *The same one who killed the cockerel.* But surely if it had been kids just larking about as everyone had thought when the cockerel was killed, they wouldn't have chanced their luck twice? They would have been too afraid of getting caught. And what was she going to tell Tommy? Poor lad, he cared deeply for those animals, in fact, Mrs Spooner often teased him that she was sure he'd take them all to bed with him if she'd let him.

As it happened, just then Tommy breezed into the kitchen, adjusting the braces on his trousers. Seeing her pale, shocked face he asked, 'What's up then? You look like you've seen a ghost.'

Gesturing to the kitchen door she stumblingly told him what she had just discovered, and grim-faced he yanked his boots on and went off to see for himself without even bothering to put his coat on.

'The murdering swines!' he ground out when he stamped back in. 'I'll tell you now, if I could get me bloody hands round their throats I'd do the same to them.' He was shaking with rage as Sunday quietly slid a cup of tea along the table in front of him.

'I'm so sorry, Tommy. I know what good care you took of them,' she said, just as Annie dosed the front door and came in, shaking the snow from her shawl.

'It's damn well snowin' again – just started,' she informed them, then seeing their grim faces she went on, 'Well, I were about to wish yer both a Happy New Year but it don't look as if it's too happy fer you pair. What's up, eh?'

As Sunday hastily told her what had happened, Annie tutted. 'The lousy buggers. Still, it'll solve the problem o' what we're havin' fer dinner today. A couple o' nice fat juicy birds'll go down nice wi' that leg o' lamb I got from the butchers.' Then, seeing the stricken look on Tommy's face, she apologised profusely and quickly poured herself a cup of tea.

'I've a good mind to stay in the rooms above the stables and see if I can't catch whoever it is that's doing this,' Tommy said over breakfast but Annie shook her head.

'Yer can't be doin' that, lad,' she said practically. 'Them rooms ain't been lived in fer many a long year an' in this weather you'd likely freeze to death. Chances are yer'd fall asleep anyway then it would all have been for nothin'.'

'I dare say you're right,' Tommy admitted grudgingly. 'But it's beginning to look like someone has got something against us.'

Daisy, who had come downstairs now, exchanged a troubled look with Sunday and without a word being said they both knew what was in the other's mind. *Mr Pinnegar!* Could it be that he was exacting his revenge by trying to frighten them? But then common sense took over and as Sunday pointed out to her friend later that morning, 'It's an awful long walk from town just to wring the necks of two chickens. Had he tried to get at one of us I could have understood it.'

'I dare say you're right,' Daisy agreed. 'But I still won't rule him out. I wouldn't put anything past that horrible man.'

More news about the said 'horrible man' came to light later in the week when Lady Huntley, together with Mrs Lockett but without baby Phoebe paid them an unexpected visit. 'We won't stay for too long,' she told them the second she had set foot through the door, 'because it's just started to snow again and young George had a job to get us here as it was. Some of the roads are virtually impassable and if we get much more, I can see us being snowed in at Treetops Manor.'

'I'll throw some rugs over the horses and give them a nose bag each,' Tommy offered.

'Yes, an' yer can tell the groom to go round to the kitchen fer a hot drink,' Mrs Spooner added.

It was as she, Lady Huntley and Mrs Lockett were enjoying a pot of coffee and a few warmed-up mince pies that Lady Huntley shared the latest gossip. 'I'm told that Albert Pinnegar is up to his tricks again,' she announced. Then, seeing the look of horror on the women's faces, she added hastily, 'Not with young girls. It's money-lending this time, apparently. One of the work-house guardians and his wife paid me a visit over the Christmas holidays and said that Pinnegar's lending out money to those desperate enough to

310

need it then charging them exorbitant interest rates. There really appears to be nothing that man will not stoop to.'

'It doesn't surprise me,' Mrs Spooner responded. 'I couldn't see him being happy pushing a broom about the market for long. But what'll happen to the poor souls that can't pay him back?'

'Ah well, rumour has it that he's got a bunch of thugs who collect his money for him, and Mr Tilsley heard that two men have already had their kneecaps broken.'

Mrs Spooner remarked crossly, 'That man is bad through and through. Fancy preying on poor desperate people! Between you and me we've had a few incidents here…' She went on to tell the visitors about the cockerel and the chickens, ending, 'O' course we've no way of proving it.'

'Well, let's hope you have no more unfortunate incidents,' Verity said. 'And there is always the chance that it was just youths.'

'I hope you're right, but in the meantime my Jacob is keeping an eye on the house and the girls of an evening.' Mrs Spooner took a long swig of her coffee and the conversation moved on to motherhood and to Daisy and Lady Huntley's forthcoming babies.

Chapter Thirty-Two

Two weeks into January it finally stopped snowing but the snow was replaced by heavy rains and suddenly everywhere was sodden and dismal. Many low-lying areas of the town were flooded and this, added to the bitterly cold winds, encouraged as many people as were able to, to stay snug indoors.

Sunday still visited the market each Wednesday but now instead of looking forward to the outings she came to dread them, for each week it appeared that Albert Pinnegar was lying in wait for her, sometimes with a couple of very unsavoury characters in tow. She didn't mention this to anyone at Whittleford Lodge. Daisy was as jumpy as a kitten since the last incident when the chickens had been killed and Sunday didn't want to distress her any more than she already was.

Pinnegar was marching about like the cock of the north again now, in fancy waistcoats and expensive suits, and each time she encountered him, Sunday found herself hating him just a little bit more than she already did, if that were possible.

This particular Wednesday proved to be no different and once she had reached the market she had visited no more than half a dozen stalls when he suddenly loomed up in front of her.

'You're looking chilly, my dear. Perhaps you'd like me to take you to the eating-house for a nice hot meal?' he suggested. His feelings towards the girl remained in conflict; they alternated between hatred and lust. He longed to possess her. *She's like a fire in my belly that refuses to be extinguished,* he thought, *no matter how she speaks to me.*

'I wouldn't go anywhere with you if I were dying of starvation,' she answered boldly, her dislike of him shining in her violet-blue eyes. 'And now if you will excuse me some of us have work to do.' She made to step past him but two of his henchmen blocked her path.

'It doesn't have to be like that.' His voice was wheedling. 'If you were to come and move in with me in my cottage, you could live like a lady. You'd never have to work or get your hands dirty again, and I would treat you like a princess.'

'Oh, just go away and leave me alone!' she cried. 'Haven't I made myself clear? I detest the very sight of you!'

The smile slid from his face, and as one of his men smirked, Pinnegar realised that they were beginning to draw attention to themselves.

'And while you're here I should also warn you to keep away from Mrs Spooner's,' she went on, sounding braver than she felt. 'We know it was you that egged the windows and killed our fowl.'

He and the two men laughed. 'And why ever would I do something like that?' he guffawed. 'I'm afraid you possess a rather vivid imagination, my dear. Although I do admit to knowing what you're all doing at any given time...'

The stall-holder had come to stand at Sunday's side now and asked, 'Are these fellers botherin' yer, pet?'

'No, it's all right, thank you.' Sunday never took

her eyes from Pinnegar's face. 'I believe they were just leaving.'

Pinnegar's lips drew together in a snarl as he turned on his heel and strode away with his two thugs in tow. Sunday flashed a grateful smile at the stall-holder and set off briskly in the other direction. Despite the brave front she'd presented to him she quaked inside every time she set eyes on Albert Pinnegar. But then she supposed she should be grateful that all he'd done up to now was approach her. There was no law that said he wasn't allowed to speak to her, so she knew that she just had to brave it out. No doubt in time he would grow weary of his obsession and leave her well alone. Even so, as she set off for home she found herself repeatedly glancing over her shoulder and was relieved when Whittleford Lodge came into view.

Once back in the warmth of the kitchen she emptied the contents of her basket onto the table and, glancing around, she asked Annie, 'Is Daisy not about?'

'Oh, she set off fer a walk along the cut some time back,' Annie answered as she examined the vegetables that Sunday had bought. 'I wish she wouldn't, atween you an' me. She's as big as a house now – an' what would happen if she were to have a fall? Yer can't tell her though.' She clucked her tongue disapprovingly. 'If yer do say anythin' she just says as she needs to get some fresh air. She's never gone for very long though, so I'd expect her home shortly.'

Sunday frowned. Like Annie she was very

worried about Daisy. Since Christmas, her friend's spirits had sunk to an all-time low and they were having trouble getting her to eat properly. Sometimes she didn't even have the energy to get out of bed and when she did, she would disappear off for solitary walks whatever the weather, shuffling along with her head bent. Still, she always came back after a little while, Sunday consoled herself and found that she was wishing for the birth to be over now. Perhaps when Daisy saw the baby she would have a change of heart and find that she could love it? She could only hope so.

She sat down with Annie and Tommy to have a light lunch after taking a tray through to Mrs Spooner but, as yet, Daisy hadn't put in an appearance.

'She'll be back soon enough. She ain't goin' to stay out much longer in this weather, is she?' Annie commented as she saw Sunday's eyes stray to the window. It was raining heavily again now and wherever Daisy was she must be soaked to the skin.

'I reckon I might just go out an' have a look for her after we've finished eating,' Tommy said then. He was concerned about his sister too, not that she'd listen to any advice he tried to give. Daisy seemed to be just existing from day to day and there was not a thing any of them could do about it.

As soon as lunch was over, Tommy fetched some more logs in and made the fires up before putting his heavy coat on and setting off in search of Daisy as Sunday got on with her chores.

The afternoon was beginning to darken when

315

Tommy reappeared and asked, 'Is she back yet?'

Sunday shook her head. 'No, there's been no sign of her.'

Tommy scowled as he removed his sodden coat and tossed it over the wooden clothes horse in front of the fire where it immediately began to steam.

'I can't understand it. I got down onto the towpath up at Clock Hill in Hartshill and followed the cut right the way to the Cock and Bear Bridge but she wasn't there. Surely she wouldn't have walked further than that in this weather?'

'Perhaps she didn't go along the canal at all today?' Sunday was as worried as he was but not sure what to do.

'Well, sure as eggs is eggs, frettin' about her ain't goin' to bring her back any sooner,' Annie said stoically. 'So you go an' put the kettle on, Sunday. This lad looks like he could do wi' a hot drink inside of him.'

By the time the evening meal had been served to the lodgers and then cleared away there was still no sign of Daisy and by then Tommy was pacing up and down the kitchen like a caged animal. Worn out, Annie had left for the comfort of her own fireside and Sunday didn't know what to suggest they should do.

'It's too soon to report her missing to the constables,' she pointed out. 'They'd just say she had probably gone to visit a friend.'

He nodded in agreement. 'I know. I suppose I'm just worried that she might...'

His voice trailed away but Sunday knew exactly what was in his mind. Daisy was so depressed that she might think of ending it all. It was what they had all been dreading and why they had been keeping such a close eye on her. Oh, if only Annie hadn't let her go out today! But then how could she have stopped her? Daisy wasn't a prisoner, after all.

'She'll be back,' Sunday assured him in a shaky voice. 'And when she does she'll feel the length of my tongue, you just see if she doesn't – worrying us like this!'

The evening wore on. Sunday sat letting the seams of a dress out for Daisy by the light of the oil lamp while Tommy sat at the side of the fire making a pretence of reading a newspaper. Sunday knew that he wasn't really reading for his eyes kept straying to the window and he was as taut as a spring.

'Are you two still up?' A voice startled them as the grandfather clock in the hallway struck ten and they saw Mrs Spooner standing in the doorway. It was actually late for her to retire too, but like them she was concerned about Daisy.

'Oh yes.' Sunday laid the dress down and stifled a yawn. 'We don't like to go to bed until Daisy's home.'

'Well, you can't stay up all night else you'll be fit for nothing tomorrow.'

'It's all right, Sunday,' Tommy butted in. 'You go on up and get some rest. I'm going to go out and look for her again. I can't just sit about round here doing nothing.'

Jacob appeared then and told him, 'I'll come with you.'

Tommy smiled at him gratefully and the two

317

men began to wrap up warmly before venturing out into the cold night. Once outside, Jacob set off to look around Stockingford while Tommy went in the direction of Hartshill, hoping that Daisy might have gone to see Cissie at Treetops Manor.

'I think I'll wait up until they get back,' Sunday told Mrs Spooner and she was surprised when the old lady went to take Tommy's chair at the side of the fire.

'I'll stay up with you. I doubt I'd sleep anyway till I know she's back safe.' But despite her kind words her chin was lolling on her chest in no time and she was snoring softly as Sunday stood by the window praying for a sight of Daisy.

It was the early hours of the morning before first Jacob then Tommy reappeared.

'I've walked miles but there's not a sight of her,' Jacob told her as he held his hands out to the fire, which Sunday had kept going. His teeth were chattering with cold and Sunday rushed away to put a pan of milk on to make him some hot cocoa. Tommy entered soon after, his face a mask of misery.

Sunday looked at him but he merely shook his head. 'Nothing,' he told her dismally. 'I'm off to report her missing to the constables at first light then I'm going to carry on searching for her.'

As an idea occurred to Sunday she felt her knees buckle with fear but she kept her thoughts to herself. What if Albert Pinnegar had taken Daisy – in revenge for getting him dismissed? The man was evil and she wouldn't have put anything past him.

Eventually Jacob went to bed to snatch a few hours' sleep while Tommy and Sunday sat at the table talking and trying not to think the worst. At some stage Sunday rested her head on her arms and slipped into a fitful doze and the next thing she knew, Tommy was gently nudging her awake.

'It's just getting light so I'm going to the police station,' he whispered. Mrs Spooner was still snoring in the fireside chair. Her wig had slipped forward, completely covering her eyes and under other circumstances the two young people might have found it amusing but as it was all they could think of was the missing girl.

Sunday agreed blearily. There seemed no other course of action open to them now, knowing what state of mind Daisy had been in. Sunday just dreaded to think what the poor girl might have done to herself.

And so, bright and early as she prepared the breakfasts, Tommy set off and all they could do was wait. Word of Daisy's disappearance had spread through the house and when Sunday served their meals the lodgers all expressed their concern. Daisy was such a sweet-natured, in-offensive girl, and they had all become fond of her.

After discussion amongst themselves the lodgers all agreed that they would go to work late and meantime form a search-party. When they were all ready to leave, Sunday waved them off. Two hours later, Tommy returned looking pale and drawn.

'Have they police heard anything?' Sunday asked anxiously.

'Not a dickey bird but they're on the lookout

319

for her now so hopefully we'll hear something soon. I did have a thought though – you don't think she might have run away, do you?'

'I wouldn't think so. Where would she go? And anyway, she didn't take any money with her or any clothes. I've checked. Surely if she was going to run away she would have packed a bag?'

'I suppose you're right,' Tommy sighed. 'But I reckon I'll get back out looking for her again now.'

'No!' Sunday laid a gentle hand on his arm. 'Jacob and the lodgers are all out looking, the police too. It's best if you and me wait here for any news now.'

Annie arrived mid-morning and she too was in a subdued mood. 'She'll turn up like a bad penny, you'll see,' she told them, trying to keep their spirits up but it didn't do much good.

The day seemed to drag by and, before they knew it, it was growing dark again and still Daisy remained missing. Jacob and the lodgers had given up the search hours ago and gone about their business. Then, as Annie was dishing up the dinner, there was a loud rapping on the door and everyone jumped.

'*I'll get it!*' Sunday and Tommy said simultaneously. They rushed to answer the door and found two policemen standing on the steps. 'Have you found Daisy?' Sunday asked before they'd had a chance to say a word and the two officers glanced at each other.

'Err ... I wonder if we might come inside?' the taller of the two said eventually.

'Yes – yes, of course. Come in.' Sunday almost

tripped in her haste to show them in to Mrs Spooner, who had been just about to go into dinner.

'Good evening, and how may I help you, gentlemen?' the old lady asked in her very poshest voice. Normally, Sunday would have found it funny but tonight she was too wound up with worry to even notice.

'Well, the thing is, ma'am…' The men removed their helmets and glanced at Tommy.

'Is it about my sister? *Have you found her?*' Tommy asked hoarsely.

'I'm very sorry to have to inform you that the body of a young girl in the family way and near to her time, was fished out of the canal this afternoon. Unfortunately, sir, the description fits that of the young lady who was reported missing this morning by you, Mr Branning. It is our sad duty to ask you to accompany us to the morgue to identify the body.'

It was the silence that followed, before Tommy cried out, *'No! Please God, no!'* that Sunday knew she would remember for the rest of her life. Then grief, too, engulfed her.

Chapter Thirty-Three

Sunday, Tommy and Jacob were helped into the back of the police cart and they set off for the mortuary. Although she was still shaken and weak, Sunday would not let Tommy go alone, and

Jacob had insisted on accompanying them as he knew how hard it would be for them both.

Sunday clutched Tommy's hand as the closed cart swayed along pulled by two jet-black police horses, but they didn't speak. When they eventually reached the hospital, the two kindly policemen escorted them inside and down to the basement.

'Here we are then, young man.' The officers stopped in front of two high doors and removed their helmets. One asked: 'Are you ready to go in, son?'

Tommy stared at him uncomprehendingly for a moment. He seemed to have locked himself away in a world of his own where no one could reach him … but after a moment he came to and nodded bravely.

'Right.' The second policeman swung the doors open and while Jacob discreetly stayed where he was, the two youngsters found themselves in yet another corridor. In the air was a smell that Sunday would never forget. As they stood there a man in a long white coat and a mask appeared from a door off to their right.

One of the policemen told him: 'We've come to look at the body of the young girl that was brought in earlier, sir. We believe it may be this young man's sister.'

'Ah yes.' The doctor stared kindly at Tommy for a moment then led the group further down the corridor.

'She's in here … would you like me to come in with you?'

Tommy nodded and clutched Sunday's hand

tightly. 'Please – and can she come in too?'

'Of course.' The man leaned against the door and they found themselves in a small room with a long trestle in the centre of it on which lay a shape that was completely covered in a crisp white sheet. Flickering oil lamps were placed at either end of the trestle on small tables, casting macabre shadows that seemed to dance across the walls and Tommy feared that he might pass out.

'Before I show her to you I must tell you that she has a very large bruise on her forehead,' the man said gently. Tommy was shaking like a leaf in the wind. The doctor then carefully drew the sheet away, revealing a young girl's face.

Tommy gasped as he stared down at her. Just as the man had told him, there was indeed a large bruise on her forehead but other than that she appeared to be unmarked. Her hair was still wet but that detail aside, she looked so very peaceful that she might just have been asleep. It was Daisy. All the strain that had shown in her face for the past months was gone and now she looked as she had used to before Pinnegar violated and abused her.

The doctor looked at Tommy and when the boy nodded, he respectfully replaced the sheet.

'I'm very sorry,' he sighed, 'but I have to ask you what state of mind was your sister in when she went out for her walk?'

Tommy gulped before saying, 'She wasn't looking forward to having the baby. It was forced on her, you see? But I'm sure she wouldn't have taken her own life. She would have known that

323

she couldn't be laid to rest with our mam an' dad in the churchyard if she did that, an' she always said that was where she wanted to be when the time came. Suicides aren't allowed to be buried in consecrated ground, are they?'

The man frowned. In circumstances such as this he should have requested an inquest, but seeing the young man's obvious distress, he answered cautiously, 'No, they're not....' Apart from the bruise on her forehead everything pointed to suicide – but then the bruise could have been caused when she hit the water, and her poor brother was so overcome with grief.

'I shall advise the coroner to record a verdict of accidental death,' he informed Tommy then, after making a hasty decision. 'And then at least she can be buried where she wished. She must have tripped and fallen into the water by accident. It's most tragic, a young girl like that with her whole life in front of her – and the baby too, of course.' A family man himself, he sighed at the waste of life.

Too numb even to cry, Tommy nodded. Yes, that must have been what had happened. He couldn't bear to think of his sister feeling so desperately unhappy that she'd actually killed herself and his unborn niece or nephew.

'The death certificate will be signed and then you can proceed with the necessary arrangements.'

'Th-thank you, sir.' Tommy put his hand out blindly as he groped his way back towards the door, leaning heavily on Sunday. Outside, one look at the two pale faces told the policemen all they needed to know, and after hearing the decision of accidental death, they fetched Jacob then led all three back to the waiting police cart.

'We'll take you home,' one of the officers said compassionately.

'Between you an' me I reckon the poor young lass *did* commit suicide,' he whispered to his colleague once they were seated at the front of the police cart and what he hoped was out of earshot of the three young people. 'I dare say the doctor took pity on her brother. At least this way the lass an' her child can rest in consecrated ground, God bless them both.'

The other policeman, who had a daughter the same age as Daisy, wiped away a tear before saying, 'Rumour has it that it was the master of the workhouse that got the girl in the family way. The guardians thought they had hushed it up but things have a habit of getting out, don't they? I don't mind telling you, at this moment in time, nothing would give me more satisfaction than to pummel that scoundrel into the ground. It's he should be being buried, not that young girl.'

The police were keeping a close eye on Albert Pinnegar at the moment, for everyone knew that he'd set himself up as a moneylender. Unfortunately, there was nothing illegal in that and until someone came forward to make a complaint they were powerless to stop him. But he'd watch him after today by God he would, the policeman vowed. The man had a lot to answer for.

The journey home was made in silence. Tommy appeared to be in shock and stared blankly ahead as Sunday sat shivering at the side of him.

Mrs Spooner and most of the household rushed into the hallway when they arrived home, and there was no need to say anything. The drowned girl was their Daisy.

Annie quickly made the sign of the cross on her chest as tears squeezed out of her eyes. 'Eeh, the poor little lass. An' that poor babby an' all.'

'Is there anything we can do for you?' asked one of the policemen who had escorted them home.

'Aye, you can, as it happens.' Beneath her paint and powder, Mrs Spooner was deathly pale and now the two spots of rouge on her cheeks made her look like a china doll. 'You could call into the undertakers and tell him that I'd like to see him at his earliest convenience.' She was leaning heavily on her stick. 'That lass is goin' to have the best send-off this town has ever seen. The finest coffin, a glass-sided hearse. An angel on her gravestone. That's all we can do for her and her little unborn baby now.'

'Right you are, ma'am. Consider it done.'

As they left, Annie took Tommy's arm and led him into the kitchen with Sunday and Jacob trailing behind.

'What you all need is a good strong cup o' tea wi' a nice tot o' brandy in it,' she said. 'Jacob, would yer fetch it fer me from the drawin' room? I'm sure the missus won't mind under the circumstances.'

'Of course.' Jacob shot off to do as he was told as Annie warmed the teapot feeling at a complete loss. There was absolutely nothing she could say that would make the situation any better.

Later that night, the five of them lit a candle and, after Jacob had said a prayer, they sat together for a while, each thinking of the gentle girl they would never see again.

Daisy was laid to rest in Chilvers Coton churchyard on a cold, grey day in a grave as close to her parents as Mrs Spooner could get her. Lady Huntley attended the funeral along with Mrs Lockett, and the Reverend Lockett did a particularly beautiful service for her that left not a dry eye in the congregation. Then Tommy stood at the side of the grave staring down at the fine mahogany coffin with the gleaming brass handles as he gripped Sunday's hand.

'I can't believe this is happening,' he whispered brokenly. 'I feel as if I'm trapped in a nightmare. I keep thinking I'm going to wake up and Daisy will be there smiling that sweet smile and caring for me as she always has.'

'I know,' Sunday answered as tears slid down her cheeks. Today was one of the very rare occasions when she couldn't prevent herself from crying.

It was to be a very long time before Tommy Branning could accept the finality of what had happened – that he was all alone in the world. Overnight had changed him from a boy into a young man.

As the mourners filed from the churchyard, Tommy and Sunday stayed behind for a few moments to say their last goodbyes, then Sunday set off for the lych-gate to give Tommy a final moment of privacy with his sister. It was as she was rounding the high church wall that she caught sight of someone lurking in the shadow of a tall yew tree. As she shielded her eyes from the drizzling rain and peered closer, she saw that it was Albert Pinnegar and her hands clenched into fists of rage. How dare he show his face here today?

As their eyes met, he walked towards her with a little sneer on his ugly face. 'What a shame,' he leered. 'Looks like I'm not going to be a papa after all.'

'One day you will answer for this,' Sunday said with absolute conviction, then she walked unhurriedly away, her head held high. When she paused to glance behind her he was gone as if he had never been there – and once again she knew that she must say nothing. Things were bad enough as they were without her adding to everyone's grief.

Back at the house Annie had laid on a feast fit for a king for any of the mourners who wished to return there, but the food might have been sawdust and Sunday found that everything stuck in her throat. Tommy sat in a trance-like state as Annie supplied everyone with a glass of sherry or something stronger if they fancied it.

Lady Huntley had come back to the house with them; she offered her condolences and accepted a glass of sherry. She knew that she would be in trouble with Ashley when she returned home. He had expressly forbidden her to attend the funeral, saying that it wasn't seemly for a woman in her condition to be seen abroad, but she had disobeyed him and was prepared to face the consequences later. All her efforts to get Tommy and Daisy out of the workhouse seemed pointless now and she could have wept at the loss of such a dear young girl, dead before her life had even begun. Tommy was clearly devastated and she wondered how he would ever get over it, and yet deep down she knew that he would. He had no choice, as she knew to her cost. Following the deaths of her babies she had been devastated too, but somehow she had managed to go on, with Zillah at her side, and Tommy too, was loved. Albert Pinnegar was a truly wicked man, and she trusted in God that one day he would be punished.

'You're looking well,' Mrs Spooner commented as they sat together. The old lady was dressed from head to toe in black and today, without her paint and powder, she looked every day of her age. It seemed so unfair to Biddy that she, who had led a long and full life, should still be there while Daisy, who was little more than a child, was dead and gone. She had become more than fond of the girl. Daisy's death had presented another problem too. The house was full now and thriving, thanks to Sunday, but how would the girl manage all the work on her own without Daisy to share the load?

'Thank you,' Lady Huntley answered politely as she felt her child move inside her. The little one was very lively today.

'There was something I wanted to ask you,' Mrs Spooner said then. 'But I'm not sure if today is the right time...' she ended uncertainly.

'Please go on,' Lavinia Huntley urged, taking the old woman's hand. She was clearly very upset.

'Well, the thing is, as you know, when Sunny suggested Daisy and Tommy should come here,

we filled the rest of the lodgers' rooms and between 'em, the young 'uns kept the place running
along smoothly. But now that Daisy's... Now it's
going to be an awful lot of work for Sunny on her
own, so I was wondering if–'

'If perhaps another girl from the workhouse
might take her place?' Lady Huntley finished for
her.

'I doubt if anyone could do that.' Mrs Spooner
dabbed at her eyes. 'But I'd like to think I could
give another little lass a chance.'

'Then leave it with me. Obviously I am not
attending the guardians' meetings at the moment
but I can certainly write to one of them and
suggest it.'

'Thank you.' Mrs Spooner had no more words
then as she stared off into space thinking of the
freshly dug grave they had just left in Coton
churchyard, of the poor little unborn innocent,
and of the loss that Daisy would be to all who
had known and loved her.

Chapter Thirty-Four

When they arrived back at Treetops Manor later
that afternoon, George helped Lady Huntley
down from the carriage and up the steps to the
front door, which was instantly opened by a little
maid who bobbed her knee respectfully.

'Please, ma'am,' she said as she took her mistress's hat and cloak, 'the master is in the library

and he asked me to tell you he wished to see you as soon as you got home.'

'Thank you, Alice.' All Lavinia really wanted to do right then was go to her room and rest for an hour. She hadn't expected Ashley to be in. It wasn't often that he graced them with his presence just lately, which suited her just fine. But she supposed she should go and see him.

After patting her hair into place in the gilt mirror she slowly waddled along to the library. The moment she opened the door she knew that he had been drinking. It was also clear that he was in a rage. She approached the fireside chair through a fog of blue smoke from the fine cigar he was smoking, sat down and said, 'You wished to see me?'

'Yes, I *damn* well did! Didn't I tell you not to risk our child's health by gallivanting about? Especially to the funeral of a bloody *maid!*'

'That "bloody maid" as you refer to her was badly mistreated,' she answered quietly. 'And I had every right to pay my last respects if I so wished.'

'And yet you were too tired to entertain my guests for dinner when I asked you last week,' he spat peevishly as he slopped yet more brandy into his glass from the decanter.

'Don't you think you've had enough of that?' she said unwisely and his chest swelled with anger. Slamming the glass down, he strode across to her.

Leaning down so that she could feel his breath on her cheek he ground out, *'I'll* say when I've had enough! You would do well to remember that *I* am the master in this house!'

'I need to rest, Ashley.' She was suddenly just too weary to argue and rose in ungainly fashion from the chair, causing his mouth to curl into a sneer.

'Look at you.' He shook his head in disgust. 'You're not fit to be seen abroad! What must people have thought?'

'I dare say all their thoughts were on the poor young soul who was being buried.' She made for the door but he stepped in her path, barring her way.

'And where do you think you're going? I haven't given you permission to leave yet.' It was becoming clearer by the minute that he was spoiling for a fight but she faced him calmly.

'I'm extremely tired and I'm going upstairs to lie down.' She had to almost push past him but he dogged her footsteps all across the hallway.

'Don't you *dare* walk away from me, Lavinia.' He was so close behind her that she feared he would stand on her skirts, but doing her best to ignore him she continued to climb the stairs – which only served to incense him all the more.

'Are you deaf?' he shouted then, causing a couple of the maids to come running. 'Get back downstairs *now* until I give you permission to leave the room, woman!'

Still she continued to ignore him, staring fixedly ahead, and suddenly with a roar, when she had almost reached the top of the stairs, he caught her arm and swung her about. The action was so unexpected that she lost her footing and the next moment she had the sensation of flying through the air as he looked on in horror. Someone screamed and then she hit the hard hall floor with a sickening thud … before darkness wrapped itself mercifully around her.

'It's much too soon!' … 'How long will that midwife be?' … 'Oh, my poor dear lamb.'

Lavinia was aware of a voice. It sounded like Zillah's but somehow she couldn't seem to open her eyes. She was on fire with pain and this time when the darkness again rolled over her she welcomed it and thankfully knew no more.

The doctor tutted as he hung over his patient.

'I'm afraid there is nothing I can do to prevent the birth now,' he told Zillah sadly. 'Labour has started.'

'But it's too soon – at least two months too soon,' the maid wailed. 'An' how will the poor soul bring it into the world if she's unconscious?' She wrung her hands in terror as she stared down at her mistress. Lavinia was the colour of wax and her lips had taken on a bluish tinge.

'Her arm is broken as well,' the doctor said as he continued with his examination. 'But that will have to wait until after the birth and then I can splint it. And in answer to your question, we can only do what we can do. The rest is in God's hands. Now fetch me hot water, lots of it, clean linen and towels, and then we must get her undressed and prepare her for the birth.'

Zillah skidded away to give instructions to the maids then hurried back up into the room to undo her mistress's clothing. It was like undressing a rag doll and tears slid down her cheeks as she was doing it. Oh, for this to go and happen now when everything had been proceeding so well. And all because of that swine's drinking! She would never forgive him for this – *never*. Especially if it cost the innocent child its life. He'd been rough with Lavinia before, of course, but never so violently as this. The house was as quiet as a grave for Ashley had collapsed in a drunken stupor and the staff were creeping about like shadows, afraid to do anything that might disturb their mistress. It was as if they were already mourning her and Zillah prayed that this wasn't an omen.

Over the next two hours she never left Lavinia's side. Occasionally the latter would wake and groan with the pain but before Zillah could offer her any comfort, unconsciousness would claim her again. *Even if it's another little lass I'll not let it go the way o' the others if God will only spare it,* Zillah thought as she continued to sponge her mistress's damp forehead. *I'll get Lavinia and the lass well away from here and hang the consequences. This time I refuse to do his biddin'!* On a few occasions, Ashley, who had roused himself and was pacing up and down on the landing, would hammer on the door to enquire how she was but each time Zillah sent him away with a flea in his ear. *Let him reflect on what he's done,* she thought and hoped that he was suffering all manner of guilt.

It soon became clear that Lavinia had developed a fever, which added to the doctor's concern. Her temperature had risen alarmingly and now he feared for both the mother and the child.

'We shall have to deliver this baby very soon otherwise we could lose both of them,' he warned

Zillah and she nodded. She was prepared to do anything to save Lavinia. The labour was progressing rapidly but with the mother unable to assist her child into the world, it was struggling.

Finally, the doctor made up his mind and, rolling up his sleeves, he told Zillah, 'Pass me that scalpel. The child's head is crowning but it keeps slipping back.'

Zillah took a deep breath before doing as she was asked, and offered up a silent prayer. And then the doctor was leaning over his patient and as Zillah gripped Lavinia's limp hand she closed her eyes tight. She couldn't bear to watch what he was doing.

After what seemed like a lifetime but what was actually only minutes, there was a slight gasping sound from Lavinia as the baby was expelled from her womb. Zillah stared down at the seemingly lifeless little body on the bed as the doctor said curtly, 'Take it, woman, and hold it upside down, for God's sake, while I try to stem this bleeding!'

Zillah hastily did as the doctor ordered and once the child was dangling she gave it a sharp slap on the backside. Nothing happened so she repeated the action and was rewarded with a mewling little cry.

'It's a boy,' she cried out as tears started to her eyes. 'She's got a little son.' But there was no time for rejoicing for the doctor was battling to save the mother now. At last the bleeding seemed to slow and Zillah let out a sigh of relief as she turned her attention back to the babe that was nestling in the crook of her arm. He was incredibly tiny and his lips, like his poor mother's, were blue.

'Get him into some warm water and keep massaging his chest,' the doctor told her. 'He's very early. Who knows if he'll survive.'

He will if I have anything to do with it, Zillah thought just as the bedroom door burst open. It was Ashley, and ignoring the still figure of his wife and the blood-stained sheets and towels, he barked, 'What is it?'

'You have your son, though the Lord knows if he'll survive.' Accusation shone in the woman's eyes but, ignoring it, he punched the air with delight.

'*A boy!* A son at last. I must get word to Mr Wilde!' He hadn't even looked at the child. Zillah felt sick with disgust as she lowered the tiny body into the bowl of warm water she had ready as Ashley turned on his heel and left.

The baby's skin was almost translucent, his breathing was shallow and there was not a single hair on his head – but then Zillah supposed this was because he had been born far too early. If this little mite survived, it would be a miracle. The clothes that had lovingly been laid ready for the past weeks almost swamped him when she had patted him dry and swaddled him, but by then thankfully the doctor was a lot happier with Lavinia.

'I've managed to stop the bleeding and she's delivered the afterbirth,' he told her. 'Now I'm going to stitch her up and set her arm, and the rest will be in the lap of the gods but there's a good chance she will recover. I think you will have to find a wet nurse for the child though. It's doubtful your mistress will be strong enough to feed him when she regains consciousness. And her milk may not come.'

'I know somebody who's just had a fine healthy girl,' Zillah told him. 'She's the sister of one of the maids here an' she lives not a stone's throw away in a cottage in Apple Pie Lane in Hartshill. I'm sure she'll help out if the master is prepared to pay her. I'll ask her if she'll move into the nursery with her own little lass, an' that way she'll be on hand to feed this little mite an' all.'

'Excellent.' The doctor nodded approvingly as he threaded a fearsome-looking needle, and after laying the baby in his crib Zillah hastened away to speak to the maid immediately.

When she got downstairs she found that Ashley had already despatched the groom with a note telling his late uncle's attorney of his son's birth.

'I shouldn't get too excited if I were you,' she said caustically. 'The poor little soul has been brought into the world far too early because of what you did, an' there's no sayin' he'll survive.'

'He *has* to!' Ashley told her, his eyes glinting dangerously. 'I'm planning a trip abroad and have put a deposit on a racehorse I've had my eye on for some time. Just fetch a nurse in or do whatever you have to. Money is no object now.'

'There are some things that money can't buy,' Zillah told him roundly. 'An' be you a beggar or a king if your card is marked an' it's your time to go then no amount o' money in the world can change it. It could be that you're about to lose you wife *an'* your child, an' if they do die then it'll be on your conscience. I just hope you'll be able to live wi' yourself.'

With that she went off to try and arrange with the maid for her sister to come and nurse the baby.

Molly Worthington arrived three hours later with her baby daughter and a bagful of clothes. Molly had readily agreed to act as a wet nurse for the Huntley baby. She was a sweet-natured young girl, with laughing brown eyes and springy dark hair, and little Marigold who was just three weeks old was the apple of her eye. Her husband had also happily agreed to the arrangement. Marigold was their first-born and as he only earned a meagre wage working on the railways in the nearby town of Atherstone, the money that Molly earned would come in very handy. She and Zillah talked as the latter was installing Molly in the nursery and it was arranged that Molly would visit her husband each evening after work in between the babies' feeds. Her husband was also welcome to visit Treetops Manor during any free time he had so, all in all, the first crisis was averted. Because of the baby's premature arrival, Lavinia hadn't as yet appointed a nanny but Molly assured Zillah that she was quite able to manage the two babies herself for the time being. In fact, she preferred it that way and so it was agreed.

Once Molly had settled her own daughter in the spare crib that had been placed in the nursery for her, the newborn was carried tenderly up to her. Molly frowned when she saw him. Next to her own plump, thriving baby he looked more like a little wizened-up old man but Zillah saw immediately that the tiny soul would have the best of care with young Molly and so she was content.

'He ain't even whimpered,' Zillah told her worriedly as Molly unfastened her blouse ready to feed him. 'Most babies would be screaming their heads off fer a feed by now.'

Molly gently laid the baby on her breast but saw immediately that this was not going to work. The baby's mouth was tiny whilst her nipple was swollen and engorged with milk but Molly wasn't going to let this stop her.

'Could you go down and see if they have a pap boat in the kitchen?' she asked as she rocked the baby to and fro. 'I can squeeze some milk into that then drip it into his mouth. At least that way we'll be able to get something inside him.'

'Bless you.' Zillah, who had been up since the crack of dawn the day before was almost dizzy now with tiredness but she was determined not to rest until she knew that the child had been fed.

'Does he have a name yet?' Molly asked an hour later. The baby had had his first feed but it had been a long, laborious job and even then she had only managed to get a few drops of milk into him. And now her own baby was stirring for a feed.

Zillah shook her head. 'Not yet, an' I'm just prayin' that his mammy will stay with us to give him one.'

'Then you get back to her,' Molly urged kindly. 'And don't get worrying about this little one. I shall feed him on the hour if need be.'

Zillah headed back to Lavinia's room with her mind slightly easier. Despite the fact that Molly had only just had her own baby she was the oldest of ten siblings, so was well used to caring for babies and children and Zillah felt that if this baby had a chance with anyone it would be with her.

Chapter Thirty-Five

'So that's what's been happening,' Cissie finished breathlessly. It was now three days since Lavinia Huntley had given birth and she had walked all the way to Whittleford Lodge to inform them of the news.

'I can't believe all this took place on the same day as poor Daisy's funeral,' Mrs Spooner said sombrely. 'We'll not be forgetting that day in a hurry, will we? But how are the mother and baby now?'

'Well, Lavinia has come round now but she's in a lot of pain so they're giving her laudanum to keep her semi-sedated. And the baby is in the nursery with Molly Worthington. Lady Huntley is too poorly to feed him herself, you see, so Molly is his wet nurse. He's only just about holdin' his own though, so I'm on my way to get the vicar to come. Mrs Lockett is Zillah's niece, as you know, so I've to tell them what's happened and ask the vicar if he'll come and christen the baby just in case … you know…'

'Is it as bad as that?' Sunday asked, and when Cissie nodded she sighed. It was heart-breaking to think that Lady Huntley had finally given birth to a live child and that he too, might soon be

340

snatched away from her.

'Zillah is so angry wi' the master she's almost spittin' feathers,' Cissie confided. 'He didn't actually push the mistress down the stairs admittedly, but if he hadn't grabbed her arm and startled her she wouldn't have lost her footing and fallen.' She blew out a breath. 'I tell you, the atmosphere at Treetops Manor is so thick you could cut it with a knife. The master ain't shown no remorse at all. In fact, he ain't been sober since the baby arrived. Talk about wet the baby's head! I reckon he could have drowned him, *and* he hasn't even been to see him properly yet either, which is another thing Zillah is fuming about. He obviously only cares about the money he will get from his uncle's estate now that he's produced a son. Trouble is, will the trust still pay out if owt happens to the baby?'

Mrs Spooner pursed her lips. 'Well, thank you for coming to keep us informed, Cissie. But now you get off and fetch Mrs Lockett and the vicar, and rest assured we'll all be prayin' for them both.' She herself took Cissie to the front door.

When the girl hesitated on the step, Mrs Spooner asked, 'Was there something else, pet?'

The girl shuffled from foot to foot uncomfortably before saying in a low voice, 'I thought you should know that there are a lot of rumours flying around the town … about Sunday.'

'Sunday?'

'Yes. People are saying that she's very free with her favours with various men. I know it's not true, o' course, but it'll really upset her if she gets to find out what's being said. We can both guess

341

who started the rumours though, can't we?'

'Pinnegar!' Mrs Spooner said immediately. Then, 'Look, let's keep this from her for the time being, shall we? There's no point in needlessly upsetting her.'

Cissie nodded in agreement then hurried away. Soon afterwards, the vicar and his wife drove her back to Treetops Manor in their cart with baby Phoebe gurgling happily on her mother's lap. Zillah fell onto her niece's shoulder and began to sob when they entered the house whilst Cissie showed the vicar up to the nursery.

His heart was wrenched with pity when he saw the baby. Molly was clearly doing all she could for him but he was like a tiny doll and the Reverend Edgar Lockett didn't hold out much hope for him at all. After unwrapping the small bottle of holy water he had brought with him he asked, 'Have his parents decided on a name for him yet?'

Molly had the answer ready. 'Yes. It will be Stephen and then Walter after the master's late uncle.' And so the vicar solemnly welcomed the child into the Church and blessed him before making the sign of the cross on his tiny forehead, all the time praying that the light of Jesus would shine on this little soul who was clinging to life.

When it was done he made his way to Lady Huntley's room to find his wife and her aunt sitting at Lavinia's bedside.

'Has she seen the baby yet?' he asked.

'No,' Zillah said. 'She's been in no fit state to. To be honest, I'm not at all sure she's even aware that she's given birth. As soon as she comes around she's in so much pain that we have to dose her up again, bless her.'

'And where is her husband, the child's father?'

'Huh!' Zillah's lips curled back from her teeth. 'That ne'er-do-well. Probably in some gin-house somewhere. It's all his fault that this has happened,' she ended bitterly.

'God is all-forgiving,' Edgar tried – but Zillah was having none of it.

'God may be but I ain't!' she declared emphatically, then looked embarrassed. He was a vicar, after all.

Verity smiled encouragingly at her aunt. 'Things will work out, you'll see,' she advised, then standing up she asked her husband, 'Are you ready, darling? This one will be screaming for her feed soon.'

Edgar stood up hastily. Phoebe might appear like a little angel but she had a right pair of lungs on her if she got hungry. It always amazed him how so loud a noise could come out of such a little person's mouth, although he wouldn't have changed a hair on her head.

'We'll be off then,' he said. 'But you know where we are should you need us, Zillah. And do please try to get some rest. You look almost as ill as Lavinia.'

'I'll rest when she's out o' the woods,' Zillah promised, then after kissing them all soundly on the cheek she sat back down at the side of the bed to continue her vigil as Cissie saw them out.

The mood was no happier in the Spooner residence and everyone was very concerned about

343

Tommy. He had not cried once since the day of his sister's funeral, nor had he said more than a word or two. He continued to work as hard as he ever had – harder, if anything – and Biddy Spooner was watching him closely.

The happy-go-lucky lad she had welcomed into her home had gone and in his place was a sullen, hard-faced stranger who seemed to be pushing himself to the limits.

'I'm worried about him, Annie,' she confided the day following Cissie's visit. 'If only he'd cry an' let all his hurt out I'm sure he'd feel better.'

'Everyone deals wi' grief in their own way,' Annie said. 'Perhaps he's best left alone at present.'

'And then there's Sunny,' Biddy went on as she fingered the black velvet choker around her lined neck. 'She's doin' the work o' two now that Daisy's gone. The poor lass looks fair worn out. I'd asked Lady Huntley to see if there was someone from the workhouse who could take over Daisy's work but it could be weeks afore she's well enough to do that now.'

'That's soon sorted,' Annie answered, straining tea into two china cups. 'I'll pop down an' see our Verity. She'll go an' enquire at the workhouse fer us.'

'What a good idea – I hadn't thought o' that,' Biddy said. 'It makes you wonder what we've all done wrong to have all this heartache,' she added gloomily. 'Talk about killin' a robin, I reckon we must have killed a whole family of 'em!'

'Rubbish.' Annie wasn't in the least superstitious. 'It ain't got nothin' to do wi' robins. It's life – an' there ain't none of us can change what's round the corner.'

'Happen you're right.' Biddy took her cup and the old friends sat in silence as they drank their tea.

The mood at Whittleford Lodge lifted slightly the following week when Mrs Lockett called to tell them that she'd arranged for a girl to come and help out from the workhouse.

'She's thirteen and the new matron assures me she's a good little worker,' Verity told Mrs Spooner. 'Her name is Nell and she's been in the workhouse since she was five, following the death of her parents. I've met her and she seems very nice and all of a flutter at the thought that you might take her. She remembers Sunday used to be kind to her. And Daisy too, bless her soul. The only thing is, she's a little bit ... er ... slow, if you get my meaning, so what do you think? I could fetch her tomorrow for you if you think she'll be suitable and you're prepared to give her a trial?'

'So long as she takes some o' the work off Sunny I ain't bothered if she's slow, so thank goodness for that.' Mrs Spooner nodded her approval. 'Poor Sunny is runnin' herself ragged. The sooner the better, that's what I say.'

And so the following day Nell was duly delivered to the Spooner residence and everyone took to her straight away. She was quite a shy little thing and spoke very rarely, but she was a good worker for all that and Sunday was so pleased to have her there. She had cleaned out and prepared the last spare room up in the servants' quarters for her; it didn't seem right to put the new girl in Daisy's room somehow and she had a feeling that Tommy

345

wouldn't have liked it. The room was still just as Daisy had left it and although Sunday had offered to clear it for him he obstinately refused to let her touch a thing. She often found him sitting in there when she went to bed and guessed that this was the only place he could feel close to his sister any more so wisely didn't comment on it. *He'll do it when he feels ready*, she told herself and sympathised with him, for she too missed Daisy's laughter, the little chats they used to have and her cheeky smile, and still found it hard to believe that she would never see her dear friend again.

On the same day that Nell arrived at Mrs Spooner's, up at Treetops Manor, Lavinia Huntley finally met her son for the first time.

Zillah had been gradually weaning her off the laudanum, lessening the doses each day, and on that particular morning when Lavinia awoke she stroked her stomach and asked groggily, 'Have I had my baby?'

'You most certainly have, pet,' Zillah told her as a sob of relief caught in her throat. It was the first lucid thing Lavinia had said for days, and although she was stick-thin and pale as a ghost she looked better than she had. 'You gave birth to a little boy, an' a right bonny little thing he is an' all.'

Lavinia's eyes fluttered open. 'A-and he's alive?' she croaked.

Zillah nodded as she tenderly brushed a lock of hair from her mistress's forehead. 'Yes, he is. He's up in the nursery with young Molly Worthington. She's been feeding him while you've been ill.'

'Ill?' Lavinia frowned and tried to pull herself up on the pillows before Zillah could stop her – and as pain shafted through her broken arm everything came flooding back and she winced. 'I – I was on the stairs ... Ashley was angry with me ... and that's the last I remember.'

'You had a nasty fall and that's why the baby came early,' Zillah explained gently.

A tear trickled from the corner of Lavinia's eye as she breathed, 'I have a son – I can hardly believe it. But is he all right? Bring him to me, Zillah?' She became agitated.

'As soon as we've got you washed and you've had something to eat I'll bring him down to you,' Zillah promised.

Later that morning Zillah went up to the nursery and fetched Lavinia's son down to meet his mother. She would never forget the look on her mistress's beloved face for as long as she lived, for it glowed with an inner light at the sight of him, even though she was still in considerable pain.

Zillah carefully lowered the baby into his mother's one good arm while Lavinia stared at him in awe.

'He's so perfect – but so tiny,' she breathed fearfully. She couldn't bear the thought of losing him now.

'Now don't start worriting,' Zillah mock-scolded. 'He's small, admittedly, because he was born so early but Molly is doing a champion job with him, bless her. She couldn't do more for him if he were her own and she's feeding him on the hour even through the night. The poor lass looks fair worn out but she's determined that he's going to survive. He looks better already, even the doctor said so.' Zillah remembered how the doctor had struggled to save them both when the baby was born. The poor man was no doubt remembering the three death certificates he had signed. At least he hadn't had to do that this time!

'Ashley must be pleased,' Lavinia said bitterly. 'I dare say he's already informed the lawyers.'

'I dare say he has,' Zillah answered non-committally. The last thing she wanted at present was for Lavinia to go upsetting herself. She had come through the worst but she was still very weak and had a fair way to go.

Lavinia focused her attention on her son then and kissed his tiny bald head. At that moment he opened his eyes and blinked up at her and she felt a rush of pure, protective love, the like of which she had never experienced before. She breathed in the sweet baby smell of him and tears of joy blinded her. This was the magical moment she had waited for all her life. Already she was looking into the future and picturing him handing her flowers at the Mothering Sunday service in the church when he was big enough. Then never again would she have to watch enviously as the other mothers accepted their offsprings' bouquets. Now she had a child of her very own, a live child to love and bring up ... and it was the best feeling in the whole wide world.

It was as Nell was cleaning the front doorstep one bright spring morning that a gentleman approached her to ask, 'Do you have any eggs for sale?'

Nell glanced up with a polite smile on her face but it died instantly when she recognised the former workhouse master. 'Tommy keeps chickens but I don't reckon he sells the eggs,' she answered timidly. 'I-I'll go an' ask him, shall I?'

Pinnegar nodded, and rising from her knees Nell fled down the hallway to almost collide with Mrs Spooner, who was just leaving the drawing room.

'Hold yer horses, gel. Is there a fire or sommat?'

'It's Mr Pinnegar from the workhouse,' Nell gasped in a panic. 'He's at the front door askin' if yer sell eggs.'

'*Is* he now?' Mrs Spooner's eyes turned into chips of ice. How dare that creature come near or by her house after what he had done to Cissie and Daisy! 'Right, you just leave him to me, lass.'

'Good morning, ma'am.' Pinnegar swept his hat off and gave a little bow when she appeared in the doorway. 'And what a beautiful morning it is. I was wondering if you had any eggs for sale?'

'An' how would you know that we kept chickens?' she asked suspiciously.

'I happened to see the young man that works for you purchasing some in the market one day. I know him, you see. I was–'

'I know exactly who you are,' Mrs Spooner said contemptuously. 'An' if you ever have the nerve to come to my door again you'll get eggs all right – shoved right up your arse! Now clear off wi' you afore I call a bobby!'

Just as she was about to close the door he stuck his leg out and stopped her, and now his face was ugly as he asked, 'And how is the Small girl

349

doing? Are you aware of her reputation? She's a little whore, did you but know it; she'll drop her drawers for any man. Can't get enough of–'

'Clear off, I said, an' wash yer mouth out wi' carbolic soap while yer at it, yer lyin' toerag!'

She slammed the door then, regardless of the fact that his leg was in the way. Yelping with pain, he stepped back, upsetting the bucket of water that Nell had left on the step; and it overturned with a clatter, soaking his trousers and shoes.

Biddy felt her heart slow to a steadier rhythm as she heard him curse. 'Serves yer right,' she shouted through the door. 'Now bugger off!'

When she turned, she found Sunday and Nell staring at her with their hands across their mouths to conceal their dismay.

'There!' she said with a loud sniff. 'That told him. Now get on, the pair o' yer. I don't pay you to stand about.'

'What he said – it isn't true,' Sunday said, her face pale with shock. Then she burst out, 'I don't think he's ever going to leave me alone!'

The woman waved her hand at her. 'He'll leave you alone all right else he'll have me to answer to,' she snapped. 'And o' course I know it ain't true. Put it from your mind. He's a lyin', horrible little toad!'

Sunday and Nell turned and hurried away to do as they were told, but Sunday was deeply troubled. When would Pinnegar finally give up and leave her in peace?

Chapter Thirty-Six

The March winds gave way to April showers and suddenly the world began to come back to life after the long, cold winter. Things were slowly returning to some sort of normality in the Spooner household. Tommy was still morose and withdrawn and they all missed Daisy dreadfully, but as Annie had told them, 'Life goes on.'

Whenever they had any spare time, Sunday would take Nell on rambles through the woods in Hartshill on their way to visit Cissie and Lady Huntley. Beneath the canopy of trees, the floor was a never-ending carpet of bluebells, and above them the soft green buds were unfurling in the spring sunshine. The blossom on the hawthorns was in full, scented bloom, and primroses and daffodils peeped from beneath the hedges. Often, the girls would pick a bunch to lay on Daisy's grave.

Lady Huntley's baby was holding his own although he could hardly have been described as thriving, but then as Zillah pointed out, he had a lot of catching up to do and they were all just grateful that he was still with them. They dreaded to think how it would affect his mother, who totally doted on him, if she should lose him now. Lady Huntley's arm was healing nicely and her many bruises had faded to a dull yellow but she was still not back to full health and Zillah fussed over her non-stop. Molly had proved to be a godsend, and between feeds she ensured that the baby spent as much time as he could with his mother. Little had been seen of Ashley since his son's birth. Mr Wilde had bestowed his first advance on him and ever since then Ashley had been out, squandering his new wealth.

'So where's his lordship now?' Zillah asked one day as she put away the clean laundry in Lavinia's tallboy.

'As far as I know he's visiting friends in London,' Lavinia answered carelessly.

'Huh! After waitin' so long fer a son I'd have thought he'd want to spend a bit o' time wi' him,' Zillah huffed.

Lavinia smiled. She was well enough to get up and sit by the window for a breath of fresh air each day now. 'I think we both know that for Ashley, having Stephen was only a means to an end,' she said. 'Now that his uncle's money is being disbursed, I doubt we'll see much of him at all – and to be honest, Zillah, that suits me just fine.'

It struck Zillah just how much things had changed. There had been a time when Lavinia had worshipped the very ground her husband walked on, but the scales had long since fallen from her eyes. Today, she saw him for exactly what he was. A selfish, narcissistic man who cared for no one but himself.

Lavinia took a sip of the coffee that the maid had just fetched for her and added, 'I'm hoping that when he does come back he'll stay in his own room. He has a son now so there's no need for him to bother me at all any more, is there?'

Zillah agreed but she still thought it was a crying shame that her lovely mistress, who was still so young and pretty, should be trapped in a loveless marriage. But then saying that, now that Lavinia had her longed-for baby, she seemed happier than she had for some long time. Only the night before, she had chattered on to Zillah about the future and the things she planned to do with her son when he was older. 'I shall buy him a little pony and get George to teach him to ride,' she had said, excitement shining in her eyes. 'And I'll get him a home tutor so that he doesn't have to go away to school. I don't think I could bear to see him only during school holidays. We shall go to church together every Sunday and in the summer we'll go for picnics.'

It had pleased Zillah to hear her making plans although she was still fearful of the baby's health. Over the last couple of weeks, he had lost his wrinkled appearance and had gained a tiny bit of weight thanks to Molly's constant care, but he was still very fragile.

'I suppose I really ought to think about trying to find a nanny again,' Lavinia mused as she stared out at the gardens. 'Molly won't be here for ever; she has her own life to go back to when Stephen is older but I haven't felt that any of the women who applied for the post were right.'

'Ah, now me and Mrs Roundtree have had our heads together about that,' Zillah interrupted then, 'an' I reckon we might just 'ave come up with the perfect solution.'

'Really?' Lavinia stared at her.

'Really.' Zillah's head bobbed. 'Yer see, the thing is, young Cissie has taken a rare shine to little Stephen. She pops up to see him an' Molly to collect the dirty laundry, an' Mrs Roundtree noticed how good she is with him. Now I know she's employed to work in the laundry, but to my way o' thinkin' it will be a lot easier to find another laundry maid than it will to find a nanny you can trust. Mrs Roundtree agrees – but what do *you* think of the idea?'

Lavinia blinked with surprise. This suggestion had come completely out of the blue and she needed time to think about it. 'We ... ell, I suppose I could consider it. But how do you know that Cissie would want to take on the responsibility?'

'I *don't* know,' Zillah admitted. 'It's just an idea at present but I reckon she'd be perfect. We know she's trustworthy an' kind, an' after havin' her own baby snatched away from her, I've no doubt she'd adore lookin' after the little master. But come on now, Mrs Lockett is due to call in today so let's get you dressed an' lookin' presentable, shall we?'

Lavinia submitted to Zillah's fussing but her mind was busy. What had been suggested actually made a lot of sense. She would far sooner let someone she knew and trusted help care for her baby than a stranger. Perhaps she would talk it over with Verity when she arrived?

The vicar's wife was all in favour of the idea when it was put to her.

'I've known Cissie for years,' she told Lavinia, 'and I would certainly trust her with my Phoebe.'

354

They went on to speak of other things then and during the course of the conversation, Sunday's name cropped up.

'Between you and me, I think she's feeling a bit scared,' Verity Lockett confided. 'It seems that Mr Pinnegar has been seen in the vicinity of Mrs Spooner's house quite often lately. Also, she has reason to believe that he has been spreading malicious rumours about her virtue. Certain men have propositioned her and been disrespectful when she goes out as a result. And every time that Pinnegar shows his face anywhere near the house, it also unnerves young Nell no end. As you may know, Nell is ... "a little slow", but she's a lovely girl. Sunday thinks the world of her and wants to protect her. After all, what reason does he have to be hanging about in their neck of the woods unless he's up to no good?'

'Perhaps he's debt collecting in that area?' Lavinia suggested as she planted a gentle kiss on Stephen's still bald little head.

'Oh no.' Verity's head wagged from side-to-side. 'He has men to do the dirty work for him by all accounts and it's God help anyone who doesn't pay up on time.'

'So why aren't the constables involved? And couldn't Sunday report him for spreading lies about her?'

'Apparently there's no law against loaning money out and I dare say if anyone is injured they can't trace it back to him. As for Sunday telling them about the lies, she has no proof of that, has she?'

'He'll trip himself up eventually,' Lavinia said

355

with certainty. 'His sort always does. Look what happened to him once it became known what he was doing to young girls at the workhouse.'

'I suppose you're right, and the sooner the better as far as I'm concerned. But how are Sunday and Tommy doing now? It was such a blow for them to lose young Daisy like that.'

'Sunday seems to be coping but Tommy is not faring so well,' Verity told her as she took Stephen from his adoring mother for a cuddle. Zillah had whisked her great-niece off to the kitchen to show her off to the rest of the staff.

'The poor lad, it must be hard for him to come to terms with it, especially after losing his parents. He's all alone in the world now,' Lavinia answered sadly. 'And, of course, Jacob is down in the dumps too from what I hear from Cissie. He no longer walks out with that young lady called Rebecca, and she's been causing trouble, so I hear.'

'I tend to think it's fortunate that they are no longer together,' Verity commented. 'Miss Rebecca Moreton is not a pleasant young lady and I disliked the way she spoke to Sunday. But at least things are looking up for the people in the workhouse now. The meals have improved and the atmosphere there seems so much better now. The shadow of fear and the bullying have gone. I heard tell that the new matron snapped Miss Frost's split cane right in two and threw it out with the rubbish, thank goodness. And once you're recovered from Stephen's birth, my dear Lavinia, we can continue to try and improve things still further there. I was going to suggest some new bedding for everyone; do you agree? The blankets they use now are completely inadequate and, frankly, could do with burning.'

Stephen began to mew like a little kitten then, ending the conversation before it could go any further and, seconds later, as if by magic, Molly appeared.

'Ah, I thought he might be gettin' ready for a feed,' she said good-naturedly. 'Shall I take him, ma'am?'

'Please, Molly, but would you bring him back when he's been fed?' It still hurt Lavinia that she hadn't been able to feed him herself although she was very grateful to Molly for stepping in. Goodness knows what her little man would have done without her.

'Of course,' Molly answered cheerily. 'Though I may be some time. He's still being drip fed although I'm hoping in a couple of weeks' time he may be able to take to the breast.'

Verity handed the baby over reluctantly and once Molly had left the room she lowered her voice and told Lavinia, 'I haven't said anything to Edgar yet until I'm absolutely sure, but I think we may be expecting another happy event in the not too distant future.'

'Why, that's wonderful!' Lavinia was genuinely pleased for her. 'I suppose you'd like a boy this time?'

'A boy would be nice,' Verity admitted. 'Phoebe would have a little brother then and Stephen would have a little friend, but I don't really mind what it is so long as the baby is healthy. I don't think Edgar would mind either.'

Now that she had told her, Lavinia noticed that

her friend did seem to have a certain glow about her and she felt envious. Edgar clearly adored his wife and little daughter and they were everything Lavinia felt a close-knit family should be. But then she scolded herself; after all, she did have her own little son now and although it was highly unlikely she would ever have any more children she would always thank God for him.

Zillah returned soon afterwards, nestling Phoebe to her and smiling like a Cheshire cat. 'They all think she's adorable an' o' course they're right,' she said proudly.

'Yes, well, you won't think that in a minute if I don't get her home in time for her feed,' Verity smiled. 'I'm telling you now, this little madam has a cry that could frighten the devil himself.'

When she had taken her leave, Lavinia told Zillah, 'I mentioned your idea about Cissie taking on the role of nanny to Verity and she thought it was an excellent notion – so perhaps you could ask Cissie to come and see me this evening when she's finished in the laundry?'

'Very well, I will – but now it's time you put your feet up for an hour,' Zillah said bossily. 'You might be on the mend but you've still got a long way to go so we don't want you overdoin' it, now do we?'

'I suppose you're right,' Lavinia agreed peevishly as Zillah helped her off with her dress and loosened her stays. She was tired of being an invalid now and just wanted to get better so that she could take her new little son out and about with her and start showing him off, as Verity did with her Phoebe.

As Sunday was strolling between the market stalls that afternoon she spotted a figure ahead of her that looked vaguely familiar. The woman stopped to examine some bruised fruit that was for sale on the end of one stall and Sunday's breath caught in her throat. It was Miss Frost, but she looked nothing like the former martinet who had once been able to strike terror into the hearts of every child in the workhouse. She appeared to have shrunk in size and had aged at least ten years since the last time Sunday had seen her. Her dress was creased and stained and a grubby shawl was wrapped about her thin shoulders. But her eyes when they turned and saw Sunday were exactly the same – cold, and unforgiving.

As Sunday approached her she drew herself up to her full height and stuck her chin in the air. 'Well? How are you faring, Small?'

Sunday would have liked to ask her the very same question but instead she answered politely, 'Very well, thank you – and yourself?'

She no longer had to bow and scrape to the woman and spoke to her on a level.

'Oh, not so badly. I left the workhouse as you might have heard. I have a room that I rent now and I'm enjoying my retirement.'

Miss Frost deliberately didn't inform Sunday that the room she rented was in one of the crowded courtyards off Abbey Street, which she shared with rats and cockroaches, or that she was now reduced to searching the stalls for the cheapest items that no one else wanted. She still had her pride if nothing else.

'I'm pleased to hear it. But now I should be getting along. Good day, Miss Frost.'

As the woman turned away, Sunday moved on. *How the mighty are fallen,* she found herself thinking. Had Miss Frost been anyone else she might have felt sorry for her, but as things were she could only remember the times the woman had shut her away in the darkness in the punishment room and the way she had always delighted in finding the worst jobs for her to do, and her heart hardened.

Two hours passed before she was ready to set off for home with her basket laden. Unknown to her she was being spied on from the shadows of a shop doorway by Albert Pinnegar. He had two of his men watching her comings and goings too, and was well acquainted with her routine now. Each Wednesday he would wait for a sight of her, his feelings flitting, as ever, from lust to hatred. She was like a magnet to him and each week his need to possess her and punish her grew greater. But she was still little more than a child, and in order to avoid any more trouble, the man knew he would have to bide his time. Meanwhile, he took pleasure in spreading salacious rumours.

Blissfully unaware of any danger, Sunday went on her way. Before she was halfway home she was sweating profusely. After crossing the Cock and Bear Bridge she paused at the side of the canal that ran beneath it to roll up her sleeves and undo the top two buttons on her dress before resuming her journey. She arrived home to find Annie in a tizzy and Mrs Spooner pacing agitatedly up and down the hall.

'What's wrong?' She dropped the heavy basket onto the table and flexed her aching arms as she looked from one to the other of them.

Annie shoved a piece of paper towards her and ordered, 'Read that!'

Sunday sank down onto the nearest chair to do as she was told as Annie wrung her hands.

Dear all,

I'm so sorry to let you all down but I've decided to go away for a while. It's not been easy for me here since Daisy died. I seem to see her everywhere and now that she's gone there's really nothing to keep me at the Lodge. At this point Sunday's hand flew to her mouth and she gasped with dismay and hurt. *I haven't decided what I'm going to do yet. Perhaps I'll train to be a carpenter or go to sea for a while, but whatever I decide, don't worry about me. I have enough money saved to see me all right for some time and I promise I will come back to visit you all one day. I know that you'll be able to replace me with someone from the workhouse, so it will give another youngster a chance. Sunday, make sure that the animals are fed, please, and Mrs Spooner, thank you for all you did for me and my sister. I will never forget it. I hope you'll understand.*

Yours affectionately,

Tommy

As the note fluttered from her hand, Sunday

361

stared ahead in shock.

'I'm so sorry, lass,' Annie muttered. 'We'll all miss him but you more than anyone.'

'I'll survive,' Sunday said past the lump in her throat and rising, she went out to check on the animals. She was feeling utterly bereft but she had become adept at hiding her feelings. She remembered how, as a child, she had been able to convince herself that one day the mother who had abandoned her would return and they would have a joyful reunion, but now she knew that this was never going to happen. She'd found solace in her friendship with Daisy and Tommy. And now they'd both left her. She had begun to wonder if she would ever have anyone to call her own; perhaps a happy-ever-after ending wasn't for the likes of her? Only time would tell. For now, she had to reconcile herself to losing yet another person for whom she had cared.

Chapter Thirty-Seven

For the first few weeks after Tommy had left, Sunday waited for the postman each day, hoping for some word from him, but as the weeks passed she had to accept that he wasn't going to get in touch, not yet at least, and she could only pray that wherever he was, he was safe. Eventually, Michael Lomax, or Mickey as he was known, joined the Spooner household to take Tommy's place. He had lived in the workhouse since the age of two when his grandmother had died and like Tommy, Daisy and Sunday before him he thought he had died and gone to heaven to land in such a happy house. Mickey was almost the same age as Sunday, and as Mrs Lockett had warned them before she introduced him to them, he was painfully shy. On the day she fetched him home it became apparent why. Mickey's skin was the colour of warm molasses, his eyes were so dark they were almost black, and his hair was a mass of tight ebony ringlets.

Micky was clearly self-conscious about his colour and they all noticed that when he spoke to them or answered them, he tended to keep his head down and not meet their eyes. Sunday and Mrs Spooner wondered if this was because of the couples who had sometimes visited the workhouse with a view to giving one of the children there a home. They had always refused to even consider Mickey because of the colour of his skin and eventually he had given up hoping that one day he might be a part of a loving family. But Mickey was a very attractive young man and from the second he arrived, Nell followed him about adoringly. Suddenly she was taking more pride in her appearance and Mrs Spooner remarked on it one day to Annie when the youngsters were both outside.

'I reckon young Nell has taken a shine to Mickey.'

Annie chuckled as she kneaded the dough for a new batch of bread. Mrs Spooner had popped into the kitchen for a chat while the house was quiet. 'You can say that again, bless her. Why,

363

she's almost a different person when Mickey's about. Have yer seen the way her eyes light up when he walks into a room?'

'Yes, I have, and between you and me I don't think she's the only one who is love-struck.' In truth, Annie had been shocked too, when she first met Mickey. Black people were a rarity in Nuneaton and she wasn't sure that he'd fit in there. However, Mrs Spooner had soon persuaded her to at least give the lad a trial and now she was glad that she had. He was a hard-working young man, she couldn't deny it. As Mrs Spooner had sternly pointed out when she voiced her hesitation, 'Happen his blood is the same colour as ours, an' when I was livin' in Jamaica I found out the colour of his skin won't wipe off on the towels neither!' After the time she had spent in the West Indies with her husband she was used to black people.

Suitably chastised, Annie had agreed he might stay.

Now, when Annie raised a questioning eyebrow, Biddy Spooner grinned. 'Ain't yer noticed the way our Jacob watches Sunny lately?'

Annie's mouth dropped open. 'Jacob? an' Sunday? No!'

'Why not?' Mrs Spooner shrugged. 'She is almost fifteen now and she's turning into a very pretty young woman.'

'Hmm, I dare say yer right,' Annie answered. 'After all, I were married when I were only a few months older than that, so I dare say he could be lookin' at her through different eyes. But how would you feel about that? I mean, I know yer like her but I thought you'd set your sights on Jacob marryin' someone who came from money, like that Rebecca he were walkin' out wi' fer a time.'

'Oh, *that* little minx! I had no time for her,' Mrs Spooner said roundly. 'I didn't like the way she looked down on our Sunny – on all of us, if it came to that. No, I reckon if Jacob has set his cap at Sunny I'd be more than happy. After all, we know her now, don't we? An' although we have no idea where she came from, she's turned out to be a little gem. Why, this place is earnin' more now than it has for years and I've her to thank for that. She certainly isn't afraid o' hard work.'

'That's true,' Annie agreed. 'But don't get buildin' yer hopes up, mind, an' start match-makin'. What will be will be – wi'out any help from you, woman.'

Mrs Spooner gave a wicked grin before hobbling off to the drawing room. 'We'll see,' she said over her shoulder and Annie laughed as she turned her attention back to what she had been doing.

Mickey settled into his new role remarkably quickly. Like Tommy before him, he adored working with the animals and he enjoyed doing the gardening and odd jobs too, so all in all in no time the house was running in a well-organised way again although everyone missed Tommy and Daisy.

The summer passed a little sadly but fairly uneventfully. Admittedly little Nell got upset from time to time when she saw Albert Pinnegar lurking nearby, silently watching the comings and goings at the house, but he never came to the door again and as Mrs Spooner pointed out, they couldn't summon the constable to him just because he was passing by. Sometimes, Jacob went out and sent him on his way, getting a mouthful of abuse for his trouble, but Pinnegar never actually threatened violence to him. Meanwhile, Sunday worked hard and the lodging house was thriving.

In late July, Mickey went to the cattle market to choose a small pony for Mrs Spooner. Sunday accompanied him and that day she got her first glimpse of the prejudice the lad had been forced to endure. As they strolled amongst the pens of animals, some people stepped away from Mickey as if by being in close contact with him they might become tainted, while others sneered and one man – one of Pinnegar's hangers on, Sunday realised – even spat at his feet. She was horrified. Mickey was one of the gentlest souls she had ever met and she placed her arm through his in defiance and glared at anyone who looked askance at him.

Throughout it all Mickey hung his head in shame and Sunday became more and more irritated.

'Hold your head up and stare back at them,' she instructed in a hiss.

'It would do no good. They don't like me because my skin is dark,' he answered miserably.

'So what?' Sunday was really annoyed now. 'What difference does it make? You're still a person and no one should be treated like this.'

When Mickey didn't answer she grabbed his

366

arm and hustled him out of the town towards the River Anker.

'We can talk there, it will be quieter,' she told him and he went without argument. Sinking onto a bench near the water, she pulled him down beside her.

'You have to learn to stand up for yourself,' she told him firmly. 'I learned that a long time ago. The weaker people think you are, the more they will pick on you.'

'But I'm different, neither one thing nor the other,' he tried to explain. 'My mother lived in London and she fell in love with a docker there. He was a black African man and soon she found out that she was having a child. When she told him, he conveniently disappeared so my mother had no choice but to come home to *her* mother with her tail between her legs. Can you imagine what people must have said when I was born? Thankfully my grandmother was a strong woman who wouldn't take any nonsense from anybody, but my poor mother died giving birth to me. Perhaps that was her punishment for having an illegitimate child – and a black one at that?' He rubbed a hand over his face. 'Anyway, my grandmother cared for me then until she died too, when I was just a nipper and that's when I was taken into the workhouse. I can still remember her clearly.' He swallowed, then concluded: 'The rest you know. The people who sometimes came to the workhouse looking for a child to offer a home to never considered me. I'm half white and half black, you see. What they call half-caste.'

'I like the colour of your skin. And at least you

367

know who your parents were and that your mother and your granny wanted you.' Sunday sighed. 'I have no idea where I came from. I was dumped on the workhouse steps the day I was born, so I dare say I'm illegitimate too. But I won't let it spoil my life, I'm telling you and you mustn't let it spoil yours, Mickey. No matter what colour your skin is you're a person and a good person, so start to stand up for yourself, do you hear me?'

With his liquid dark eyes looking dangerously shiny, Micky sniffed and nodded as Sunday rose and said, 'Now let's go and buy that pony, shall we? And remember to stare them right back in the eyes.'

With their arms linked together, the two youngsters set off again, and before too long they had got what they had come for.

The pony was a placid animal recently retired from the pit and destined for the knacker's yard until Mickey rescued him. 'I think we should call him Treacle,' he told Sunday as they led the pony home.

'It does suit him but let's wait and see what Mrs Spooner thinks, eh? He is her pony, after all.'

As it happened the old lady thought it was a splendid name and she fell in love with the gentle creature on sight. He was brown and white with soft brown eyes and suddenly Mrs Spooner was off out, here, there and everywhere in the cart that Mickey had restored to its former glory. The little pony had given her a new lease of life and was quickly spoiled by all of them.

Before they knew it they were into September

and the weather began to change. The nights drew in, and once again the fires needed to be lit in the mornings each day, a job that Nell and Mickey took their turns doing.

On one particular Monday when low grey clouds were scudding across the sky, Nell and Sunday entered the kitchen in the late afternoon after finishing the laundry between them. Sunday was now quite capable of cooking all the meals yet still Annie turned up as regular as clockwork to help out, especially with the evening meal. She had discovered quite quickly that retirement, especially without Daisy and a bairn to care for, could be quite lonely and she enjoyed the hustle and bustle at the house.

'Ah, here you are, lass,' Annie addressed Sunday the instant she set foot through the door. 'Take this through to the dinin' room fer me, would yer?'

Sunday frowned at the covered dish Annie was holding out to her. The lodgers didn't usually dine for at least another hour.

She held her hands out to oblige but Annie then told her impatiently, 'Take yer apron off an' tidy yer hair first, can't yer, gel?'

That was odd. Annie wasn't normally so fussy but the girl supposed she'd better oblige her so she quickly did as she was told, carelessly running her lingers through her hair.

Nell and Mickey were looking on and Sunday noticed that even Mickey was grinning.

'What's going on?' she asked warily and Annie scowled at the two young people and flapped her hand at her.

'Never you mind. Now just get through to the dining room and do as you're told for once!'

Sunday took the dish and set off, then as she pushed the dining-room door open, she gasped in amazement. All the lodgers were there with Mrs Spooner as well as Jacob, Mrs Lockett and Lady Huntley. Even Zillah was there, smiling at her. Cissie would have come too, she found out later, but she was back at Treetops Manor helping Molly with the two babies. A little dig in the back propelled her into the room and she was aware that Mickey, Annie and Nell were close behind her too.

Completely bewildered as to what was going on, she stood there with her mouth hanging slackly open as they all burst into song.

'Happy Birthday to you, Happy Birthday to you...'

'Oh! But how did you know?' she gasped as colour tinted her cheeks.

Lady Huntley giggled. 'I was the one who had to sign your release papers when you left the workhouse, if you remember, and your date of birth is on there. Mrs Spooner felt it might be nice to mark the occasion with a little party, seeing as you're fifteen today.'

'Oh!' Sunday was speechless for one of the very few times in her life as she gazed at the table that was laden with fancy treats. Now she suddenly realised why Annie had been sending her off on errands and doing her best to keep her out of the kitchen and the larder for the last couple of days – she had been preparing all this. No one had ever done anything like this for her before and the girl wondered why it was always so much harder to hold back tears when someone showed her an act of kindness than when they treated her unkindly.

Chapter Thirty-Eight

Within minutes the party was in full swing and Sunday was thoroughly enjoying herself. Miss Bailey was belting out a tune on the piano and Annie was hurrying about sloshing gin into anyone's glass who would stand still for long enough.

Jacob was particularly attentive and made sure that Sunday's plate was kept full until she had eaten so much that she was sure she would burst.

Eventually Sunday collapsed onto the sofa next to Lady Huntley who was looking distracted.

'A penny for them?' Sunday said brightly and the woman started.

'Oh, sorry, my dear. I was miles away.' She sipped at her drink, a rather nice sherry that Mrs Spooner kept in for special occasions, and confided, 'I was just thinking what a coincidence it is that today is your birthday. My daughter, the last one who died, would have been fifteen today too.'

'Oh, I'm so sorry.' Sunday gently rubbed her hand.

Mrs Spooner, who was sitting at the other end of the sofa, glanced up at this, and saw Zillah looking visibly uneasy. *There's more goin' on here than meets the eye,* Biddy found herself thinking, but tonight was neither the time nor the place for interrogations so she put her suspicious aside.

And then Jacob suggested, 'I think it's time we gave Sunday our presents and told her what her surprise is, don't you, Aunt Biddy?'

The old woman nodded and he hurried away to return with a large box which he plonked down on Sunday's lap.

'I hope they're the right size,' he told her. 'If not, you can blame Auntie.'

Sunday carefully untied the string and removed the lid then gasped as she withdrew a fine worsted day dress in a rich burgundy colour trimmed with black velvet. And that wasn't all. Beneath it was a beautiful lilac gown in the very latest fashion, the sort that ladies wore for afternoon tea. The clothes dazzled her, but grateful as she was, she wondered when she would ever get the chance to wear them.

Mrs Lockett was the next to give Sunday her gift, an assortment of lace-frilled handkerchiefs, each one lovingly hand-sewn.

'They're so pretty,' Sunday told her with genuine delight. Each of the lodgers had bought her a little gift too. There was a fountain pen from Miss Bailey, her own writing set from Mr Greaves, a large new carpet bag from Miss Falconer, and so it went on until the girl's head was spinning. Finally, Lady Huntley handed Sunday her present – a beautiful bonnet inside a hat box. She had never owned anything like it in her life, but again she asked herself, *When am I ever going to wear such clothes?* They were far too fine to wear when shopping in the market or cleaning in the house, but she was grateful to each and every one of them, nevertheless.

'And now for your last surprise, Sunny,' Mrs Spooner told her then. 'You're coming on a little holiday with me and Jacob.'

'A holiday?' The girl blinked, completely baffled. 'But where to?'

'To London.'

'London!' Sunday thought she must be hearing things. It seemed like the other side of the world to a girl who had never ventured further than the marketplace in her home town. 'But how will we get there? And where will we stay?'

'We shall be going on the train and the hotel is already booked,' the old lady told her with a smile. 'I'm sure you'll enjoy seein' all the places you've only ever read about in books. My dear husband took me a few times, God rest his soul, so I'll enjoy goin' again too. We'll be leaving next Monday and we'll be staying for a week. That's why everyone bought you new clothes. We shall need you to look the part if you're visitin' the capital. Though you will be expected to help me with me dressing and so on while we're there, so no slacking.'

'But what about everything here?' Sunday asked worriedly. 'There's an awful lot for Nell and Mickey to do on their own.'

'That's all taken care of,' Mrs Spooner assured her. 'Annie will be moving in here while we're away to supervise, and if all the jobs don't get done... Well, it's only for one week, ain't it? We can soon catch up when we get back home. So, what do you say? Are you up for it?'

'Oh yes!' Sunday said hastily. She was getting excited already although the thought of going on the train was more than a little daunting. She had often watched them pull into Trent Valley railway station, all steam and smoke and absolutely huge! They reminded her of the fire-breathing dragons she had seen in storybooks. But then, she reasoned, if Jacob and Mrs Spooner had travelled on them before, they must be safe, mustn't they?

By the time the little party ended Sunday was already counting down the days until she set off on her adventure.

'Yer so lucky,' Nell told her wistfully that night as they climbed the stairs to their rooms.

'I know.' Sunday was glowing. Mrs Spooner and Jacob had become the nearest thing to a family that she had ever had, apart from Tommy and poor Daisy, of course, and she couldn't imagine leaving them now, although she still sometimes dreamed of opening her own home for foundlings when she thought of the babies in the nursery at the workhouse. Of course, now that she was older she realised that that was all it would probably ever be – a dream. First she would need to be able to afford to buy a property large enough to house them, and then she would have to find a way to clothe, feed and educate them. Even though Mrs Spooner was generous, on the wages Sunday earned she would never have enough, even if she lived to be a hundred. Still, she was more than grateful for what she had.

That Wednesday when she made her weekly trip to the market she spent a little of her wages on a pair of smart buttoned boots from the rag stall. They were made of a lovely soft tan leather and would look far nicer with her new clothes than the ones she had bought before, which were more workaday. These fitted her so perfectly they might have been made for her, and she could wear them anywhere – even in London. Back at the Lodge, she put them on to show Nell, and twirled about in them.

'Eeh, everyone is goin' to think yer a real lady,' Nell sighed enviously. But she was happy because Sunday had treated her to a little box covered in shells, and inside had put a bright shiny new penny.

Sunday laughed. 'Oh, I doubt that!'

But Nell was adamant. 'Yes, yer will – an' yer prettier than any of 'em an' all.'

The big day finally arrived and as Sunday got ready to go early that morning she was so excited and nervous that she struggled to do up the buttons on her bodice. She had chosen to wear her new day dress to travel in, along with her new bonnet and shawl, and when she was finally ready and surveyed herself in the cracked mirror in her room she hardly recognised herself.

'You'll do,' she told her reflection with a grin, and lifting her new carpet bag she hurried down to the kitchen, noting that Mrs Spooner's trunk and Jacob's bag were already waiting at the side of the front door. She smiled; by the size of Biddy's trunk anyone would have thought they were going away for at least a month, but then she did like to dress up, and seeing as it was her only pleasure, Sunday didn't begrudge the old lady her frills and furbelows.

Jacob followed her down the stairs looking very

dapper in a new embroidered waistcoat and a dark morning coat. As he eyed her admiringly, Sunday felt slightly self-conscious but relieved that he didn't comment.

Annie had no such scruples. 'Why you've scrubbed up a treat, pet,' she declared when Sunday entered the kitchen. 'Anyone could take you for gentry in them clothes.'

Nell instantly burst into floods of tears and began to swipe her face and her runny nose with her apron.

'Oh, now come on, Nell. It's not as if I am going away for ever – it's only for a week. Cheer up!' Sunday gave the girl a cuddle but that only seemed to make things worse so she hastily stepped away from her.

'You look really nice, Sunday,' Mickey told her shyly but then they heard Mrs Spooner in the hallway.

'Sunny – are yer ready, gel? We do have a train to catch, you know.'

Annie rolled her eyes. 'Get a move on, lass,' she said, giving her a nudge. 'Sounds like the cab Jacob ordered yesterday is here.'

They all trooped out into the hallway to see the party off as the driver loaded the luggage onto the cab before helping the ladies inside.

Sunday lowered the window and leaned out to give Nell one last kiss. 'Be good now – and don't forget, I shall be back in the blink of an eye and I'll bring you something nice.' The driver swung up into his seat then and urged the horses on, and Sunday waved until Annie, Mickey and Nell were just tiny dots in the distance.

'That's it then,' Jacob said with a grin when she closed the window. 'We're on our way.'

'Huh! And I just hope you ain't forgotten anything,' grumbled Biddy.

'Of course I haven't, Aunt. I'm quite capable, you know,' Jacob told her with a wink at Sunday.

Mrs Spooner was even more elaborately dressed today in an enormous mauve silk crinoline with a fine purple fringed shawl about her shoulders and a hat to match. Like the dress she wore, the hat was heavily adorned with silk flowers and feathers that fluttered in the slight draught from the window, and there didn't seem to be an inch of flesh showing that wasn't covered in gold and precious gems. She was bound to attract more than a few curious glances, Sunday thought, but even so when she looked at the old woman she felt a rush of affection. The cab rattled along and within no time they arrived at the station, where Jacob halled a porter to put their valises into the luggage van.

The train was already standing at the platform and Sunday eyed it nervously. It seemed so much bigger close to, and smoke was belching out of it, filling the air with an acrid smell.

'Here's an empty carriage,' Jacob said as they walked along the platform peering in at the windows. 'This will do nicely.' He helped his aunt aboard and Sunday followed apprehensively. Suddenly she was wondering if this had been such a good idea after all but it was too late to back out now so she nervously took a seat. Soon after, there was the sound of doors slamming as the station-master hurried along the platform. When he was sure that everything was ready the guard then raised his green flag and slowly the monster roared into life and puffed out of the station in a cloud of smoke. Within minutes they had left the town behind and slowly Sunday felt her nerves begin to unwind. Jacob kept up a constant stream of chatter, pointing out places of interest as they passed through them. Mrs Spooner was soon soothed into a snooze by the gentle rocking motion of the train and now Sunday was enchanted as she gazed at the fields full of sheep and cows and the farmers busily harvesting.

'I never knew the world was so big,' she said in awe and Jacob chuckled.

'Oh, this is just a fraction of it. Wait until you go abroad. There are so many places to see: Rome, Paris, Vienna, New York to name just a few and they can all be reached by sea and rail now.'

'It's highly unlikely I'll ever see any of those places,' she pointed out. 'I'm just a maid, remember?'

'Ah, but a very pretty maid if you don't mind me saying so. And you're intelligent too. With your looks and your mind, you could marry anyone you wanted to … although I hope you don't, of course.'

Sunday glanced at him from beneath her long dark lashes but didn't reply. She didn't quite know how to, if truth be told, so instead she settled back in her seat to enjoy the rest of her journey.

Chapter Thirty-Nine

When they stepped down from their carriage at Euston station, the smoke from the trains had risen to form a fog high overhead in the rafters, and porters were rushing about with trolleys as passengers issued orders at them.

'Stay close. If you lose sight of us we'll never find you in this crowd,' Mrs Spooner advised as Jacob summoned one of the porters to fetch their belongings from the luggage van. Sunday didn't need to be told twice. She shrank as close into the old lady's side as she dared, feeling completely out of her depth. Jacob and the porter reappeared soon after and they picked their way towards the exit. Sunday had thought market day back at home was busy – but it was nothing compared to this. A huge church reared up over the way, reaching into the sky, and horse-drawn carriages were clattering across the highway nose to tail. Jacob, however, seemed totally unfazed by it all. He had stepped into the road, Sunday was sure at risk of his life, and hailed a cab in no time. The driver quickly jumped down from his seat to load their luggage onto the hold at the back then once Jacob had given him the name of their hotel in Westminster they clambered inside and set off.

'Phew! I wonder when this was last cleaned out?' Mrs Spooner remarked as she gazed with distaste at the grubby straw on the floor, but

Sunday was too intent on gazing from the window to notice. Now that she was here she was keen to see as many of the sights as she could.

'The driver will be taking us along The Strand to Trafalgar Square and then down Whitehall, to the Houses of Parliament,' Jacob informed them. 'It won't take long.'

Sunday gazed out, drinking it all in before they passed mighty Charing Cross station and then turned left along Whitehall. When Big Ben came into view, a tingle of excitement coursed through her. They bowled past into Parliament Square and on down the Embankment, turning off and heading down a wide street to their hotel. 'Everywhere looks much more impressive at night,' Jacob informed her. 'I thought we might go for a stroll after dinner if you're not too tired.'

'Just so long as you keep to the gas-lit thoroughfares,' his aunt warned him. 'There's places here where they'd cut your throat for sixpence and you have to beware of pick-pockets an' all.'

Jacob winked at Sunday. 'Yes, I know, Aunt. Don't worry, I wouldn't dream of venturing anywhere that wasn't safe. Would you like to come too?'

'Would I hell as like!' Mrs Spooner snorted. 'I want a nice hot dinner and an early night after comin' all this way. I'll do a bit o' sightseein' tomorrow.'

When they arrived at the Belgravia Hotel, Sunday was amazed to see two gentlemen in very plush red and gold uniforms standing either side of the impressive entrance. They rushed down the steps to help Mrs Spooner and Sunday alight

380

from the carriage the instant it stopped, as a porter hurried forward to collect their luggage. The foyer they were shown into took her breath away and she stood speechless, gazing about as Jacob went to the desk to announce their arrival.

'We're on the first floor,' he told his aunt and she nodded her approval as a porter led them towards a lift. Sunday had never been in one before and was a little nervous when the iron gates clanged shut, but she enjoyed the experience all the same. They emerged onto a long landing. A luxurious carpet ran all along the centre of it, and gilt-framed pictures and heavy mirrors were set at regular intervals along the wall. Once again Sunday began to feel out of her depth but Jacob and Mrs Spooner appeared perfectly at ease. They might have been used to such surroundings every day of the week from the way they behaved.

The porter who had shown them upstairs stopped at a door, telling Jacob, 'This is your room, sir. The ladies are in the next two.'

'Thank you.' Jacob reached into his pocket and dropped some coins into the young man's hand. The latter then moved on to the next room which was Mrs Spooner's. She disappeared inside and Sunday was led to her room; she was taken aback to find that her bag was already there and a young maid was unpacking it.

'Oh really, you don't need to do that. I can do it myself,' Sunday told her, deeply embarrassed as the young woman shook out Sunday's best gown and hung it in the armoire.

'S'all right, miss. This is wot I'm paid to do,' the

girl told her with a cheeky grin. She had a curious twang to her voice and Sunday guessed that she must be London born and bred. Hastily she fumbled in her bag for some coins, and when the girl was done and made to leave she dropped them into her hand and thanked her. Sunday giggled to herself, wondering what the maid would have thought had she known she was unpacking for another maid.

In her new clothes, in London and being waited on for the first time in her life, Sunday Small felt like a princess! She then turned her attention to the room and wandered about touching all the beautiful fabrics reverently. This was a far cry from the comfortable but basic room she had at Mrs Spooner's, and for a moment she was saddened as she thought of how much Daisy would have loved it. The bed had a thick feather mattress that she sank into when she sat on the side of it and Sunday wished that it was bedtime already, although her stomach was beginning to tell her that it was approaching dinnertime. They had eaten the basket of food that Annie had packed for them for lunch on the train, but that was a long time ago and she was hungry again. Since living at Whittleford Lodge she had become used to eating good meals and she had filled out considerably.

To her delight, Sunday found that a door in the corner led to her very own bathroom and she promised herself that later that evening she would bathe in there, but for now she knew that she ought to go and call on Mrs Spooner. She might be being treated like royalty but she was still expected to cater to the old lady's needs – and would do so willingly. After having a hasty swill in the sink in her bathroom she then tidied her hair and slipped next door to Mrs Spooner's room and tapped on the door.

'Come in!'

Sunday found her sitting in a chair by the window enjoying the view. From here they could see all the way across the surrounding rooftops to the River Thames. It was late afternoon and the light was fast fading from the day so she was making the most of it. Jacob was there too, sitting in another chair reading a newspaper and he smiled at her as she entered.

'My room is lovely, thank you so much for bringing me,' Sunday told Mrs Spooner.

Biddy smiled. 'You've earned a treat, lass. Thanks to you the lodging house is thriving again. In fact, I've been thinking of extending it some time in the future but let's enjoy our break first, eh?'

'Aunt was just saying that she'd prefer to dine in her room tonight,' Jacob informed her then. 'I've said that we'd be happy to stay with her but she says we're welcome to go down to the dining room if we wish.'

'Oh no, I wouldn't think of leaving you, Mrs Spooner,' Sunday protested. 'I'd be quite happy to eat in here too.'

'In that case I'll ring for a maid and ask for a menu.'

Once they had chosen and placed their order, they sat back to relax for a while. Mrs Spooner's room was considerably bigger than Sunday's with a table and four chairs and a small sofa placed against one wall... Sunday must have dozed off, for she was embarrassed when Jacob gently shook her arm to tell her, 'Dinner has arrived. Come on, sleepyhead.'

'Oh, I'm so sorry.' She felt her cheeks burn as she hastily jumped up. 'I didn't mean to fall asleep. I didn't realise how tired I was.'

She saw that the table had been laid with a crisp white cloth and silver cutlery, and a young maid was taking various covered silver dishes from a trolley and placing them in the centre of it. It all smelled delicious and her stomach growled in anticipation making her feel even more embarrassed. Mrs Spooner was already seated.

'Come on.' Jacob gallantly pulled a chair out for Sunday. He then shook out a white linen napkin and laid it across her lap before giving a little bow. 'There we are, madam. Would you like me to serve you?'

'Oh, sit down and don't be so daft,' she told him. 'I'll serve you. That's what I'm here for.'

The meal was a happy affair and Jacob and Sunday chatted about all the places they wanted to visit as Mrs Spooner listened benignly. They tucked into a thick pea soup followed by perfectly cooked lamb chops, crispy roast potatoes and a selection of vegetables, and ended the meal with a helping of superb chocolate gâteau covered in thick cream that even Annie couldn't have bettered. Sunday felt so full she was sure she would burst.

'Oh, that was wonderful, thank you.' She sighed in blissful satisfaction. 'Shall I clear all these dirty pots back onto the trolley now?' she asked innocently.

Mrs Spooner chortled with laughter. 'No, you will *not*, my girl. That's the maid's job. While we're here you're to do nothing except help me out a bit when I need it. So I suggest you help me get ready for bed then you two young things can go and have an explore. Don't go too far though. They get some right terrible fogs in London and they come down so quickly you can barely see your hand in front of you. I remember me an' Mr Spooner got lost in one once when we were strolling back to our hotel from the theatre.'

'We'll be fine,' Jacob assured her, then to Sunday, 'I'll leave you with Aunt Biddy then I'll meet you downstairs in the foyer in half an hour. Make sure you wrap up warmly. It gets chilly at night now.'

Sunday happily did as she was told, and when Mrs Spooner was tucked up in bed with a penny romance novel she hurried downstairs. Biddy always passed the books onto Sunday now when she had finished reading them and the girl thoroughly enjoyed them. Jacob was waiting for her and he took her elbow and led her towards the door, saying, 'You're looking very nice. Now, where would you like to go?'

As they emerged into the dark city streets, Sunday found herself blushing. She had never stepped out alone at night with a young man before and felt suddenly shy.

'Oh er … let's just go for a walk,' she suggested, very conscious of his hand on her elbow.

'In that case we'll head for the Mall.' He smiled

down at her and she suddenly realised how tall he was. 'I'm sure you'd like to see Buckingham Palace.'

'I would,' she told him as they strode beneath the flickering gas lamps. After visiting the palace, they hopped aboard an omnibus and Sunday gazed happily out of the window. Mrs Lockett had always been very keen for her pupils to have a glimpse of the towns and cities beyond their home town, and Sunday had loved looking at pictures of London. Just as Jacob had told her, the River Thames did look completely different by night. The gas lights flickering on the surface of the water lent it a romantic air and above them the dark velvet sky was dotted with twinkling stars.

'We'll visit Westminster Abbey and St Paul's Cathedral tomorrow if you like,' Jacob suggested and she nodded eagerly. Her happy mood diminished somewhat when they walked back to the hotel and she saw the ragged beggars sleeping in alleyways, huddled together for warmth. At home, these people might have been in the workhouse. Here, they lived on the streets.

A man with a white stick suddenly staggered out of the shadows, holding out a tin mug. 'Can yer spare a penny fer a poor blind man, little lady?' he whispered pathetically and Sunday immediately began to rummage in her reticule but Jacob hurried her on.

'You mustn't,' he warned. 'He wasn't really blind, otherwise how would he have known you were a young lady?'

'Oh!' Sunday was shocked but knew that Jacob

must be right.

Sure enough, the supposedly blind man began to curse them and Jacob tugged her away, out of earshot.

'I'm sorry,' Sunday mumbled.

'Don't be, you weren't to know,' he said warmly. 'But you have to have your wits about you here. This place is teeming with pickpockets and ruffians.'

Sunday glanced about nervously. The flickering street lamps were casting dancing shadows across the pavements and suddenly she wished she were back in the hotel. She'd just realised how utterly exhausted she was too, so she wasn't sorry when Jacob steered her safely home.

Up on the first floor she thanked Jacob for an enjoyable evening and wished him good night, then on impulse she decided to look in on Mrs Spooner before she herself retired, in case she needed anything.

She tapped on the old lady's door, waited then let herself in, and instantly she saw that her employer was fast asleep, propped up against the pillows in her bed. But this was Mrs Spooner as she had never seen her before. The old lady's wig was discarded on the dressing table, and with her wispy grey hair floating about her head and without her heavy layers of paint and powder she looked suddenly very old and fragile. Sunday had often helped her to undress but Biddy had always insisted on having complete privacy afterwards, seeing to the rest of her toilette herself. Now the girl saw why. Mrs Spooner was understandably reluctant to let anyone see her like this, so not wishing to upset her she quickly turned about and tiptoed from the room.

The incident did bring home to Sunday, however, that Mrs Spooner might be even older than she had thought and she found herself wondering what would happen to herself, Nell and Mickey if their beloved employer should die. But then, feeling utterly selfish and guilty for having such thoughts, she let herself into her room, revelling in the sheer luxury of it. For now, she was just going to enjoy herself. The future would see to itself.

Chapter Forty

The following morning after Sunday had helped Mrs Spooner to get dressed in yet another outrageous gown, mint-green this time, and enjoying a hearty breakfast in the hotel dining room the three of them set off on a sightseeing tour of London in a horse-drawn carriage. Sunday made the most of every minute. She was aware that she might never come to the capital again and didn't intend to miss a single thing.

On the steps of St Paul's Cathedral was an old woman selling birdseed, and Jacob bought a bag so Sunday could feed the cluster of pigeons flapping about their feet. Another old lady was selling posies of violets, and Jacob bought one for his aunt and one for Sunday, much to their delight. It was the very first bunch of flowers Sunday had ever been presented with and she only wished that they could last for ever.

'I shall press a couple between the pages of a book so that I can put them on Daisy's grave when I get home,' she told him, and he smiled at the kind thought. Although Sunday put her usual cheerful face on things he knew how much she was missing her friend.

The following day, Jacob took them on a boat trip on the River Thames. They sailed all the way down to the Tower of London, and as Sunday thought of all the young queens who had been imprisoned there in years gone by she felt sad – although this was also one of the highlights of her trip.

'It just goes to show that being rich and famous isn't everything, doesn't it?' she commented thoughtfully. 'It's far more important to have good family and friends and a safe place to live, with people you love.' She couldn't help but feel a deep sorrow. Now that she had finally accepted that her mother was never going to try and find her she realised that Mrs Spooner and the people at Whittleford Lodge were probably the closest she was ever going to get to having a family of her own. Sensing the girl's pain, Biddy squeezed her hand but then Sunday was smiling again and the moment had passed.

'Why don't you two get yourselves off to the theatre this evening?' Mrs Spooner suggested the next day. 'I'm too old to be gaddin' about at night but there's no reason why you two young things shouldn't go.'

'I think that's an excellent idea,' Jacob agreed

and instantly went off to get tickets while Sunday and Mrs Spooner sat enjoying an afternoon tea amongst the potted palms in the dining room.

Jacob soon returned, looking very pleased with himself. 'I've got us tickets to go and see Lillie Langtry in *The School for Scandal* at the Prince's Theatre,' he told Sunday, waving the tickets in the air. 'It's near Piccadilly Circus and Leicester Square. It's also quite close to Chinatown, but we won't be visiting there; the place is full of opium dens.'

'You can wear your best gown,' Mrs Spooner told Sunday, 'and I'll get one of the maids to come and put your hair up for you. You have to look the part if you're going to the theatre.' She was well aware that she should have chaperoned the girl, but seeing as they were in London, and not likely to meet anyone they knew, it would no doubt be all right. She trusted Jacob to behave like a gentleman.

Sunday had never been to the theatre before and took special care when she was getting ready. As she had promised, Mrs Spooner sent a young maid up to her room, who piled her hair onto the top of her head in an elaborate style before teasing it into ringlets. She told Sunday that the queen often wore her hair like that. Sunday then put on her new lilac gown. It was an afternoon gown really, but seeing as she didn't have an evening gown it would have to do. When she glanced in the mirror, she saw that the workhouse girl was gone and in her place stood an elegant young woman. If only Daisy and Tommy could see her now, with her hair like Queen Victoria's!

'You look a treat, miss,' the maid who had dressed her hair told her cheekily. 'Just mind your bonce on them lift doors on your way down.'

When Sunday stared at her bewildered, the girl giggled. 'Bonce – head to you. Sorry, miss, I forget everyone ain't from London like me. But now I really should be orf. Have a lovely evenin'.'

Sunday gave her a hug and a sixpence, then grabbed her shawl and hurried along to Mrs Spooner's room. She didn't want to make them late.

'Why, Sunny lass, you look a picture,' Mrs Spooner said approvingly. 'But now let's be havin' you! Jacob's got a cab waiting outside.'

'Thank you so much for bringing me,' Sunday suddenly said, and leaning forward she quickly pecked the old woman's cheek, making her face flame beneath her rouge.

'Oh, get off with you.' Biddy waved her hand at them and, giggling, she hurried away.

Sunday would never forget the night that followed; it would live on in her memory with its colours undimmed. She enjoyed every minute of it and wished that it could go on for ever. When she walked into the theatre on Jacob's arm she got more than a few admiring glances but once the show started she never took her eyes from the stage for a single second.

'Oh, wasn't Miss Langtry just wonderful! And so *beautiful!*' she said dreamily on their way home in the cab.

Jacob gently took her hand. 'Yes, she was – but she wasn't half as beautiful as you.' He then turned Sunday's hand over and kissed the palm of it as her cheeks burned. 'I don't know if you're aware of it, Sunday,' he went on, 'but I've grown very fond of you. It began at Christmas when Rebecca was so rude to you. I think up until then I'd looked upon you as little more than a child, but that night I suddenly realised that you were growing up. Now don't look so worried,' he said hastily as he saw her expression. 'I realise that this might come as a surprise but what I want you to know is I'm prepared to wait until you feel ready – if you think you could ever feel anything for me... Do you think you might?'

'I ... I don't know,' Sunday stuttered. This was all so unexpected. 'I do like you – very much.' She thought back to the crush she'd had on him when she'd first gone to live at his aunt's, but that had soon passed. And so much had happened since then.

'Then that'll have to do for now, but just remember what I said – and who knows what could happen in the future?'

'Aren't you forgetting something, Jacob?' she said quietly. 'I'm your aunt's maid.'

He laughed. 'Oh, I don't think that would trouble her.'

Suddenly for Sunday the night was slightly spoiled. She was flattered that Jacob liked her and, after all, he was very kind, and handsome too – everything a girl could want. *Not so very long ago I would have been thrilled if he'd said this,* she told herself as she tactfully withdrew her hand and tucked it beneath her shawl. Jacob could offer her love, and security – those things she had always yearned for, yet she knew that this wasn't enough if she couldn't love him in return.

Sensing that she needed time to think, Jacob remained quiet, and for the rest of the journey the only sound to be heard was the clip-clop of the horses' hooves.

On their final day, Mrs Spooner took Sunday shopping at Liberty in Regent Street and once again it was a completely new experience for the girl. There didn't seem to be anything that the enormous shop didn't sell. There was a perfume counter where Mrs Spooner enjoyed herself, trying out at least half a dozen new scents, until the air around her was so cloying that Sunday could hardly breathe; there were shoes, hats, scarves, gloves, jewellery, everything a woman could wish for, and Mrs Spooner was in heaven. She bought Jacob a fine leather wallet and then, turning her attention to Sunday, she told her, 'And now, young lady, we're going to get you a nice warm coat for the winter. Don't bother arguing, it's my treat and I insist. I need to get a little gift for Annie too.'

Biddy soon had the assistants rushing back and forth with coats of every design and colour as Sunday obediently tried them all on until at last she found one that she declared was just right. It was a similar colour to the burgundy crinoline she had had for her birthday, and it was so warm that when Sunday tried it on she felt as if she had been wrapped in a snug and very elegant blanket.

'But it's *far* too expensive,' she breathed in Mrs Spooner's ear.

'Let me be the judge o' that,' Biddy Spooner said airily, then to the assistant: 'We'll take it. Wrap it up for us would you, dear?' And she gave the name of the hotel so that it could be delivered that same day.

Armed with other, smaller packages she then headed for the tea room with Sunday jogging behind her, trying to keep up, similarly loaded down. Mrs Spooner ordered afternoon tea for them and Sunday was glad to sink into her chair. As she had soon discovered, shopping with her employer was almost as hard work as being at home.

She was grateful, however, to get a little respite from Jacob, who had shied away from what he called 'women's shopping'. Since he had declared his feelings to her their relationship had undergone a subtle change. He was still the perfect gentleman but she could sense him watching and waiting for her answer and she found it a little unnerving, so much so that she was looking forward to going home now and getting back into some sort of a routine.

Admittedly, she hadn't ruled out the possibility of building a life with Jacob; she would have been a fool to discount it. But sensibly, she knew that she was still very young to be making such a momentous decision and she didn't want to be rushed into anything. It was almost as if her head was telling her one thing and her heart was telling her another. Her head was telling her that she might never get another offer from such a decent young man again; her heart was telling her that when she met the right person she would know. It was all very confusing. *I just need a little more time,* she convinced herself as she and Mrs Spooner waited to be served. A maid placed a three-tier stand of tiny sandwiches in front of them, whilst another arranged a silver teapot and two delicate china cups and saucers before them. They had been shopping for most of the day – in fact, the time seemed to have flown by so now they both tucked in, enjoying every mouthful.

When it was empty, the stand was replaced by a similar one, on which were arranged a number of very appetising-looking fresh cream cakes, dainty iced cakes and scones.

'Come on,' Mrs Spooner encouraged as Sunday refilled her cup for her. 'They charge ridiculous prices here so we may as well eat up. I hate to see waste, I do.' She then bit into a large cream horn as Sunday selected a truly extravagant chocolate éclair. Ten minutes later, Sunday was feeling slightly sick, and when Mrs Spooner again pushed the cakestand towards her she held her hands up in a gesture of defeat.

'I couldn't eat another single mouthful,' she giggled. 'At this rate I shall be having to let the seams in my dresses out.'

Mrs Spooner grinned. 'I reckon my hatred of seein' food go to waste comes from when I was a nipper,' she confided. 'Before I met my husband I often went to bed with an empty belly. There were a large family of us, see, an' the lads used to wolf down everything they could get their hands on. My mam reckoned they had hollow legs, so even when I married and didn't have to worry any more about where the next meal was coming from, I never forgot those times.'

It wasn't often that Mrs Spooner spoke of her poor background and Sunday felt touched that she had confided in her.

'Anyway, that's enough o' that,' Mrs Spooner said then, clicking her fingers for the bill. 'I reckon we've still got another couple of hours left to get some more shoppin' in, so chop chop. I still need to find Annie a little present, an' a bit o' something for Nell and Mickey too.'

Sunday was only too happy to go along with the suggestion as she wanted to buy some small gifts for the folks back at home too.

By the time they got back to the Belgravia Hotel, where Jacob was waiting for them in the foyer, Sunday felt as if her arms were at least six inches longer.

'Now you see why I didn't want to come along.' He grinned as he took the bags off them both. 'I know my aunt when she goes on a shopping spree.'

He escorted the two ladies up to their rooms then Sunday excused herself as Mrs Spooner began to show her nephew all her new things.

'I think I'll get my packing done now to save having to do it in the morning,' she said.

'All right, dear. Jacob ... what do you think o' this?' Sunday slipped away as Mrs Spooner began to haphazardly tip her purchases out onto the bed.

The packing took no time at all and although Sunday was tired and had intended to have a rest before dinner she found that she couldn't settle. In less than twenty-four hours she would be home and her very first holiday would be over. She wasn't altogether sorry although she had enjoyed herself immensely. It had been wonderful not to have to keep glancing across her shoulder in case Mr Pinnegar was there every time she ventured out. He seemed a million miles away here but soon now they would return home and his taunts would start all over again. She shuddered at the thought but she had missed Nell, Annie and Mickey and couldn't wait to tell them all about the sights she'd seen and the places they'd visited.

She put on her best gown again and paid particular attention to her hair that evening after helping Mrs Spooner dress for dinner, and when they arrived in the foyer where Jacob was waiting for them, as usual he complimented them both.

'May I just say how ravishing you ladies are looking this evening?' he said. Then, with one on each side of him, their arms tucked into his, he led them through to the dining room for dinner. The meal was delicious, all five courses of it, although Sunday was still so full from the afternoon tea that she couldn't really do it justice.

When it was over they retired to the lounge where they had coffee, then Jacob asked, 'Would you like to go out somewhere, Sunday? It is our last evening here and I'm sure my aunt wouldn't mind.'

'That's very kind of you,' Sunday answered demurely, 'but I'm rather tired as it happens so I think I'll go to bed early, ready for the journey home tomorrow.'

'I'm ready for my bed an' all, lass. All that shopping has caught up with me.' Mrs Spooner

397

smothered a yawn as Jacob looked hopefully at Sunday again, hoping to change her mind but without success.

He didn't argue. Instead he saw them both to his aunt's room and bade them good night, leaving Sunday to help his aunt prepare for bed.

'Have you realised our Jacob's got a soft spot for you?' Biddy asked in her usual forthright way as Sunday was unlacing her stays.

Sunday's blush was her answer and the woman told her sternly, 'You could do a lot worse for yourself, yer know. Everything I own will be his when I pass on. Think on it, lass. You'd never go short of anything.'

'I'm a little too young to be thinking of settling down just yet,' Sunday answered diplomatically and hoping to change the subject she added, 'I hope we'll find everything is all right at home when we get back.'

'Why wouldn't it be? Annie is more than capable.' Mrs Spooner yawned again then, so after tucking her into bed and settling her with a magazine, Sunday scooted off to her own room where she sat on the bed staring pensively into space.

Her two biggest dreams had almost died now. The first had been to find her mother, the second to own a house big enough to take in foundling children. Both seemed so unrealistic now. Perhaps marriage to Jacob was the only way to go, after all? The trouble was, she didn't love him – even if he could help make her second dream come true. Some instinct was telling her to wait for something – but as yet she didn't know what it could be.

With a sigh she started to get ready for bed.

Chapter Forty-One

Mrs Spooner noted that the atmosphere on the way home was somewhat strained but she wasn't overly concerned. As her mother had always told her, 'the path to true love never runs smooth'. And so now that Sunday was aware that Jacob thought fondly of her, the way the old woman saw it, all she had to do was sit back and let nature take its course. After all, Sunday was a bright girl and she'd soon realise how lucky she was to have a chap like Jacob look kindly on her.

They were all relieved when the train eventually chugged into the Trent Valley railway station at Nuneaton and whilst the porter fetched their pile of luggage and many new packages from the guard's van, Jacob went off to find a cab. In no time at all they were loaded up and heading for home, and Mrs Spooner was secretly glad. She'd enjoyed her break but had begun to realise that she was getting a little old for gadding about.

'Ah well, at least the house is still standing,' she said with a wry grin when the cab pulled up outside. But the grin was soon wiped off her face the instant she set foot through the door to be welcomed by Annie, who looked as if she had the weight of the world on her shoulders.

'Well, I'd have expected a smile instead o' bein' met by a face like a wet weekend,' Mrs Spooner said. 'What's up with you, woman?' Then sniffing the air and wrinkling her nose she asked, 'And what's that awful smell?'

'We've had a terrible time of it since yer've been gone,' Annie answered, screwing her apron between her hands. 'You'll need to sit down fer this. I hardly know where to begin. The first night yer were gone we locked up as usual an' everythin' was fine an' dandy. But then when Mickey came down the next morning he found the chickens squawkin' about the yard. Someone had released them from their coop although they hadn't harmed any of 'em this time. That damn wily old fox did though – two of 'em he had fer his supper. Two mornin's later we found someone had opened the stable door in the night an' Mickey caught up wi' Treacle wanderin' along Haunchwood Road. Also, the night after yer left, someone set a fire right outside the kitchen door, an' then … an' then … Nell got attacked.'

'*What!*' Mrs Spooner was horrified. 'Is she all right? And how much damage did the fire do? Was anyone burned?' The other incidents, although worrying, were nothing compared to this.

'I'll make yer a cup o' tea. I dare say yer all ready for one then I'll explain everythin'.' So saying, Annie bustled off to the kitchen as Sunday helped the old lady to take off her outer things.

Ten minutes later with a pot of tea sitting in front of them in the drawing room, Mrs Spooner asked again, 'Is Nell all right, Annie?'

Annie nodded and began to explain. 'Yes, I'll tell yer all about that in a minute but I'll start at the beginnin'. As I said, the fire happened the night after yer left. We'd noticed a couple of shifty-lookin' blokes hoverin' about outside earlier in the afternoon an' they made me feel a bit nervous like, so I'd asked everyone to keep a watch out for 'em comin' back. I was in bed dead to the world that night but thankfully Mickey had got up to check on the sow. She's due to drop a litter any day as yer know an' he's been keepin' a beady eye on her. Anyway, as he came down the stairs he smelled burnin' and when he went into the kitchen there were flames lickin' up the inside o' the back door. I dread to think what might have happened if he hadn't come down when he did.' She let out a long, whistling breath as she thought back, then went on: 'Anyway, he managed to put the fire out afore it came right into the kitchen although we've had to have the carpenter come to measure up fer a new door. It could have been so much worse though. Had he not come downstairs we could all have been burned to death in our beds. Outside the back door he found a pile o' twigs an' branches on the step, them that hadn't burned. Someone had deliberately made a fire there an' then scarpered.'

'Did you report it to the constable?'

Annie sniffed indignantly. 'Well, o' course we did – but there weren't nothin' he could do. There weren't a soul in sight by the time Mickey had put the fire out, so as the constable pointed out, it could have been anybody. We couldn't even give them a description o' the men we'd seen loiterin' around outside 'cos they wore caps an' mufflers an' we didn't get to see their faces. The constable just told us to be extra vigilant. Mickey's slept in the chair in the kitchen ever since, bless him. An' that ain't the worst of it.' Tears sprang to the old lady's eyes. 'Once the fire were under control Mickey went to check on the sow, only to find that some cruel bugger had stabbed her! All her piglets died with her – it was a sight I never want to see again in what's left of me life.' She gave a sob.

Sunday sat stroking Mabel who was cuddled as close to her as she could get, with her large golden head in her lap. It was one thing to slaughter animals for food – but why would anyone deliberately stab a creature for no reason except spite! And then she felt sick as a face popped into her mind. *Pinnegar!* Or, more likely, his men.

'O' course I sent fer the butcher to take her away the very next mornin'. There were no sense in wastin' perfectly good meat.' Annie, the ever-practical, had pulled herself together. 'I told Mickey he could go an' get another sow from the cattle market soon as ever yer got back, but the lad were gutted.'

Mrs Spooner looked dazed, hardly able to take everything in. What a homecoming this was turning out to be! She almost wished she'd stayed in London.

'So now tell me what's happened to little Nell.' The way she saw it, she might as well know everything and get it over with.

'Well, 'cos Sunday were wi' you in London I sent Nell into town on Wednesday an' on the way home she decided to take a short cut fer some o' the way along the canal towpath.'

Sunday blinked. Even the mention of the canal turned her stomach now after what had happened to Daisy and she avoided it like the plague.

'Anyway, she were on a quiet stretch when suddenly a bloke stepped out from the hedge an' afore she knew what were happenin' he knocked her to the ground an' started beatin' her. The poor little soul ain't no further through than a broom handle so she stood no chance o' fightin' the lousy bastard off! But then he lifted her skirts an' it don't take much to guess what he were goin' to do.' Annie shuddered as she took a noisy slurp of her tea. 'Thank goodness at that stage Nell saw a horse on the towpath ploddin' towards her pullin' a barge at the same moment as the bloke did, so the swine took to his heels an' left the poor lass lyin' there yellin' blue murder! It were the bargee who kindly brought her home, an' a rare old state she were in, I'm tellin' yer. Mickey shot straight off to fetch the doctor an' the poor lamb has been in bed for the rest o' the week although I think she's on the mend now, physically at least. God knows how long it'll be afore she feels confident enough to go out on her own again though.'

Mrs Spooner let out her breath on a sigh, then as a thought occurred to her she asked, 'The chap who attacked her – what did he look like? Was it Pinnegar?'

Annie shook her head. 'That were the first thing that occurred to me but she said she didn't think so. He had a scarf tied round the bottom half of his face and he was wearing a hat so she didn't get a good look at him, but she said it couldn't be him 'cos the chap were too skinny.'

'Hmm, well, if you ask me, for all these incidents to happen within the space of a week is more than

403

sheer coincidence. I wouldn't mind betting Pinnegar was behind 'em, though suspecting an' provin' it are two different things,' Biddy said.

She made up her mind. 'From now on I don't want the girls going out on their own,' she stated firmly. 'And I shall be asking Jacob and Mickey to keep an eye out. I want the front and back doors locked at all times and I might even consider getting a guard dog. If we were to put a kennel in the yard at least it would alert us if strangers trespassed on the property. I'm afraid Mabel here is no use for that sort of thing. She'd probably lick an intruder to death.'

Everyone nodded in agreement as Annie cut into a sponge cake that was still slightly warm from the oven.

Sunday declined a slice. She'd lost her appetite as she thought of what might have happened to poor little Nell. It brought back her own narrow escape from the housefather. 'I'll just pop up and check on Nell if you don't mind,' she said, and excused herself. With Mabel trotting along at her heels she went into the hall, picked up her bag and made her way to the top attic floor. After depositing her bag in her room she went and tapped on Nell's door.

'Who is it?' a timid voice answered.

'It's only me. We just got back.' Sunday inched the door open to find Nell curled into a ball beneath the blankets on her bed, but the instant she saw her friend the tears started to pour down her cheeks and she sat up and held her arms out.

'Oh, you poor thing.' Sunday wrapped her arms about her, appalled at the first sight of the girl.

One of her eyes was almost shut and large purple bruises covered the whole of one side of her face. Her chin was badly grazed too, probably from where she had been pushed down onto the towpath, Sunday supposed. 'It's all right, I'm here now,' she soothed as she rocked Nell gently to and fro. 'And from now on one of us will come with you every single time you go out until they catch whoever did this.'

'The coppers said there ain't much chance o' that happenin',' Nell sniffed. 'The nice man from the barge ran after him when he found me, but he weren't quick enough to catch him an' he got clean away. Mickey went lookin' for him too, when the barge man brought me home but he were long gone by then ... Sunday, I'm frightened!'

Sunday passed her a handkerchief and Nell noisily blew her nose then winced with pain as she struggled to sit up. One of her ribs was cracked from where her attacker had kicked her, and all in all just as Annie had said, she was in a rare old state.

'At least you're safe now,' Sunday said gently. 'And we'll all make sure that this never happens again. Now lie down and try to rest and I'll go and bring you up a nice cup of tea and a slice of cake.'

Nell obediently did as she was told as Sunday made her way back down to the kitchen. Jacob was there and he asked immediately, 'How is she?'

'Not good.' Sunday heaved a sigh. 'Do you think your aunt is right – about all these incidents

405

being connected, I mean?'

'It rather looks that way,' Jacob answered worriedly. 'But now that we're back, I can help. I'll stay down here for a few nights for a start-off, to give Mickey a rest in case those blackguards decide to come back, and if they do I can promise you they'll be sorry. I was good at boxing at school and nothing would please me more than to give them, or the man who attacked Nell, a damn good thrashing. Meantime I don't think it's a good idea for either of you two girls to go out on your own or together for a while. Mickey is to come with you if I'm at work.'

Sunday thought what a thoroughly nice chap Jacob was. Any girl would be lucky to have him as a suitor … so what was holding her back?

'Anyway I'm off to unpack,' he told her then and with a smile he left her to prepare Nell's tray.

The following day, Lady Huntley came to call after news reached Treetops Manor of what had happened. With her she brought Stephen, tightly swaddled in a shawl.

'It was Cissie who heard all about it when she went into town,' Lavinia told Mrs Spooner. 'But is everything all right now?'

'Well, there ain't been no more incidents. Jacob an' Mickey have took it in turns to sleep in the kitchen just in case,' Biddy Spooner answered as she stared down at the infant in her arms. He was such a tiny, sickly-looking little thing and his skin had a yellow tinge to it to her mind, but his mother clearly thought he was adorable if the way she kept her eye on him was anything to go by.

'And how are things at Treetops Manor?' Mrs Spooner asked then as the baby's mother leaned over to wipe a trickle of milk from his tiny mouth. Molly had fed him just before they came out and Lavinia was watching the clock closely. Stephen was still being fed little and often; it was the only way he could keep his milk down.

'Oh, much as usual.' Lavinia gave a wry smile. 'Ashley is often away in different parts of the country. Now he has access to money again, he likes to attend all the big race meetings. Horses are his passion. It grieves me that he barely looks at our son even when he is at home. But that's fine, this little man has the rest of the household doting on him.'

Sunday came in then bearing a pot of coffee and some of Annie's biscuits. After she'd laid the tray down she looked at Lady Huntley and asked, 'May I hold him?'

'Of course, my dear – but do be gentle.'

Mrs Spooner gladly handed him over. Babies were lovely but they did tend to be messy little things. However, Sunday was enchanted with him.

'Why, he's just like a little doll,' she said, smiling as she planted a kiss on his forehead and admired his shawl. 'Isn't this like the one that Phoebe has?' she enquired.

Lady Huntley nodded. 'How observant of you – and yes, it is. I gave some baby things to Mrs Lockett before I knew I was expecting Stephen. I ordered them from a very exclusive shop in Mayfair in London when I was expecting my first baby long ago, and sadly they had lain unused for almost fifteen years.' A flicker of sadness crossed her face as she thought back to her lost daughters. 'At least they are all being used now though,' she said and Sunday felt sorry for her. She could see the woman's pain in her eyes. It must be terrible enough to lose one baby let alone three, one after the other, as Lady Huntley had.

'Cissie talks about Stephen every time I see her,' she said then, on a happier note. 'She seems to be quite besotted with him.'

'I think all of the staff are.' Lady Huntley chuckled. 'I dread to think what it's going to be like when he's pottering about the place. I fear he's going to be spoiled rotten.'

'Quite right too!' Mrs Spooner said stoically. 'What's the point of havin' little ones if you can't spoil 'em, eh? Imagine how lovely it will be when you can go out and do things together.'

'Oh, I *do* imagine it,' Lady Huntley cried. 'I can't wait to be able to take him to church with me and out into the garden.'

'It'll come soon enough.' Biddy narrowed her eyes as Sunday bent to place the baby back in his mother's arms. There it was again – that little feeling she got whenever she saw the two of them together. She couldn't quite put her finger on it. Perhaps it was simply her strong belief that Sunday would make a loving mother herself one day.

'Right, well, I'd better get on then. Good day, Lady Huntley.' Sunday tripped from the room to go about her chores, leaving the two women to chew over all that had happened while Mrs Spooner had been in London.

Chapter Forty-Two

Two weeks later, Nell was able to resume gentle tasks about the house although she adamantly refused to go to market, even accompanied by Mickey. The encounter on the canal towpath had clearly unnerved her badly and she would venture no further than the laundry room and the back yard.

'She just needs time to recover from what happened,' Mrs Spooner declared. 'So in the meantime you can do the market trips again, Sunny. But Mickey will come with you, mind. I don't want either of you girls venturing out on your own for now at least.'

It was now October and the weather had taken a turn for the worse, so on market day, Sunday wrapped up warmly in her smart new coat and bonnet and joined Mickey in the little cart.

As they clip-clopped up Haunchwood Road he told her worriedly, 'I've to take Treacle to be shoed at the blacksmiths and then I've to look around the cattle pens for a new sow. That should take an hour or so. Mrs Spooner said I wasn't to leave you alone, so you can come with me, if you like.'

Treacle was Mickey's pride and joy, as were all the animals. He loved them as much as Tommy had.

'Oh no, I will be fine on my own. There should

409

be plenty of people about.' Sunday gave him a re-assuring smile as she clung onto her bonnet. There was a strong wind and it was threatening to snatch it away. 'Annie has given me a list of things to get for her, so I'll be seeing to that. We can meet up afterwards.' The trip to London had increased her confidence.

Sometime later, Mickey dropped her off in Queen's Road at the entrance to the market before agreeing where they should meet later on.

Sunday gave him a wave, and with her basket over her arm she set off to start on the shopping. The sky was grey and leaden and this, combined with the wind, didn't make it the most pleasant of days. However, Sunday would never stop enjoying her freedom from the confines of the workhouse so she went happily from one stall to another. She had almost finished her shopping when the rain started, a gentle drizzle at first that soon turned into a real downpour. With a muttered curse she headed for Stratford Street away from the stalls and dived into an empty shop doorway. Her new bonnet was her pride and joy and she didn't want the rain to ruin it so she decided she would stay there till the rain had slowed a little. After setting her basket down she started to brush the rain-drops from her new coat. It was then that she became aware of someone blocking the light. Glancing up, her stomach sank as she saw Albert Pinnegar planted there with two of his henchmen standing close behind him, leering at her.

'Tasty little whore, ain't she, Henry?' the smaller of the two said to the other. 'Albert's told us how free she is wi' her favours. I wouldn't mind liftin' her skirts an' havin' a peek at her silk drawers meself.'

Ignoring the man's lewd comments and determined not to let them see how afraid she was, Sunday raised her chin and addressed Pinnegar, saying, 'What do *you* want!'

He was glaring at her and she saw immediately that he was angry. 'Enjoy your week away with your latest fancy man, did you?' he spat, ignoring her question. His hands were clenching and unclenching into fists and his eyes were wild.

He must be talking about the week she had just spent in London with Jacob and Mrs Spooner, Sunday thought – but how on earth did he get to hear about it? Then common sense told her that people always gossiped. After all, it wasn't often a maid was given such a treat and Pinnegar had probably thought she and Jacob had gone alone.

'If you're talking about the week I just spent in London, surely you must know I accompanied my *employer* and her nephew.'

'Huh! I bet that didn't stop you from pleasuring him, you slut. Word has it that you shared a room in a posh hotel.'

'That's not true!' Sunday's face grew hot with mortification and as he took a step into the doorway she shrank back against the wall. She was absolutely convinced that Pinnegar was the one behind the fire at the Lodge and the attack on Nell, but she couldn't accuse him without proof. Looking out, she saw that there weren't many people about now; like herself they had all sought shelter from the rain and she suddenly felt very vulnerable.

411

'Look – when are you going to leave me alone?' she asked him desperately. 'Why can't you just accept that I have no interest in you?'

His chest swelled and his face turned a dull brick-red colour. *'You* have no interest in *me?'* he hissed from between clenched teeth. 'Let me tell you, young lady – I wouldn't touch a little whore like you even if you handed it to me on a plate for free. But you are in my debt. You owe me! It was because of you and that friend of yours that I lost my job at the workhouse and I won't be happy till I've paid you back, in full. Oh yes, my lady, you will rue the day you crossed Albert Pinnegar!'

Sunday's heart was hammering so loudly she feared it would leap out of her chest but to her great relief he turned about and stamped away then with his henchmen following like two ugly mastiffs. She sagged against the wall. That confrontation had been just a little too close for comfort. When was she *ever* going to be free of him? She was now beginning to feel seriously unnerved. If he had been responsible for the fire and setting someone to attack Nell, then she was now putting those closest to her at risk, for Pinnegar would clearly never stop hounding her until he considered he'd had his revenge. There was only one thing she could do now; she would have to move from Mrs Spooner's to somewhere where he couldn't find her.

A sick feeling started in the pit of her stomach at the thought of it, but deep down she knew it was the only solution. She would never be able to forgive herself should anything happen to those she cared about. The prospect of leaving the only place

412

where she had ever found happiness made her feel weak with dismay. Lifting her basket she stepped back out into the street. It was still raining heavily but suddenly her best bonnet didn't feel so important any more as she glanced up and down to make sure that Pinnegar had really departed. He was like a bad penny, turning up when she least expected him. Satisfied that he had gone, she lifted her skirts and raced towards the blacksmiths.

Oh, Daisy, I'm so afraid, she told her departed friend silently.

'Excuse me, ma'am,' Molly said as Zillah admitted her to her mistress's bedchamber early one cold November morning. 'I don't want to alarm you but I think you should send for the doctor. I've been up all night with Master Stephen. He has a fever and I can't seem to bring it down. Marigold has one too. I fear they've caught the measles from Mrs Lockett's little girl, Phoebe. The rash is just coming out on them both.'

Lavinia Huntley immediately got out of bed as the colour drained from her face. 'Zillah, send George for the doctor. Tell him it's urgent,' she told her as she slipped into a peignoir. It was a lacy little affair trimmed with feathers and Molly thought it quite inadequate for such cold weather. But that was the gentry for you, always having to look their best.

'You should have fetched me in the night,' Lavinia scolded as she raced for the door with her heart thumping. Little Stephen was her whole world; the sun rose and set with him, and she couldn't bear to think of losing him now. If she

413

did, she told herself, it would be all her own fault for visiting Verity, although no one had known at the time that Phoebe was sickening for the measles. She had visited to meet their new son, Michael, who had thankfully been safely delivered at the right time.

'I didn't like to disturb you. And anyway, there was nothing more you could have done for him than I have,' Molly answered. She looked worn out and Lavinia felt guilty as she noted the dark shadows beneath the young woman's eyes.

In the nursery there was a fire burning brightly but Lavinia saw that Stephen had been laid on top of his blankets and stripped down to his binder. Marigold was in the other crib and she was fretful too.

'I've been sponging him down with cool water all night but it doesn't seem to have made any difference,' Molly told her worriedly.

Lavinia scooped his little body into her arms and began to rock him to and fro, deeply alarmed to feel how hot he was. It was as if someone had lit a fire inside him and his face was red and wet with sweat.

'He's had a slight cold for a few days now, as you know,' Molly went on, 'but it was late last night when he seemed to take a turn for the worse and the rash started to come out. Marigold has it too, but she doesn't seem as bad as Stephen.'

'Well, she wouldn't, would she?' Lavinia glanced enviously over at the plump child who was whimpering in the other crib. 'She's always been so much stronger than Stephen.' Then, seeing how distressed Molly was, Lavinia's voice softened as

414

she told her, 'You mustn't blame yourself, dear. You've been marvellous with him. In fact, he couldn't have had a better nurse than you.'

The two women then fell silent as they each prayed for the doctor to come quickly.

The examination of both babies was done and as the doctor removed his stethoscope his face was grave. 'Marigold doesn't seem too bad, but I'm afraid the infection has gone to Stephen's chest.' He glanced sympathetically up at the child's mother who stood so still at his side she might have been carved from stone. 'All I can do is leave a sleeping draught to help him rest while you continue to sponge him with cool water to bring the temperature down, and try to trickle some liquid into him.' He paused then before asking, 'Is his father here?'

Lavinia made a great effort to stop herself from flying into a panic at these words. 'N – no, he's still in London, I believe.'

'I see.' The doctor straightened and stroked his chin. 'It would be wise to ask him to return home if you manage to locate him.'

Lavinia nodded numbly as she took her son into her arms and sat down heavily on the nearest chair with him. For now, words failed her; she was too choked with fear to say anything.

Molly saw the doctor to the door where he promised to return later in the day.

'Is it all right if I feed Marigold, ma'am?' Molly asked as she crossed to the crib.

Again Lavinia nodded as Molly bared her breast and placed the child to it. The infant instantly

415

started to suckle noisily and Lavinia felt a moment's resentment. Marigold was a robust, healthy little girl whilst Stephen... She stopped her thoughts from going any further. She shouldn't be blaming Molly's child. It was Ashley's fault for causing their son to be born before his time.

By mid-morning word had gone around the house that Master Stephen was grievously ill and once again the servants shuffled about like shadows, their faces strained. They all loved the baby but they loved their kindly mistress even more and couldn't even begin to contemplate what losing him might do to her. The measles epidemic that had swept through the town had already claimed a number of children's lives, and now they prayed that their little master wouldn't be the next victim. Earlier in the day Mrs Lockett had paid a quick visit to see how he was, and it comforted Lavinia to know that she and Edgar were praying for him too.

Zillah ran up and down the stairs between the nursery and the kitchen all morning fetching trays of tea and treats to try and tempt her mistress to eat and drink, but Lavinia refused them all. She left her baby briefly, just once, to get dressed, if that's what it could be called, for she merely dragged on the nearest clothes that came to hand and rushed off back to the nursery without even brushing her hair or washing her face. Now was not the time for vanity. She was fighting for her son's life.

'Here, let me take him now. You go and have a rest,' Molly urged once the late afternoon had snatched the light from the day, but Lavinia shook her head as she placed a wet cloth on his rosebud mouth and tried to dribble some water into him. The rash was red and angry on both the babies now but already Marigold was gurgling some of the time and seemed to be much better.

'No, you go and get yourself something. I don't want to leave him.'

Molly quietly lifted Marigold and carried her down to the kitchen where she reported to the staff who were anxiously waiting for news.

The doctor returned after his afternoon surgery but there was no change in the child and he felt helpless because there was absolutely nothing he could do for him; so he quietly left, with instructions that they should send for him should there be any change whatsoever.

It was when Molly returned to the nursery that Lavinia suggested, 'Why don't you go and spend the evening with your husband at home, dear? Stephen isn't going to need feeding until he's on the mend, and he's keeping Marigold awake with his crying. There's no point in us both staying up all night.'

The offer was tempting. It had been some long time since Molly had lain in her own bed with her husband's strong arms about her so she quietly collected together what she and Marigold would need for the night and left, sensing that Lavinia wanted some time alone with her son.

Soon it was darkest night but Lavinia's vigil went on. Tirelessly she mopped the precious little brow and trickled water into his mouth as she talked to him, whilst Zillah sat in a corner looking worriedly on, feeling more useless than

417

she had ever felt in her whole life.

At one point Lavinia carried her son over to the window and drawing back the curtains she looked out into the stormy night. Leafless branches dipped and swayed in the wind as if they were engaged in some macabre dance as she whispered, 'Look at that big world out there, darling. It's all waiting for you and when the spring comes round again we're going to have such good fun. Young George will put a rope swing up for you and build you a treehouse. And you will have your very own pony too, just as soon as you're big enough to ride. It will be a little one at first, of course, and you can come with me to choose it. I wonder what colour he will be and what you will call him? We'll go for picnics too. You'll like that, won't you? And every Sunday we'll go together to church and afterwards you can play with Phoebe for a while. Won't that be grand? In the summer we'll pick wildflowers to place on your sisters' graves. You had three little sisters, you know, but sadly they are all in heaven now. But you're strong, my darling. You'll stay with me, won't you?'

In the corner, tears poured down Zillah's face. It seemed so unfair. There were women in the courtyards in Abbey Street in town who bred like rabbits. Many of the babies never made it to their first birthday because of lack of food and warmth. Their parents were so poor that when their offspring died they would pay the under-taker a penny to bury them in the same coffin as the next person who could afford a proper burial. And here was Lavinia's baby, who had had nothing but the best of care since the day he was born, fighting to survive.

At some stage in the early hours, Zillah fell into an uneasy doze from pure exhaustion. The dawn chorus of the birds in the trees woke her the next morning and, rousing, she stretched painfully, noting that the fire was almost out. Hastily she raked out the ashes and threw some lumps of coal onto it, and it was then that it hit her, the silence. Stephen wasn't crying any more. She turned her attention to Lavinia. She was sitting in the nursing chair with the baby still clutched to her breast and Zillah's heart skipped a beat. He was so unnaturally quiet and still. Tentatively she crossed the room and laid her hand gently on his forehead. His skin was cold and clammy to the touch.

'Why don't you give him to me now?' she asked Lavinia chokily. He had slipped quietly away in the night and looked at peace now.

Lavinia shook her head, her eyes dull and glazed. 'No – you go and leave us, Zillah. I want a little time alone with him.'

Zillah opened her mouth to object but then thought better of it and tiptoed out of the room. She would go down and ask George to ride into town to fetch the doctor and the undertaker. Then when his mother had said her goodbyes she would wash the little soul and prepare him for his final journey.

Chapter Forty-Three

Cissie arrived at the Spooner residence in floods of tears later that day to break the bad news.

'I can't believe it,' Sunday murmured in shock. Cissie pulled out a kitchen chair, sat on it and noisily blew her nose. 'It happened in the early hours according to Zillah, but she'd dropped off to sleep so the poor missus must have sat cradling his little dead body for most of the night. He was stiff as a board before Zillah realised what had happened and the missus wouldn't let the undertaker take him from her for ages. They had to almost prise him out of her arms.' She gave a sob.

'Will he be buried in the orchard with his sisters?' Sunday asked in a wobbly voice.

'No, the vicar came and said that because he had lived he should be buried in a churchyard. The girls never breathed so that's why they were allowed to be buried in the grounds of Treetops Manor. The mistress ain't at all happy about it but there's nothing she can do to stop it.'

'Does the master know about it yet?' Mrs Spooner asked then and there were tears in her eyes too. Biddy Spooner wasn't quite as hard as she liked to make out.

'No,' Cissie said. 'The last the missus heard of him he was staying with his cronies in London, but Zillah says they have no contact address for him so there's no way of letting him know.'

'*What?* You mean he might miss his own son's funeral?' Sunday was appalled.

'That's about the long and short of it if he don't turn up. They can hardly put it off indefinitely, can they?' Cissie answered, before adding, 'And between you an' me I don't think he'll be that much bothered anyway unless little Stephen's death affects the legacy. He hardly ever even looked at the poor little scrap anyway.'

'Poor Lady Huntley,' Mrs Spooner said feelingly. 'That child meant the world to her. All she's ever wanted was to be a mother for as long as I've known her. God knows how this will affect her.'

Cissie nodded in agreement as she rose from the chair, saying, 'Well, I'd best be off. I've promised to go and break the news to Mrs Lockett as well, and it's a good walk from here.'

'There'll be no need for that, lass,' Mrs Spooner told her. 'I'll get Mickey to harness Treacle and he'll run you there in the trap. You sit down an' have a rest while I go an' find him. You look fair worn out.'

The old woman hobbled away as Cissie sat there looking bereft.

'Well, I'd better get on,' Sunday said reluctantly. 'Take care, Cissie, and be sure to let us know when the funeral will be.'

Cissie nodded numbly and then Sunday scurried away. She had been all set to tell Mrs Spooner that she was leaving that evening. She truly believed that if she stayed on at the Lodge, she would be putting everyone there at risk – for who knew what Pinnegar might try next? But now, after giving it some thought she felt she should

421

bide her time, until after Stephen's funeral at least. In the meantime, she could search about for another position. The thought of leaving all the people she had come to care for cut like a knife, but that was precisely why she needed to go. What a terrible week it was turning out to be. Thinking of the tiny dead boy, Sunday wanted so badly to give in to her grief and cry her eyes out ... but then she feared that, once started, she would never be able to stop.

Stephen was laid to rest in Chilvers Coton churchyard a week later following a funeral service conducted by the Reverend Edgar Lockett. It was a dull drizzly day to match the mood of the mourners who attended it. Mrs Spooner went whilst Sunday stayed at home with little Nell, who was distraught. Verity Lockett was particularly upset. After all, Marigold and Stephen had caught the measles from her Phoebe. Thankfully both of the little girls had been strong enough to fight it, but now Stephen was gone.

The whole of Treetops Manor was in mourning. The staff had become used to Molly dashing between the kitchen and the nursery and the sounds of the babies crying for their feeds – and now there was nothing but silence. The mistress was also giving them grave cause for concern, for since the undertaker had taken Stephen away in his tiny coffin she had not once spoken nor ventured from her room until the day of the funeral, and only then because Zillah had coaxed her into going.

'It ain't natural,' Cissie whispered to the cook,

Mrs Barlow. 'Zillah reckons that the mistress just sits gazin' out of the window. She ain't even cried.'

'The poor lass is grievin' hard,' the woman said sadly. 'An' don't forget – she's been through this a number o' times before.'

'Even so, it might have been a bit easier on her if her husband had been here,' Cissie said venomously.

'Huh! I doubt that,' Mrs Barlow answered as she loaded savoury patties onto a plate before handing it to the maid to carry to the dining room. She'd prepared a meal for any of the mourners who might wish to come back to the Manor following the service. 'That young bounder Ashley were neither use nor ornament. Happen the mistress will prefer to grieve on her own. But now Mrs Roundtree's asked if you'd pop up and collect all the baby clothes from the nursery and get them into the laundry room while the mistress is out o' the way. It will only push the knife deeper in if she goes up there an' sees his little things lying about.'

Cissie didn't relish the task one little bit but she nodded anyway and headed for the back stairs.

Once in the nursery, tears pricked her eyes as she saw Master Stephen's tiny clothes strewn about. Her thoughts unexpectedly turned to George then, and despite her grief, a little smile lifted the corners of her mouth. Just the day before, he had told her that he had feelings for her and she could barely believe her luck to think that a well-set-up young man like him would ever look her way! He knew all about the illegitimate baby she had given birth to and her poor beginnings, yet he was still prepared to look kindly on her. For her at least life wasn't all bad and, who knew, perhaps one day if things turned out as she had hoped, she and George would be married and she would have more babies, although none of them would ever replace the one she had lost, of course. On this slightly happier thought she glanced about to make sure she had missed nothing and set off for the laundry with her arms full of baby clothes.

It was almost a week later when the sound of hooves was heard on the drive outside, and shortly afterwards, the door at Treetops Manor was flung open. Ashley entered the hall and throwing his hat towards the little maid who had rushed to greet him, he demanded, 'Where is everyone? And why is this place so damnably quiet? It's like a graveyard in here!'

He frowned as the girl burst into tears and darted away just as the drawing-room door opened and his wife appeared.

'Ah, there you are, Lavinia. I was just asking the maid why it's so quiet. Something feels different.'

Lavinia stared at him without expression. How like Ashley, to just walk in as if he had only been gone for an hour or two instead of weeks. Today she made no pretence of being pleased to see him.

'May I ask where you have been?'

He was preening in the hall mirror, straightening his cravat – yet another new one, she noted – and smoothing his hair.

At the tone of her voice he glanced at her in the mirror and, noticing her pallor, he turned to face her. 'After staying in London I was invited to a friend's in Kent for a few days. But have you been ill? You look quite ghastly.'

'Would you really care if I had been?' Then, without waiting for his answer, 'No, I haven't. It was your son who was ill, as it happens.'

'Ah, probably the time of year. I believe babies are prone to get coughs and colds in the winter, aren't they?'

'It was neither a cough nor a cold.' She turned away and walked into the drawing room and he followed her, closing the door behind him.

'Stephen had the measles,' she told him when she had stopped in front of the roaring fire. She noted he didn't look particularly concerned but then this didn't surprise her.

'I see – and is he recovered?' As he spoke he was about to lift the cut-glass decanter to pour himself a drink but her next words stopped him in his tracks.

'He died. Two weeks ago. His funeral took place last week.'

Astounded, his mouth gaped open as he stared at her, then collecting his wits together he threatened, 'If this is some sort of malicious game you're playing, I have to tell you I find it in extremely poor taste.'

'I assure you it's quite true.' Her blue eyes were almost black as she faced him, her back ramrod straight. 'And you could not even be contacted. His own father!'

'But I ... how could I have known?' He began to pace, trying to take in what she had told him. However, Lavinia considered she had already

425

spent quite enough time with him and began to walk towards the door.

'Wait…' He put his hand out to stay her and she paused.

'What will I tell Mr Wilde?'

Her nostrils flared as she answered passionately, 'I have just told you that our son is *dead* – and all you can worry about is your uncle's money. Why, you are even more of a scoundrel than I thought. Pack your bags and leave immediately. I never want to set eyes on you again! And take your valet, Matthews, with you.'

'Now you can't mean that. This is my home and you are my wife.' He held his hand out to her but she slapped it away.

'Only when it suits you,' she ground out. 'But it stops here! You have gone too far and from this day on you are as dead to me as your daughters and your son. I don't care if your uncle's attorney cuts you off without a penny. Were you on fire in the gutter, I swear I wouldn't piss on you!'

Deeply shocked, he took a step back. Never in all his years with her had he heard Lavinia swear or be coarse, but the woman standing before him was no longer the sweet-natured malleable girl he had married. Grief had hardened her. Like all bullies, he was afraid of those stronger than himself.

'But what about my allowance?' She had always been generous to him despite the fact that he had never done a single day's work in all the years she had known him.

'I have already instructed my solicitor and the bank to stop it – so you had better pray that Mr

Wilde will look on you kindly.'

He saw a measure of satisfaction glittering in her eyes and knew in that moment that she meant every single word she said. This was no idle threat.

'Look,' he said in a low voice, 'I realise I should have let you know where I was. I should have been here – but give me another chance, that's all I'm asking. You *must* know how much I care for you and how much I cared for our son,' he pleaded as he broke out in a cold sweat.

'Really? I don't believe you.'

He looked at her with that charming lopsided smile that had once made her legs turn to jelly as he saw his comfortable way of life slipping away from him. Then, stepping forward, he said contritely, 'You poor, poor darling, what you must have gone through.'

But she made no move towards him and only continued to silently regard him as if he were of no consequence. It seemed to the man then that, along with the death of their son, her love for him had also died.

His temper flared as panic set in. 'You can't make me leave this house, you bitch! What is yours is *mine*. I'm your husband, remember? It's the law of the land!'

'Under normal circumstances you would be quite right,' she conceded. 'But have you forgotten that my father had the commonsense to make you sign a document before our marriage in which you agreed that my wealth should remain my own? Obviously dear Papa wasn't as blinkered as I was. But now if you will excuse me I am going to my room. I am grieving for our son even if you are

427

not. I would be grateful if you could be gone by the time I come down.'

Hot fury flowed through him as he ranted, 'Fine then – I'll go. But you'll soon come crawling, begging me to come home!'

A mocking smile hovered on her lips as she paused at the door to stare at him for one last time. 'Believe me, hell will freeze over before that happens.' And with that she sailed from the room, closing the door behind her. She had finally done what she now knew she should have done years ago, and she also knew that had her beloved father still been alive, he would have applauded her.

Chapter Forty-Four

January 1886

The New Year was a quiet affair as everyone was still mourning the death of baby Stephen. Sunday was also painfully aware that it was now a whole year since Daisy's death, so one way and another they were all glad when the celebrations were over and the household was running normally again. Sunday finally felt it was time to approach Mrs Spooner with her future plans. She had delayed her departure long enough. There had been a number of incidents during the last weeks, only minor ones admittedly, but she knew without a shadow of a doubt that Albert Pinnegar would never stop hounding her whilst he knew where she was. The inevitable could be put off no longer. Each one of those so-called minor incidents was a reminder that Pinnegar was always there, hovering in the background like a big black crow about to attack a helpless worm.

Her chance came on a cold and frosty January morning when she carried the old lady's mid-morning coffee into her.

Mrs Spooner had been unwell with a nasty cough and cold and was sitting bundled up in blankets before a blazing fire when Sunday entered the room. 'May I have a word?' the girl asked.

'Words cost nowt,' Mrs Spooner answered before blowing her nose noisily on a large white handkerchief. 'Sit yourself down, lass, an' spit it out whatever's on your mind.'

Sunday perched on the edge of a chair, hardly knowing how to begin. This was proving to be even more difficult than she had thought it would be.

'The thing is…' She gulped deep in her throat and forced herself to go on. 'It's so hard to say this but I'm just going to come out with it. I'm leaving.'

Mrs Spooner's eyebrows disappeared into the fringe of the wig that was perched somewhat crookedly on her head. 'What do you mean, you're leaving?'

'I've been intending to go for some time,' Sunday said in a low voice. 'But with little Stephen dying and Christmas coming up… Well, I thought it best to wait a while which was probably the wise

429

thing to do because I've found myself a new position.'

'But why? I thought you were happy here.' The old lady looked so hurt that Sunday was ashamed.

'Oh, I *am* happy here,' she said sincerely, reaching out to take the wrinkled hand in hers. 'But I also realised some time ago that while I'm here I'm not just putting myself at risk any more but all of you – and I would never forgive myself if any of you got hurt because of me. You know Mr Pinnegar will never leave me alone. All the incidents – the fire, the attack on Nell and the animals – I'm convinced they were caused by him so I'm going to move out of town. Not too far, just far enough away that he won't be able to find me.'

The old woman opened her mouth to object but then snapped it shut again. She wasn't overly concerned about herself but she knew that young Sunny was right. Pinnegar would hound her for as long as there was breath in his body *and* for as long as she stayed within the local area. Things had come to a pretty pass, and everyone was on edge. Something had to change, and it was brave of the girl to step forward.

'I shall be sorry to lose you, Sunny pet. You brought sunshine into this house,' Biddy told her mournfully. 'Will you come and see us sometimes?'

'Of course I will, although not for a while because of Pinnegar. I'll leave the address of where I'll be working, but you must promise faithfully that you won't give it to anyone, only our very closest friends.'

'As if I would!' Mrs Spooner snorted with an indignant toss of her head. 'But where are you goin'? Are they decent people you'll be working for?'

Sunday nodded as she crossed her fingers behind her back. Word had it that the farmer and his wife with whom she was going to live were harsh taskmasters – but time would tell and Sunday had never been afraid of hard work. 'I think so. It's about four or five miles away, I believe. They have a farm in Mancetter, which isn't so very far away.'

'No, it ain't as the crow flies,' Mrs Spooner agreed, then leaning forward she asked, 'Is there nothing I can do to make you change your mind?' Yet even as the words left her lips she knew that she was wasting her breath. Sunny could be a stubborn little bugger when she set her mind to something, which strangely enough was one of the things the woman had come to love about her.

'Have you told the others yet?' she asked.

'No – only Annie so she could line up a replacement for me. I didn't want to go and leave you in the lurch. She's already spoken to Mrs Lockett about getting someone from the workhouse to train in my place. I wanted to speak to you about it first before I told the others though. I hope you understand why I'm doing it.' Sunday welled up but choked back her feelings. 'I want you to know that I've been happier here than at any other time in my life – and I'll always be grateful to you for the opportunities you've given me.' The release of another girl from the workhouse to replace her would be the only good

431

thing to come out of this sorry mess, Sunday thought dismally. At least that youngster would gain her freedom now.

Mrs Spooner let out a deep sigh. 'And what about our Jacob? He still looks on you fondly, you know.'

'I'm fond of him too, but I don't feel ready to commit to anyone just yet and I think he's accepted that by now,' Sunday said honestly.

'That's fair enough ... but I'll miss you, lass. We all will, if it comes to that. When were you thinkin' of goin'?'

'I thought the end of the week.'

'I see. Then there's not much more I can say, is there? Just remember – there's always a home back here for yer if things don't work out.'

Sunday rose, her eyes overly bright, and quickly left the room with Mabel trotting at her heels. That evening, once the meal was over, she pulled Jacob to one side to have a quiet word with him. She felt it was the only fair thing to do but his aunt had already told him of Sunday's impending departure so it came as no surprise to him.

'I never really thought you were interested in me in that way,' he said, and tried to smile. 'And I wish you all the very best, I really do. You are a fine young woman, Sunday Small. If ever you do find a chap you want to settle down with, he'll be a lucky man.'

Sunday gave him a quick peck on the cheek. Thankfully he didn't seem to be overly upset and she wondered if he already had his sights set on someone else. Jacob had an eye for a pretty girl so he wasn't going to miss her for long.

Friday came all too quickly and soon Mickey was loading Sunday's possessions – far more than she had arrived with – into Mrs Spooner's trap while Treacle stood contentedly munching from a nose bag. Mrs Spooner had insisted that Mickey should take her to her new position, and now they were all assembled at the door to see her off.

'And please don't forget, if Tommy should turn up–'

'I know, give him your address but ask him to keep it to himself,' Mrs Spooner said patiently. Sunday had never completely lost hope that her friend would come home one day.

Sunday nodded numbly, aware that she was dangerously close to crying. Hastily, she embraced Mrs Spooner then hugged Nell, who wouldn't let her go and was sobbing into a large white handkerchief as if the end of the world was nigh. And then Sunday scrambled up onto the seat of the trap beside Mickey. He urged Treacle on and Sunday waved at the dear familiar faces as the trap began to move.

'Goodbye, I'll come and see you soon,' she shouted, and as the trap began to climb Bucks Hill she sank back in the seat, aware that there was no going back now.

Mickey was quiet on the journey, and when eventually they pulled onto the track leading to Yew Tree Farm and the farmhouse came into view, he sucked in his breath.

'It looks a bit run down,' he commented worriedly.

433

'Mrs Barnes, the farmer's wife, has been ill, which is why they need someone to help out,' Sunday said. She refrained from mentioning that the Barnes family had set on and sacked three girls in as many months, according to what she had heard. In truth she wasn't looking forward to working there at all but it was the only option she had at present.

The trap drew into a farmyard that was liberally dotted with weeds and Sunday bit her lip as she glanced at the dirty windows of the farmhouse. What had she got herself into this time?

Mickey swung down out of his seat, as agile as a cat, and helped Sunday alight before lifting her bags from the back, then side-by-side they approached the back door.

Sunday rapped on it and almost instantly someone shouted, 'Come in!'

They entered the kitchen together to see a woman, heavily wrapped in blankets, seated in a chair at the side of the fire.

'You must be the lass my Harry has set on,' she said bluntly, without a word of welcome. And then, scowling at Mickey, she added, 'An' what's *that!*'

She was staring at the poor lad as if he was something the cat had dragged in and Sunday bristled with indignation.

'This is my good friend Mickey. He was kind enough to bring me here.'

'Ah. Well, now he has, he can sling his hook. We don't like foreigners around here, especially darkies.'

Sunday opened her mouth to object but

Mickey placed his hand on her arm and shook his head. Sadly, he was used to facing prejudice.

'I was just going, missus,' he said, keeping his eyes fixed firmly on Sunday. Then with a nod he headed for the door, telling her, 'You know where we are should you need us. Goodbye, Sunny.'

When the door had closed behind him, Selah Barnes asked, 'Why did he call you Sunny? What's your real name?'

'My last employer used to call me Sunny, but my name is Sunday.'

'Huh! What sort of a name is that?' the woman snorted. 'While yer here I shall call yer "Girl".'

'As you wish,' Sunday said placidly. She then held out two envelopes to her new employer, saying, 'These are the references your husband told me I would need. One is from my last employer, Mrs Spooner, and the other is from the Reverend Lockett.'

The woman waved them aside. 'What use are a few fancy words on a bit o' paper to me? I speak as I find an' I'll judge yer by the amount o' work yer do. I'll expect it done properly, mind.'

Sunday glanced around the kitchen. It was absolutely filthy, far worse than the state Whittleford Lodge had been in. It was going to take her days to get this place back into some sort of order if the rest of the rooms were as bad as this. Every available space seemed to be cluttered with old papers, dusty bowls full of forgotten items, and huge cobwebs hung from the stained ceiling. Just as in Whittleford Lodge when she had first arrived there, the flagstones on the floor were so filthy the colour of them was indistinguishable.

435

Her new employer had by now begun coughing into a large piece of huckaback. It was hard to tell how old she was because her illness had obviously aged her, if the lines of pain about her eyes and mouth were anything to go by. Her hair was greying at the temples and scraped back carelessly with a couple of large combs, and her skin had an unhealthy tinge to it. She was also painfully thin and yet her eyes were a sharp piercing green, which led Sunday to believe she was younger than she looked.

'Well, are yer just goin' to stand there all day gawpin' like a simpleton, or are yer goin' to knuckle down to work?' the woman said harshly. 'We ain't employin' you to hang about an' do nowt.'

'I have no intentions of just hanging about,' Sunday snapped back. 'But first I would like to see where I'm going to be sleeping if you don't mind so that I can put my things away and change into my work clothes.'

The woman waved a finger towards a ladder in the far corner of the room. 'You'll have to make do wi' the room under the eaves. Me an' me old man an' me son use the bedrooms down here.'

Sunday nodded and carried her bags over to the ladder. When she'd manoeuvred them up the steps, which was no easy task, she dropped them onto the bare floorboards and looked around in dismay. It was freezing cold up there and, like downstairs, the place was positively insanitary. The roof sloped sharply on either side of her and she knew that she would have to be careful not to bang her head. A straw mattress was thrown on

436

the floor and there was a jug and bowl and a rickety old chest of drawers leaning on its side – but other than that the room was empty. Sunday couldn't help thinking of her clean and comfortable attic room back at Whittleford Lodge but she resolutely began to unbutton her best dress and slipped into one of her work ones before tying an apron across it. Luckily there were some nails hammered into the roof beams so she hung her best dress and her coat on them. The rest of the unpacking would have to wait until later, but she would tell the woman that she needed some time to sweep and wipe down the place before she retired. She would need some clean bedding too, if her new mistress owned any such thing. It was then that she saw what looked suspiciously like rat droppings on the floor and she shuddered. Every instinct she had told her to lift her skirts and race back to Mrs Spooner's as fast as her legs would take her, but Sunday had never been one to shirk her duties so, squaring her shoulders, she headed for the ladder again.

'Right, what would you like me to do first? And how should I address you?' she asked when she was down in the kitchen once more.

'Get some dinner on, Girl – me man an' me son will be in soon. An' while yer here yer can call me missus.' She gestured towards a door then, telling her, 'You'll find meat an' everythin' yer need to make a stew in there. Me 'usband says yer can cook?'

Because of Annie's guidance Sunday was able to answer truthfully, 'Yes, I can.' When she opened the pantry door she was pleasantly surprised to find that it was very well stocked with food. *Well, at least I'm not going to starve even if I get worked to death,* she thought with a grin. There were jars of home-made pickles and jams, a selection of vegetables and fruit that must have been carefully stored, as well as a large ham and a couple of meat joints on a marble slab. She picked out some potatoes, carrots and Brussels sprouts and a piece of cold roast beef that could be carved into slices for the meal, but when she reached the sink she was confronted by leaning towers of dirty pots and pans. Before she could get started, she'd have to tackle this lot. So she fetched the kettle that was luckily bubbling merrily away on the fire and set to. Once the stew was simmering over the fire, Sunday scrubbed the large table that stood in the centre of the room then turned her attention to the floor. She was sweeping away the dirt and debris when the farmer, accompanied by a surly-faced young man, entered the room, bringing a blast of icy air with them.

'Ah, so you arrived then,' the farmer said, throwing his grubby hat onto the clean table. Sunday had approached him in the market some weeks before after hearing that he was looking for indoor help at his farm. She hadn't liked him then and she liked him even less now. His son didn't look to be of a friendlier disposition either. He was tall and broad-shouldered with a ruddy complexion, and as she thought of the playful banter she had shared with Mrs Spooner's lodgers a lump formed in her throat.

'This is our Bill,' the farmer told her then,

nodding towards his son.

The young man was avidly watching her and Sunday felt as if he was undressing her with his dull grey eyes, but she inclined her head politely all the same. There was no sense in getting off on the wrong foot and things might improve with time.

The two men seated themselves at the table and, wiping her hands on her apron, Sunday went and took down two bowls from the dusty dresser that stood against one wall and ladled stew into them before fetching a loaf from the pantry.

The two men fell on the food like pigs, grunting and slurping as if they hadn't eaten for a month but neither of them thanked her or commented on the quality of the meal. She then spooned a smaller portion into a bowl for the missus but the woman merely pushed it around with the spoon and hardly ate anything. When no one invited her to join them, Sunday finally helped herself to a portion and sat at the table as far away from the men as she possibly could.

Once the men's bowls were empty they held them out to her for another helping and when they had eaten that too, they belched, rose from the table and left the room without a word.

Manners cost nothing, Sunday thought as she carried the empty bowls to the sink, but she didn't say anything; she merely went back to sweeping the floor.

It was dark when the men next appeared and the missus told her, 'Make a pot o' tea and set out bread, cheese an' pickles from the pantry, Girl. You'll need to bake tomorrow. Yer can make bread, can't yer?'

'Yes, I can,' Sunday answered stiffly as she went off to do as she was told, noting that neither man had even attempted to wash his hands before going to the table. After the meal the farmer sat reading the paper whilst the son disappeared off to the local inn, still wearing the clothes he had been working in all day. The missus was dozing by the fire by then and Sunday asked her, 'May I go up and clean my room now? And may I have some bedding?'

'You'll find beddin' in the ottoman in my bedroom. It's through that door over there – but don't go touchin' nothin' else, mind!'

'I am not in the habit of touching things that don't belong to me,' Sunday said indignantly and bustled away to return minutes later with clean sheets and some blankets. She hoisted them up the ladder, and once upstairs she wrapped her shawl about her in the chilly air as she shook the mattress and made her bed up. All she had to see by was the light of a candle so the main cleaning would have to wait until morning, for it was as black as pitch up there. By now she was exhausted, and deciding that she'd had quite enough for one day she washed in the cold water that she'd poured into the jug earlier in the day and after hooking her nightgown out of the bag that she hadn't had time to unpack, she slipped it on and climbed into the bed shivering. The blankets were itchy and she curled into a ball feeling thoroughly sorry for herself.

Suddenly the happy life she had led at Mrs Spooner's seemed a distant memory but she knew that she was going to have to grit her teeth and make the best of things, for her own safety and that of those most dear to her.

Chapter Forty-Five

'I was wondering if I might have Sunday afternoon off this week,' Sunday said to the missus early in February. She had been working on the farm for over a month now, and she was keen to see Cissie. There was little danger of Mr Pinnegar finding her at Treetops Manor.

The woman looked shocked. 'I would have thought yer'd settle in afore yer went askin' fer time off.'

Sunday stood her ground and faced her squarely. 'Everyone, even servants, is entitled to some free time,' she answered spiritedly. 'It was part of the agreement I made with your husband before I came here that I should have *every* Sunday afternoon off. I've been here for over a month now and not had any time at all to myself as yet since there was so much to do. And you can't deny I've worked very hard.'

Selah Barnes sniffed. 'Perhaps just one Sunday afternoon a month then,' she said grudgingly. 'But you're not to go nowhere till you've cooked the dinner an' cleared the pots.'

'I wouldn't dream of it.' Sunday fully intended to take every Sunday afternoon off from now on as had been agreed but didn't bother to argue the

441

point just then.

If the woman heard the sarcasm in Sunday's voice she chose to ignore it. She had to admit the girl had the house looking as neat as a new pin from top to bottom now – not that she would have told her that, of course. That was what she was paid to do, after all.

There had been times during that month when Sunday had come close to packing her things and just walking out, particularly after Bill was starting to become over-familiar with her every chance he got, but somehow she had forced herself to stay. Only the day before, she had slapped his face after he had pinched her bottom as she staggered to the sink with an armful of pots. She had carefully placed them down on the enormous wooden draining board and then crossing back to him, she had lifted her arm and whacked him. The trouble was, it had made him laugh rather than deter him from doing it again.

'I like a lass wi' a bit o' spirit.' He had grinned as he rubbed his reddened cheek and Sunday had stalked off up to her room in a sulk. The man was hateful and every day she spent with him made her detest him a little bit more.

'Play yer cards right, Girl, an' our Bill might just put a ring on yer finger. Him an' his dad will need someone to keep house for 'em after I've gone,' Selah Barnes had told her weakly when Sunday finally ventured back down the ladder after making sure that Bill had gone out again.

The very thought turned Sunday's stomach but all she said was, 'I don't intend to let anyone put a ring on my finger for some long time, thank

442

you, missus.' She was tempted to add that even when she did, it certainly wouldn't be her brute of a son, but she was too polite to say so.

The woman started to cough again then, and despite the fact that she was very difficult to get on with, Sunday couldn't help but feel sorry for her. She was clearly dying of consumption if the blood-stained rags Sunday had to leave in the soak bucket each night were anything to go by. Sunday waited on her hand and foot and tried to make her as comfortable as possible, yet she had never heard her son or her husband offer Selah one kind word. Nor was there a single word of thanks for all that Sunday herself did – not that she expected it any more. It had become clear within the first week that she was classed as no more than a skivvy.

Leaving the dough that she was kneading on the table, Sunday crossed to the sink to fetch her employer a drink from the pail of fresh water she kept there. All the water was supplied by a well in the farmyard and sometimes she felt as if she spent half her life walking to and fro from it.

The woman took it and sipped at it noisily before saying, 'Go an' fetch me pearls from the bedroom, would yer? An' yer can brush me hair then when you've finished that bread.'

Sunday quickly covered the dough and left it to rise on the hearth before doing as she was told. She fastened the string of pearls about the woman's scraggy throat before reaching for the hairbrush. She found it poignant that the woman insisted on wearing her pearls each day. They looked rather out of place on her neck, which at least was clean now, thanks to Sunday giving her a warm wash every day when the men were out in the fields – but appeared to be the only things of worth that Selah owned, apart from her worn gold wedding band. She had once told Sunday in one of her rare friendlier moments that the pearls had belonged to her mother, and she clearly treasured them. Now as she twisted the woman's thinning hair into a plait, Sunday felt her heart grow lighter. For the last month she had felt like a prisoner at times but now at least she had her afternoon off to look forward to – and she couldn't wait to hear from Cissie how everyone she cared about was doing.

Sunday was a day like any other until after lunch. Sunday washed and dried the dishes then climbed the ladder to her room to get ready for her outing. Once upstairs she glanced around with a sigh. Only the week before, she had insisted on some arsenic-laced bread being laid up there and sure enough she had woken the next morning to find a rat, almost as big as one of the farmyard cats, lying dead only inches away from her mattress. Bill had thought it was a huge joke and had taunted her with it when he went up to fetch it down, leaving her near hysteria; ever since, she had hardly slept a wink. *But it won't be for much longer,* she promised herself. Even living in the workhouse had been marginally better than working at Yew Tree Farm and she intended to start looking around for a new position just as soon as the weather improved.

Crossing to her bag, she started to lift out her

coat and good boots. She hadn't had cause to wear them since arriving but today she wanted to make an effort. It was as she was unpacking them that she noticed the brown paper package tied with string that had been handed to her when she left the workhouse. It probably contained the garments she had been wearing on the day she had been left on the steps of the workhouse … but even now, after all this time, it had remained unopened. For some strange reason hidden to herself, Sunday hadn't wanted to look at them. The tiny items must surely have been handled by the woman who had given birth to her, and until recently she had hoped that her mother would come back to claim her. Superstitiously, she had feared that opening the package would break the spell and jinx her dream of ever coming true. But, a little voice in her head told her, *there's no chance of that happening now, so what could be the harm in looking at them?*

Laying the small parcel on the floor she finished getting ready, keeping her eye on it the whole time. Should she or shouldn't she open it? And then finally curiosity got the better of her. Sitting on the side of the mattress she pulled the parcel towards her, carefully untied the string and turned back the paper, which was now brittle with age. What was revealed made her gasp, for inside was a small nightgown and a beautiful lacy shawl fit for a princess. They were clearly very expensive items and now her mind whirled. Her mother must have had money to afford such things! There was also something about the shawl that was vaguely familiar but for the life of her she couldn't think what it was. After fingering the delicate items for a moment or two she tried to conjure up a picture of the woman who would have dressed her in them, feeling the sense of abandonment she had experienced as a child all over again. Then resolutely she wrapped them back up and placed them in a drawer before shrugging her coat on. What did it matter now who her mother had been? She clearly hadn't wanted her and Sunday was used to fending for herself now. Tying the ribbons of her bonnet beneath her chin, she made her way down the ladder into the kitchen, careful not to trip on her long, elegant coat from Liberty's.

Bill was standing by the kitchen table when she descended and his eyes nearly popped out of his head at the sight of her. He'd never seen her in her best clothes before and whistled beneath his breath.

'I were just sayin' to me ma that you might make me a good wife,' he told her as if he were doing her some great favour. 'Yer a bit skinny admittedly an' yer were brought up in t'workhouse but I might be prepared to overlook that. Yer a good worker though, so what do yer say?'

Sunday could hardly believe her ears. 'Was that some sort of a marriage proposal?' she enquired icily.

'Aye, I dare say it were so – what's yer answer?' He hooked his fingers into his braces and swaggered, certain that she would jump at the chance of being his wife.

'I have no intentions of marrying you or anybody else for some long time,' she said primly.

'And now if you'll excuse me I must be off. It is my free afternoon, after all.'

He scowled as he watched her walk towards the door, clearly amazed by her response. 'Well, think on it then. You'll do no better. You're a pauper bastard, after all, wi' no idea where yer came from – an' most blokes wouldn't touch yer.'

'I'll bear that in mind,' Sunday told him sarcastically, and without another glance in his direction she marched out of the farmhouse.

It was less than an hour's walk to Treetops Manor and she fumed all the way as she thought of the cruel remarks he had made ... but then, not wishing to spoil her afternoon she tried to push the thoughts aside, and as she turned into the drive her spirits lifted again just as they always did whenever she visited this lovely home. One thing was for certain, now that Bill had set his sights on her, the sooner she was gone from Yew Tree Farm the better. After making her way round to the kitchen door she tapped and entered – and there was Cissie sitting with George at the kitchen table.

'*Sunday!*' The girl's whole face lit up at the sight of her friend and she shot across the room to wrap her in a warm hug. 'Oh ... it's just *so* lovely to see you. Are you settled at the farm? We've all missed you so much. Come and sit down and tell us what you've been up to.'

Sunday giggled, not able to get a word in edgeways as Cissie dragged her to the table and lifted the big brown teapot.

'Take your coat off else you won't feel it when you go back out,' she urged. 'And get this warm tea down you. You look frozen through. We've got

447

so much to tell you.'

She glanced at George then and blushed prettily before confiding, 'Me and George are betrothed now. And the mistress has given us her blessin'. I'm going to live in the rooms above the stables with him after we're married so I can go on working here. Well, at least until our family starts to come along,' she ended with a shy peep at her man, who beamed at Sunday.

'Why, that's wonderful news!' Sunday was genuinely thrilled for them, especially Cissie, and you only had to look at the couple to see how much in love they were.

George then stood up and said his goodbyes, as he had work to be getting on with, in the stables.

'I was wonderin' if perhaps you'd be me bridesmaid when we do get wed,' Cissie said when he'd gone, and Sunday nodded eagerly.

'It would be my pleasure – but when is the big day to be?'

Cissie became solemn. 'To be honest it's a case of the sooner the better for us, but we have to respect that Lady Huntley is still in mourning for Master Stephen so we've put it off till early next year.'

'Poor thing, how is she?' Sunday asked as she sipped at the hot sweet tea.

'Not good.' Cissie sighed. 'She rarely goes out any more. But then they say time is a great healer and in the meantime Zillah fusses over her like a mother hen. Zillah asked me earlier on today to pack away the rest of Stephen's baby clothes in the nursery; she says it's too upsetting for the mistress to have to keep seeing them lying about.

I was working up there this very afternoon as a matter of fact but I came down for a break. Perhaps yer could come an' talk to me while I carry on?'

'I will,' Sunday agreed. 'But I ought to pop in and see Lady Huntley first. She's been so good to me one way and another over the years, and I haven't seen her since the baby died so I'd like to go and pay my respects.'

'Right you are. You can come up with me and I'll show you which is her room.'

And after briefly catching up on how Mrs Spooner and everyone at Whittleford Lodge was faring, the two girls made their way upstairs chattering away non-stop. There was so much to talk about.

'That's Lady Huntley's bedroom door there,' Cissie whispered once they reached the first-floor landing. 'I shouldn't go mentionin' Master Ashley if I were you though,' she advised. 'She booted him out when he returned after the baby's funeral but he dropped on his feet. That type allus do. He's wealthy in his own right now, an' livin' the life o' Riley by all accounts. Still, they do say that what goes around comes around, don't they? So happen he'll get his just deserts one day – an' it won't be a day too soon as far as I'm concerned. The rotten sod put the mistress through hell. I reckon she's better off wi'out him.'

She gave a cheery wave then and set off for the nursery floor as Sunday straightened her skirts, smoothed her hair and advanced on Lady Huntley's bedroom door. She hadn't set eyes on the dear woman since her baby's death and had only

449

heard worrying news … but she and Lavinia Huntley had always been easy in each other's company, so she hoped the meeting would not be too difficult.

Chapter Forty-Six

It was Zillah who answered the tap on the door and she beamed in welcome when she saw who it was standing there.

'Well, I'll be…' she gushed, grabbing Sunday's arm and giving her a hug. 'Look who is here, Lavinia. Isn't she a sight for sore eyes? We've been wondering how you were getting on.'

Lady Huntley was sitting reading and at a glance Sunday saw that she had lost a lot of weight. There were bags under her eyes too, but she smiled when she saw Sunday and held her hand out to her.

'It is indeed lovely to see you, my dear. I know Mrs Spooner has worried about you although you've written to her a couple of times. Come and sit by me and tell us all about what you've been up to.'

Zillah took the seat at the side of her and Sunday shrugged. 'There's not much to tell really,' she admitted. 'This is the first time I've left Yew Tree Farm since I've worked there and I've been getting the house straight for them. Mrs Barnes has been ill for some time so it was in rather a state although I'm sure she wouldn't appreciate

450

me telling you that.'

'I see.' Lady Huntley stared at her and Sunday had the feeling that she could see right into her soul. 'And are you happy there?'

Sunday lowered her eyes and mumbled, 'It's all right, I suppose.'

'I sense there's more to this than you're letting on,' Lady Huntley said. 'Do they mistreat you?'

'Oh no, nothing like that,' Sunday told her hastily. 'It's just...' She paused, thinking how best to explain it. 'Mr and Mrs Barnes aren't the nicest of people, and the son, well, he's a brute, to be honest. Only today he told me he would do me the honour of marrying me – although I am only a pauper bastard from the workhouse!'

Lady Huntley's nostrils flared. 'How *dare* he say such a thing! I hope you put him in his place.'

'Yes, I did,' Sunday assured her. 'But it made me realise that I can't stay there now. I shall start to look around for a new position just as soon as I'm able.'

'There will be no need for that,' Lady Huntley answered firmly. 'Because I have the perfect post right here for you. Mrs Roundtree has informed me that one of our maids will be leaving at the end of the month so I shall need to replace her. Would you be interested in the post?'

Sunday stared at her, hardly able to believe her luck. After Mrs Spooner she couldn't think of anyone she would sooner work for – and surely she would be safer from Pinnegar when living at Treetops Manor than she had been at the lodge? Even he wouldn't dare to stalk her here. There were always so many of the staff about and he

451

would be afraid of being seen.

'I'd be very interested,' she chirped as Zillah looked on with a broad smile on her face. 'But I won't tell the Barneses that I'm leaving until nearer the time, if you don't mind. I think they'd make things difficult for me if they knew.'

'That's settled then,' Lady Huntley said with a smile. 'Before you go, you can see Mrs Roundtree and ask her to measure you for your uniform. She can have it all ready for you then and you'll have a room right next to Cissie's.'

Sunday had to stop herself from clapping her hands with delight and in that moment she realised just how unhappy she had been at the farm. She did feel slightly guilty at the thought of leaving Mrs Barnes, who was undoubtedly very ill, but decided she would tell them the week before she was leaving so that they had time to find a replacement to care for her.

Lady Huntley took her hand and patted it, clearly as happy as she was about the thought of her joining them at Treetops Manor, and it was then that Sunday said tentatively, 'I was so sorry to hear about baby Stephen, ma'am. He was a grand little boy.'

'Yes, he was.' Lavinia's eyes were suddenly full of tears but she smiled bravely and went on, 'But I consider I was very lucky to have him, if only for a short time. I never had that privilege with my daughters and, as I learned long ago, life has to go on.'

Sunday was about to change the subject, reluctant to cause the dear woman any more pain, when Lady Huntley said, 'Did you know that Tommy

452

has returned to Mrs Spooner's?'

Sunday's mouth gaped with shock before she whispered, 'No.'

'Yes, indeed. He turned up shortly after Christmas, so Mrs Spooner was telling me when she visited last week. And what a change there is in him. He's an apprentice to the carpenter in the town now and doing very well, by all accounts.'

Sunday's heart raced as she thought of him. He had always been so kind and so protective of her and Daisy, even when they had been in the workhouse. It was nice to hear that he was doing so well for himself.

'He is planning to rent a little cottage in Coton eventually, but until then he's staying at Mrs Spooner's.'

'And have they had any more problems with Mr Pinnegar?' Sunday wanted to know.

Lady Huntley shook her head. 'Apparently not. After you left, everything died down and they haven't had any incidents at all – although word has it that the ghastly man is making quite a few enemies with this new money-loaning scheme of his. He wants to be careful because some of the men he's mixing with would cut their own grandmother's throat for sixpence!' Lavinia's face had become quite animated.

Sunday didn't much care what happened to him. Even now, just the mention of his name could bring her out in goose bumps.

'On a happier note, Mrs Spooner informed me that Jacob and the young lady he's recently been stepping out with are becoming rather close.' Lady Huntley's eyes twinkled. 'Ellie is a lovely

453

lass and I have a feeling they'll become engaged before too much longer.'

Sunday was genuinely pleased to hear it. She had been very fond of Jacob but not in a romantic way so the knowledge that he was seriously courting would ease her guilt.

'And Mrs Spooner?' she asked then.

'Oh, the usual winter coughs and colds but she's holding her own,' Lady Huntley chuckled. 'I'm beginning to think that our dear Biddy will live for ever.'

'I hope she does.' Sunday grinned. 'Please send them all my love. But I ought to be off now. It will be dark in no time and I promised Cissie I would see her again before I go.' She refrained from saying that she was meeting her in Stephen's nursery. 'Thank you so much for offering me a job here. I promise I shall work hard for you.'

Lady Huntley grinned. 'Not too hard, I hope. Shall I tell Mrs Roundtree to expect you to start on the first of March? And don't forget to let her measure you for your new uniform before you leave.'

'Yes, please. And I won't forget. Goodbye for now, Lady Huntley. Goodbye, Zillah.'

Zillah saw her to the door and unexpectedly planted a kiss on her cheek. 'Bye, pet. I'll see you soon.' She looked almost as happy about the idea of Sunday working there as Sunday herself did and the girl headed for the nursery with a warm glow in the pit of her stomach. Once again it looked like her luck was about to change for the better.

Her happiness evaporated like mist when she

entered the nursery to find Cissie diligently folding Stephen's baby clothes and packing them away in brown paper in trunks that would be carted off to the attic, probably never to see daylight again.

The nursery was a sad, empty place without a baby in it. His shawl was flung across the back of a chair and the tiny blanket in his crib was turned back, just as it had been the last time he slept in it. The fire had long since died out; cold ashes had spilled out onto the hearth and Cissie wept as she went about collecting up his things. They still smelled of milk and baby and it broke her heart. The mistress was unlikely to ever bear another child. Her final chance to be a mother had died with Stephen.

'It's so sad, isn't it?' Sunday whispered. 'Lady Huntley was so very happy with her little son.'

Cissie wiped her eyes as Sunday began to stroke some of the exquisite baby clothes.

'Yes it is, poor soul. Seems she were never destined to be a mother.'

Then absent-mindedly fondling a pretty lacy shawl, Sunday lifted the mood again when she told Cissie about her job offer. Her friend was delighted.

'Why, that's the best news I could have had.' She stopped what she was doing for a moment to give Sunday a sisterly hug. 'Just think, we'll get to see each other every day then, and you can help me plan for me weddin'.'

'Here, you'd better pack this.' Sunday handed her the shawl, wondering why she had a strange tingling feeling as she did so. 'But now I'd better get down and see the housekeeper before I leave. Lady Huntley says I've to be measured for a uniform.'

'You'll love working here,' Cissie promised her. 'We get treated very well.'

The girls said goodbye for the time being then and Sunday headed for the kitchen again in search of Mrs Roundtree. Lady Huntley had already sent Zillah to tell her that Sunday would be coming to work there, and so the kindly woman was expecting her. She whipped her off to the sewing room where she seemed to measure every inch of her.

'I'll show you where you'll be sleeping before you go,' she offered, and took her up to a sparsely furnished but spotlessly clean room right next door to Cissie's. To Sunday, who had been sleeping on a straw mattress on the floor in a freezing attic, it looked like heaven.

'It's lovely,' she said happily.

'Hmm, well I dare say there'll be some late-night chinwags going on if your mate is right next door,' Mrs Roundtree said shrewdly, 'but just so long as it doesn't affect your work and you don't disturb anyone, I'll turn a blind eye or rather ear to that.'

They made their way back downstairs and after saying goodbye to George, Sunday set off back to the farm, feeling a great deal happier. *Bill can behave as badly as he likes from now on,* she thought to herself, *because I won't have to put up with it for much longer.*

It was almost fully dark by the time she arrived back at the farm, and Selah Barnes started on her straight away.

'You've took yer time, ain't yer?' she whinged.

456

'The men are starvin'. Get some tea on the go.'

'When I've changed my clothes I will,' Sunday answered boldly. She didn't even care if they sacked her now. She could always sneak back and hide out with Mrs Spooner for a couple of weeks until she took up her new position. She would get to see Tommy again then...

Even the draughty cold attic couldn't dampen her spirits that late afternoon and after lighting the candle she began to change out of her best clothes, humming happily to herself. She was standing there in her petticoats when she suddenly had the feeling that someone was watching her. Whirling about, she was horrified to see Bill's head sticking above the top of the ladder.

'What on earth do you think you're doing?' she demanded angrily, snatching up her dress to cover her modesty.

He licked his thick lips and grinned. 'Now don't get goin' all coy on me,' he teased. 'After all, once we're wed I'll see it all anyway.'

'I told you – I'm not ready to marry anyone,' Sunday sputtered indignantly. 'Now go away this minute!'

With a chuckle he clattered down the ladder leaving Sunday feeling very vulnerable indeed. Why hadn't his mother stopped him from climbing up there? Selah had known she was getting changed. And what if he were to do it again? With shaking fingers, she hastily drew her work dress on and went to prepare the tea, ignoring Bill's hungry eyes as best she could. *Thank goodness I'll be leaving soon,* she thought, because who knew what he might attempt next?

Chapter Forty-Seven

The next two weeks were a nightmare. Sunday had no way of blocking the entrance to the attic so she slept little and kept waking to check that Bill wasn't climbing the ladder to join her. She knew that if he did, she could scream – but also guessed that neither the farmer nor his wife would come to her aid. If she married their son, they would have a built-in full-time skivvy for life – so they were not going to stop him from doing whatever it took to make her agree to wed him, were they?

Lack of sleep made her feel dull and listless so when there was a tap on the door one wild windy night just as she was serving up the supper, she took little notice although she had never known the Barnes family to have visitors before. Bill went to answer it.

And then she heard a voice that she had never forgotten – and slamming the dish containing the bacon and leek pie onto the draining board, she raced across the room and pushed Bill aside.

'Tommy! Oh, Tommy, I thought I'd never see you again!' She was shocked at the change in him. He was even more handsome than she had re-membered and seemed so much older somehow.

Bill was glaring at the young man on the step. 'Who the bloody hell is this then?' he demanded.

'He's a friend,' Sunday said, as Bill made to

shove her back into the room. 'And I haven't seen him for a long time so I want to have a word with him.'

'Not in *my* house yer won't,' the missus shouted from her seat at the side of the fire. 'Tell him to clear off. I told you before, we don't want strangers comin' round here! An' you've got to dish the dinner up, Girl.'

'Dish it up yourself,' Sunday retaliated. 'If I can't invite Tommy inside then we'll go and talk in the barn.' With that she stepped out into the cold night and, taking Tommy's hand, she led him across the yard through a number of indignantly squawking chickens and into the shelter of the barn.

It was hard to make out his features in the gloom but she could sense him towering over her and her heart began to hammer.

'Sorry if I've got you into bother coming here, but it's so wonderful to see you again, Sunday,' he said, and even his voice sounded different now too. More grown up somehow.

'Oh, don't get worrying about them. They're horrible, the whole lot of them,' she fumed.

'So why are you here then if they treat you like that?'

She could hear the concern in his voice and it touched her. 'I won't be for much longer but they don't know it yet,' she confided and she then went on to tell him of her new position at Treetops Manor.

'But why ever did you leave Mrs Spooner's in the first place?'

She lowered her head. 'Because while Mr

459

Pinnegar knew I was there he would never have given any of us any peace,' she explained. And then she said something that she had never dared to voice. 'And because I still wonder if he didn't have something to do with Daisy's death. Oh, Tommy, I know she was at her lowest ebb but I still find it hard to believe that she would have taken her own life or been clumsy enough to fall into the canal.'

'I've thought the same,' he said in a low voice. 'Trouble is, we have no proof. If I had and I knew it was him, I'd kill him with my bare hands. I'm just so sorry I couldn't protect you or Daisy.'

He reached out to her then and without thinking she leaned against him, loving the feel of his arms as they slid around her and the clean, manly smell of him; he smelled of wood and soap.

'I'm sorry I ran off as I did,' he sighed. 'But I needed time away to think things through and sort myself out. Ever since our parents died I wanted to be my sister's protector, and when she was being used by Pinnegar, I didn't even notice, Sunday. And when she got with child and then drowned, I asked myself what kind of brother I was. Useless! I felt that I'd let her down.'

'But you didn't,' Sunday objected with her head tucked beneath his chin.

'I think I know that now, but I didn't then.'

Their conversation was stopped from going any further when the barn door was suddenly pushed open and Bill appeared, bearing an oil lamp. The light fell on them stood close together and his mouth twisted.

'Mam says yer to get yer arse inside right now,'

he said to Sunday. 'An' what are you doin' wi' this feller? Yer betrothed to *me,* in case yer'd forgotten!'

'I most certainly am not.' Sunday stepped away from Tommy and stood hands on hips, glaring at him. 'I've already told you at least a dozen times that I'll *never* marry you, so when are you going to get it through your thick head?'

'We'll see about that.' Bill then turned his attention to Tommy and ordered him, 'Get off my land afore I call the coppers to yer.'

'For doing what? Since when has visiting a friend been an offence?' But Tommy began to move towards the door all the same, not wishing to make things worse for Sunday. 'I'll be at Mrs Spooner's should you need me,' he told her and with a final hard stare at Bill he strode away, to be swallowed up by the darkness.

Sunday was so humiliated and angry that she placed her hands on Bill's chest and pushed him out of the way with a strength she hadn't known she possessed before storming back into the kitchen.

'That'll be the last time yer invite one o' yer fancy men back here else you'll find yerself out on yer arse, Girl,' Mrs Barnes railed at her and suddenly something in Sunday snapped.

'That would suit me just fine,' she retaliated. 'You can get some other mug to run around after you because I shall be out of here first thing in the morning.' With that she ran up to the attic and began to ram her belongings into a bag.

Very slowly her anger subsided as she listened to the conversation grumble on downstairs. She knew that they were calling her all the names under the sun but she didn't care. She couldn't wait to be away from the place and with her itchy blankets wrapped tightly about her to ward off the cold she sat whiling away the hours and praying for daylight to come.

The sound of someone clattering about the kitchen early the next morning made her start and she realised that at some point during the early hours of the morning she must have fallen into an exhausted doze. This is it, she told herself resolutely, and lifting the two bags she had arrived with she started down the ladder. They could get their own damn breakfasts. She was off!

'And where do yer think you're off to in such a hurry?' Mrs Barnes demanded as she reached the bottom of the ladder.

'I told you last night I was leaving.' Sunday's chin jutted defiantly as the woman surveyed her with a sly look in her eyes.

'You ain't goin' nowhere till yer've give me me pearls back, yer little thief, else I'll call the coppers.'

'*What?*' Sunday's mouth dropped open. 'I haven't got your pearls. You know I haven't!'

'Well, they've gone missin' an' who else could 'ave taken 'em, eh? Bill, check her bags!'

Before Sunday could stop him Bill had snatched her bags from her and tipped the contents all over the floor.

'But I never...' Her voice trailed away as her eyes settled on the pearls lying on the fancy baby shawl. She was so shocked that she was momentarily struck dumb. And then it hit her. Bill must

462

have crept up the ladder and placed them in her bag when she had dozed off. Even so, it wasn't the pearls that her eyes were fastened on but the shawl ... as it finally struck her why the little garment had seemed so familiar. She felt as if she had had all the breath knocked out of her body as Mrs Barnes carried on ranting.

'See? Yer nothin' but a common little thief,' the woman said triumphantly. 'An' you offer to so much as set foot out that door an' leave us all in the lurch, girl, an' I'll have the coppers on yer tail quicker than yer can say Jack Robinson!'

But her words were going straight over Sunday's head as her mind reeled with shock. Giving a strangled cry, and before anyone could stop her, she turned on her heel and raced back to the ladder again.

Once back in the attic room she sank to her knees as she desperately tried to put her thoughts into some sort of order. She had been left on the workhouse steps wearing an identical shawl to the one Mrs Lockett's baby wore – and that shawl had been given to Verity by ... none other than Lady Huntley! Stephen had had an identical one too – but what could it all mean? Unless...

Slowly everything began to fall into place like the pieces of a jigsaw. She recalled Lady Huntley telling her that she had ordered all the baby clothes from an exclusive shop in London's Mayfair before the birth of her beloved first, stillborn daughter. None of the items had been worn, apart from to bury the tiny corpses in, but had been lovingly stored. Sadly, her second daughter had also been stillborn, but ... *her third daughter had*

463

been born on Sunday's own birthday and would have been the same age as her ... which could only mean...

Heart hammering, Sunday pressed her fingers against her pounding forehead. She remembered Zillah telling Mrs Lockett how much Mr Huntley had wanted a son – it was something to do with his inheritance from his late uncle – so could it be ... could it be that *she* had been the third-born daughter and because she wasn't the son he had hoped for, she had been abandoned on the workhouse steps? But no – there were *three* tiny graves in the orchard at Treetops Manor.

Even so, now she wondered at the colour of her hair and eyes: they were the exact same colour as Lady Huntley's. Surely it was all too much of a coincidence? Could it be that Lady Huntley was really callous enough to sacrifice her newborn daughter for her husband's whim? If Sunday was indeed Lavinia's daughter, then everything about her was a well-calculated lie, for how could she pretend to be grieving for her son when she had abandoned her daughter so callously? Yet even as the thought occurred to her, Sunday rejected it. She had come to know and care for Lady Huntley and could not believe that the gentle woman would do such a wicked thing.

None of it made any sense but Sunday was determined to get to the bottom of it. But how? she asked herself. Perhaps she should just ask the woman outright? She cringed at the thought, for if Mrs Huntley truly had no knowledge that her last daughter had been born alive, what would Sunday's accusations do to her? And what if she wasn't her daughter? Perhaps she could voice her suspicions to Mrs Lockett instead... Over the years, the kindly woman had become almost like a surrogate mother to her, but was it fair to involve her?

Sunday scrubbed at her eyes with the palms of her hands as her head spun in confusion. Perhaps it was just as well that she wouldn't be able to go and work for her for a while. She was only too aware that should she try to leave now, Mrs Barnes would have her arrested for theft. No, much as she hated it she would continue to live here – if it could be called living, that was – and to skivvy for the Barnes family. But she would never marry Bill. She would rather throw herself from the top of the quarry than do that!

Suddenly the rosy future she had planned back with her dear friends was gone in the blink of an eye. There would be no chance now of saving a little each month towards her dream, and grabbing the chamber pot from the side of the bed she leaned over it and was heartily sick.

When she went back downstairs sometime later, in her work clothes, the men had left and Mrs Barnes was in her usual position at the side of the fire.

'We'll be havin' no more silly talk about yer leavin' then,' she stated and Sunday couldn't be bothered to argue with her even though she knew the woman had tried to set her up to look like a thief. 'Good!' Selah nodded with satisfaction. 'If you'd been called up in front o' the magistrates fer stealin' you'd likely have been sentenced to a stretch in jail – an' who'd employ yer once yer

465

came out?'

'No, I'll be staying,' Sunday answered flatly as she tied her apron about her waist.

'Right, then get crackin' on the dirty laundry. You've wasted enough time as it is this mornin', an' when that's done yer can come back in an' start on the dinner. The mister slaughtered one o' the pigs yesterday so we'll be dinin' on pork fer weeks.'

Without a word, Sunday headed for the laundry room.

Chapter Forty-Eight

They were almost into March when Sunday decided that it was time to get word to the housekeeper at Treetops Manor that she wouldn't be taking up the position she had been offered there, after all. How to do it was the problem. She couldn't bear the thought of going there again, even to see Cissie, not until she felt clearer about her suspicions and what this might mean. And then it came to her – she could get word to them via Mrs Spooner, and there was no time like the present.

Marching into the kitchen, she told Mrs Barnes, 'I shall be going out this afternoon.'

'What do yer mean, you'll be goin' out indeed,' the woman challenged with the little strength she had left.

'Exactly what I said,' Sunday answered without

wavering. 'I've told you I intend to take one after-noon a month off and I've decided this month's will be today. If you don't like it, you can lump it.'

'How dare yer talk to me like that, yer little trollop!' Mrs Barnes wheezed, going red in the face, but ignoring her Sunday climbed the ladder to her room to get ready. When she came down some minutes later the woman was still chunter-ing indignantly but Sunday needed to get going. She set off towards Clock Hill at a smart pace and without looking back.

On the bridge that spanned the canal she paused to stare down at the narrowboats. *How nice it would be to just climb aboard one and sail away to where no one could find me,* she thought glumly. Her emotions had undergone a number of changes since the epiphany about the shawl, ranging from hurt to anger. The worst of it was, there was no one she could talk to. She had thought again of visiting Mrs Lockett but then realised that this wouldn't be fair on her. Verity Lockett was related to Zillah, who was also Lady Huntley's maid so it would place her in a difficult position. Likewise, she couldn't confide in Mrs Spooner either, fond of her as she was. Biddy and Lady Huntley were great friends, so until Sunday had decided what she wanted to do about her suspicions she must keep them to herself.

With a sigh she moved on until Whittleford Lodge came into sight. A lump formed in her throat as she thought of how happy she had been there. It had almost been like being a part of a family for the first time in her life and she ex-perienced a fresh surge of resentment towards

Albert Pinnegar. Why couldn't he have just left her alone?

She was halfway down Buck's Hill when she had the feeling that she was being watched. She whirled about, but could see no one there. *You're starting to imagine things now,* she scolded herself and quickened her footsteps, but still the sensation persisted. It was a relief when she finally skirted the house and headed for the kitchen where she saw Nell washing up at the sink. Annie was rolling pastry at the table but at sight of her they both stopped what they were doing and hastened to let her in, bombarding her with questions.

'Eeh, lass. We've really missed yer an' that's a fact. Are you all right?' asked Annie, thinking that Sunday looked rather pale.

'An' do yer like workin' on the farm? Do they have dogs an' cats?' from Nell, and all the while Mabel was also jumping up her, adding her greeting to theirs.

Sunday knelt to stroke her and got her face thoroughly licked in the process.

'Just let me get my breath back and I'll answer all the questions you like,' she pleaded as she rose and plopped onto a kitchen chair.

'Make a fresh pot o' tea, pet,' Annie instructed Nell as she took a seat at the side of her, and Sunday made an effort to look cheerful.

For the next ten minutes the questions came fast and furious. Sunday was careful not to let them know how unhappy she was as she answered them as best she could, but eventually she asked, 'Is Mrs Spooner in?'

'Aye, she's in the drawing room.' Annie cocked

her head towards the door. 'An' it's right glad she'll be to see you an' all.'

As Sunday rose, Annie's face fell. 'You will be stayin' fer tea, won't yer?' she asked hopefully but Sunday shook her head.

'I'm afraid not, Annie. I'd love to but I have to get back to the farm. Mrs Barnes has been right poorly this week so I'm needed there.'

'I see. Well, don't get leavin' it too long afore yer come again, pet. As long as you're safe to do so, that is.' Annie planted a resounding kiss on her cheek and Nell got all weepy as she headed for the door.

Sunday found her old employer done up to the nines in all her finery as usual when she entered the drawing room and once again she received a rapturous welcome.

'Come an' sit by me an' tell me all you've been up to,' the old lady said, patting the seat at the side of her. 'Lady Huntley were tellin' me you'll be startin' work fer her at Treetops Manor shortly.'

'Actually, that's what I've come to talk to you about,' Sunday said as she sat down and spread her skirts. 'The thing is, I won't be going there, after all, and I wondered if you could let her know for me.'

'Not goin'? Why ever not?'

'Mrs Barnes is very ill and I don't feel it would be fair to leave her.' Sunday crossed her fingers beneath the folds of her skirts, and avoided the woman's eyes as she lied to her.

'Well, I have to say I'm surprised.' As Mrs Spooner looked at her shrewdly, Sunday felt colour rise in her cheeks. She had never been a very good liar. 'I got the impression yer weren't too fond of working at that farm and there'd be far better opportunities for you at Treetops Manor. You wouldn't have to work so hard or do such long hours either. And you'd be nearer your friends. Lady Huntley is goin' to be very disappointed indeed, and so is Cissie.'

Sunday said awkwardly, 'It can't be helped. I can hardly leave Mrs Barnes in the lurch, can I?'

'Huh! From what I've heard you wouldn't be the first. Word has it they can't keep staff there 'cos they don't treat 'em right, but then I suppose the decision is down to you at the end o' the day. But if you're quite sure, of course I'll get word to her for you.'

Thankfully they went on to speak of other things then. Of what the lodgers had been up to and how Jacob was.

'He's took a rare shine to the new girl,' Mrs Spooner told her cautiously, keeping a close eye out for her reaction. 'She's in town at the moment pickin' up some bits an' pieces for Annie.'

'I'm happy for him,' Sunday assured her truthfully. Jacob would make someone a very good husband but she knew that it could never be her. He deserved to have someone who really loved him, not someone who would simply be marrying him for security. 'And if they do make a go of it she'll be a very lucky girl.'

Mrs Spooner sighed. She would have liked to welcome Sunday into the family but respected her for being true to her heart. 'Oh ... an' there's somethin' else,' she said, suddenly remembering, and rising slowly she leaned heavily on her stick as she crossed to the mantelpiece and carried an envelope back to Sunday.

'This letter came for you t'other day. I was going to get it to you.'

'A letter for *me?*' Sunday was amazed and couldn't for the life of her think who it might be from. But yes, it was her name on the envelope so she thanked Mrs Spooner and slipped it into her pocket to read later. The urge was on her to open her heart and confide her fears, but it wouldn't have been right.

All too soon it was time to set off back to the farm again and she rose reluctantly. It had been so nice spending time in the only home where she had known happiness. She was a little disappointed that she hadn't seen Tommy again, but he was probably out at work and as Mrs Spooner hadn't mentioned him she hadn't liked to.

'Let me get Mickey to run you back in the trap,' Mrs Spooner offered then but Sunday declined. She was terrified of bumping into Albert Pinnegar again but didn't want to expose Mickey to any more insults from the Barneses.

'I'll be fine,' she promised. 'And if I hurry I'll be back before it's dark.' She hugged the old woman, whose eyes were suddenly overbright, and after promising that she would return very soon she set off back to the farm. She had almost reached Woodford Lane when she remembered the letter in her pocket so she stopped to open it and then gasped with delight.

It was from Tommy, and as she read it her heart warmed.

Dear Sunday,

I hope I did not make things difficult for you when I called at the farm a while back. I am now working for the carpenter in town as you know and I have rented a tiny two-up two-down house in Shepperton Street. I would love to see you if you have any spare time off from your duties. Perhaps you could come and have tea with me one Sunday? I have written the address below and look forward to hearing from you,

Best wishes

Tom x

Tom! He had signed his name Tom. It made him sound so much more grown up, but then he was nineteen now. With a smile she folded the letter and put it away carefully then continued on her journey. Once again she couldn't rid herself of the feeling that she was being followed and the hairs on the back of her neck stood up as she hurried on. She had almost reached the track that led to the lane when just for a brief second she could have sworn that she saw someone moving in the darkening shadows. Fear made her break into a run. What if it were Albert Pinnegar or one of his henchmen following her? She didn't pause again until the farmhouse was in sight, at which point she stopped to get her breath back but only for a moment or two. She had been gone for less than three hours, almost a third of that time spent on getting to and fro, but she knew that she would be made to suffer for it when she arrived, and she was soon proved to be right.

'You took yer time, didn't yer?' Mrs Barnes greeted her the second she stepped through the door. 'The fire's almost out an' not so much as a bite prepared fer the men when they come in from their work. You're bone idle, Girl, that's what you are.'

'Then get someone else to take my place.' Sunday was in no mood for the woman's complaints whether she was ill or not. 'Now if you'll just give me a chance to get changed I'll come down and make the fire up. *Then* I'll start to prepare the evening meal.' With that she made for the ladder, leaving the farmer's wife muttering beneath her breath. Sunday was beyond caring now and no longer even attempted to be pleasant. She merely spoke when she was spoken to, or had to and that was enough.

The men came in shortly after to find a cold meal spread out on the table for them. Bill snorted as he eyed the cold pork pie, cheese, ham and pickles.

'So what's this then? Ain't a man entitled to a hot meal when he's been out workin' all day?'

'She's been off flyin' her kite,' his mother told him nastily with a glare at Sunday.

Bill narrowed his eyes. 'Have you now. An' who have yer been with?' he said jealously.

Sunday paused in the act of sawing the loaf. 'What I do with my spare time is nothing to do with you, *or* who I do it with,' she said.

She watched, feeling sick, as he lowered himself onto a chair and began to ram food into his mouth. *Even the pigs in the sties outside have more*

473

manners than him, she found herself thinking as she went to fetch the jug of ale the men insisted they should have with their evening meal each night. She banged it down on the table, causing some of it to slop over onto the tablecloth, then loosening her apron she slung it across the back of a chair and headed for the ladder that led to her room.

'An' just *where* do yer think yer goin' now?' Mrs Barnes demanded. 'There's still the washin'-up to do, Girl!'

'I'll do it tomorrow,' Sunday retorted and disappeared up to her room.

That night, she tossed and turned as sleep eluded her. The visit to Mrs Spooner's had brought home to her just how much she had lost – and now her future stretched pointlessly ahead of her. The only good thing to come of knowing who her real mother was – if indeed Lady Huntley *was* her mother – was the fact that she now knew that she was no bastard, for all the good it would do her. She wished again that she could allow her emotions to find release in tears, but over the years she had strictly schooled herself not to cry. How Miss Frost had loved it when the children she had punished wept! She was thinking of the hateful matron and the equally hateful Mr Pinnegar when she became aware of a noise downstairs: if she wasn't very much mistaken, she had just heard the ladder to her attic room creak. That could only mean one thing: someone was climbing it and she would have bet her life that that someone was Bill. It was dark as pitch in the attic, the only light shining through the hatch from the dying fire in the kitchen below. Frantically she peered into the gloom looking for something that she might use as a weapon to defend herself, but the only thing she could see were her ugly old work boots that she wore about the farm. Grasping one, she slid out of bed onto the cold floorboards and on her hands and knees she crawled across the room to the opening.

Seconds later, the top of Bill's head appeared and with every ounce of strength she possessed she brought the boot down on top of it. He let out a yelp of pain, then as his hands loosed from the ladder he crashed back down onto the floor below, landing in an undignified heap.

'What the bloody 'ell did yer do that for, yer silly bitch!' he screeched as he sat with his head in his hands.

The door to Selah's bedroom opened and she limped painfully across to her son, asking, 'What's to do 'ere then?'

'I whacked him when he was trying to climb up to me – that's what's to do!' Sunday shouted down through the hatch.

'Yer silly little cow,' the woman scolded, helping her son to rise to his feet. She held up her candleholder. A huge bump was already forming on her son's brow. 'Yer should be flattered he's payin' any interest in a little bastard from the work'ouse! This farm'll be all his one day when owt happens to me an' his dad.'

'I'm not a *bastard* and I wouldn't want *him* if he were going to inherit a castle,' Sunday stormed, but she was shaking all over with shock after her

475

narrow escape from rape. Now that Bill had tried it once, there was nothing so sure as that he would try it again.

Chapter Forty-Nine

The atmosphere was strained at breakfast the next morning but Sunday went about her duties as usual, trying to ignore the whole pack of them. Who did Bill think he was anyway, doing her some great honour by trying to force himself on her like that. And she had no doubt whatsoever that this was what he had intended to do. He certainly hadn't climbed the ladder for a game of tiddly-winks, yet here were his parents, treating her as if *she* had done *him* some grave injustice. She didn't even feel guilty when she saw the huge bruise on his forehead. It served him right and she'd do the same again if he repeated his attempt to deflower her! Maybe next time he'd break his horrible neck.

Out in the laundry room she took out her frustration on the washing as she pummelled it in the dolly tub, and all the while her mind was busily working. By lunchtime she had devised a plan. It was the only option open to her now. She would wait until the early hours of the following morning and then slip away under cover of darkness, when she was sure that they were all fast asleep. They wouldn't be able to stop her this time. She dreaded being out alone in the dark but knew that she had no choice if she were to escape. She planned to go to Mrs Lockett at the vicarage. Verity would help her, she was sure of it, but as yet she had no idea where she would go from there. For now it would be enough just to get away from the farm before Bill got the better of her.

The day seemed endless but at last she was able to get up to her room where, instead of climbing onto the uncomfortable straw mattress, she hastily rolled her belongings into a bundle and shoved everything into her largest bag. Eventually she heard the family retire to their rooms and she strained her ears into the darkness, hoping that Bill was in too much discomfort to repeat the previous night's attempt to come to her. Thankfully all was soon silent save for the creaking of the house as it settled and the sound of an owl in the tree outside. She waited until she heard the sound of the old grandfather clock strike one then cautiously began the climb down the ladder, praying that she wouldn't be heard. When she finally reached the bottom, which was no mean feat when juggling her bag, she stole across to the back door and, placing her bag down, she grappled with the bolt. It was very stiff and when she finally managed to shoot it across, the sound cracked around the room like a gunshot. Sunday held her breath but thankfully all remained quiet so she opened the door and stepped out into the chilly air. The dog in the kennel came out, his hackles rising, but when he saw it was Sunday he slunk back inside and she moved on.

It wasn't until she was a good mile away from the farm that she finally paused to rest for a moment. Thank goodness no one appeared to be following her. She was away from the hated Barnes family and hoped she would never have to clap eyes on any of them ever again.

It was a very long walk to Coton, and by the time the Chilvers Coton church spire came into view, she was completely exhausted and also reluctant to involve Mrs Lockett in her problems. And then it came to her: Tommy, or Tom as he now pre-ferred to be called, would help her – she was sure of it – and he lived close to the church. Thankfully she knew most of the people who lived in the cottages in Shepperton Street so it was fairly easy to guess which one Tom was renting. She judged that it must be three or four o'clock in the morn-ing by now and she hated to disturb him – but what choice did she have? After approaching the door, she tapped on it and waited anxiously, praying that she was at the right cottage. After a while she was beginning to think that no one had heard her but then the door suddenly inched open a crack and Tom's bleary eyes peered out at her.

Almost instantly he was wide awake. Taking her arm, he helped her inside and hastily lit the oil lamp that was standing on the table. She was em-barrassed to see that he was dressed in nothing but his trousers with his braces dangling and she quickly averted her eyes as he asked, 'What on earth are you doing out and about all alone at this time in the morning, Sunday? Has something hap-pened?' Then without waiting for an answer he crossed to the dying fire and after raking out the dead ashes he threw some more logs onto it. Then he pushed the trivet holding the soot-blackened kettle into the heart of the flames.

'Now. Tell me what's going on.' He led her to a chair and gently pressed her down onto it and she blinked as she stared up at his smooth skin and strong shoulders. He really was a man now!

'I'm so sorry to disturb you at this hour,' she said, clearing her throat. 'I was planning to go to Mrs Lockett's because I didn't know where else to go and...'

As her voice trailed away and her chin drooped to her chest he took both her hands in his own. 'You did exactly right to come to me,' he told her softly. 'Now start at the beginning...'

And suddenly everything was pouring out of her as if a tap had been turned on. She told him about the way the Barnes family had treated her and what Bill had done last evening. She then told him about her suspicions about Lady Huntley and as he listened intently he whistled through his teeth. It was such a relief to confide in someone that she felt as if a huge weight had been lifted from her chest.

'Have you confronted her?' he asked.

'No, what would be the point? Lady Huntley is gentry and if she really did wish to get rid of me, why would she go back on her decision now? Everyone knew that her husband wanted a son, so I must have been a huge disappointment to her. That's probably why she got rid of me.'

'I find that hard to believe,' Tom said stoutly. 'If you ask me, there's something fishy going on here. That doesn't sound like her at all. Look how good she's been to you and other children from the workhouse! Her husband might have wanted a boy but I wouldn't mind betting she'd have been delighted with whatever baby she gave birth to. It just doesn't add up, does it?'

'No, it doesn't and I don't know what to think, I'm so confused,' Sunday said miserably as Tom went to collect two cups from the draining board and spoon tea leaves into a teapot.

'Well, the only way to get to the bottom of it is to ask her outright,' Tom sensibly pointed out. 'Perhaps you have it all wrong and there's some perfectly reasonable explanation for you being wrapped in that shawl when you were left on the steps of the workhouse. Perhaps it was one of her maids who got into trouble and stole the shawl because she was in no position to keep you?'

'What? On exactly the same day as Lady Huntley had her baby? That would have been too much of a coincidence, surely? And what about the colour of my hair and my eyes? They're exactly the same colour as hers – is that a coincidence too? Oh, Tom, one minute I *want* her to be my mother and the next I resent her because she could be.'

'Then if you can't speak to her, perhaps I could do it for you?' Tom suggested, but Sunday shook her head, clearly in a panic.

'Oh no, please don't do that! I don't know what I want to do about it yet.'

'All right, all right, of course I won't if you don't want me to,' he promised. She was becoming very agitated so he quickly changed the subject, saying, 'And as for that Bill, I'll sort him out tomorrow. By the time I've finished with him he won't try to interfere with young lasses again a hurry, you can bet on it!'

'Oh no, Tommy – I mean Tom! You mustn't do that either, please. You'll just make things worse. For now, it's enough that I'm away from there.'

She patted the waistband of her gown where her money was safely sewn into a little pouch. She'd left the farm without the wages that were due to her since asking for them might have raised suspicions that she intended to leave, but she was thinking of asking the Reverend Lockett if he would collect them for her. Surely the Barneses would not refuse a man of the cloth? And for now she still had the money she had saved while she was working for Mrs Spooner, so if she was very careful she would be all right for a few weeks at least and by then hopefully she would have found another job.

'Tomorrow I shall start to look for another post and rent a room in town somewhere. I just needed a safe place to stay for tonight if you don't mind too much. I shall be perfectly comfortable in the chair by the fire.'

'You will not sleep in the chair,' he objected. 'You can go and hop into my bed. I'll sleep in the chair and there's no need for you to go and rent a room. You can stay here.'

'Oh, and wouldn't the gossips just love that?' she said with a wry smile. 'Imagine what they would say. Pinnegar and his henchmen have already spread it all around the town that I'm a loose woman, and if it got out that I'd stayed here it would just add fuel to the fire.'

Tom paused in the act of pouring the boiling water into the teapot and a slight flush rose in his cheeks as he said, 'They wouldn't if you were to

481

marry me.'

Sunday was so shocked that for a moment she could only stare at him but then she said, 'I don't think there's any need for you to go to those lengths,' although she was deeply touched that he cared enough to offer. 'I shall be perfectly all right so long as I can keep out of Pinnegar's way. He's still got it in for me, you see, even now. That's why I left Mrs Spooner's and went to work at the farm, but I think he found out where I was, because lately I've sensed that someone's been following me – and once or twice I've thought I've seen someone hovering around the farm. Thank you, Tom, for taking me in.'

Her eyes roved about the little room then and Tom said sheepishly, 'Sorry it ain't very special. I'm out working for most of the time so I haven't had time to fancy it up much. It needs a woman's touch.'

Sunday couldn't have agreed more, although she didn't say so. The room was indeed very sparsely furnished with only the barest of necessities, although she noted that it was spotlessly clean. There weren't even any curtains hanging at the window but she could imagine how comfy it could be with a bit of tender loving care.

She yawned then and seeing how exhausted she was he quickly poured the tea, ordering, 'Here, get something warm inside you then go and get tucked up in my bed. We can talk more in the morning.'

She gratefully accepted the chipped cup he slid across the table to her and soon after she went and sank into Tom's bed and within minutes despite all that had happened was fast asleep, feeling safe for the first time since she had left Mrs Spooner's. It was strange that, she found herself thinking just before sleep claimed her. She had always felt safe with Tom.

She woke next morning to find a note standing against the sugar bowl on the table,

Dear Sunday, I didn't want to disturb you but I have had to go to work. We will talk more later, Love Tom xx

She smiled at his thoughtfulness then went to have a thorough wash in the tiny kitchen. As she had told him the night before, she didn't want to become the talk of the town so the sooner she found herself somewhere to live and got another job the better.

It was mid-morning before she found a room to rent. There were any number available but some of the ones she had looked at were so filthy she had cringed at the thought of entering them let alone sleeping in them. Others had been far too expensive but the one she was shown in Edward Street was within her means and fairly clean so she accepted it immediately and handed over two weeks' rent in advance. She had left her bag at Tom's. There had seemed no sense in carting it about with her but now her priority was to find employment. She could collect her bag later.

She found a job late that afternoon. It wasn't ideal because it was in a baker's in the centre of the town, which meant that Mr Pinnegar might easily spot her, but now that Tom was back in Nuneaton she wasn't quite so afraid of what he might do. The

483

pay was modest and the hours were long but even so she was grateful for it and promised to start work very early the next morning. As the baker, a huge rosy-cheeked man had explained, they had to start early to get the first batch of cakes and bread into the shop before opening time.

With her accommodation and somewhere to live settled, she then went to the vicarage where she asked the Reverend Lockett if he would kindly collect her wages for her from Yew Tree Farm. When she explained to him what had happened, both Edgar and his wife were appalled at the way she had been treated and Edgar promised he would visit them the very next day.

'You should have come straight here to us,' Verity Lockett scolded gently. 'We would never see you without a roof over your head, surely you know that?'

Sunday was grateful for her concern but deep down she knew that she could never have stayed there. She might have brought trouble down on them when Pinnegar discovered where she was and she couldn't risk that happening to the dear little family. Especially now they had Michael, their new baby son, to care for.

'I'm fine now really, but very grateful to you,' she told her friends sincerely and then after a short while she went back to Tom's to find him already home from work and cooking them a meal.

'I hope you like steak and onions with jacket potatoes?' he said when she appeared. 'I've learned how to look after meself although I admit I can't cook anything fancy. But now tell me how you've got on today.'

484

And so Sunday seated herself at the table and told him all about it, and soon after they ate the meal he'd prepared for her and very nice it was too. They then washed and dried the pots together and he tentatively remarked, 'I've been thinking about what you said about Lady Huntley and I reckon you should have it out with her. At least then you won't be constantly fretting over it.'

Sunday's curls danced about her shoulders as she said proudly, 'I most certainly will not. If she didn't want me then why should she want me now? No – what's done is done and I certainly won't go begging her to acknowledge me as her daughter!'

Tom sighed. He knew how stubborn Sunday could be but he thought she was making a big mistake. Lavinia Huntley certainly didn't strike him as the sort of woman to ever abandon a child. Everyone knew how much she had always longed to be a mother and how badly she had taken little Stephen's death. Even so, he was sensible enough not to argue, for now at least, so changing the subject he suggested, 'Well, at least we'll be able to eat together each evening if you like. You might get a bit tired of pork chops and cold mutton, but it will be better than eating bread and cheese in your room on your own.'

'I'd like that,' Sunday said quietly. It would be something to look forward to at the end of a long working day.

Later that evening, Tom walked Sunday to her new home. It would have been nicer, he thought, if she had agreed to stay with him, although he could understand her reasons for turning him down. Folks hereabouts liked a bit of scandal and it wasn't considered seemly for two young people to live together without being wed. Still, at least he would see her every day now – and that was more than he could have hoped for.

Chapter Fifty

Sunday had been working in the baker's for a week when the inevitable happened. She was serving at the counter early one morning when the shop bell tinkled and Albert Pinnegar strolled in. Seeing her there, all the old feelings of desire, frustration and anger rose in him, threatening to choke him. Quickly recovering from the shock, he pulled himself together.

'Well, well, and look who's here.' He grinned maliciously as he twiddled with his waxed moustache. 'I heard you'd run away from the farm. News travels fast around these parts.'

How very convenient it was, to have her back in town and close at hand, he thought. 'I didn't run away, I chose to leave,' Sunday muttered as she looked away from his hated face. Why, oh why couldn't he just disappear in a puff of smoke, never to be seen again!

'What can I get you?' she asked then as if he were any other customer.

'I'll have one of your large cottage loaves.'

Sunday briskly wrapped a loaf in brown paper and placed it on the counter. 'That will be fourpence, please.' She took his shilling piece, gave him his change in two threepenny bits and two pennies, then ignoring him completely she attended to the next customer who had come in closely behind him.

She could see the hatred he now felt for her burning in his eyes. Outwardly, she was as cool as a cucumber but inside she was quaking. He could always have that effect on her and she tried to quash the memories of his violations on her body. When he left a few seconds later she breathed a huge sigh of relief, but then she found herself glancing towards the door for the rest of the morning.

It was early afternoon, just after Sunday had had a short break for lunch, that the shop door opened again and in waltzed Mrs Spooner. Now here was someone she was pleased to see and the girl's face broke into a smile. However, there was no answering smile on Biddy's painted lips.

'So what do you think yer doing working here?' the old lady snapped, rapping her cane on the floor for Sunday's full attention.

'I left the farm,' the girl explained, glad that there were no other customers at present to eavesdrop on the conversation.

'Hmm, an' I can guess why. That randy son o' theirs try it on again, did he?'

When Sunday nodded the old woman scowled. 'So why didn't yer come to me then? You know I said there's always a home fer you at my house.'

'I didn't want to bring any more trouble to your door,' Sunday muttered meekly, which caused the old woman to snort with annoyance.

'Huh! That Pinnegar has somethin' to answer for, so he does, scarin' harmless lasses an' preying on innocent folk. Why, I'd like to clout him around the head wi' me cane, knock some sense into the bugger. Now, are yer coming home or what?'

Home. What a wonderful word. Sunday swallowed before saying, 'You know I wouldn't risk that. If I came home, he might start another fire, and this time not everyone might get out. It's just too dangerous.'

Biddy harrumphed again as Sunday asked, 'How did you find me?'

'Our new maid Mary-Jane recognised you yesterday when she walked by the shop 'cos she remembered you from the workhouse. You didn't think you'd be able to keep your whereabouts quiet workin' in a place like this an' servin' folks all day, did you?'

'I suppose not.' Sunday lowered her head, feeling suddenly ashamed. She should have let Mrs Spooner know where she was at least. 'I thought being here in the town with lots of folk about, I'd be safe.'

'Well, if I can't get you to come home with me you could at least promise that you'll keep in touch and pay us all a visit from time to time. Come on, Sunny, what are yer playin' at? Lady Huntley is upset that she hasn't seen you either. Why couldn't you have gone to work there as arranged?'

The mention of Lavinia made hot colour flood into Sunday's cheeks but she managed to answer calmly, 'I suppose I didn't want to go there after

488

all, when it came down to it, but I will come and see you. How about this Sunday afternoon? I might even go to church this Sunday morning now that I'm living back in the town.'

'Make sure you do,' Mrs Spooner said gruffly, then without so much as a by your leave she stamped off, leaving Sunday feeling buoyed by the old lady's love. Thoughts of Lady Huntley followed – and again she got the sick feeling in the pit of her stomach at the idea of being so callously abandoned by her all those years ago. Her thoughts then moved on to Tom and her heart did a little flip. She loved the way he fussed over her and the thoughtful little things he did. The time they spent together was precious and she was so glad that he'd come back into her life. Perhaps they could walk to church together on Sunday? In a slightly happier frame of mind she began to scrub the counter down.

It was shortly after that when Edgar Lockett came in and handed Sunday an envelope.

'Your wages from the Barnes family,' he told her. 'I'm sorry I couldn't get them to you before. It's been so busy this week, I don't seem to have enough hours in the day.'

She thanked him and dropped the envelope into her pocket then watched as he shuffled about from foot to foot, his eyes downcast, before saying, 'I ought to tell you that Mrs Barnes has passed away. Last night it was. According to the doctor it was her heart.'

Sunday was sorry to hear this although she couldn't be a hypocrite and pretend to be upset. The woman had never bestowed so much as one kind word on her in all the time she had lived at the farm, despite everything she had done for her. And perhaps a heart attack was a merciful release from her lung disease.

'How are the menfolk coping?' she asked.

Edgar sighed. 'As well as can be expected in the circumstances. She's going to be buried at Mancetter church.'

'Well, thank you for letting me know.' She hoped that Edgar didn't blame her. Selah could have died at any time. 'And thank you for getting my wages.'

He smiled before turning and striding away and Sunday thought yet again what a kind and gentle man he was.

It was later that day that a maid at Treetops Manor answered the door to a tall, sober-looking gentleman in a smart suit who handed her his top hat, cane and gloves, and asked to see Lady Huntley.

'I don't know who he is,' she told Zillah when she hurried towards the drawing room to find her. 'I forgot to ask – I'm sorry. But I've put him in the library.'

'Right you are, pet.' Zillah approached Lady Huntley, who was sitting in the windowseat reading, to tell her of her visitor.

'Come with me, would you, Zillah?' she asked. 'I wasn't expecting anyone.'

'Of course.' And side by side the women made their way to the library wondering who the unexpected caller might possibly be.

The second they entered the room, the man stood up and bowed, his face solemn. 'Lady

490

Lavinia Huntley, I presume?'

When she nodded, he coughed to clear his throat before beginning, 'Perhaps you would like to be seated, my lady? I'm afraid I have some bad news for you.'

As Lavinia groped nervously for the nearest chair, assisted by Zillah, he produced a card from his waistcoat pocket and she quickly read it. *Mr Victor Peregrew, Solicitor.*

'I work for the firm that has been handling your husband's affairs since he inherited his fortune from his late uncle,' the man went on.

Lady Huntley raised her eyebrows. 'I don't quite understand, sir. What could that possibly have to do with me?'

Again he looked uncomfortable before going on, 'Unfortunately, there has been a tragic accident and it is my regrettable duty to have to inform you that your husband, Sir Ashley Huntley, was killed two days ago.'

The room pitched as her hand rose to her mouth but then, taking a deep breath, she asked, 'What sort of an accident? And are you quite sure that it was Ashley?'

The man said heavily, 'There is no doubt about it, I'm afraid. He was out shooting with a party in Ledbury and someone's gun went off ... by accident.' He cleared his throat. 'It appears that your husband had been having a little liaison with the wife of the man whose gun went off, so the police are, of course, investigating. I am sorry to distress you with that detail, my lady. But whatever the outcome there is no doubt whatsoever that the deceased was Sir Ashley Huntley. I am sorry to be

491

the bearer of such bad news. Please accept my sincere condolences, my lady.'

Lavinia was so deeply shocked that she could only nod as she tried to take in what he had told her.

He shifted towards the door then, saying, 'I shall leave you now to absorb what I have told you, but with your permission I will return at a suitable time to discuss your situation as you are, of course, your husband's next of kin and will therefore inherit all he had. Good day to you, ladies.' He took another bow and then quietly left the room.

Lavinia hardly noticed, for in her mind's eye she was seeing Ashley as he had been when she first met him, young and handsome, so loving and attentive. On the day they were wed they had moved to Treetops Manor with her head full of dreams of the children they would have. The house would ring with laughter and they would live happily ever after but all that had soon changed and her disillusionment began. And now … he was gone. She supposed that she should be weeping but found that she couldn't. Her eyes remained dry. The all-consuming love she had once felt for him had died with her dreams many years ago, the last vestiges swept away with the death of their tiny son, and now she found that she couldn't be a hypocrite and play the part of a grieving widow.

'He's gone, Zillah,' she said flatly and stared about the room. It was full of beautiful furniture and yet like her life it was empty and always would be now.

Zillah, meanwhile, was wrestling with turbulent thoughts. Ashley was gone. Could she now share the terrible secret that had haunted her day and night for all those years? But first she must decide the best way to tell her mistress – and then pray that Lavinia would forgive her.

Due to a fault with the ovens the baker's was late closing that night and Sunday was concerned that Tom would be worried about her. She had a spare key to his cottage now and whoever got in first after work would start to prepare the evening meal. She grinned; it would undoubtedly be him tonight so they would probably be having something simple again. She took a loaf with her and an apple pie that was going begging. They ate together each evening and it was fast becoming the highlight of her day.

It was raining as she set off from the shop and she pulled her shawl across her head. There was no sign of Pinnegar or his men so she decided to take the shortcut to Tom's home, past the River Anker and across the Pingles Fields. Most evenings, the area was full of children and families but this evening it was almost deserted due to the weather. Regretting her impulse to take this route, she hurried on and soon was approaching the passage that ran beneath the railway lines. It was a dismal place and the walls were always running with damp but tonight it seemed even darker in there and she quickened her footsteps, keen to get to the daylight at the other end of it. She silently scolded herself for ever coming this way, but it was too late to turn back now. She was almost halfway through when she became aware of footsteps behind her; in fact, someone was almost directly upon her. She couldn't make out their face in the darkness but from the size of them she judged the person to be a man. A shudder of terror passed through her.

She made to step aside, trying to dodge away from her pursuer, but then she saw lights flashing in front of her eyes as something heavy smashed down on the back of her head. The pain was excruciating. As she staggered, crying out, the darkness swallowed her up.

When she came to, she groaned – or at least she tried to but there was something in her mouth, some sort of gag. She opened her eyes but could see nothing and for a moment she panicked, thinking she had gone blind before realising that she was tied to a chair and was in total darkness. She tried to spit the gag out for it tasted disgusting, but it was tied tightly and all she could do was make gurgling noises in the back of her throat. Who could have done this to her and where was she? Why had they left her alone? And then as her senses came back to her she realised it must have been her old enemy, Albert Pinnegar. Her hands were bound so tightly at the back of the chair that her fingers were tingling and her legs were tied too. She wriggled and squirmed, hoping to loosen the bonds, but all she seemed to do was tighten them. There was a dull pain throbbing away at the back of her eyes and she wanted to sleep but she was too afraid to do so now.

I'll plead with him when he shows his face – if he takes away the gag, she told herself. And yet she couldn't convince herself that it would do any good. Terror began to set in. What if he never came back? 'What if *no one* ever came? She would die here all alone in the darkness. It was a daunting thought and she renewed her efforts to free herself, making the chair she was tied to swing dangerously to and fro. But it was no good, she was only making things worse and tears of frustration filled her eyes. She began to shiver with a mixture of cold and fear as she tried to think where she might be, but though she strained for any sounds there was only silence save for a dripping noise coming from somewhere. Her headache was getting worse and now she felt sick, which made her panic again. If she were to vomit with the gag in she would likely choke, so she tried to breathe through her nose and calm herself. For now there was nothing else she could do. She was entirely at the mercy of her captor, God help her! And there was still so much she had wanted to do with her life. Why, only that day she had decided that it was time to confront Lady Huntley with her suspicions, for try as she might she couldn't find it in her to dislike the woman and felt that Lavinia deserved a chance to explain, just as Tom had pointed out. *Tom.* The thought of him brought the tears stinging to the back of her eyes again. He would no doubt be going mad with worry about her, just as he had when Daisy had disappeared – and there was not a single thing she could do about it.

After checking the range yet again, Tom strode to the doorway and peered down the road for at least the twentieth time in as many minutes. Even allowing for her working late, Sunday should have been home ages ago and now he was getting seriously worried. It wasn't like her to just not turn up without getting word to him and their meal was almost ruined. *Perhaps she didn't feel so well and decided to go straight home to her lodgings,* he thought as he stood chewing on his lip. There was only one way to find out so, lifting the dish out of the oven and putting a plate over it to keep it warm, he slipped his coat on and set off in the rain. It took only a matter of minutes to reach Sunday's lodging house where a stony-faced landlady coldly informed him that no, Miss Small had not yet arrived home and that she did not at all approve of her young ladies having gentlemen callers. Suitably chastised, Tom stood on the pavement outside with his hands in his coat pockets wondering what he should do next as the cold rain dripped down the back of his neck. The baker's, that was it. The man wouldn't be too happy about having his evening disturbed but at least he might be able to tell him if Sunday had mentioned that she was going somewhere. Tom got a similar reception at the baker's to the one he'd had from the landlady and now he was extremely anxious. With a sigh he set off for home but then he brightened. It could be that she was already there waiting for him. He arrived back to an empty house.

The next morning, bright and early, Zillah informed Lavinia Huntley that she had to make an urgent visit to her niece, Verity. Lavinia was mildly surprised. It wasn't like Zillah to go haring off anywhere but she gladly gave her permission and ordered the carriage to be brought round to the front of the house for her. The maid was a little too old to be making the long trek into town on foot now. Normally Lavinia would have gone with her but the sight of baby Michael was still too painful and made her think of Stephen. Zillah had seemed distracted and on edge ever since the news of Ashley's death had reached them, which was faintly surprising. She had never made a secret of the fact that she couldn't abide the man, so Lavinia couldn't understand why his demise should affect her so badly. However, she had other things to occupy her mind that morning. The undertaker would be calling to see her to arrange her late husband's funeral. She felt obliged to give Ashley a good send-off. They were still married, after all, and it was the last thing she would ever have to do for him.

When Zillah arrived at the vicarage she found Verity doing a simple puzzle with Phoebe on the hearthrug in the cosy parlour and the baby fast asleep in his crib.

Verity was delighted to see her but recognised at once that her aunt was in a very agitated state.

'Come and sit down and tell me what's wrong,' she urged as she yanked the bell-pull at the side of the fireplace. She would get her maid to make her aunt a hot toddy; that might help to restore her. Once the drink had been ordered, Zillah sat silently wringing her hands until the tray had been brought in, then, taking a sip of the steaming mixture of lemon, rum and hot water, she slowly and painfully began to tell her niece of Ashley Huntley's death and the terrible secret she had

497

been forced to keep for so many years.

By the time she had done, Verity's face had paled and she was almost reeling with shock but there was no recrimination in her voice when she asked, 'So what are you going to do now?' Her voice was little more than a squeak. She couldn't even begin to imagine what her aunt must have been through.

'I'm going to tell her everything,' Zillah responded. 'And I want you to come back with me and be there while I do it. I realise it's a lot to ask of you.'

Verity sadly shook her head. 'I'm afraid this revelation, coming on top of Ashley's demise and the loss of Stephen may be too much for her to bear.'

Zillah drank down her toddy in one gulp then stood up, nervously twisting her fingers together. 'I know, but it can't be put off any longer. I'm no spring chicken and I can't contemplate going to meet my maker with this on my conscience. What my dear lady decides to do when she knows will be up to her then.'

Verity rose slowly and shook out her skirts, telling her aunt, 'I'll get ready immediately. Mrs Young will watch the children for me for a while. And if it's any consolation, I believe you are doing the right thing. It is time for poor Lavinia to learn what really happened on the night her last daughter was born.'

Chapter Fifty-One

The undertaker had only just left when Zillah and Verity arrived back at Treetops Manor. When the maid had let them in and taken them to the library, Lavinia stood up and smiled a welcome, assuming that Mrs Lockett had come to offer her condolences.

'Hello, Verity, how nice to see you. I suppose Zillah has told you what's happened?'

'Yes, she has,' Verity answered. 'And I'm so terribly sorry, dear Lavinia. Edgar and I will help you in any way we can. However, that isn't the reason why I'm here. Perhaps you'd better sit down, for Zillah has something very important to tell you.'

This was the second time in two days she'd been told she might need to sit down, Lavinia thought apprehensively. What could have happened now? Once she had done as she was asked, the two women came to sit opposite her and Zillah bowed her head, summoning her courage and wondering where she should start.

'What I'm about to tell you will come as something of a shock...' she said, and paused to moisten her lips. 'And I just pray to God that when you know of it, you will be able to forgive me.'

Lavinia frowned. 'Good heavens! Go on.'

'Well, it happened the night your last daughter was born. Ashley wanted a son, as you know.

Girls were no good to him. You had a terrible birth with that one if you remember, and by the time she was delivered you were unconscious. In fact, I feared we were going to lose you for a time... Anyway, Ashley came storming in and was furious when he discovered you'd given birth to another girl. He ... he told me that I was to smother her with a pillow and have her body buried next to the other two.'

Lavinia's hand flew to her mouth. 'You're telling me she was born *alive?*'

Zillah nodded miserably. 'Aye, she was, but he threatened me, said if I didn't do as he wished he'd have you locked away in Hatter's Hall and I'd be put in the workhouse. He would pay a doctor to class you as insane if I didn't obey his instructions.'

'What are you saying, Zillah? That you *killed* my baby!' Lavinia felt as if she were about to faint and Verity rushed to sit beside her.

When Zillah mutely shook her head, Lavinia frowned, confused. 'But you *must* have done. I went to visit her little grave as soon as I was able to. Oh, my poor dear baby girl.'

'Inside that grave is nothin' more than a pillow wrapped in a shawl,' Zillah said in ringing tones.

Lady Huntley gasped. 'So... So ... what happened to my baby then, if she wasn't born dead?'

Zillah closed her eyes for a second before going on. 'After the midwife had left that night I took the baby and hid her in my room, then I wrapped a pillow in a shawl and took it out to the grave that Matthews had dug ready. He believed that I was burying the child but she was safe in my

500

room all the time. Much later, when I was sure that no one was about I carried her all the way to the workhouse, left her on the steps there and rang the bell. Then I hid until someone came and I knew that the little scrap was safe. I didn't know what else I could do!' she said desperately. 'If you cast your mind back, you'll recall that our Verity had recently started work there so I knew I would hear how the child was faring through her, although I didn't dare tell Verity who the child was, of course.'

'B-but she would be nearly sixteen now. Is she still alive?' Lavinia asked tremulously as hope flared in her eyes.

'She is that – and you know her well. Sunday Small is your flesh-and-blood daughter, God bless her.'

'*Sunday!*' Lavinia gulped for air as she tried to take it in. She had a daughter, a *beautiful* daughter, and all this time she hadn't known! And yet now that she came to think about it, hadn't she always felt a special bond with the girl? They had the same colour hair, the same colour eyes. Why, *oh why* hadn't she sensed who she was!

'I didn't dare tell you while Ashley was alive, for God knows what he might have done,' Zillah went on. 'But it's weighed heavy on my conscience, and now I reckon it's time you knew. C-can you ever forgive me, pet?'

'It's not *you* who needs forgiveness,' Lavinia said immediately. 'You simply did the best you could in difficult circumstances, and you saved my daughter's life. All this is Ashley's fault. May his black soul burn in hell for what he forced you to do. Now what I need to do is tell Sunday who she really is and pray that she will forgive *me!* Oh, I have a *daughter.*' Tears poured down her cheeks, and Verity and Zillah each took one of her hands in theirs and held her for a long moment. And then she cried, 'Come along ... we must go and find her immediately and explain what's happened.'

Zillah's breath hissed out on a sigh of relief and she suddenly felt lighter than she had for years. The secret was a burden she had kept and carried for all of Sunday's lifetime. Without even stopping to collect a coat Lavinia raced out to the waiting carriage with the two women following closely. Mrs Spooner had told her that Sunday was working in the baker's shop in town now. She was sure to be there at this time. But not for much longer if Lavinia had anything to do with it. She intended to bring the girl home to Treetops Manor where she belonged, and where she would take her rightful place as daughter of the house.

The journey into town seemed to take for ever but at last they pulled up in front of the baker's shop. Gathering her skirts into one hand, Lavinia jumped down from the carriage without even waiting for George to help her and ran inside.

The baker's wife was standing at the counter and she gawped at the woman in surprise. It wasn't often she had the gentry venture into the shop, it was usually their maids.

'I wish to speak to Miss Small,' Lavinia said, staring expectantly across the woman's shoulder.

The woman scowled. 'I'm afraid she ain't turned in fer work today, me lady.' She looked none too pleased about the fact.

'Oh … I see.' Lavinia Huntley looked somewhat deflated before asking, 'Have you any idea where she might be?'

'Well, I dare say she'll be round at her lodgin's in Edward Street or at her young man's. He comes to meet her some nights. Tom, I think he's called, an' I reckon he lives in Shepperton Street. Oh, an' if you see her, tell her to get round here straight away if she wants to keep her job.'

Her only reply was the slamming of the door and in a huff she began to arrange the loaves on the counter.

Next, Lady Huntley tried both the lodging house and Tom's address with no success, although Tom was at home. He'd been so worried about Sunday that he'd taken a day off work to look for her after spending a sleepless night waiting in case she turned up as she had before.

'And you say you didn't see her last night either and she didn't return to her lodgings?'

Tom shook his head and then voiced the thing he feared: 'You don't think old Pinnegar got his hands on her, do you?'

Lady Huntley visibly paled at the thought. They were standing outside Tom's cottage when a man who was passing stopped to say, 'I don't want to poke me nose in where it ain't wanted but I couldn't help but overhear what yer said. If it's Albert Pinnegar yer on about he ain't gonna get his hands on anyone. I just bought the local newspaper an' he's made the local headlines – look!'

Removing a newspaper from under his arm he

503

unfolded it, sniffed importantly and read, '"Former workhouse master Mr Albert Pinnegar was found dead in his cottage last night with a knife in his heart." It's here in black an' white, look.'

Quickly snatching the newspaper from him, Tom read the rest of the piece.

'He's right,' he muttered to Lady Huntley. 'It says the police already have the man who they believe did it in their custody. He was one of Pinnegar's rent collectors. Apparently Pinnegar had tried to cheat him out of his wages so they got into a ruckus and the chap pulled a knife on him. Someone heard them arguing as he passed Pinnegar's cottage and saw the chap through the window.'

'Good riddance to bad rubbish, that's what I say,' Zillah snorted. 'But if he hasn't got her, where can she be? It just isn't like Sunday to disappear off without a word to anyone.'

'I think it's time we reported her missing to the constables,' Lady Huntley said then and her heart was aching. For this to happen now, just when she had discovered that the girl was her daughter was heart-breaking, and the thought that she might lose her before she had even had the chance to claim her was almost more than she could endure. She felt sick with worry as she wondered where the poor girl might be.

Their next stop was the local police station in the town where a solemn-faced constable listened to what they had to say.

'We thought it might have been Albert Pinnegar who had taken her,' Tom told him. 'But we just found out that he was murdered last night.'

The policeman nodded. 'So he was. We have the chap who we think did it in custody an' a right shifty character he is an' all. He's denying everything, of course. But can you think of anyone else who might have a grudge against her?'

'Well, she recently refused an offer of marriage from the son of the Barnes family from Yew Tree Farm in Mancetter, but I don't reckon Bill Barnes would be daft enough to do something like this.'

'Hmm, well, it might be worth getting one of my constables to pay them a visit,' the officer remarked, making a hasty note on his pad.

Tom stared thoughtfully into space then suddenly he groaned as he gasped, 'There is *one* other person who always had it in for her...'

Sunday had no way of knowing how long she had sat, alone, thirsty, in pain and fear. The minutes and the hours seemed to drag by and her body ached from being tied in the same position for so long. The smell of damp and decay was overpowering and she thought she must be in a cellar somewhere. Biting down panic, she was beginning to think that no one was ever going to come. Suddenly a light appeared at the top of a steep wooden staircase and someone holding a flickering candle appeared. The girl blinked as her eyes tried to adjust to the light, but it wasn't until her jailer was standing right in front of her that she realised who it was.

'You thought you'd got away with it, stealing my man from me, *didn't you?*'

Sunday stared up into the eyes of Miss Frost, but

this was not the prim and proper matron that she remembered. The creature before her was unkempt, and the smell that issued from her person and her clothes was making Sunday choke behind the gag. Her eyes had a maniacal gleam in them and the girl was terrified. Her old enemy had gone completely mad – she must be!

As the woman began to dance around the chair, Sunday strained her neck to try and keep her in sight.

'I've been watching you ever since you left the workhouse. Always trying to tempt my Albert away from me, weren't you, you little hussy? *And* you lost me my job. A punishment room is where you belong – where you've always belonged. And this is one I have made ready for you.' It was then that Sunday saw the knife gleaming in her hand in the candlelight and she began desperately to struggle against her ties again. She didn't want to die here in this cold, dark cellar. She'd never see Tom again. She blinked with shock as the truth hit her like an avalanche: that she loved him!

That was why she enjoyed being in his company, why butterflies fluttered to life every time she saw him. And now she might never get the chance to tell him.

As she leaned forward, the woman's foul-smelling breath hit her full in the face and Sunday retched. Then Miss Frost gently drew the knife down the girl's cheek, cackling with pleasure as she saw a trickle of blood appear.

'I'm going to teach you a very painful lesson,' she taunted her victim. 'But not like when Albert died last night. His end was too swift when I plunged the knife into his heart. I couldn't bring myself to torture him even after he'd broken my heart and spurned me. *But he had to die!* Daisy's death took longer though. You should have seen the fight she put up when I pushed her and that brat she was carrying into the canal! And the animals at Mrs Spooner's...'

Sunday's head was reeling. Anger ripped through her as she imagined how terrified poor Daisy must have been in the moments leading up to her death. But it was too late to help Daisy; it was Sunday's turn now and it was clear that Miss Frost was going to show her no mercy.

Suddenly, the woman kicked out and the chair she was tied to toppled onto its side, knocking the breath from Sunday's body. Only a miracle could save her now; she was going to die and she prayed that her end would be swift.

The woman began to dance dementedly around the chair again, kicking out and sending ripples of pain surging through Sunday's defenceless body.

'Go on then ... *cry!*' the woman screamed, reaching out and slicing the gag from Sunday's mouth. 'I want to see you cry! You never would, would you? Even though it meant that I punished you twice as hard as anyone else in the workhouse. But you will cry now, my lady, before I'm done with you. *There's no one to protect you now!*'

Suddenly there was a noise from above and then the clattering of footsteps on the stairs. Miss Frost stared up in shock and began to back away from her. And then two police constables seized the knife and handcuffed her while Tom dropped to his knees before Sunday and began to fumble with the ties that bound her.

'Oh, my poor love!' He was openly sobbing as he wrestled with the ropes. 'If anything had happened to you...' Then suddenly she was free and he was holding her to his chest as waves of dizziness washed through her. Just for a moment another face appeared over his shoulder. Lady Huntley's.

'*Get her away from me!*' she screamed, suddenly finding her voice, and then she fainted in Tom Branning's sheltering arms.

Chapter Fifty-Two

As her eyes blinked open she winced with pain. Every inch of her ached and she was tired. So tired that she just wanted to go back to sleep and never have to wake up again.

'Sunday? Come on, sweetheart, open your eyes.'

She groaned but when she did as she was told she found Tom leaning over her and instantly started to feel a little better.

'Here, take a sip of this.' He held a cup of water to her cracked lips and nothing had ever tasted as good as she gulped at it. 'That's it, now lie back and rest.'

Her hand rose to feel the pad on her cheek and he smiled at her reassuringly. 'It's all right. Miss Frost cut you but the doctor's stitched it up so neatly he promises it will barely be noticeable when it's properly healed.'

'And ... Miss Frost?' Her voice came out as a croak.

'Safely locked away in Hatter's Hall where she'll never be able to hurt anyone again,' he promised her.

'Eeh, yer gave us a right scare back there,' another voice said, and glancing over Tom's shoulder, Sunday saw Mrs Spooner. In fact, she realised now that that was where she was, back in her old room at Whittleford Lodge. But there was another anxious face peering at her too, and as she realised who it was she began to get agitated.

'Please, make her go away!' she begged, pointing a wavering finger.

Deeply distressed, Lady Huntley began to back towards the door. 'If you'll just let me explain...'

But Sunday, exhausted as she was, was having none of it. 'I know exactly who you are – my so-called mother. I worked it out a week ago and I never want to set eyes on you again – *ever!'*

With a sob Lavinia fled from the room as Tom bent over Sunday, trying to calm her but she was tired again now. So tired that she couldn't seem to keep her eyes open and, within seconds, she was fast asleep again.

The next time she awoke, the room was in darkness save for an oil lamp that stood on a small table at the side of the bed.

'Feeling more like yourself, are you, lass?'

Sunday turned towards the voice to find Zillah sitting there.

'Yes, I think so,' she muttered as Zillah gently lifted her head and gave her a sip of water.

'Good, because I have something here for you. I've made Tom go for a little rest. He's barely left your side since you were brought here.'

She held an envelope out to her but Sunday was too weak to take it and asked, 'What is it?'

'It's from Lady Huntley ... now don't go getting yourself all worked up,' she chided as Sunday's head swung from side to side. 'It's your inheritance,' she went on. 'You've clearly guessed that my lady is your mother and you've made it more than clear that you want to have nothing to do with her, but she wants to do right by you, you see? This is a letter telling you that as soon as she can possibly get the papers drawn up, Treetops Manor and a sizeable amount of money will be yours to start your foundling school with your young man. She remembers you told her once that this was your dream, to be able to give orphaned and abandoned children a happy childhood so this is your chance to do just that. She will be moving away and I will be going with her.'

'I don't want *anything* off her,' Sunday said churlishly. 'She abandoned me as if I was nothing! I've managed quite all right without her help up to now and I don't want her conscience money.'

'Ah, but it isn't quite like that,' Zillah told her patiently. 'So now I'm going to tell you what *really* happened on the night you were born – and you can believe me or believe me not.'

When she had finished her tale, Sunday lay as still as a statue staring up at the ceiling. Everyone knew how devoted Zillah was to her mistress, so was she telling the truth or just trying to show

Lavinia Huntley in a better light? It was all very confusing! And yet she had never known Zillah to lie before.

'I'm going to go away and let you think on what I've told you now,' Zillah whispered. 'Meanwhile, the police are here and they'd like to speak to you. Are you up to it, lass?'

When Sunday nodded weakly, Zillah crept from the room, quiet as a mouse.

Sunday made her statement and told the police all she could remember, and shortly after they had left Tom came back into the room. Taking her hand, he gently kissed each of her fingers in turn. 'Feeling a bit better, pet?'

She nodded, sending shards of pain shooting through every inch of her body. 'Yes – but how did you know where to find me? If you hadn't come when you did ... Tom, you saved my life!'

'Ssh now ... we don't need to think about that. It didn't take much figuring out when I discovered that old Pinnegar was dead. I thought of Miss Frost straight away, and then one of the policemen said he'd noticed she'd been sleeping rough in some derelict pit cottages on the way to Bedworth. And that's where we found you. The rest you know.'

'It was Miss Frost who killed Daisy ... and Mr Pinnegar,' she told him then and his eyes filled with tears.

'Aye, I heard the police talking out there.' He cocked his head towards the door. 'Apparently they already knew that it wasn't the bloke they'd arrested that killed Pinnegar because someone had informed them they'd seen Miss Frost running from his cottage with a knife in her hand. They've already let the chap go. But of course I didn't realise it was her that had killed my sister.' He lapsed into silence for a few moments. 'Still, I suppose we'll have to try and put that behind us now and remember Daisy as she was before.'

Staring at her solemnly, Tom cleared his throat then said awkwardly, 'That time when I asked you to marry me, Sunday I meant it, you know.'

'So ask me again.'

He blinked in surprise, then dropping to one knee at the side of the bed he said softly, 'Sunday Small, I love you more than life itself so will you do me the very great honour of becoming my wife?'

'I'd love to,' she answered, and then he was kissing her and there was no one else in the whole wide world but the two of them.

Two days later Sunday was well enough to come downstairs and sit on the chair in the drawing room to be fussed over by all and sundry. 'I could quite get used to this,' she told Mrs Spooner teasingly and the old woman laughed.

But then becoming sober, Biddy asked, 'Have you thought any more about what Zillah told you about Lady Huntley?' Since that night no one had dared mention the subject but now Mrs Spooner felt that it was time to tackle it. She'd never been one for brushing things under the carpet.

'I don't want to talk about it,' Sunday muttered, turning her head away from the woman.

'Well, none of it will be sorted until you do,' Mrs Spooner warned, then after rising from her chair she instructed Tom, 'See if you can't get her to see sense, will you?' And with that she hobbled from the room.

Tom glanced at the pout on Sunday's face and asked, 'Are you quite sure you want to shut her out of your life, Sunday? I believe every word that Zillah said – and why should the woman be blamed when she didn't even know you were alive? The poor soul was told that she'd given birth to yet another stillborn child. Can you even *begin* to imagine what that must have been like for her? And then to be told the truth when her husband has just died … that she'd had a daughter all along! Why, she was almost beside herself with worry when we were trying to find you. All she's asking for is a chance to try and make up for all the lost years with you. Everyone knows how much she has always longed for a child. Won't you at least consider giving her a chance?'

'I'll think about it,' Sunday said stiffly and Tom decided to change the subject.

Could he have known it, she thought of nothing else all week and finally on Saturday evening she made her decision. 'Will you be going to church in the morning?' she asked Mrs Spooner.

'As if I'd miss it. It's the Mothering Sunday service tomorrow.'

'Then may I come with you?'

'Just so long as you realise that Lady Huntley's liable to be there an' all. I don't want you causing any trouble in church.' She eyed the girl suspiciously but Sunday merely smiled.

'As if I would.' And it was left at that.

The following day dawned bright and sunny and they all piled onto Mrs Spooner's little trap and set off for the church. Primroses and wild violets adorned the countryside and the sound of birdsong accompanied their journey, mingling with the chime of church bells. It looked set to be a very special day. The evening before, Jacob and Ellie had officially announced their engagement, and today Tom and Sunday intended to ask the Reverend Lockett if he would marry them.

Everyone in the Spooner household was excited at the prospect of the two forthcoming weddings. Treacle plodded slowly along, and as she and Tom sat squashed together on the little wooden bench seat with his arm tight about her, Sunday felt at peace with the world. The couple had had a long talk the evening before and he too was smiling like a Cheshire cat.

When they arrived at All Saints Church in Chilver's Coton, the congregation were making their way through the churchyard to the entrance to the church but Sunday and Tom paused to buy two bunches of violets from the little old lady flower-seller who stood at the gate and who was doing a roaring trade. They then picked their way through the cemetery until they came to Daisy's grave, where Tom gently laid his flowers and murmured his love to his sister, telling her the news about him and Sunday before heading back to the porch. Sunday smiled as she saw the children from the workhouse snaking their way along the path, followed by the kindly new housemother. She was pleased to note that they were chatting happily and that they all looked well-fed and well-clothed now.

The church was full to capacity when they entered but then that was no surprise. The Mothering Sunday service was one of the most popular of the year and the church was packed with excited children bearing posies of wild flowers that they would present to their mothers at the end. Cissie and George waved to them and Sunday waved back. It seemed that love was in the air.

Mrs Spooner, Sunday and Tom took a seat towards the back of the church. The front pews were already full, but over the heads of the congregation Sunday spotted Lady Huntley sitting with Zillah at the front.

Eventually a hush fell, and after singing some hymns and saying some prayers, the reverend conducted one of the most moving services Sunday had ever heard. In it, he extolled the virtues of what being a mother entailed.

'A mother's love begins even before her child's birth and burns more brightly than the brightest star in the universe until the second she draws her last breath,' he told the hushed congregation. He smiled at his wife, who was sitting in the front pew staring at him adoringly as she tried to get little Phoebe to sit still. 'It is an all-consuming, unselfish love that never dims,' he ended, and then the children slowly began to offer their mothers their gifts. It didn't seem to matter that most of the gifts had no monetary value whatsoever if the ecstatic smiles on the faces of the mothers was anything to go by.

Tom gave Sunday's fingers an encouraging

squeeze and when she nervously glanced at him he nodded, smiling broadly. And so she rose from her seat and quietly walked along the aisle with her heart pounding until she came to the pew where Lady Huntley was sitting.

'These are for you ... Mother,' she whispered, shyly offering the posy of violets she had brought from the flower lady at the lych-gate.

'Oh!' For a moment Lavinia Huntley was struck dumb as tears began to course down her cheeks. Then with a strangled sob she grasped her daughter and hugged her to her. Suddenly Sunday was crying too – really crying for the first time in years – as she nestled comfortably in her mother's arms.

'Oh, my darling girl. You've come back to me at last,' Lady Huntley wept.

Tom beamed and winked at Zillah as, arm-in-arm, mother and daughter walked down the aisle and out into the sunshine, oblivious of everyone around them, chattering away to each other fifteen to the dozen, their faces illuminated by love. As they passed, the young man heard Sunday say excitedly, 'And as for your offer of using Treetops Manor as a home for foundling children, when Tom and I marry, we would be very happy to take you up on the offer ... provided that you stay there too to help us, Mother. Tom will do all the odd jobs about the place, he's very handy, and I shall do everything I can, but we are still very young, you see, and so will need someone to look to for advice.'

Turning aside, Tom Branning hastily brushed a tear from his own eye. A great endeavour stood before them: the establishing of their home for lost and lonely children, where no child would feel unwanted, and where each child would belong.

He, like so many others at the church today, would never forget this precious Mothering Sunday service.

When the Reverend Lockett lit the first candle in honour of mothers everywhere, he had said it was 'a light in our darkness, a symbol of love'. And that, to Tom and Sunday – two workhouse children – showed the path ahead, lit by that same light.

Acknowledgements

I would like to say a huge thank you to Kate, James, Eli and everyone at Bonnier for all their love and support, not forgetting my wonderful agent, Sheila Crowley, and my brilliant copy editor, Joan Deitch. xx

Dear Friends,

I'm so excited to be sharing *Mothering Sunday*, the first of my brand-new days-of-the-week series, with you all. I do hope you enjoyed it as much as I loved writing it.

Mother's Day is always such an important time, a time when we can show our mums how much we appreciate all they do for us, so I found myself getting into this novel straight away. Of course, things are much more commercialised nowadays, but back in the time the book was set, children went to church with their mothers and presented them with just small gifts, which I think is lovely. As any of us who are mothers know, it is the gesture rather than the expense of the present that means so much. I have a loft full of little cards that the children have made for me over the years and they're more precious than gold. Sadly, I lost my mum seven years ago so it's always hard for me now on Mother's Day when I visit Chilvers Coton churchyard with flowers for her grave.

A lot of research went into this novel but whilst Nuneaton Workhouse was an actual place I must tell you that all the characters, including the horrid Miss Frost and the abominable Mr Pinnegar, are purely fictional, figments of my imaginaton.

I truly came to adore little Sunday, bless her; all

she ever wanted was a mother to love her. How heartbreaking is that? And then there were Daisy and Tommy, the kind Lady Huntley, the flamboyant Mrs Spooner and the gentle Miss Beau; so many other characters I was sad to wave farewell. Having said that, you will get to see some of them again in the next book, which focuses on Monday's Child. In *The Little Angel* you will meet Kitty, who is almost too pretty for her own good! I really hope you enjoy her story.

It was back in June 2004 when my first book was published and what a busy time it's been since then; I can't believe that *The Little Angel* is my thirtieth novel! I'm never happier than when I'm locked away in my office with my imaginary characters and can't see ahead to a time when that will change.

When I'm not writing my own books I'm usually reading someone else's. Of course, Catherine Cookson was, and still is, one of my all-time favourite authors so one of the highlights of my career was when I was allowed to write sequels to her trilogies. I felt very honoured and hope that Catherine would have thought that I did her wonderful stories justice.

Surprisingly, one of the most common questions asked by my readers is, 'Which of your own books is your favourite?' I can always truthfully answer, 'The one I am working on now,' because if I don't strive to make each one better than the last I would feel that I was letting my fans down. For the duration of writing each book I feel what my characters feel; I laugh and cry with them and always feel sad when it's time to let them go. But that never lasts for long – there's soon another idea popping into my head and then I'm off again!

And so now it's time to put my thinking cap on for Tuesday's Child, but first I might allow myself a few days off to potter in the garden, another love of mine. As I write this we're entering October so I've no doubt there will be plenty of pruning to do!

I shall look forward to hearing your thoughts, as always, on *Mothering Sunday*.

Take care.

Much love,
Rosie xx

Annie's Fruit Scones

Ingredients
225g/8oz plain flour
4 tsp baking powder
pinch of salt
55g/2oz butter
28g/1oz sugar
Milk to mix
55g/2oz chopped cherries or raisins

Method
Preheat oven to 220°C.
Sieve flour, baking powder and salt into a bowl.
Rub in the butter.
Add the dried fruit and sugar and mix together, adding the milk gradually until you have a soft dough.
Roll out to 2cm/¾ inch thickness and cut into required shapes.
Place on an ungreased tin and bake in a very hot oven for approximately 10 minutes. To test if cooked, press firmly at the sides. Scones are cooked when firm to the touch.

Serve warm with butter and jam. Enjoy!

This Large Print Book for the partially sighted, who cannot read normal print, is published under the auspices of

THE ULVERSCROFT FOUNDATION